DECAY

DECAY

THE SEVENTH AGE

BOOK 3

Table of Contents

LUCY'S LEXICON

ALL COMMENTS ARE MY TACTICAL ANALYSIS AND BASED OFF CURRENT INFORMATION – LUCY. *AND PHOEBE'S!* (WITH CONTRIBUTIONS BY DOCTOR DANEKA) I WROTE SOME SHIT—AKIRA

The Sons and Daughters. Homebase: The Second City. Primary Goal: Take down the Unification or die trying. Then try again.

- [ ] AKA Boss—Patron for the Lady of Fate. I CALL HIM BIGGER BOSS—A.

- Lucy—Demon Hunter Helldiver. *The leader we go to when shit needs to get done -P.* (Just how many handaxes and wooden stakes can one person carry?—D.)

- Mike Auburn—Naïve idiot who actually pulled it off. Slayer of Golgoroth. Got killed. Then lost in Purgatory like an idiot. LOST? OR HUNTING? ALSO LIKE… GHOSTS COME BACK YO.—A. *He taught the world how to become magical. They won't forget that.—P.* (They won't LET us forget that. We are typically hunted for good reason.—D.)

- Jane Auburn—Aka JK-47. Mike's sister. Killed the Death Lord of Suicide. Caretaker of cats and currently … also dead.

She really looked good on camera, swoon... -P. SHE SHUT YOU DOWN HARD, PHOEBES—A. *I am allowed ... to fangirl, okay? -P*

- Akira—Boss's assassin, insect shapeshifter, and bearer of the coat with many patches. *AND* CURRENTLY THE ONLY ONE OF YOU KIND ENOUGH TO KEEP JANE'S CATS ALIVE.—A.

- Doc Daneka—Psychic vampire who feeds on emotions. Also happens to be an actual therapist. Unfortunately his father has gone insane and started calling himself Lazarus. (The sins of the father are not reflected upon the child.—D.) *Yeeeaaah... look Doc, that connection to your dad is going to come back.—P.* WAIT, DO YOU HAVE YOUR DAD'S NUMBER? CAN WE FUCK WITH HIM?—A.

- Phoebe—Prophet of the blood, head of recruitment for the Sons and Daughters, her visions likely come true. *Likely? LIKELY?—P* YOU DID PREDICT THAT ODIN HIMSELF WAS GOING TO PAT ME ON THE HEAD. GUESS WHAT... HASN'T HAPPENED YET! I WANT MY HEAD PATS—A.

- Edward Morris—Mind-Controlling Vampire—Runs Chicago now. *Good ol' Morris, holding down our fort.—P.*

Dystopia. Homebase: Texas. Primary Goal: Provide stability to the world as governments collapse by empowering corporations across the world with magic.

- Peter Culmen—CEO of Triumvirate Enterprises. Also known as Mr. Anonymous, one of ten Warlocks who helped shatter the world. Recent events have made him something of an occasional ally. *Even we need money and favors to fuel our war—P.* (It's telling that even though his entire city has embraced technomagic, they still remain engaged globally).

I love visiting uncle peter! He always lets me eat visiting vice presidents and then calls it profit!—A.

- Jack—One of Peter's new Silicon-based lifeforms. Proof that someone addicted to demonic or angelic blood can transition off and find new hope. He's head of Dystopia's security. fyi, jack can make any kitchen appliance deadly and produce tasty food.

The Society of Deus. Homebase: The Twin Cities. Primary Goal: Promote magical elitism through education and instruction—with vampirism. It's where you go if you want to spend every day in class and every night training for their undead army. Unfortunately, it's a nice city; the coffee is superb.

- Damien Vryce—The warlock who betrayed Lazarus and stole his soul back, shattering the world and becoming a Lich. Then ran into hiding to dodge the wrath of every angel and demon hunting for his pasty ass. (He is still the most powerful entity that isn't in the Unification.—D.) *It's hard to track a master of possession who swaps bodies, but I think I've figured out a tell.* So is he a hero? Or our enemy? On one hand—brought magic back. On the other... kinda killed Mike.

- Gabriel D'Angelo—Sorcerer and current Primus for the Society of Deus. *Gabriel has been working with Dystopia to create emergency services in the wastelands of America.*

- The Gargoyles (Onyx, Jade, and Obsidian)—Stone creatures used to defend sorcerers of Deus. They used to be mortal Chicago police officers before they fell when the Sons and Daughters assaulted Chicago, and Vryce molded them into their current state. The friends we had are no longer.

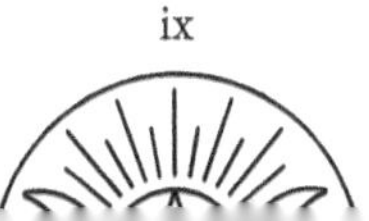

- Slade and Cael—High Sorcerers who serve Vryce. Slade has a penchant for fire magic, and Cael weaves druidic spellcraft. (Cael is also an excellent fisherman.–D).

- Charles Walsh—Former Unification member and has fully joined the Society. A sorcerer with mastery over time magic, Charles acts as something of a Dean in their universities.

The Archive. Homebase: Denver. Primary Goal: Basically, to allow governments to die with grace while poaching their best talent. Any budding empire in this new world should watch out for their spycraft.

- The Praenomen—A truly cunning entity who engineered the first successful strike against the Unification, brought Dystopia in check, and slayed the demon king Bollard. I like her. (You like her because she's ruthless.—D). *She played us and Boss like a fiddle.—P.* LOOK, SOMETIMES YOU NEED TO HIRE A KILLER, AND SOMETIMES YOU NEED TO BRING A SHOVEL.—A.

- The Whisper—Master infiltrator. Faceless vampire and impersonator. Perhaps our greatest chance to embed someone in the Vatican.

- Alex Kristov—Lead Scientist at Atlantis and Scientific Liaison to multiple companies. Peter's apprentice. Abandoned Dystopia before their last crisis and is helping the Archive build new weapons to take down cryptids.

- Calamity—A Faerie with a knack for making bombs and bullets create bigger explosions. Or misfire entirely.

- Left Behind—A confused demon with a penchant for unweaving magical wards. Handy when you need to kill a sorcerer in their own sanctum.

The Unification. Homebase: The Vatican. Primary Goal: The Unification, also known as the Church of Lazarus, wishes to restore the world back to before magic returned. Or rule over it as necromancer gods by killing everyone. Comprised of countless secret societies, they still hold all the cards.

- Lazarus—The first Lich. Returned from the dead two years ago, in theory. Lazarus appears to be the name for the Thirteenth Death Lord, the Seat of Heaven's Wrath, and is a perfectly mortal sociopath. (The fact that a human can control a global conspiracy is impressive though.—D.) *He's your father. Of course you would say this.—P.* WHAT MAKES HUMANS ANY LESS DANGEROUS IN THIS WORLD?—A.

- Death Lords—Thirteen Lords of Death that rule over various aspects of Purgatory.

- Alexandria of Ur—Thousand-year-old vampire. Dangerous. Despises that magic and vampirism are so easily accessible in the world and will kill anyone who isn't of "noble" lineage.

- Lucian Montague—Death Lord of Misfortune. The beggar lord. We don't have any real intel on him. *Sorry Lucy, all I know is he's next.—P.* LOOK, ANYONE IS BETTER THAN THE LORD OF SUICIDE.—A.

Memorial: Those who have died for good. For better or worse.

- T—A Sorcerer who betrayed the Society of Deus when this all began. Without him, the Sons and Daughters would never have banded together. Unfortunately, his soul was sucked into hell. R.I.P., Brother.

- Kevin Thayer—Journalist and reporter who covered Jane during her rise to popularity when corporations branded magic. Was gunned down by a machine gun ... in the middle

of a battlefield filled with cryptids who enjoy the taste of souls. Kevin did leave his mark by showing us Sons and Daughters the power of the media and swelled our ranks.

- Frankie—Best damn zombie cab driver Chicago has ever seen. Yet Bollard put him in the ground inside the Society of Deus before he could warn us. Unfortunately, even though Frankie *is* a zombie, we can't unbury him without knowing *where* he is at. Eternity trapped six feet under.

- Symon Vasyl—Former Archive vampire with a specialty in sabotage. This French bastard gave his unlife to drive a wedge between Peter Culmen and the Unification last year and hasn't been seen since.

- Bollard—A demon who imprisoned Lazarus and helped set him free. Then, when he realized humans would eat any demon heart for power, tried to build his own army of magical creatures just to save them from the real monsters—us. The Praenomen consumed his heart and stole his power.

- Lord of Suicide—The Death Lord of Suicide. Built his armies in North America by convincing people to take a drug that granted powers but ultimately ended their lives. Was eventually killed in Dystopia by Jane Auburn.

Lexicon: Terms we use. New recruits to our army should familiarize themselves with these.

- Demon. The guardians of purgatory. Everything from your classic hellhounds, hot succubae, and giant balrogs. Their blood makes magic you thought didn't exist real. Eat one of their hearts (tastes like peaches), and you'll become vampiric. Cursed to feed on the blood of others but way stronger than you ever imagined.

- Angel. The guardians of heavenly principles. Think, like, making the wind blow or rivers flow. They are often unconcerned with humans entirely, but if you catch one and eat its heart (tastes like apples), then you'll become more psychic and can fuel more complex spells without the need for divine blood.

- Cryptid. Creatures of folklore and legend brought back into this world in great numbers. Like cockroaches, these buggers pop up anywhere and everywhere and are the main source of power acquisition. Summon yourself a cryptid, eat its heart, and you'll get a quirky little power based on what you ate. They say... you are what you eat, after all.

- Witch. A human who uses the blood of magical creatures to cast spells and isn't bound by any creed, religion, or style. As long as they have magical blood, their magic will work.

- Sorcerer. A human who ate the heart of an angel and can cast spells without external blood. Can cast higher magic or grander rituals than most but is still as durable as a regular human.

- Vampire. A human who ate a demon heart and exhibits a variety of undead powers.

- Freak. A human who ate the heart of a cryptid (or bought power from a company) and has a singular power or mutation.

- Warlock. A sorcerer who managed to summon, bind, and eat both the heart of an angel and demon and shred their soul by doing so. It's a very stupid idea to become one of these, as you are nothing more than a hollow husk of arcane power. Only a handful of idiots ever really pulled this off. Each of them is capable of ending the world.

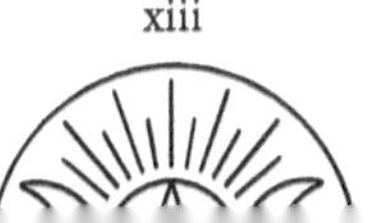

- Lich. Best we can tell, it's a warlock who managed to piece their soul back together or stitch enough souls into one body. A true violation of heavenly principles. All known liches are bound to Purgatory to fulfill a service. Even angels and demons work together to stop someone that has the power of humans, angels, and demons combined out of fear.

- Purgatory. The land of the dead where all human souls go when they perish. Within Purgatory, anything ever lost can be found if you hunt enough. Now it's a gold mine of magical or forgotten artifacts that were lost to history—for the right explorers. Purgatory both overlays our world and seems to metaphorically stretch *down*. We don't know how far.

- Helldivers. Professionals of any type who have learned the rituals to dive into Purgatory and navigate its corridors in search of lost treasure.

- Sparkles. The best damn pizza-loving demon! Also, Sparkles might steal your tacos.

They stepped on dreams for centuries.
They hoarded their power behind their empires.
They cultivated magic to grant their wishes.
All while we slept.
If we were poor, it was because we were lazy.
If we were jobless, it was because we didn't want to work.
If we were sick, it was because we didn't work out.

But they had magic. They had demons.
They were monsters.
Rich. Famous. Powerful. Monsters.
Yet they wanted to be the one thing they didn't have.
They wanted to be god.
So they used magic to grant that wish.

It woke us up.

Magic has returned. Companies have branded it.
Power is accessible to all.
For our crime, the sun itself has turned black.
As if the very gods have closed their eyes upon our world.
So, in this darkness, grab a crowbar and eat a heart.
It's time that we bring retribution against Them.

Big Foot

Big 'Ol

Ghost Lands

Distopia Part 2

LIGHT MOUNTAINS

MOUNTAIN RANGE

Jackelope Mt.

Archive

Dev

Nava

Desert

Skin Walkers
ignore voices at night
*and in WOODS

Distopi

? Lake monster?
Furry Vamps
Awoo
MOUNTAINS
Tiny Devil
SPOOKY
Sons & Daughters
Out of Date ?
Ravenous Drummel Dump
Mountain Border
Turds
Rhymes with Witches
Lazarus

CHAPTER 1

"Abandoned and alone in this forsaken world? Burdened under the sins of mankind? Let the Church of Lazarus be your guiding light. For in the darkest corner of Hell, even a powerful man will cry out for salvation. Abraham pulled Lazarus from Hades to save us all. Follow his lead and be redeemed."

–Emergency broadcast

John Daneka's skin was screaming for him to stop, but he knelt in the center of a circle of ash surrounded by masks. Despite the awful pain, his lips curled into a smile, nicotine-stained teeth showing. Fear and suffering meant nothing to him; if he succumbed to his mortal weakness now, then his plan would be ruined. When the black sun rose at dawn, John would be gone, and Lazarus would march into the chamber of gods of death and make the world right again. At least, that was his plan, and the only move he had left on the chess board. The real soul of Lazarus perished due to the incessant betrayal that plagued all secret societies, and in order to maintain the tiniest speck of hope—John burned himself alive and became the false prophet. If he could maintain the charade, the lie would eventually be irrelevant, and the power to cleanse the world would once again fall under his

mantle as the Lord of Heaven's Wrath. Even if the masses called him Lazarus instead.

"Now move, damn you," he hissed at his charred, trembling hand, barely holding onto a scrap of tin near a brazier. *Even under the gaze of Venus, my flesh still fails me. It's unbecoming to debase myself into swears, but lighting myself ablaze to keep the future alive is not the wisest course of action.* His teary eyes trailed up the candlelit walls in the chamber as if begging the ancient dead gods for a temporary blessing. The Cabinet of Masks within the Vatican was a common retreat these days for John. He felt it a fitting refuge given his position within the Church of Lazarus as, well, Lazarus. A little-trafficked chamber adorned with masks from pantheons Rome had rolled over with their propaganda and preserved like hunters mounting trophies. For it was but a mask he wore and a lie he weaved to the world after his failure three years prior. Failure burned into his very flesh along with the grave clothes of Lazarus himself.

With each rise of the black sun, he grew weaker. Mortals feasted upon the hearts of the divine, stealing their strength and becoming monsters, and without bold action, he risked becoming irrelevant.

The dead returned to the lands of the living, and Lazarus couldn't be fit to crawl yourself out of the pits of Purgatory, could he? What a weak willed lackey of a dead god. John's hatred for his current troubles allowed him to push past the pain, willing his fingertips to fold the tin in half at last. A single spark of joy welled within him before the tin square fumbled out of his hand, clanking against the marble floor and sliding to the edge of the heptagram. The tin clattered and slid, threatening to disturb the ashen edge John had neatly prepared. He flailed after it, tripping over the tattered clothes that dangled from his bony arms and tipped over the brazier, sending the red-glowing coals bouncing around the chamber. The erratic dancing flames made the mask of Aphrodite appear biblically demonic as she gazed on with disapproval.

"Fuck." He breathed heavily, coughing seven specks of blood inside the ritual circle. The flames died before his eyes. Their last kiss of light sparkled along the tin amulet resting inches from ashes. The cool floor was, at least, ointment to his wounds. Plus, John reasoned, he did go through the trouble of having his hunters burn a Medusa alive. "Come on, ol' chap, you're the Lord of Heaven's Wrath. Prophet of the Unification. Lazarus himself. Savior of the world. Not a college freshmen praying to the porcelain throne." *Therein lies my problem. I'm a liar.* He peeled himself off the ground, elbows first, as he no longer had the muscles in his right arm to perform a simple push-up; if not for the mysterious grave clothes of Lazarus animating his flesh, he would have perished long ago.

It would be a trivial matter for him to grab the bowl of Medusa blood resting as a sacrifice to Aphrodite and drink deeply of its healing powers. Casting a simple spell using divine blood would heal his wounds and repair his flesh, but doing so would cost him everything for a mere temporary fix. Unlike the rest of the vampires, sorcerers, Lords of Death, and more within the various tendrils of the Unification, to truly become Lazarus—he needed to remain pure. No matter how much pain and fear from the horrors of humanity's ambition he felt. *I'm a liar, but I chose this lie to save the world. I will unwind this magical chaos and revive an omniscient God once more.* He quickly pushed down the hubristic thoughts that he, himself, might very well become that God if his plan worked. Purpose, rather than power, drove his faith, even if that faith now focused inward upon himself.

Pushing through the barrier of pain, he snatched the tin amulet and scooped the boiling gum-like material that spilled from the brazier. *Resin from a Boswellia tree, copper tin engraved with a bronze stylus folded thrice, coated and smoked over frankincense, and the acquisition of wealth, wisdom, and love shall be mine.* John completed the steps of the ritual, knowing full well it was powerless. Spells and magic may be real, but without the blood of a creature, it was nothing more

than a meditative exercise—an exercise that pushed the pain back into the recesses of his soul every morning.

Folding the tablet in a pouch of linen and fixing it underneath mummified wraps along his ribs, Lazarus rose from his position with strength of will. The bowl of Medusa's blackened blood no longer tempted him.

"A gift from the Unification to you." Lazarus bowed before the masks of gods. "Once this substance was rare, guarded only by our secret societies for those who needed its power to shape the world. Now it might as well be cat food. So, feast away while you can. When my Church has finished with this world, your blood will be obsolete. Until tomorrow, my dead friends." He reached down, grabbed a simple oak-carved cane, and walked through the ashen heptagram. "Dawn is nearly upon us, and I've got a speech to deliver." *Time to do what I do best.*

Within the Sistine Chapel, one-hundred and fifteen monsters waited for Lazarus to arrive. In the years following the shattering of the world, when the sun rose black and magic returned to the world, Vatican City had become the seat of power for the Unification. Each of the monsters represented a secret society that existed in any corner of the globe. A vampire or two from the Thule society, sorcerers from the Order of Golden Dawn, werewolves and witches from Skull & Bones, all bickered amongst themselves over why they were summoned. Some claimed they were dragged here by monsters under orders; some said they were tricked; some, like Alexandria of Ur, wondered if they should have worn something more presentable than Victorian lace and a corset.

For centuries, the Unification served as the only dispatcher of divine blood, for their helldivers guarded the secrets of plunging into

Purgatory to slay a demon who guarded the dead. Blood that would make magic real. Every secret society that wished to influence the world had to debase themselves before the council of thirteen that ruled the Unification for a vial or two of blood once every decade. In an ambitious bid to increase the supply, all organizations entered a decades-long pact to shape world governments and spend the last remaining supply on earth to enact a great ritual that would resurrect Lazarus from the dead.

Like many ambitious plans, it worked—just not in the way many of the wicked creatures would have enjoyed. Their coveted power was now in the hands of every fool in the world. Magic was commonplace; corporations branded and sold it in boutique corner shops. Lazarus wasn't the only being to return either... Millions of dead souls escaped their prisons in Purgatory and returned to the world, along with cryptids, demons, angels, and just about any mythological creature a babushka would shake a stick at. Their governments and power structures had collapsed, barely holding on for life, replaced by corporations and anarchist movements around the world in their own little fiefdoms.

So once again, even three years after the dawn of the black sun, the members and representatives of the Unification found themselves huddled in the walls of the world's most powerful secret society—the Vatican. Summoned by the very figure they resurrected, they hoped Lazarus had a plan to tip the scales of balance back in their power.

Behind their whispered words and polite bickering, their gazes darted to the ten green-robed masked figures seated in front of the altar and then the two empty chairs. Each chair represented the twelve Lords of Death, albeit missing two. Each wore a mask that served to represent which aspect of death they presided over. One for murders, one for pestilence, one for famine, old age, and so forth. Every three years, an election was held for who would be chosen from the rank-and-file to don a mask and become a Lord of Death. The lead-up to such a process often involved several daggers, blackmail,

and currying favor from the countless societies of magic that hailed from cultures across the globe. It had now been three years since the world ended, and with two vacant seats, everyone in attendance was eager to peacock their way into a vacant chair.

Or even replace one of the existing Lords—at least in their dreams.

Lazarus entered from behind the altar, flanked by two figures shrouded in white robes each holding a green flame. He took up position, gaze falling upon the room, and inhaled sharply through his teeth. This was the day Lazarus was waiting for. The three-year election of the Lords of Death. Only his seat as the Lord of Heaven's Wrath was not in question, purely out of status, not power. For nearly everyone in the room was centuries older in material power than he. Some Lords had ruled over Purgatory for a millennium, but this was his chance. His chance to fix the world.

"My humble, assembled colleagues," Lazarus's charred hand placed over his heart, "as stewards of this world, we have failed it. By your combined might and ambition, you broke divine law. Each body in this chamber was involved in the creation of ten warlocks around the world. You fed these sorcerers the heart of an angel and a demon. Shredded their souls and gave birth to truly inhumane creatures who could desecrate the barriers of humanity's innocence." His fist slamming on the altar echoed through the chamber.

Any who still stood placed their butts firmly in their uncomfortable seats. The vampire Alexandria poured herself another glass of crimson with an amused smirk, muttering under her breath that it was indeed a sight to see.

Lazarus let the sound rattle off the walls and fixed his gaze on Alexandria. *A thousand-year-old undead. Creator of civilizations and the very one who retrieved my grave clothes. She's the most likely candidate for a seat, but for heaven's sake, she flirts with everything, living and dead.* If it wasn't for the layers of mummified cloth over his already charred face, the very mortal Lazarus might have blushed at

her perfect features. Even if she was dressed in black, Victorian lace up to her neck, the corset left little to the imagination.

"Even worse," Lazarus continued surveying, moving his gaze across the room to other potential candidates, "you fed thousands of innocent souls to sacrifice, consorted with demons, and lost control of the warlocks, allowing one of them, Damien Vryce, to reclaim his soul from Purgatory and become a lich. A position reserved only for those who have a seat among these twelve." He gestured to the Lords.

The Lord of Murder, so old all that remained was a black skeleton animated by necromancy alone, clenched his fingerbones into a fist.

"Our coveted power is in the hands of those who betrayed us. The power of angels, divine right, and magic we controlled to bring order to the world—is scattered across our earth. Each day, the sun itself rises black! The morning star itself cannot bear to look upon our sin!" Lazarus's impassioned raspy voice reached hearts.

"Hear, hear!" Members shouted, stomping their feet or banging their pews.

"Let us reclaim what is ours!" an Italian sorcerer shouted. "The fate witches of Italy can fix karma!"

"Osirica of Egypt," a black woman in gold robes rose, shouting over the murmurs with a deep and musical voice that commanded respect, "is positioned to guide us through these times. For too long Africa has been ignored, but we are the seat of life. The first craftsmen and women who built the Valley of Kings. Let Ta Set Ma'at rise again. The palace of truth shines its light brighter today than ever before."

The double doors to the papal chamber creaked open, and Lazarus saw a beggar attempt to slip in quietly and fail doing so. Right after the representative of Osirica spoke, the chamber doors slammed shut. "Sorry, sorry! Had a spot of trouble." The scarred zombie with mottled long blonde hair, Hawaiian shirt, and beach sandals scooted through pews while sipping unicorn blood out of a coconut in a gross disregard for etiquette. "'Scuse me, pardon, mind the daggers, flight ran late. You know how it is—can't flap your arms fast enough. Mind if

I sit here?" The beggar didn't wait for a response before sitting down next to Alexandria, who wrinkled her nose at first before smiling with fangs.

"By all means," she purred.

"So. So. So very kind of you to join us, Mr. Montague." Lazarus smiled. *Fuck. Of course, the beggar lord got the invite. Because why wouldn't Misfortune show his head one last time?* "Osirica," Lazarus deftly brought the room under control with a wave of his hand, "you shall have your chance. For today, the need for the Unification ceases. Each of you brought me back into this world to guide you, and I've watched and listened to you for years now. Hearing your prayers. I will fix this world as the God you each yearned for. A world of divine order and control. Nobility restored once again. Purgatory brought to balance and divine righteousness in the hands of those faithful. For today, the Church of Lazarus and the Unification become truly one." Lazarus folded his hands and watched the looks of cautious curiosity unfold on the faces of the monsters and Lords. Indignation in some, opportunity in others.

Mr. Montague whispered under his breath, "Because Sunday school is what everyone signs up for out of choice. Didn't we eat most of the Catholics?"

Alexandria laughed audibly before covering her mouth.

The Lord of Murder rose. "Lazarus, you are correct. We summoned you into this world, for the divine blood in your veins will help us fix the problems we face in Purgatory. Yet I believe I speak for all of us when I ask the question that has hung on our teeth as we've watched the world burn. How?"

Thank you. Lazarus gave a peaceful smile to the Lord and placed his hands inches above the two green flames in the hands of his flanking attendants. "As the Lord of Heaven's Wrath, it is time we cleanse the world in a righteous fire. We are the masters of necromancy. We command the legions of the dead. The goal of the Unification was always to unify humanity under a single banner. To bring back God

with their faith. In this world of ash, our path to restoration is simple." He snuffed out the two flames by pinching each with his scorched fingers, never noticing the pain.

"We crusade once again. We bring the wrath of the divine to the unworthy. When our armies have unified the world under one banner, I will fix this world and restore the sun. In short..." He paused and looked deep into the eyes of each Lord of Death.

"We kill humanity."

CHAPTER 2

A small cellphone video recording plays. Mike Auburn, pale and vampiric, pushes through a crowd of people while elbowing a cop in the face. His green trench coat, coated in patches, is fresh—still without tatters and bloodstains. "Oh, I'm letting you go, Officer. Tell Captain Slade that I'm bringing a horde of demons to Vryce's little tower tonight. Your operation is busted, and I'm going to show these people what you guys are really up to. Now get the fuck out of here before I name you dessert." Mike smiled with fangs.

–Recorded footage of the Sons and Daughters

"I mean really... how do you *kill* a god anyway?" Mike Auburn wondered aloud in front of Balor's tomb. The twelve-foot-tall giant was impaled against a concrete slab with red spears the size of construction I-beams. Three eyes of Balor were closed, only two of them peacefully. The third eye was skewered by a spiral-wound piece of petrified wood that jutted out, like an angel had thrown it down from heaven to silence a deity whose gaze was no longer needed. Viscous liquid from the eye still trickled down Balor's naked form, pooling into a moat which had given birth to violet-shaded flowers. Mike ensured his boots never crushed one, despite how clumsy he

could be as he approached. Even though Balor was killed and imprisoned in Purgatory, the thought of laying a hand on the god seemed both forbidden and enticing to Mike.

"Kill its..." Jane grunted as she planted both feet into a dead Barghest and heaved its massive doglike frame off the edge into the abyss below them, "...followers. Same as taking down any famous person: convince everyone they aren't worth their salt, and your product is better." The five-foot-four ghost of Jane Auburn kipped up from her bum and leaned over the edge, watching the hellhound fade from view and strained to listen for it hitting bottom. "You gonna help, or are you just going to stand there slack jawed like you've never seen a naked god?" Her lips scrunched in disappointment over the lack of impact. "Why is my tiny ass doing all the heavy lifting here?"

Mike glanced back over his shoulder at Jane as he crawled up the gnarled tree that provided the throne for Balor's body. He was a decade older than her by all his accounts, and her complaints were probably valid. Mike was rugged, clearly a person who worked with his hands, and the stubble on his face always gave the impression he cared enough to shave but distracted enough to forget after a few days. Jane was much shorter, covered in scratches, bruises, and several stab wounds but still appeared like the female star of an action movie—every mark only made her cooler. Unlike her, Mike didn't appear as a crispy critter shot with several lightning bolts and burned alive, and he was thankful for that. Still, other than their noses and cheekbones, Mike figured people probably wouldn't even know they were related. *Brown hair, brown eyes is the older brother of a short blonde with green eyes? One of our parents got a little busy.*

"Fucking shittle bricks on biscuits," Jane shouted in surprise when a dying hellhound twitched at her feet, and she began stomping its head.

I take that back. We are totally related. Sorry parental units A and B, possibly C.

The view was unlike anything he'd seen in Purgatory, and even the tomb of Lazarus wasn't as impressive. Balor rested on a large circular platform suspended by chains and pillars, and the red-skinned god was, at least to Mike, more than impaled by the beams. *Did they have Godzilla take him out?* Whoever did it, Mike figured they had reason to fear Balor's escape because the entire cavern was filled with scribbled arcane wards on every crystal, rock, and outcropping. Not a single one looked like a natural growth, more like whoever built this room was trying to achieve a hypnotic geometric pattern. He shook his head to snap out it. Staring at pretty rocks and violet flowers in the realm of waiting wasn't why they were here.

Neither was Jane cursing his name while she dragged another dead demon off the ledge.

"Hey! Those hellhounds didn't kill themselves, you know. Besides, you had the audacity to die without a pack of cigarettes on you." Mike's fingerless gloves hovered over Balor's chest, feeling the heat and subtle heartbeat pulse within. The pulse of power echoed through Mike's soul. *It's not dead.* Heat, not unlike the great demon Golgoroth, boiled and pumped beneath the crimson skin. Its pulse quickened as if it could sense Mike's presence. Balor felt ... impatient. *That's a mood, buddy. Gotta say, like your style if you are still eager after a minor case of decapitation.*

"Addict." Jane's voice snapped him out of the focus.

"Fuck. Yeah, guess I am. I'd kill Satan himself right now for a pack."

"Well, why did *you* die without a pack of smokes then?"

"Oh, I had smokes." He looked back at his sister with a boyish grin on his stubbled face. "The lightning strikes exploded my lighter."

"Maybe... I dunno, don't piss off warlocks with the ability to control weather then?"

"What's the fun in that?" Mike turned back and went for it. *Please don't explode!* He palmed Balor's chest while clenching his eyes shut. Mike and Jane were completely out of their league down here, and they both knew it. An ironworker and bartender weren't exactly

occult experts and master helldivers equipped to deal with looting the lands of the dead.

To Mike's pleasant surprise, Balor did not explode upon being touched. Mike had nothing to base that fear on, but who really understood the rules of ancient gods and demons anyway?

Oh, sweet heaven and holy tacos. Balor's heart pulsed faster. For over a year now, Mike had wandered Purgatory looking for a sign, a way back into the lands of the living to continue the fight against the Unification—the bastards who broke the world and ruined the lives of millions. Unfortunately, they had power. Lords of Death, vampires, and entire governments were under their thumbs. But it was power that Mike showed the world how to steal. *Find them, kill them, eat them.* It was an insanely simple recipe when he thought about it. Summon a demon, angel, or creature of myth—kill it and eat its heart. Doing so could transform a person into something out of legend, even if it came with drawbacks. The power obtained was unquestionable.

After a year of searching Purgatory, Mike had finally found another heart worth consuming. Demons, he learned, really didn't care about dead human souls... but they actively guarded all sorts of myths. Even when he was alive, Mike could see into Purgatory. *Same with Jane, I guess.* Every other human here was blind and deaf, and since they could see, that meant they could find a way out easier than most. But he wasn't going back empty-handed like the last time. This time, bastards like Vryce would be made to listen. He just needed that certain *something.* Something that could tip the balance back in his favor. The heart of a god.

"I know what you're thinkin.'" Jane reached down and picked up a heart Mike had pulled from a hellhound. "Nom a deity, right? Can't say I disagree, given how crazy powerful people are becoming in this world, but... doesn't change our current situation." She chucked the heart over to Mike.

"We're dead." He sighed and caught the heart.

"Bingo." She finger gunned.

"I think we can still eat these." He bounced the heart in his hand. "Demons and monsters seem real to us. They have a heat to them, like a baked potato."

"I mean, sure, you CAN go eat anything. Do you know what will happen? I sure don't."

His broad shoulders slumped, and he licked the heart. It still tasted like sweet peaches even after all these years, but other than a nice rush, it didn't magically restore him back to life. *Maybe not yet for Balor.* "I suppose you're right. Not like I haven't tried a few already... It's the lack of seasoning."

"Probably the lack of a body. I'm pretty sure we aren't the first ghosts in the history of Purgatory to kill a demon. Besides, that heart is probably the size of you. We need help." She scrunched her nose and narrowed her eyes at him, firmly planting one hand on a hip.

Mike stepped back over the violet flowers and plopped the squishy pomegranate-shaped heart in the flower bed before walking over to his sister. Jane had grown up. At twenty-four years old, the blonde-haired, green-eyed spitfire would certainly cause trouble. *I missed my opportunity to scare the fuck out of any potential dates.* Mike was quite a bit taller than her at six foot one, but he wrapped an arm around her and shook her with love. When he looked at her from afar, he couldn't help but notice her death marks. A thousand scratches and claw marks ripped her abdomen and back to shreds. Death by a thousand cuts, and he hadn't been there to protect her. Then again... Mike knew he really wasn't there for any aspect of her life. *Fitting that our reunion would be in death.*

Despite the time between them, Jane buried her head in his chest. "What are we going to do?"

"Shenanigans" was the only comfort Mike could give. Purgatory was a strange place. As far as he could tell, it was ... down. Down below the world where everyone they knew lived and thrived. At its peak, the lands of the dead overlaid the lands of living, but a millennium of civilization built upon itself pushed layers and layers of

Purgatory farther into the abyss. Every soul he or Jane encountered in Purgatory was blind. They couldn't feel, see, or touch anything they encountered, cursed to wander the catacombs of history like mindless entities for eternity. Mike knew that if they could find their way back to the surface, the dead could cross back over as a ghost of sorts, but getting out was like winning the lottery. *Only those lucky enough to wander to the surface crossed over.* "Do you remember the path you took to get down here? Not going to lie—I didn't leave breadcrumbs."

She punched him. "Idiot. And... actually... I'm something of an expert helldiver. While you were off doing your best impression of a tourist, I was leading entire armies through Purgatory. Thank you very much." She booped his nose and backed off, skipping over the flowers and heading around Balor's tomb. "This way, cupcake." She nodded.

There were really only two paths. One was the narrow irrigation canal that Mike had come down, littered with guardians he had slain along the way that entered from the bottom part of the cavern. Since demons were wardens of blind prisoners, they assumed that every ghost was equally deaf, dumb, and blind, and so they put up little resistance when they found out otherwise. The thrill of killing demons in Purgatory rarely happened for Mike anymore, but he clung to even the smallest feeling, no matter how faint. As long as he still had feelings, he reasoned, he still existed.

The other narrow pathway, one that connected to the circular platform where Balor clung to existence, led to a set of massive stone doors with raised carvings of deer and a half-man, half-birdlike figure.

The small ... support was easily a hundred feet away or more, which made the gigantic doors infinitely more imposing.

"Before you say a thing," Mike held a finger over Jane's lips, "yes, I'm fully aware that we take the ominous door pathway instead of the way I came in. I was referring to *after* we get out of this lair."

"Riiighhht..."

Of course, that door just happened to have two small demons standing guard, each with their right leg significantly shorter than

their left and a malformed hunch and dressed in rags. Even from this distance, Mike could see that their left foot twisted backward, and each wielded a javelin with nasty-looking barbs, ready to stab any of the ghosts who blindly wandered out of the depths.

Of course, she wants to go toward the creepy little demons. "I'm going to go on a limb and say that you didn't head in this way."

"Oh, hell no." She led him past Balor and balanced perfectly on the four-inch wide stone beam that spanned a hundred yards to the next set of doors. "I followed your trail of carnage. However, going back to where I came from is pointless. I killed the Lord of Suicide there, and there's a few million dead souls from Texas jamming up any exit. Our only way back up is through to the next city. Plus, as much as you want to eat that heart, I need to remind you..."

"Yeah, I'm dead. Got it." Mike flailed a floppy hand in her direction. "But if everyone else can come back from the dead, I figure fuck it. Might as well chart a path to the good shit, eh? But seriously, don't fall. It will take us like six months to get back up here."

"What makes you think I don't want to eat a god?" Jane said while easily walking backward with perfect balance.

"You mean you aren't already one?"

"Only in my dreams."

Mike easily found his footing on the narrow path while contemplating why he had encountered other deity prisons in his time here and came up empty-handed. Most were withered husks drained of any blood, or piles of ash, but guarded, nonetheless. *Maybe it's out of memorial? Or maybe upper management never gave new orders. I suppose it's an easy paying gig if your job is standing guard for a few thousand years.* The fact that a single misstep would send either of them plunging down into an abyss with no known end didn't faze him in the slightest as he pondered. *When I was a vampire and we helldived, I found Lazarus. Dumb mistake killing him in retrospect even if he did ask for it.* He bit his lip. The only reason he'd been able to find Lazarus was because the Unification held a global ritual with scores of

helldivers in a treasure hunt to find their next god—and he ended up in the same room as Vryce when it mattered. Balor had been trickier. Mike had to start asking questions in between the punches and actually pay attention to find this prize. He honestly figured there would be thousands of trapped magical creatures down here, but instead, it was a graveyard for carrion. *Where the hell are all the dragons anyway?* He skipped a little closer to Jane without worry.

For years, he built skyscrapers in Chicago, and a concrete oblivion was no different than Purgatory oblivion. *One foot in front of the other, and then lunch!* Mike re-tied his red bandanna, scooting his brown hair back out of his eyes so the little demons remained in clear sight. If past encounters had taught him anything, they wouldn't even put up a fight until they realized that Mike and Jane could see them. Both, as they had learned for better-or-worse, were descendants of Lazarus. *Whatever the fuck that means.* But Mike wasn't going to look a genetic gift horse in the mouth. With all the death and misfortune that surrounded the siblings, being able to see, touch, and feel in Purgatory naturally made them the biggest badasses on the block.

Jane broke into a sprint. Halfway on the cobbled stone beam to the demons standing on the platform, her legs fired like pistons, and her boots kicked loose cobblestone as she raced into action. The little buggers made several *chk-chk* sounds in alert to each other and leaped ten feet into the air themselves, throwing their javelins at the duo. Jane tripped forward, ducking the first spear and rolling like an acrobat on the beam. Hooking her right leg while down, she tumbled sideways off the edge, nearly giving Mike a heart attack in the process as she used the momentum to swing underneath and catapult herself back up into the air.

Like a semi-truck, Mike clobbered forward instead as Jane easily cleared his head in the air. With an iron grip, he latched onto her extended hand and dug his heels in, spinning once again and launched Jane forward. Aerial movement came easily to her. He marveled at how she pivoted her body weight and spun with a perfectly

timed kick into one demon's gnarled forehead with a hearty crunch before backflipping neatly onto solid ground.

The other demon hissed a curse in a language—Mike had no damn clue what it was—before running up the large doors higher still. "Chullachaqui!" Its shrill voice echoed from just above the deer antlers before it scurried up through a small hole in the ceiling, echoing the cry again and again in alarm.

"You were supposed to kill that one..." Jane kicked bone off her foot by tapping it against a wall.

"Yeah, well... I didn't get to live life as an acrobat apparently. We better move though. Once they start screaming..." He shouldered into the door, cracking it open slightly.

"More start coming. I know. We are about to have a horde of creepy demon babies on our six." Jane braced herself and joined Mike in heaving the door open. Although, at a hundred pounds lighter than Mike, it didn't have the same impact.

"Creepy." He slammed again. "Demon. Babies?" Together, with the third impact, the double doors groaned open. "You know what that is?"

"Duh. It said its name. It's a Chullachaqui. Guardian of rain forests that lure people into jungles. If you grind their eyes up and snort it like cocaine—you gain the ability to solve puzzles." She blinked. "Dude, you can buy it from Avalon. Little buggers' mate with humans or steal children to increase their numbers, so... they aren't uncommon."

Mike choked. *Avalon?! What. The. You know what... I wanna know, but I don't.* "What the hell happened while I was dead?"

"Beats me, mate. I just saw the commercials." She strolled into the next room. "Huh."

"Huh is never good."

"So, how do you feel about more dead gods?"

Mike squeezed past through the opening.

A labyrinth unfolded itself underneath them. Eldritch green and orange streams of light flowed above roughly hewn amethyst walls.

Minotaur guardians, roving one-eyed humanoids, and clawed creatures with hearts of ice prowled outside of the tombs. Within this chamber, Mike saw not a single dead human soul. Rather, locked and imprisoned in every corner of the labyrinth below was a scene akin that of Balor. A corpse or creature was pinned upside down to a tree by a variety of weapons. Some were impaled with flaming swords while others were shackled with silver nails as their eyes were plucked out by sparrows. More harrowing to Mike was the fact that not all were dead. Several of them still screamed and begged for their release. For some of them, Mike was clueless as to their origin... but the giant blue ox chained to the floor next to Paul Bunyan was certainly one he recognized.

The sounds of screeching and alarms echoed in the room as the vaulted ceiling started to move and wings began to unfold while red eyes opened one-by-one.

"I think we are going to need more help." Mike tapped Jane's shoulder and pointed up.

"Only way out is through. Hope you can run fast."

"Well... I stopped smoking a year ago." Ghosts didn't need to breathe, Mike figured. *I really don't want to know what happens when you die a second time.*

CHAPTER 3

"Companies that profit off your ignorance are false idols. Ye shall overthrow their altars of digital currency and burn their groves of demons with fire. We shall topple their graven images of their profit-inspired gods and eradicate their names from history in the purification of this world."

–Church of Lazarus radio

"**D**id he just say to kill all of humanity?" Lucian Montague leaned over to Alexandria in the Sistine Chapel.

"Hush little darling, don't say a word." The vampire had a sultry purr to her voice and a growing smile.

Ah. Yup. She's in for it. Someone has daddy issues. Lucian rolled his eyes and turned his attention back to Lazarus. The Lord of Heaven's Wrath looked every bit the part he was cast to play, clad head-to-toe in mummified grave cloths with a moth-eaten robe and growing shadows behind him. From the stained glass windows, the black sun's pale ghostly light cascaded over the altar in a rainbow of prismatic hues that colored the tips of Lazarus's fingers green, as if he were wielding the very flames he had just snuffed out—a divine sign that even when heaven's light had dimmed, faith could restore vibrancy to a gray world. The cathedral was stunned in silence, many leaning

forward on their pew. *It's just glass, you idiots. Ugghhh, please tell me this event has pie or donuts.* Each had the same look in their eyes as Alexandria. *This is going to end fantastically. Fuck me, I guess...* He shrank down in his pew and grasped an old Susan B. Anthony coin for a spot of luck.

Lucian had to hand it to Lazarus. The bastard cloaked his evilness behind divine justice like any decent cult leader. Although, he had to admit they did work their asses off to bring him back from the dead. *Maybe summoning a dead guy for a third time was a bad choice. We should have just picked a random number from a phone book.* Still, something didn't quite sit right with Lucian. He had walked the earth when they brought Lazarus back the first time, and it may have been a hot minute, but he didn't remember Lazarus being a genocidal maniac.

The Lord of Murder rose, giving a standing ovation.

"Anyone who saw that coming, please stand up..." Lucian muttered.

The rest of the room followed suit. Even Alexandria rose like a fangirl with deep applause. Out of the hundred-and-fifteen representatives chosen to be here, only Lucian remained seated, laughing to himself as he traced the smooth edges of the old dollar in his hand and wiggled his toes in worn boots. "Welp ol' lady. Time to do my work, I suppose." He tried to take a deep breath but choked on grave dirt that was still in his throat. *Right... right... still dead.* The tattered organs he once called lungs heaved and choked as he lurched forward, rocketing himself up and intentionally tripping over Alexandria and deftly slipping the coin into the heel of her shoe before spilling out onto the red carpet in the aisle.

Alexandria just-so-happened to tip forward, her long hair catching on the Lady of Fate's ornamental mask, which was yanked off and tangled when she straightened. The Lady of Fate, a brown haired, brown eyed German girl in her early twenties, reddened instantly and rose from her seat—punching Alexandria square between the eyes and planting the vampire back in her seat while trying to cover her face.

Sensing combat, stone gargoyles lurched forward and watched the proceedings before they launched themselves from their perches fifty feet above, descending upon the duo. The Lord of Pestilence dove to protect Fate and found himself in the gargoyle's clutches before a single spell could be cast. Unfortunately for the gargoyles, touching a Lord of Death was forbidden, and just as they flew over Osirica of Egypt, the magic that sewed the guardians together was unmade—causing the Lord to fall right into Osirica's hands. A look of panic overtook her, realizing she was touching the Lord of Disease—she screamed.

Chaos soon unfolded.

While supernatural powers were flung left and right, Lucian crawled on all fours up to the various chairs of the Lords. Right to the seat he once owned. He'd given up the mask to his own chosen replacement a few times now, but inevitably, they would suffer a tragic accident. After the great Unification ritual to bring Lazarus back, Lucian handed it to a barista in Rome to take over, and it wasn't long before one of the vampires mistook him for lunch. "Hello, old friend," he said, picking up the golden mask, tipping his head just enough to the left as a gout of magical fire pierced the air. The golden mask was worn and aged, cracked in three places, but made from coins comprised of a hundred empires that fell for one reason or another: Constantine, Atlantis, the United Kingdom, and more. Lucian traced a finger over the edges before calmly sitting down and placing the mask on his zombified face. *Was hoping my vacation would be longer, but alas, even as the Lord of Misfortune, it's no wonder I've got the occasional bout of bad luck. Glad I didn't hit Vegas this weekend.* Lucian bathed in his sarcasm. He never had good luck.

Once the mask hit his face, the undead beggar with mottled hemp sandals faded from view, replaced by a strikingly handsome gentleman with perfectly stick-straight long blond hair and violet eyes. The sandy and torn Hawaiian shirt repaired itself like a magical schoolgirl transformation before becoming pristine and freshly

pressed. Lucian cockily raised an eyebrow at Lazarus and held out his now ring-covered hands. "What can I say? I spent the past few decades binge-watching shows in Japan. What have you been doing?"

"Waiting for today, old friend." Lazarus had remained calm at the altar, watching the chaos unfold with an unamused set of weary eyes, like he was simply waiting for the rampant display of powers people could now channel to finish.

"They'll put their dicks away soon enough." Lucian craned his neck back to look at the brawl he'd caused. "Election day for our seats always ends up like this."

"Speak for yourself, beggar." The Lady of Fate pried her mask from Alexandria and cleaned off locks of torn hair. "I knew you'd show up, but did you really have to pick on me today? Besides..." She looked between her legs as if checking to make sure another prank wasn't hidden under her chair.

"Trust me, Lou. You've got more iron between your legs than half the world put together." Lucian chuckled. "Sorry, love."

Alexandria clutched the side of her head before coyly looking at the rest of the room. In a flash of speed, she sat next to Lucian, grabbing the unclaimed mask that sat next to him. "This makes us even."

"By all means, I can't think of anyone more fitting to take over the Seat of Suicide." Lazarus bowed his head and allowed Alexandria to remain.

Nor can I. Lucian couldn't help but be happy with himself. With one unlucky coin, he changed the entire mood of the room from "kill all humans" back into a familial brawl among colleagues who had worked together for ages. For a brief moment, he was content. Elections for the Lords may only happen once every three years, but they always drew from the same pot of candidates: liches who guarded over souls in Purgatory or those bold enough to borrow the power of their masters. Alexandria was just a vampire, an old one at that, but she would soon learn about the hundred chains that came with the power behind that mask. It would take her another ten years to even

grasp a fraction of its power. *Then again, the Lords of Suicide never last too long. Neither does Misfortune, I suppose. It's why I keep trying to get rid of the damn thing. But this room has gotten more crowded with entitled pricks, and at least I can endure the misfortune and save someone else the trouble.*

Once Alexandria donned the mask, the chapel violence died down. Whatever opportunity they once had had now been stolen.

Lazarus's fist hit the altar, and once again, all eyes in the room were upon him.

"Now where were we…" Lazarus folded his hands and strolled to the right of the altar and down the steps. Pacing through the chapel like a lion in a cage and cowing any who he gazed upon, he continued, "Ah yes… I remember… bringing Heaven's Wrath to the world."

Shit. He's still on about it. Lucian quickly raised his hand and waved it around like a schoolboy. Unfortunately, his moment of interruption was at an end, and with the Lord of Murder boring holes in the back of his head, Lucian thought it best to just lower his hand. *Look, I know this gets you hard and all, but calm the fuck down, skull boy.*

<I can hear your thoughts, worm.> The Lord of Murder invaded Lucian's mind.

<Aww, our love has been far too strong for so long…> Lucian winked.

<Steal ownership over my empire of dead again, and I will feed your soul to maggots.>

<Still angry about that? Not my fault your serial killers always seem to make a mistake and are taken down by a spot of bad luck,> Lucian lied.

"We need to kill humanity, not out of hatred, but out of love." Lazarus continued to stroll, oblivious to the telepathic conversation among the Lords. "Humanity has become a fractured God. We in the Unification have known since our beginning that their belief, their faith, makes them stronger. Yet now, more than ever, they are distracted. It became more difficult to helldive, to push past the barrier of Innocence and acquire the divine blood you need to shape

the world. But now we have all the blood we need. In some countries, you can order it for next day delivery." He took a long pause. "Preposterous."

<I'll keep killing your paupers before they whither in old age.>

<Please do. They've already had a hard life. Have you ever been broke, Murder? Oh wait... no. You literally stole the first murdered soul in history from both Fate and me. Fuck you.>

<You are a maggot who feasts on our scraps, waiting for a piano to drop.>

<And yet, I keep finding myself by your side. Memento Mori, bitch. Even Emperors look the same as beggars when they die. They both shit themselves.>

The Lady of Fate cut into their conversation. *<I will be both of your nightmares if you don't cut the prattle.>*

<Yes, ma'am.> Lucian resolved himself to behave. Out of all the Lords to not trifle with, the Lady of Fate was at the top. They enjoyed ... a friendship over the centuries, and she tolerated his pranks like a mother tending to a childish boy, but he knew when to silence himself.

Lazarus paced back down the second aisle with hands folded behind his back. "The problem we face now is the Warlocks that were created. One, in particular, managed to pull back his soul from Purgatory in the great ritual. The rest have slowly betrayed each of us for their own fiefdoms. Even our youngest Warlock in Texas betrayed us, selling our gifts to companies around the world. They are short sighted but dangerous. They've already killed the Lord of Suicide once, and if we do not act now... this world will be bathed in a thousand years of darkness. However..." He held up a single finger.

Oh, here we go.

"Now we are no longer shackled behind secrecy. We are masters of magic, necromancy, and have the very Lords of Death on our side. We are *unchained* by secrecy. Allowed to act openly. So, each Lord will lead an army to every corner of this earth and purge the unfaithful. Turn the dead souls into our soldiers and evacuate the faithful. Once

our crusade is complete... a new world order will be established. The wicked will seek repentance and find their place in Gehenna. We can then do what we were given the divine right to perform: tend the gardens of this Earth."

Lucian couldn't help himself any longer. He rose, bowed deeply, and let himself be bathed in the green and violet lights of the black sun before speaking with a trembling voice. "Shouldn't the living have their choice, my Lord? We are, after all, each liches and Lords who seek to only teach them the lessons they need before returning to the Room of Guf." Lucian always had a problem with that name. For one, it was biblical in the classic sense, and the second, born souls really haven't returned to realm of unborn souls for quite some time. God, as it were, had checked out long ago after creating the world. *Or died. Dying is certainly a possibility. We certainly aren't innocent in that regard, and in trying to fix that—we done fucked up.*

"The treasury of souls in the seventh heaven was desecrated by the Warlock Vryce, Lord of Misfortune," Lazarus said as he flicked angelic blood from his reliquary in Lucian's direction. "Once the seal was broken by the usurper's hands, it spoiled the realm. What unborn soul could enter this world and remain pure? Once one warlock claimed an unnamed soul to restore his, what is to stop others from following in his footsteps? The living made their choice when they consumed the hearts of demons and peddled their souls for petty magic." His words stung at the hearts of many in attendance for many fit that bill, seeking material power over inner purity. It reminded them that Lazarus was all too aware of their unchecked ambition, and given the choice to steal the pure essence of an unborn soul for power, they would. But worst of all, it was the sting of jealousy that one of their own, Warlock Vryce, actually *did* it—and they didn't think to do it first.

Even Lucian wasn't immune to the judgement. For he too had taken the plunge in consuming the flesh of the divine. Starving and hungry for a single apple, Lucian's first heart eaten was nothing more

than a spot of unluck that he stole from a wealthy noble thousands of years ago. A life of misfortune and pain had long taught him the error of his ways.

"Since you care the most about their well-being... why don't you handle the most difficult country? The United States has long held a penchant for rebellion, and since Lady Alexandria will need some time to acclimate herself to her new role, you shall oversee bringing the country of heathens to their knees." Lazarus's order was absolute.

Of-bloody-course. The same country that Vryce is hiding in, another rebel Warlock in Peter Culmen, and the lot that killed good-ol Suicide. At least I'll get to see Vegas. "My lord, I have no armies of the dead. My paupers are simply unlucky, the smallest number of any other Lord or Lady here." Lucian attempted an appeal, but he knew his fate was already sealed. His gaze moved over to Lou, the Lady of Fate, who wore a slight smirk. *Yeah... I'm screwed.*

"Wars do not begin with the dead, my friend. With the consolidation of the Church of Lazarus and Unification, armies once wielded by governments will assist you. Along with of course... necromancers and sorcerers from every society and the council of twelve other Death Lords. At least, those they can spare for their own conquests of course."

The Lord of Murder, with his glowing red eyes behind the black skull that comprised his face, patted Lucian on the back. "I'd say that I'd love to murder the United States, but I'm going to take Russia. Rasputin has been a bit of a devil of late, and we all know that despite their bravado, that newborn country is nothing more than a fleck in history. I'm sure you'll succeed swimmingly. I'll send you my best."

"If I die, Fate gets my soul..." Lucian retorted.

"Fine, I'll send my worst then."

"Fate still gets my soul."

"That's why you get the worst. I'd have a great spot for you in my museum of dead legends. You should really see what I've done to the

labyrinth these days—when you aren't busy bawling your eyes out on your Seat of Gilded Crowns."

"My lover's got humor." The Lady of Fate smiled. "Lucian will find what he's looking for. Freedom? Victory? Validation... Death would be lucky for him. If anything, a few centuries of suffering as rednecks feast on his blood will teach him another lesson."

Lazarus descended from the altar with his two attendants. Each dipped their thumb in the reliquary of angelic blood and smeared a thumb print on Lucian's mask. "You are officially ordained and released to your charge. Go forth and earn the glory you've long sought at our council. Call it a bit of foresight, but having the Lord of Misfortune hear the rest of the assignments would be inviting baneful magic into our house, my child."

Lucian kept his head down as the thumbs ordained his mask. *I'm a little teapot...* he sang rapidly to control his thoughts in the room. A stray thought would let any number of creatures pluck it like a cherry, so by focusing on anything but what he really wanted to think, Lucian masked, even if he was screaming the song in his head as he performed his polite bow. His pace was that of a scurrying old man shuffling down an aisle of monsters envious and lusting after the scraps of his soon-to-be empty throne, but his mind ignored them. A thought was gnawing at the base of his skull that he knew must be suppressed until he was at a safe distance. *Is it still sight these days? Nobody is scrying on me, right? At least out of the building.* A radioactive mind worm that wriggled in his decayed skull begged to burst out of his eyes.

He hurriedly undid the double doors again and broke into a sprint out of the chapel. Wooden sandals echoed on the marble floors as the Vatican guard stood at attention until the rays of the black sun kissed his skin. Lucian tumbled down the long staircase, letting the pain cloud his thoughts and bathing in the laughter of soldiers going about their day in the streets of Rome. It wasn't until Lucian lay prone, tongue tasting shit on a sewer lid on a small cobblestone alleyway several blocks away that he let his brain finally speak the truth he just saw.

"Why didn't Lazarus touch the blood...?" The Unification survived on the blood of the divine. It's how they did their magic. They weren't gods, just mortals who plucked the fruit of knowledge to shape the world. To deny the blood was to deny power. Lazarus either *couldn't* use the blood because he was lying or he *wouldn't* touch the blood because he was already divine.

Lucian couldn't help but cackle in laughter at the absurdity of the thought. He was ordained to murder a continent by altar boys. Something was wrong... and unfortunately for those in the United States, his answers would be over their graves.

Closing his eyes, Lucian allowed himself to descend into Purgatory. It would be a long walk across an ocean to meet whatever paltry armies the Church of Lazarus would give him. Taking a commercial airline was just begging for trouble, and terrible food service, but at least, Lucian would get to restock his coins in his favorite city of all time. New Orleans was his destination. The city plagued by bad luck always managed to claw itself back. A city of romance and myth. His current Seat of Gilded Crowns.

CHAPTER 4

"The black sun offers plant life no sustenance. The bleak paradise of Dystopia claims that their science can feed the world. How long will you live under the thumb of corporations for food? Denied the very freedom to tend to our gardens and toil soil? The Church of Lazarus can show us a new way to rewind the world. All we require is your faith and your acts of service."

–Printed message stapled to light pole

Jane loved vertigo. The feeling of plummeting through the abyss, tumbling wildly out of control and watching the world whiz past before her very eyes in a dizzying circle made her feel at home. Her past life was a whirlwind of chaos, and she thrived in being the eye of a storm. She and Mike made the snap choice that the best place to hide wasn't by running above the prison on the labyrinth's walls but to dive down inside. It would be too easy for every demon to see them at once if the two were inch-worming their way across the high walls like caterpillars, and at least down below, they could fight or sneak a smaller number rather than cling for life as magic and spear assaulted them. Mike fell like a hippopotamus, but she tumbled into a forward somersault with all the grace of a treasure goblin flailing for a jewel just out of reach. *I miss my rocket boots. Oh look… demon squirrel.*

She honestly didn't care if she splatted face first into the floor. Pain wasn't something she felt as a ghost, and in an odd way—she enjoyed the freedom that gave her. So, while Mike focused on a soft landing, dragging his hand along the wall and tumbling to remain quiet, Jane enjoyed the menagerie of monsters she saw mid-tumble. Gargoyles, demon-rat-squirrel things, plague doctors, minotaurs, and more—each danced once before the soul-forged emerald and amethyst walls blocked their views.

She hit the ground like a wet noodle and just lay there. *On one hand... freedom. On the other... there is no rush or sense of peril. THIS IS BORING!*

"Shhhhhhhiiiiiiiiiittt, Jane, you okay?" Mike skidded to her side.

"Way to catch me, jerkface." She twisted her arm back into position, lurched into a runner's sprint, and bolted down the hall. "This way."

"Sorry sorry... sorry... wait up..." Mike whispered platitudes and trailed behind her.

The labyrinth was massive from what they saw earlier. Intentionally a maze designed with various earth minerals for every sector, Jane recalled seeing four: Emerald, Amethyst, Sapphire, and Gold. The walls interlaced with each other to form a massive spiral with smaller prisons on the outside and a single cell that was heavily guarded in the middle by all four types. The walls were easily thirty feet tall, the ceiling now vaulting more than a hundred feet above them with gargoyles and vreeches waking up from the alarm. Their only chance of getting through was using the walls as cover and slipping into a prison to hide or keep moving. Even though Jane didn't feel pain, she still didn't want to experience whatever torture demons had up their sleeves. Although the thought did conjure several images in her imagination, she quickly pushed them down out of embarrassment and focused on finding a way out of Purgatory for now. *Get it together, girl. No use in truckin' around in this gold mine without the tools to drill*

for oil. She hissed at herself upon realizing her mind was flustered… and that she was slightly lost.

At the first intersection, Jane skidded to a halt and peeked. To the north, the walls became more emerald in make, and a sleeping minotaur was being woken up by a gargoyle landing on its knees. To the west, straight through, it led closer to the middle with a mix of emerald and amethyst, a clear path at the moment, and then from the south, she spied a posse of … plague doctors? They were very much still living. Human and filled with the aura of life—dragging a cart of souls stuffed in jars on wooden rickety wheels. They stopped outside of a prison and were opening large iron bars to place a jar inside.

"So… straight ahead?" Mike whispered right in her ear.

Jane jumped back and nailed his face with the back of her head—wincing reflexively. "Dude. Don't sneak up on me." She punched his thigh. "No, not west. Not yet. We have to get there soon; I think I saw the other exit when falling. This whole place is a spiral with two entries. But… not now. We gotta get moving still." She pointed up. Like a swarm of spiraling bats, creatures flew through the entrance they had just come through, several circling above their initial drop point.

Mike let out a small curse, then straightened himself up like he belonged, simply walked out into the intersection, and turned north with his hands buried in his pockets. He strolled right to the minotaur like it was an old friend.

Are you fucking insane!? Jane gulped and tried to pull off the same act, following behind. "Ummm…"

"Don't worry. I got this. Superpower of mine—just go with it."

This is how we get turned into ashtrays.

The minotaur and gargoyle were bickering with hisses and snarls, and a swift backhand crunched the gargoyle's maw before any eyes were laid upon the ghostly duo strolling through dead-god-gardens. Its black horns tilted sideways as it studied them, massive hands

tightening around an axe taller than Jane. Mike gave a casual nod and waved his hand and kept walking forward.

Peeking behind her, Jane noticed that one of the plague doctors holding the cart with a raven-beaked mask and golden-rimmed googles glared at them but didn't alarm the other three. Her eyes nearly bugged out of her head as they got closer. *Okay. We can take them... right?* She nodded. *Yeah. Totally.* Her mind raced back to the reality TV shows she watched about cryptid combat back in Texas... and in every scenario, a captured minotaur might as well been an old-world war tank. Vastly tougher than they looked. She was pretty sure anti-freak cannons were invented just to punch their hearts out of their chest.

Just as Jane was getting ready to sprint into action, they were close enough to the monsters that she could feel the heat radiating off them. Mike still didn't stop walking though. He just ... kept going at the same pace, waving his hand, and putting it back in his pocket. Then repeating the process. He bumped right into the gargoyle's side, bounced back slightly, then walked forward again to repeat it.

Alright, bro. Marbles. You've lost them... She sighed and bumped blindly into Mike's back. Then repeated.

The gargoyle pointed at the pair and chuckled, kicking Mike down the next intersection to the west. Mike just calmly stood back up and kept walking, blindly waving at nobody in particular.

Jane braced herself and walked face first into the minotaur's crotch. *This is not an invitation!* A flash of white danced before her eyes as the monster snapped the axe hilt into her temple, sending her sprawling to the ground. Stunned that Mike's dumb plan was actually working, Jane picked herself up and continued forth. *I have so many questions.*

Even more questions when the insane plane did work, and the gargoyle took flight, and the minotaur headed down the path they had just come.

The walls surrounding them were almost purely emerald now with breaks every fifty yards or so with prison chambers. Some had thick iron bars, others had no door, and some had doors with etched occult wards laced in blood like a scarlet letter upon them. Inside the nearest prison, a scrawny old man with a long-tattered beard was chained to the wall. He still wore a pointed hat and green tunic while a floor filled with rotted petrified apple saplings decorated his chambers. Both Mike and Jane paused, neither finding the strength to look away from where someone had attached spigots to the man's heart, harvesting his blood like tree-sap into the planted saplings. Slow, shallow breaths wheezed through open door.

"Guess we know what happened to Johnny Appleseed..." Mike said somberly.

Jane marveled at Mike and his chopped brown hair that would make anyone want to pet and ruffle it like a pet dog. A red bandanna survived his death, and he still clung to that as tightly as he did the fingerless workman gloves his spirit wore. Every ounce of his clothing had that distinctly worn look about it. Unlike Jane who bore death marks all over her body, Mike looked exactly like he did the day he became famous. Except for his iconic anarchist trench coat, he was the spitting image of himself on TV. In a broadcast she had seen a thousand times, Mike let the secrets of eating demon hearts out to the internet—by eating the heart of Golgoroth and becoming an extremely public vampire. Blasting the entire concept of how to steal magic to everyone in the world was certainly a way to make yourself famous. She wasn't sure if that made things better or worse, but at least his death meant they were reunited. Even if she was jealous that if you eat giant demons, you don't keep the death wounds. *Maybe all of his are like a bunch of rotten organs on the inside and worms. Yup. Mike has worms. I'm convinced.*

The cart squeaked down the labyrinth.

She pulled Mike into the prison, just in case anything flew overhead, and cupped his cheeks, pulling his attention solely onto her. "Hey, notice me. I have questions."

Mike's eyes were pools of sadness and frustration, not at her, just ... always. He grabbed her shoulders back and centered her between him and the draft-tap god. "I notice you. Ask away."

"That stunt you just pulled—"

"Been dead longer than you. Demons assume almost every ghost down here in Purgatory can't see, is blind, and just wanders around. The dead who do leave sure as hell aren't clamoring to get back in once they cross the veil. As soon as I saw those Unification sorcerers feeding souls... I knew our odds were better against the wardens." He tussled her hair. "White-guy-construction-worker superpowers, sis. Nobody notices us when we blend in. Nobody ever pays attention to the help, the laborer—"

Jane silenced his oncoming rant with a finger over his lips. "Question two. Why don't you ... look like me? You know, with all the marks of how we died. You were ... ACTUALLY fried by lightning."

This question caused Mike to clench his jaw and debate answering. She could feel the oncoming "you don't want to know" or half-lie bubbling up in his gut. *Don't you dare try to protect my feelings.*

"Vampire," he blurted with a nod. "Yup. I uh... I went full vampire. Like, fuck it, right?" Mike let her go and went over to the Johnny Appleseed. "I actually ate Golgoroth's heart, a demon of war. After that, I was undead as they come. Sun burned, wooden stakes through the heart, the full nine yards. Even had to drink human blood. Even if I cut my hair, the next night I was back to normal."

"Yeah, well, I injected synthetic cryptid blood from Elcoll into my veins for super speed so... meh!" Jane couldn't resist sticking her tongue out.

"How did that work out for you? No side effects?"

"Just my metabolism eating me alive and sending me to an early grave... What the fuck are you doing? Question time is over." *His insides are totally worms.*

"You flip on a dime, eh?" He laughed and checked the pulse of Appleseed. "The Unification was getting blood for centuries to power their magic while the rest of us suffered in ignorance. I think we stumbled onto one of their farms. They kill the competition and drain them dry."

Mike lifted Appleseed's hand and let it fall back down with a sickening *thwop* against the gemstone wall and the soft clatter of chains. "Reminds me of Lazarus. He was just like this in his tomb. No door, no real guards, just ... clinging to existence."

"Well don't kill this one then. No need. You can order magic fertilizer from Haystack that won't grow petrified plants. We need to move though. Those bird-masked people are wheeling that cart closer." *We can't do fuck all about this anyway right now. One man doesn't save the world.*

Mike slowly nodded before pocketing a petrified apple and peeking out the door to check up. "Yeah, well, their blood can't help us now... if we get out." She saw his eyes sparkle as if the nicotine-addicted hamster in his brain was coming alive with a scheme. "We may not be able to use their power but—"

"—the rest of the gang can." She nodded. "Plus, I know people in Dystopia who owe me. If anyone can fix a bunch old dead guys nobody knows..."

Mike's gaze was fixated on a swarm of vreech demons flying past before grabbing Jane's wrist and running west, keeping themselves crouched low against the emerald walls and past several more prisons. "Nobody knows?" he uttered in defiance as they passed a barricaded door with occult wards. Several iron bars were jutting *out* of the door, and the methodic sound of a hammer hitting steel echoed from within. "That was Johnny-fucking-Appleseed. Planted all the

apple trees! Didn't you learn that in school?" He knocked on the door. The hammer stopped.

A tall bald black man with iron-colored eyes peered through the small peephole. "You two better be fixin' to set me free."

"You John Henry?" Mike asked while still crouched.

"In the flesh."

"Thought so." Mike flashed a smug look to Jane. "If you haven't broken out, we sure as hell can't get past this ward. Can you wait for us to get back? We need..."

A vreech screamed from above and descended. The leather-winged demon folded into a bullet dive and began to spew hellfire down the corridor. Jane quickly pulled Mike away from the door and began running, praying to herself that the scoring green-fire didn't catch them. The next intersection was a solid sprint away. Digging her feet in, she focused on the rhythmic timing of her run, letting the sense of death behind her fuel her pace forward. *One. Two. One. Two.* She smashed into the emerald wall with her shoulder and didn't get a chance to recover before Mike grabbed her by the collar and raced down south along walls with dusty gold flames.

Jane saw the plague doctors abandon their cart and race down the hallway after them, each casting a spell that summoned forth translucent shackles that barely missed her neck. *I hate sorcerers.* The dual-colored walls soon became a solid gold as they passed into the next sector. Prisoners they raced past seemed more alive, and Jane was certain she spied at least one she knew—the Slenderman, calmly sipping tea in an open cell but held as a prisoner from the very torches of golden light that surrounded him.

"West! Go west!" Jane shouted as she ran past Mike again, pointing ahead. Gargoyles, vreeches, sorcerers on their tail, and minotaurs barreled down on their position, rumbling the floor with each heavy hoof-fall. The first path west already had guards. "You had to talk to a guy, didn't you?!" Jane shouted as she scanned for an opening at the next.

"Who doesn't know American folklore?!" Mike ran like a semi next to her, taking the second path west and shouldering through a gargoyle, tumbling past, and booking it forward.

"I don't! I don't fucking know American folklore because America sucks giant donkey balls!" Jane planted a boot on the gargoyle's face and jumped to catch up. They were headed in the right direction and looped around the center where most of the guards were. "It should be just ahead!"

"We aren't going to make it. Fuck it..." Mike skidded into an open-air prison that was larger, only a mere fifty yards away from the exit Jane saw—to her eternal frustration.

"You gotta be shitting me. What good is a giant ... blue ... bull?"

"Help me!" Mike shouted as he tugged on the chains of the largest ox Jane had ever seen as a minotaur's axe cut her ponytail clean off.

She dove into the room and frantically started kicking the pylon. "A little help!" she yelled at the ox.

The ox, easily over ten thousand pounds in girth of pure muscle, roused angrily at the two ghostly intruders but was even more challenged by the minotaur. Its eyes turned red, and Jane witnessed actual smoke, cartoonish in nature but blackened like a coal furnace, spew forth from its nostrils as it railed against the chains.

The minotaur ignored the ox and brought its silver axe clear overhead to chop Mike in twain.

Jane abandoned the pylon plan and launched herself at the cloven feet, hoping to destabilize the monster. Curling herself up into a tiny ball, she crashed into the immovable legs. The minotaur didn't budge. Instead, she found herself stepped on and pinned down to the ground. Even as a ghost, she suddenly felt out of breath from the demons' touch, and the view of Purgatory she took for granted began to darken. Like she was being put back in place like a good little girl. Stripped of what little power she had left.

The sound of an axe hitting flesh made her feel sick, but she never expected Mike to roar like a frenzied beast. Suddenly her vision came

back as the giant blue ox burst over her and crashed the minotaur through the wall. The giants easily plugged the width of the corridor, and every creature outside was focused on the rampaging blue beast that charged inward to the center of the prison.

"That's Babe." Mike clutched his own chest. "Man, I miss being a vampire... Enhanced strength is something I miss."

Jane looked down at the chains to see what happened. They weren't ripped apart or cleaved in two. Instead, the sixth link down was simply undone with a gap in the link.

"I'm an iron worker, Jane. Support chains like these need to be tightened or shortened. There's always one for sizing."

"Show off..." *Look at me—I gave everyone magic. I know dead old guys and giant blue steaks. Tsk. You're adorable.*

"Let's get out of here."

Sneaking through the western exit was significantly easier now that there was a rampage underfoot. Jane and Mike easily approached a set of golden double doors encrusted with American coins and a slogan in a plaque that was framed above:

A MAN'S ONLY WORTH IS HOW MUCH WEALTH HE CAN GENERATE.

Split down the middle of the double doors was an arcane symbol both of them recognized: the official alchemy guild symbol used by the Society of Deus. Jane had seen it on TV countless times and had even fought side-by-side with their armies once. Mike ... tried to kill their leader, Primus Vryce.

"Psychopaths, aren't they all..." Mike sighed as he pushed one open and walked through.

"Without them, we'd all be dead."

"We are ... dead." He held up a finger.

The current room was a posh Victorian loading dock. A dozen elevators fed by pullies, lit gas lamps that flickered a soft orange, and the soft brass instrumental music of an old scratchy record player. Pallets filled with small clay jars and wax seals were neatly stacked and labeled in Italian, but Jane knew those were filled with harvested blood. Everything clicked into place. *They really are farming myths and legends for magic well before the end. No wonder it's so cheap!*

A voice speaking Italian, interrupted only by the sharp tap of hard-bottom shoes on smooth flooring, echoed closer. Both Mike and Jane took cover behind a crate of bottled blood. From what she could see, one was adorned in the white robes of the Church of Lazarus. They were wearing a black skull mask with rubies for eyes and seemed to be issuing orders to the other. Nothing about the masked figure struck Jane as living, but she wasn't a Death Lord either. Instead, she wore frame-hugging leather underneath her robes with a rapier and had stark-white hair that flowed down her back. *She's beautiful.*

The other creature was an Ukobach demon, a minor demon that Jane was super familiar with. The short, naked, red-skinned fiend carried a pan full of coals. It was about five foot in height with eyebrows and a nose that begged to be punched in the face. *Fucking fast food demon. If I hear one more ad about your chicken wings...* The pair paused in front of them, and the elegant and deadly lady gave some final orders. As the Ukobach fell to its knees and kissed her shoes, Mike tapped Jane's ankle.

Do you speak Italian? he mouthed.

Fuck no? she gestured back silently.

Well, what did they say?! he pantomimed.

Jane had an idea. *It's my turn, shortcake.* She gave Mike a wink and patted the top of his head while telling him to wait. They watched as the demon remained bowed until the Church of Lazarus delegate left, closing the door behind her. The minor demon dared not lift its head.

"I got this, bro," Jane whispered and jumped into view on top of the pallet. "Hey. Chicken wings."

The demon rose, startled by the sudden appearance of Jane in a room she didn't belong but didn't sound any alarms or screams. Instead, it leveled the pan of hot coals just beneath Jane's chin. "You don't have rank over me. So speak, descendant of Lazarus."

"What makes you think I don't have any rank over you? Do you know who I am?"

The demon studied her for a few seconds, its large, black-saucer eye sockets drinking in the story of her soul. "Death by suicide."

"By the Lord of Suicide," Jane corrected and bounced off the crate, standing on one leg and bending over the coals to blow on them. "I'm a representative from the Church of Lazarus. Texas division. You are ... one of the many Ukobachs in charge of shipping Barhgest Burgers to the Devil's Steakhouse at T-Cellular arena, yes?"

Jane just knew Mike was probably flailing behind his crate. *Wtf is right... Watch me work and squirm.*

"I am sorry, my liege." The demon bowed. "There are so many of suicide running through this realm of Purgatory in the past year, it's hard to keep up with who is whom."

"Well, do you have our delivery of Barghest Burgers? For every one of your kin you sell to us... don't you get ... taller? When people die of gluttony by your hand." Jane held her hand a foot above the demon.

"Th-that is none of your con-cern. My height is triple the others.'" It batted away her hand. "We are under new management now. Bosses are changing often these days it seems. Upper management is making movements."

"Hrmm... unfortunate. Because I hear that Midwinter Black coffee..." Jane stepped closer, "recently discovered that if you grind Ukobach eyes, their brew is potent enough to raise the dead. If we can't sell Barghest Burgers... maybe the vreeches will cut a deal to sell us Ukobach eyes. Unless..."

The demon fell to its knees, peppering a hundred kisses on Jane's feet. Mike couldn't help but stand up with the most confused look Jane had ever seen a grown man make.

"Please, anyone but Midwinter. We've done good? We kept the art of frying foods with no sun! Yes. Grease. Fat. Flavor. New Orleans still has best food. We rule here and grow tall."

Jane knelt down and pinched the demon's ear, forcing its head back to look up at her. "So, if you aren't serving or don't want to be served in Texas, then tell me about your new orders. Maybe I might want a new job too? I don't have to go back to Dystopia or find dear Lord of Suicide and report back, do I? Maybe we can go to New Orleans?" Jane added an extra pout to her voice for added effect and let the Southern twang she could summon from hell itself bathe the demon in its full captivating effect.

"The Lord of Murder is making moves." It winced at the pinch... but its foot thwapped the floor like a happy dog at the pain. "It wants us to fatten up the gods in this sector and harvest anything that remains. The Lord of Misfortune is coming to kill everyone in America, so these gods won't exist soon. He... he... he wants all their hearts, blood, eyes, and souls before Misfortune finishes. Says we can use any dead we want to fatten up fast. A fried soul is a faithful soul, they say!" The demon's rotten lips curled around a smile.

"Now who's a good little boy..." Jane scritched its chin. "See... if there are no living people, no reason to be in the meat business. Poor Misfortune gets to come to a new nation, and all its spoils will be raided before he even gets here."

The demon could barely keep its lidded eyes open. "Yyyyesss... no living... no meat... no coffee. No Midwinter. Yyyyou are a smart suicide. Already did it once! No need to do it twice. Join Murder. They say... they say he's almost got Golgoroth's replacement on his side."

Mike moved forward at that name, and Jane could tell he wanted to grab the demon by its throat and just strangle it. She batted him away before he could get close.

"Well, no living means ALSO means no need for people to eat fried foods or enjoy fireworks. Wouldn't that put you little buggers of gluttonous enjoyment out of work? You *are* demons of pleasure, after all."

These thoughts raced around its head, but the hamster inside its skull wasn't strong enough on the wheel to fully power the light behind the Ukobach's eyes.

"So here is what you are going to do. You are going to fatten up and make all those legends in there strong again, okay?" Jane flexed her arms. "Do what that fine lady told you to a T. Do not accept no for an answer from any vreech down there. Get all your little buddies down here if you need and feed those gods 'til they are big enough to roll down the Mississippi, ya hear?"

The Ukobach nodded furiously.

"I'm going to go up to New Orleans with my bodyguard here, and we are going to talk to Mr. Misfortune about finding you work in a place with nothing but ghosts, mmmkay? If you do a good job keeping these guys big and healthy until we come back... you might have a place in a new business."

"Yes, ma'am. Yes, ma'am. My... my name Fed."

"Well, I'll call you Mr. Fed." Jane extended a hand for a shake. Mr. Fed gladly took it.

"Get on with it then. There is a big ol' steak running around in there." Jane's smile at that moment would melt anyone's heart, and apparently, the heart of a fiend who fed people until they choked on their own vomit.

The siblings watched the demon rush out of the room with vigor in his orders from the Church of Lazarus and waited for the doors to close.

"So... I've got questions," Mike finally asked.

"Demons speak any language known to humanity. They are the ultimate translators, and corporations scare the fuck out of them. I mean, screw Angel-Be-Gone, just tell them that a company is

launching a new product line based off their kin and…" She twirled her fingers.

"I feel like I missed a lot in the time I was down here."

"We make a good team, don't we?" She offered a fist.

Mike fist bumped back. "Fuck yeah, we do. Finally ready to go back up?"

"Looks like we got another Lord of Death to kill."

"And a tomb full of legends to save."

They pushed a crate of divine blood onto one of the elevators and began their ascent back to the lands of the living. *Still sucks I won't be able to actually EAT a Po'boy.* Jane sighed while tugging on a pulley. From the look on Mike's face, she knew he was having the same thought.

CHAPTER 5

"Grasp your destiny or watch your dreams turn to ash. Magic has returned. Companies branded it. Religion tries to steal it. Divinity is at your fingertips—but it takes knowledge hidden from your eyes for centuries. The Society of Deus is not your enemy. Enlightenment is for everyone."

–St. Paul University Brochure

Damien Vryce hated the French Quarter. New Orleans had much to offer as a whole, but this small segment of tourism felt as invasive today as it did when he walked the streets three centuries ago. Vryce knew it was formed in the seventh century; he had been there to witness it. There when the romance and mystery had once been a spectacle for newcomers, a place where old magic was hawked on display in a vain attempt at survival from wealthy landowners. Cultured civilization gave up the old ways well before magic faded from prominence, but those same civilizations still paid to keep a witch in their pocket for emergency's sake.

It wasn't the people Vryce disliked, at least in most cases, but rather the ignorance that often washed away true magic. He'd stayed away from New Orleans for several decades, much like how he avoided Chicago's St. Patrick's Day parades. Pagans celebrating

the very bastard who chased them out of Ireland rubbed him the wrong way.

Yet today was a new day.

The black sun he worked to summon forth hung gloriously in the sky. Its muted rays and permanent eclipse bathed the oldest quarter in its faded violet light, allowing the gaslight torches to flicker and cast the perfect set of dancing shadows on weathered streets. Vampires, ghosts, shape-shifters, fortune tellers, and regular people mingled in broad daylight to conduct their affairs and share culture both old and new—the dream he'd long sought to see born. A chance for every human to shed their ignorance and embrace the hidden world beyond the veil of innocence. A chance for creatures of the night to walk once again, no matter the time of day.

"Those bold enough to grasp power can have power." Vryce breathed in deeply as he set foot on Rue de Chartres. It was a smaller foot than he was used to, a small teenage foot in a brand mortals called Doc Martins. He wasn't exactly sure how good of a podiatrist Doctor Martin was, but his boots were highly recommended by students in the Society of Deus, and Vryce was doing his best to blend in.

As a fifteen-year-old girl, dressed in pressed black slacks, a formal black shirt with a blue tie, and an off-black men's pea coat—Vryce looked like a tomboy. His brown hair was pulled back and tied by something his great-great grandchildren called a "scrunchie," and golden spectacles dangled on a button nose that framed both his heterochromatic eyes, one golden-green, the other a deep shade of unnatural black. As the world's premiere master of possession (the time-honored art of stealing the bodies of others), Vryce had walked this earth for over six centuries in the shoes of countless lives. Yet the body he resided in now was as much his as his original form, albeit with a chromosome altered during the early stages of gestation. *A new age calls for a new form. Besides, I shan't run into problems. A mortal coil is nothing more than a vehicle for the conscience.*

The smell of rotten sewage assaulted his nostrils, and somehow, that made his stomach grumble out of desire for food. He stopped at the nearest corner after stepping off the streetcar and set down his viola case and black Brook & Talbots branded-leather adventure bag to clench his stomach. *Why this smell makes me hungry, I'll never understand. I miss drinking blood. Far more efficient.*

"You okay, miss?" A stranger bold enough to approach asked.

"Yes." Vryce straightened instantly. "Pardon? It's been a while since I visited, but I hear there is a bazaar of oddities and curiosities nearby? Mind..."

"Yeah, I can help you out. Lookin' for Fortune Row, eh? Head past St. Louis Cathedral, you'll see a big sign for a gumbo shop and turn left on St. Louis. You'll find Bourbon Street about a block up," the stranger said while snapping his jaw back into place. A ghost from a bygone era but alarmingly polite.

"Bourbon street? I was hoping..."

"For something in Theme? You've got that look of a girl who knows what she's after. Sorry to disappoint, bambin. Everything is on Bourbon this week for the festivities. All them soldiers arriving drawin' all the crowds."

"Right. Thank you." *Let's see... he's about a hundred years old dead. Polite. Helpful. French-American.* Vryce reached down into his adventure bag and rummaged around before pulling out three vials of mercury. "If you find yourself compelled by a necromancer. Drink one, throw one at the ground, and the other at his eyes." An act of unprovoked altruism that did not directly benefit him was ... rare. But Vryce had spent centuries within the Unification fending off metaphorical daggers while eliminating his rivals all the same, and this was meant to be a vacation. A chance for him to start a new life for the next several centuries.

"Oooh... dark one aren't you, la jolie? Thank you. You uh, want an escort? They call me—"

"No. I'll be fine. Thank you." Vryce picked up his belongings and headed forth. Getting a ghost entangled with his affairs was a recipe for a year of haunting which he didn't have time for.

To say that Vryce was looking forward to a much-needed vacation was an understatement. His quaint form weaved deftly through increasingly dense crowds in anticipation of seeing how this city had survived magic crashing back in. If his own Twin Cities up in Minnesota had founded entire universities and militaries based off its use, then New Orleans surely would have taken the chance to bring back the old ways. The black sun reached a nexus of noon on a cold day, and packed streets of mixed crowds were engaging in festivities despite the chill. Within the bay, Vryce could see entire shipyards filled with tankers, and old galleon ghost-ships anchored and awaited their turn to disembark. The city streets, however, were an illuminated bouquet of neon signs and old gaslit lanterns for cafés that promised warmth, delicious alchemical brews, and pastries. Pastries he hadn't had the chance to taste in his own body for six centuries.

"If only the dead didn't make the very air taste like a wet grave." He pinched his nose. *Thank the gods I don't have the heightened senses of a vampire at this very moment.*

The streets may have been lined with plastic bags and overrun waste, and a vampire may have been spilling blood from a man just out of Vryce's vision, but he didn't care. The excitement of finally seeing a showcase of magical oddities and fortune tellers was the entire reason he took the cross-continental road trip he did. The majority went on foot, and he was certain that his great-grandchildren Gabriel and Delilah could handle their respective agenda. For the moment, Vryce wanted to experience life and wonder again. He sacrificed the world for the return of magic and was beyond eager to see what they'd done with it.

Ducking underneath soldiers wearing Church of Lazarus clothing and elbowing past politicos from the ravenous leftovers of Washington, D.C., Vryce fought his way through dense consumers

and partygoers. *One would think that noon would be a quieter time, but I suppose the undead need not fear the sun any longer.* This new form was shorter than he was used to, and all around him was nothing more than the middle of people's backs. Being verbal and saying please barely mattered as other packs of humanoids jostled him, and Vryce became more aggressive in his approach, using his viola case to jab taller people in the ribs. Doing so was an ill-calculated maneuver that left his other side open for large lady to thwack his neck with her own oversized. That single act caused his balance to falter, sweeping and jostling him around like a frog in a witch's stew as the crowd bustled and shifted.

People ignored the girl struggling to regain footing, often smooshing and knocking Vryce around despite the sharpness of his elbows. He had a newfound respect for his tiny homunculi that clamored underfoot of his gargoyles. By the time Vryce had wedged himself halfway through, he was rather sure that several parts of his human form that were taboo for touching were indeed touched. *I may have to kill half later.* Wholesale annihilation of ignorance was behind him for the moment. Even if he had to make a demeaning crawl between the legs (dragging his Brook & Talbots dufflebag with him) of a Unification necromancer fresh off a boat for progress in order to finally step foot on Bourbon Street, he swore to recognize the limitations of smaller female frames forever. *How does Delilah keep her aura of command with such undiluted mastery?*

"I hate the French Quarter." Vryce pushed his spectacles up with a single finger, the viola case strap tucked in the crux of his elbow.

For fourteen city blocks, an entire parade of colors, nudity, drugs, and alcohol paraded through with purple lights and brightly colored yellow-and-green fanfare. The parade wasn't his issue. Lining every block was a collection of stalls and bazaars he could tell with a single glance were peddling the most basic of magic. *What did Gabriel call this? The basic bitch of woo-girl witchdom?* Vryce didn't know what a woo girl was, but he certainly heard their battle cry.

Vryce almost set his bags down before spotting the filth and vomit that dribbled along the sidewalk and decided against it. Shouldering the Brooks bag bandolier style, he swapped the viola case to wipe his hands clean from the stench of human contact while surveying his vacation hot-spot prospects, *trying* to keep an open and optimistic mind. It didn't surprise him that the level of … talent … was below his desire. *Can't fault mortals for latching onto the basics at first. Even toddlers need to walk.* Yet the taste of disappointment still hung within him like the lingering smell of rotting flesh. *They could have at least purchased a basic guide.* Nonetheless, he was here to scout, potentially guide, and also bear witness. Standing on the sidelines wasn't going to reveal any hidden talents lurking among the plethora of street vendors.

Strolling against the tide of the parade on the south side, Vryce ignored the card sharks and sleight-of-hand gambling games at first. A handy skill, but a skill that wasn't anything new. Nestled between two gamblers was a small apothecary stand selling incense, oils, and other bottled cryptid humors with a tarot array laid out. The owner had an aura of frustration about her as she struggled to attract attendees deeper to her table or speak at a volume loud enough to stand out. Curiously, he stepped up.

The short-cut blonde woman had crow's feet and smiled through her teeth—shooting a sideways glance to the dice-hawker to her right. "Finally, someone with taste. A quick path to fortune leads many to ruin. You look like a lost soul in need of guidance, dear, so allow me to help," she said, shuffling the cards.

Vryce picked up a small rustic bottle of dark brown liquid off the table with his free hand. "Perhaps. What is your specialty?"

"That, my dear, is an all-organic bottle of a Romani recipe of love." Her wrinkled hand moved adjusted her glasses. "I'm half Romani, and as a neo-pagan, we've spent many moons bottling the love of Aphrodite and the Sky Father into an aroma essence that will attract the husband you are looking for. The fact you picked this means you are on the prowl for love. Given how gorgeous you are for a woman

of your age, I hardly think you'll need help attracting someone, but a little oil goes a long away in bringing out your spirit animal of sensuality."

Vryce dropped the bottle back and quickly removed his hand, unaware of the slight rose-tint in his cheeks. "Neo... pagan... Romani... spirit animal?" The mental gymnastics of appropriated occultism hurt Vryce's brain, as if this lady had just crammed every basic bit of Coachella culture into a blender and made a frappe out of it.

She smiled more. "Yes, we women need to bind our familiars somehow. Would you like a sample?" She grabbed Vryce's wrist, and before he could react, she spritzed him.

At least the smell of cinnamon, patchouli, and cedar was more pleasant than other odors.

"I'm sorry, but I'm not looking for love." He smiled while wiping it off on his coat. "I'm also not a woman. So, tell me, Susan, do you manifest your magic through will? Have you stepped through the circles and imbibed blood? Or are you channeling a different way?"

Susan looked confused. "A little mind reader, are you? Well, no wonder you can't find love. A girl like you who doesn't acknowledge what she is won't ever be invited out." She gestured to her cards. "I don't even need to pull one to tell you that a dress would be more suited for you."

Vryce simply pointed to the sign that said *Susan's Sorcery*. "How much for a reading then? Tell me one true thing." He folded his arms, already suspecting where this was headed.

"A case of bottled water, three bitcoins or equivalent."

One transaction later, Vryce patiently observed the charade of fortune reading.

"You've come from a broken home and found yourself lost. The card of death means great change is about to be upon you, but life will change when you meet your emperor. His wisdom will provide you the steady hand and protection you need in this world." Susan went through all the motions of a proper cold read, but even Vryce noticed

that her gaze darted to a cheat sheet taped to the six-foot table. "Now today is only a special, but finding your emperor will be a long journey. I can help be your spirit guide in awakening your inner woman so you can bear multiple children. Think about how magical that would be in this world, to bring new life in."

"You are a tragic disappointment." Vryce curled long hair behind his ear. "Even these dice-dealers next to you have more skill. For starters, your oil is nothing more than basic herbs rebottled, and your skill with the cards is non-existent. Magic has returned, but out of your own ignorance or fear, you've refused to actually imbibe the blood or lack the willpower to do so. Also, you aren't of Romani descent. I'd wager given the aging patterns that you are Polish and German, but raised in Alabama and survived the rising of the black sun thanks to the forces in Dystopia. Displaced after the war, and now here in New Orleans having to work with the very creatures you despise whilst trying to build your own cult. I'd pack up your things. Remaining here will only allow you to taint these streets with your pungent odors."

Vryce had already turned his back and was continuing his journey to a mix of dayumns, and the loudest shrill "EXCUSE ME!" from the now fuming and fist-clenched Susan who followed behind Vryce as he continued shopping, swearing several curses that he easily ignored. Even as he sampled another fortune teller's crystal ball, a spirit channeler, and even a charm salesman, Susan followed along to warn and complain loudly behind him. None of the other stalls so far had any magic at all, and Vryce's reaction was certainly as endearing to each.

Between two buildings curled another small teenage girl in ragged black jeans and a leather coat that Vryce spied. She was nearly fetal in defense from two men who were trying to drag her out farther.

"Fucking witch, you owe us!" One spat and kicked her in the ribs before the other heaved her prone on the sidewalk mere feet away from Vryce.

The crowd flowed around them as if they were invisible, more interested in laughing at Vryce ignoring the vain attempts of an angry Susan and several other disgruntled fakes he called out.

The girl remained limp out of survival with burst lip and a black eye already forming; she just closed her eye from the sting of alcohol that was poured on her. Vryce was familiar with this song-and-dance, and if history was any teacher, a trip to a pyre and stake-burning was next for the poor girl.

"Excuse me, *gentlemen*," Vryce enunciated the final word intentionally. "What has this witch cursed you with to cause such ire?"

"Pound sand," the larger one said, fixing his green baseball cap down and snarling through his unkept beard. "All you cunts are the same. Runnin' away and stealing like little whores."

Susan shrilled from behind. "I told you she'd run. *Females* who dress like boys aren't the ones you want to buy."

Vryce's gaze shot to the side and glared at the crowd following him. Emboldened by their numbers, a small half-circle had formed behind him with Susan at the front. "Excuse me? What do you mean ... buy?" His voice was barely a whisper, but the content cut through the sound of the parade.

"You in a pretty dress would be nice." The second man reached down and picked up the girl by the neck. "It's a dangerous world out there. Vampires, demons, and monsters, yeah?" He nodded at Vryce. "Someone's gotta protect our future."

"And that someone is you?" Vryce chuckled. "Or... is it supposed to be ... them?" He pointed back to the half-circle. "Is... is that the game here? You ... buy ... people with talent in the craft?" Casually, he strung the viola case strap over his shoulder to free up his hands. He would not forget a promise made mere moments ago.

"Big mouth on a little lady."

"She's a witch for sure," Susan chimed in. "We could bottle her blood."

The half-circle closed, and the parade still marched on.

Vryce calmly opened a vial of Barghest blood under his peacoat with his thumb and gestured several circles with his index finger while reciting a small Latin incantation and looking into the eyes of the girl. Their minds merged, and their thoughts flowed as one.

<I do not know you, but I can teach you. What is your story, and why are you here?>

At the speed of thought, a flood of memories poured from the girl. Her name was Lumine, and she had consumed the heart of a minor demon of Agares, a crocodilian servant of the demon lord when she was twelve years old. Several like her were all kept nearby in a flat, initially promised food and a way to stop the hunger, in exchange for their blood being bottled. More flashes danced in Vryce's mind detailing how many along this bazaar kept those they called "freaks" chained for their power without having to risk fighting a demon themselves.

<It's impressive, and lucky, you were able to eat such a heart, even if minor. The hunger you feel now will never subside. You need to drink the blood of mortals and magical creatures for sustenance. It is why you are so weak now and unable to help yourself. If I free you from this torment now, will you promise me a favor in turn?>

The girl nodded.

<When I am done with my display, you will drink to regain your strength. Then you will rescue your brothers and sisters by your own hands. Do we have a pact, Lumine?>

"Grab her," the cap-wearing man shouted, choking Lumine further.

Vryce calmly set down his Brook & Talbots bag and opened it up as the half-circle lunged forward at him. Deft hands grabbed a spool of copper wire and uncorked one vial of bone dust from a three-hundred-year-old skeleton and rolled forward, winding the wire between his fingers and inhaling the dust.

Susan barreled forward, kicking over the bag and surprisingly grabbed Vryce by the hair with an intensity he didn't expect, right as other man firmly clenched just above his elbow. A third, the one with

the crystal ball, wrenched free the viola case on his back and tried to help pin Vryce down before his spell could be cast.

But it was already too late.

A cat's cradle of copper and blood intertwined his delicate fingers as he utilized centuries of sleight-of-hand training to finish the web and twisted with a wrist lock—once. *"Tu mondo puppa in minibus es."* Vryce couldn't resist curling his lips in a smile as the bodies of everyone on the street froze. Not just the half-circle. Not just Susan or the two men. But every person who walked past and had ignored them this entire time. The dancers at the tail end of the parade who were clearly watching but chose to do nothing, and even a shop owner who had locked his door shut a few seconds ago. All froze.

With a twist of the cradle, like puppets on strings, their arms bent like marionettes to their sides. Vryce remained kneeling next to Lumine, whose knuckles had turned white as she made tiny fists after being dropped to the ground. "You see, blood is the power that they lack for their spells, but also training. This cat's cradle, is a microcosm of hermetic principals for my control." He extended the cradle, letting the blood mix with bone dust and rotated his hands. In doing so, the crowd of people were forced to shamble in an orderly set of lines in front of the kneeling duo. "Willpower is a trained asset. It's very difficult to control a large number of people like this with a direct spell, so we focus our will on something smaller. As above, and so below." He nodded to the crowd.

"Who... who are you?" Lumine asked, massaging her bruising throat while marveling at the way Vryce's fingers deftly danced. Despite her injuries, Lumine eagerly leaned in toward Vryce out of curiosity, and her body language did not betray that he was a threat.

"A mentor with many enemies." *New Orleans isn't a waste after all.* "Now Lumine, as skilled as I am, this spell will not last forever in my current state. So, pick one that I won't kill. That one is for you to kill and regain your strength."

Lumine placed her hand on Vryce's knee and studied the crowd. Their faces paining to scream or shout, and their eyes dancing freely in panic even if their bodies refused to move on their commands. Even the dead and ghosts fell victim to his spell and soon realized that being supernatural or undead did not make one immune to sorcery.

Lumine pointed at Susan.

"Hrm. I'll admit. I did not see that coming..." Vryce quickly jerked the cradle taut and then clapped his hands together. The entire crowd went limp as their necks were snapped and twisted, blood and ectoplasm alike leaked from eyes as all within the spell were swiftly sentenced to death. Echoes of spines popping riddled off the walls to a moment of silence as those outside the spell's radius finally took note of what had transpired.

Susan, however, remained held, and very much alive. Lumine let her teeth grow into a vicious smile of crocodilian nature and lunged forward like the young vampire she was, finally getting the taste of the only substance that would satiate the eternal hunger she now had. Vryce could still feel the flow of pleasure from Lumine as she slated her thirst for revenge.

<Remember our pact.>

A wave of gratitude washed through her thoughts as Susan drew her final breath.

Vryce undid the cradle and searched the ground for his bag, viola, and spectacles while humming to himself. Magic had returned, but training was still needed. For a moment, he allowed joy to spread through him over a good deed performed. He felt a little like his old self—a favor earned from a powerful young prospect and the satisfaction of displaying the power he was known for.

Yet his bag was nowhere in sight. A bag that contained enough reagents and blood to handle any threat he encountered as a human. *Must have missed one.*

"Well, today is certainly going to be an adventure." He sighed.

Chapter 6

The Society of Deus has officially banned the consumption of any citizen—undead, dead, or living—within its borders unless express permission is given. While we understand that some entities are significantly more delicious than others, please understand unsanctioned feasting will result in your destruction.

Thank you. —Society of Deus P.S.A.

Chill nestled into Vryce's bones as he stepped into the shadows along a cobblestone pathway. The afternoon sun provided little warmth, and the Lilith Moon was already visible just over the bay. Breathing into his hands and rubbing them furiously, Vryce ignored the tenderness and red lines from the copper wire to focus on his quarry. Bodies of the fallen littered the street behind him, and along the two- and three-story balconies, gawkers were capturing photos of the scene. Some gave the occasional shout in his direction, but Vryce knew nothing would come of it. New Orleans wasn't under the protection of any particular lord or vampire. At best, a roaming squad of anti-freak unit police might attempt to take him in—a problem he already factored into his calculations should they arrive, and the very reason he needed to acquire the vials of blood and components in his bag.

Whoever stole this is bold. Why is it that I'm always the one they steal from? The Unification steals my soul, Alexandria steals from my libraries, Delilah steals my agents, and Gabriel for some blasted reason constantly steals my gargoyles. Cracking his neck to remove a kink, Vryce picked up his pace away from the parade. The cobblestone pathway was narrow, only room for two across, and so far, he'd encountered no courtyard entries or cold-iron gates into a warded haven. An inventory check of his pockets came up empty in a vain search for a spare vial of vitae. If combat was required, he would be at a significant disadvantage unless he used the power stitched to the viola slung over his right shoulder. A fragment of his true soul, bound and stitched to the phylactery, one of seven in the world, was but a sliver of his power—but enough to handle most threats. *No need to overreact just yet. There are Unification soldiers in this city, and playing a single note would certainly cut my trip short.*

Ever since the black sun rose, Vryce had kept a ... relatively low profile, only engaging in using his recovered true magic when needing to hammer in an unsightly nail that would become a threat. The very fact he existed and had overcome impossible odds was a self-created miracle, and he wasn't going to risk it by drawing unneeded attention to himself. *Within reason, of course.* From apprentice, to sorcerer, to vampire, and then warlock—Vryce broke divine law and reclaimed the fragments of his shredded soul so he could command the very spheres of creation and bend local reality to his will. It certainly raised the ire of the other liches and every angel and demon that existed. They were bound by the shackles of servitude for eternity, and in an ironic twist of fate, Vryce chuckled over being bound in an entirely different way despite his freedom from servitude.

"I need to hide like a mouse from an owl," he mused right as he saw pair of cloaks take a sharp right ahead. "At least until I can fight twelve Death Lords at the same time..." *Even if it takes me a thousand more years.* "Excuse me!" Vryce shouted and leaned into a sprint, clutching the viola case to prevent the clumsy bounce.

Rounding the corner was a childish mistake.

Six cloaked sorcerers from the Church of Lazarus were walking in sets of twos while rifling through the contents of his bag. Each footfall of their boots fell in unison with the one next to them, and beneath their cloaks, Vryce could clearly see shouldered automatic weapons and military garb. They paused at once and slowly turned their bloodshot eyes back in his direction—wolves looking upon a little lamb they just caught.

Vryce drank every ounce of information. *Six soldiers, sorcerers, one or two perhaps undead.* The markings of their Death Lords on their cloaks were familiar to him. A dancing black skeleton holding coins signified the Lord of Misfortune, and the red skull with wicked teeth represented the Lord of Murder. *Unlikely alliance. They typically do not play well together.* The cobblestone path he came from was too narrow for any real escape, but behind the six soldiers was a large open street back into public view. Hanging vines with white flowers lined both sides of this street from three-story red-brick houses. *Each window is boarded shut, but with a drop of blood, the vines could be useful.*

"Yes?" A soldier of Misfortune asked while closing Vryce's bag. The rest turned fully and took a passive stance but subtly revealing how armed they were by pulling their cloaks back. Each of their shadows grew in size and animated their hostility despite the owner's stoic demeanors.

Vryce unlatched his viola case. "Gentlemen, I believe you have accidentally taken something that doesn't belong to you. So, I've come to reclaim it."

"This?" The soldier slung the bag over his shoulder. "A little dangerous for a young sorceress like yourself to be wielding. A little dangerous for the citizens of New Orleans, it seems, as well."

"Mortals make their own choices, do they not?" Vryce extended a hand, fingers poised to snap as if he readied a spell. "New Orleans is unclaimed territory, and I've no quarrel with your cult today."

Several soldiers *tsked*. "Cult? Maybe to some," he acquiesced. "But you represent exactly why magic should be policed." The Misfortune soldier broke rank and took a step closer, and his shadow grew long claws. "You're a bit young to be a member of the Sons and Daughters, you don't dress like a Second City Helldiver, so, young lass, are you a lost member of the Society of Deus?" A pistol unholstered and was leveled back at Vryce's hand. "Or a holdover from the ravenous pricks of the Pentagon?"

I've certainly had better odds. It's been a few years since I tested how many bullets a mortal can take. "Maybe we got off on the wrong foot with you taking that which is mine. With one snap, you'll each be my puppets to do with as I wish—and we both know I'll snap before that bullet hits. Rock beats scissors; magic beats bullet."

"Only if you have ammunition." The soldier lowered his gun and pulled the trigger.

The echo of gunfire caused Vryce's eyes to widen and reflexively snap his fingers. Ready to summon forth his armies and twist their shadows to his whim, his fingers started to bind invisible strings as the pain in his right thigh crept into the back of his mind. Hissing through the pain as his vision blurred, Vryce abandoned his bluff and raced for his viola.

The five other soldiers descended upon him before a single note could be plucked. Their shadows sprung to life and bound Vryce's hands to the grimy ground. Freezing chills wracked his nerves from the shadows' touch, and no amount of struggling in this body of a teenage girl was going to break their steel-like grips. *THIS HURTS WAY MORE THAN I REMEMBER!*

Vryce, for the first time in centuries, actually screamed in pain as tears flowed freely. He wasn't sure which pain was greater—the sharp tearing pain in his thigh or the frustration at his limitations and invisible bindings. As helpless as he was when he was almost burned on a pyre for consorting with the demonic in England six hundred years ago. Just like then, his fate rested in the hands of the Unification. They

"saved" him then, and here he was again... infinitely more powerful—and bound just the same.

"See," the soldier of Misfortune crouched and grabbed Vryce's brown hair, yanking it back to force eye contact, "mages like you always get cocky. You're smart enough to not become a blood addict but cowardly enough to refuse eating a heart. So, all your components are here..." He tapped the bag. "Luckily for you, that makes you human. A pure one at the moment. Like a flower in a garden of weeds. A perfect sacrifice." He looked at the others. "Bag her. We only need a few more."

"Wait!" Vryce stalled. "Come on, Misfortune. Who is your regional director? I'm not exactly sacrifice material." *Sacrifice?* Vryce rolled his eyes. *They are prepping a summoning ritual.* "You are correct about a few things. I'm indeed human, but you've seen my work. How do you know I'm not agent for the Lady of Fate?"

The soldier shifted, fingers lifting up Vryce's chin. "And if you are?"

"I should have probably led with that." He winced, and one eye closed. "You know as well as I that she gives her specialists freedom. I'm from the Order of the Eastern Star. Here in New Orleans for the same reason you most likely are. The Unification's Seat of Gilded Crowns rests beneath us in Purgatory, no? How many gods still remain to drain dry? Out of the ten chambers on this globe, surely Lazarus isn't going to let farms of divine blood rest unguarded." The knowledge of the Unification's inner workings came easily to him. *I can offer secrets for decades.*

"So that's where you acquired such potent vitae... dangerous indeed." The soldier switched languages to Italian and uttered a command check to verify if the Lady of Fate had sent any troops or specialists recently.

Vryce knew exactly what he said and responded back in perfect Italian. "I'm not a recent conscript despite my age. I've been monitoring this region since the Lord of Suicide perished in Texas a year ago."

Swapping languages fluidly, knowing the position of their Death Lords, and secrets about the Seat, was certainly causing the soldier to pause. Vryce found himself pulled into a kneeling position, but his viola was still a touch out of reach. All he needed was to lay a single finger on its cherry oak frame—and this matter would be solved. "I can verify my standing. My seal and writ are under an arcane ward upon my instrument."

"Fate must smile upon us then today." He opened the case fully to inspect.

Vryce contemplated flinging himself onto it, but the blood seeping through his trousers was already causing him to see white stars. *I won't make it.* "I'm going to bleed out..." he said faintly.

The viola case slammed shut. "Yes. You're going to bleed just like we have a leak of information. Unsurprising given this is the nation of usurpers. Do you think that you're the first former Unification operative who has tried to bluff us?"

"Bluff?" Vryce let out a weak laugh.

"If you were currently active, you'd know why our galleons are gathering in the bay. Especially given your Lady's involvement."

Maybe I'll have better luck with the demons you summon. "Well... let's see how good your summoning circle is, I suppose," Vryce said, resigned as his vision flashed white from a gun smashing into his temple.

The world turned black.

CHAPTER 7

*The temptation to drink the blood of legends runs strong.
Heed our warning: claiming this power destroys that
which you are. Happy shall they be that taketh and
dasheth thy little ones against the stones if they've consumed the flesh of fiends. For they will be raised as
fiends themselves. Do not feed your children the blood
of demons, lest you be devoured in turn.*

–Message printed on torn church parchment

Lucian Montague strolled through the depths of Purgatory toward his divine prison—the Seat of Gilded Crowns. The seat itself was truly nestled deep in Purgatory, almost tumbling to the edge of oblivion where all of creation ceased to exist. There, forgotten objects and unlucky trinkets of treasure piled up like an ever-growing trash heap. As long as humans continued to exist, they would continue to suffer misfortune, and their prized possessions would be nothing more than a forgotten memory. At various times in history, Lucian would mystically tether his stolen throne to many continents. But ever since he and the fellow liches that comprised the Lords of Death decided to fix Purgatory by bringing Lazarus back from the dead— it'd been in New Orleans.

There was no other reason than Lucian liked it. He didn't care how many labyrinths and prisons the Church of Lazarus built on top of it while he did his best impression of an absentee landlord. He was ultimately the only defecting vote from the plan to create the warlocks hundreds of years ago. He was the only one who reminded each member that at one point—they were each just humans who shattered a supreme divine law of reality, and he was the only one to gleefully laugh when the first reports came in of warlocks betraying their death cult during the great ritual for their own power. Just as they had done—albeit on a much tinier scale. Lucian never really broke a world. The last Death Lord just found someone unlucky enough take the mantle. Unfortunately for New Orleans, the apocalypse was about to double-tap it into oblivion.

A three-night stroll to the bottom of the Atlantic Ocean was a pleasant journey. He even enjoyed the sights of sharks feeding on the lost souls that had the misfortune of being washed out to the tempests from their more land-bound afterlives. Sharks, by their very nature, served an important part in the celestial hierarchy by sending the truly lost to oblivion, and Lucian knew those dead would know the peace and quiet. A peace and quiet that he'd never known. *Hey, unless these undead fuckers in the U.S. find a way to end my curse. One could always hope!*

He let out a long sigh that gurgled with sickly green water through his yellowed teeth while stepping out of the bay. After a second of consideration, he elected not to put on his mask to become presentable, a choice made by taking in sight of what had become of his second favorite city. Warships of Lazarus's armies had already made the journey and docked just outside of New Orleans. The marching dead assembled around the city just beyond what thin veil of innocence remained left in the world. Lucian didn't fault humans for holding onto the tattered remains that the worst had come, for erecting an intentional veil of ignorance subconsciously that kept the

deeper bowels of Purgatory still hidden from them despite the world's events thus far.

He only pitied them.

In trying to accept their new world as something *survivable*, they continued to keep themselves oblivious to the armies that slowly marched around them, hidden beyond a barrier of innocence so thin that both children and monsters could see clearly. Only the rational adults thought they could keep the absurd at bay, and the very thought of this nearly broke Lucian into a fit of cackling mad laughter on a wooden dock. *Oh, this world is hopeless. I... I can't help it... We are all ... so screwed.* He tugged at the tatters of skin and bone as he clutched his skull to prevent himself from laughing, wracking his own brain bucket with his bony hands. Legionnaires crawling onto land must have thought him mad.

"Ah, hell with it," he finally rasped and cracked his old bones. "Maybe the insane despot is right. Doesn't change one simple fact. DADDY IS HOME, BITCHES!" Lucian splayed his arms out wide and finally let loose the cackle while fixing the mask made of coins back to his skull. "Time to shake this thing up and make love before we all burn in the fires of oblivion." His clothing changed to match his mood—a hideously colored suit knitted in a variety of colors with a straw, wide-brim hat. A flick of his wrist summoned a cane from his vault deeper in Purgatory, a gnarled petrified piece of wood from the original garden of Eden. With a soft twirl and a skip in his step, the Death Lord of Misfortune began to enjoy his stroll, right as the thunderstorm rolled in overhead in the "real" world.

"Ya'll are missing out on the beauty of this city by only seeing half of it..." he muttered to nobody in particular as he became drunk with giddiness over the view. The black sun still hung on the horizon despite the thunderstorm, a typical southern gout of rain that always ruined well-laid festivities. Its rays glistened like a prism of colors that danced like a perfectly orchestrated symphony to Lucian—purples, reds, and yellows reflecting off the already vibrant paints the

inhabitants decorated their buildings with. To most, they saw New Orleans as it was currently, a bit run down and covered in graffiti, while still filled with festivities despite the world's calamity. To those who saw past the veil of innocence and into Purgatory—New Orleans was a multi-level paradise built on top of one disaster after another. Each calamity the city ever faced was etched into the very soul of the land even if people tried to bury it.

Just beneath the memory of North America's oldest inhabitants, the Chitimacha, lay his labyrinth of Golden Tears. To be honest with himself, Lucian hadn't really stepped in to check on what the Unification had done with the place in a few decades, and it didn't really matter to him. *Probably just binding up dreams of would-be myths for a farm. Let me guess: they put that stupid farmer planting apple trees. He's barely a footnote!* Still, the Mississippi River washed countless lost treasures into his vault, and the city was a magnet for the misfortunate looking to turn their luck around. His city did it with style, even though he did respect Vegas and Reno for noble attempts. In Lucian's city, his paupers and souls that gathered here already knew they were screwed and accepted that fate—which made their afterlife better. *If you are going to be stuck in Purgatory forever because God is dead, might as well enjoy some good music.*

Not far off the harbor, inside a janitorial closet for Shrimpies, Lucian tapped twice on a jury-rigged elevator floor and grabbed an old hemp rope while humming to himself, beginning his descent into the Labyrinth. His entrance was as far removed from gaudy as one could get, a simple escape hatch and a single rope that had held up since the city's founding that led to an old chamber pot room beneath a mansion rightfully condemned to hell by freed men bringing their fury upon cruel soulless masters. As Lucian descended, rain from his timely storm crossed the barrier and leaked through on the foreheads of those very souls he'd imprisoned in his floor. Each soul he had personally forged into a yellowish green brick that lined his bathroom. Each of the souls was someone who exploited the less fortunate. *The*

Lord of Murder was right about one thing... I may ... have poached a few souls from the other Lords. Sue me. They were fuckers. He twisted his alligator-skinned shoe on one out of spite and opened a rickety door that almost fell off its rusted relic hinges into the main hallway.

With one quick look, Lucian did an about-face right back into his escape. "Nope."

Firstly, the Labyrinth was crawling with fiends; as expected, the Unification had turned it into another one of their farms for dying gods and myths. Secondly, it was now crawling with soldiers, necromancers, and more from nearly every other Death Lord—but mostly Murder. But mostly, it was the very happy Ukobach demon pleased to see Lucian's return, flailing his arms and racing to greet him.

"Lord Montague! You've returned! Brought a storm I see... Hopefully ... a hurricane, yes?"

Lucian groaned with head tilted back, knowing that his fate was sealed. "How many times do I have to tell you? I had nothing to do with Katrina." He spun around and bared his true zombie form to the demon. "I'm the bastard who made sure those who died were able to give a final message to their families." *And was punished for breaking the veil of innocence and jeopardizing "the great ritual."* Lucian made air quotes for his internal monologue, and by that point, the fiend was already wrapping his long arms around the scrawny Death Lord. "Hello, Fed."

"You... you are very early, yes." The short, red-skinned demon patted Lucian down as if he was packing heat. "Was not expecting you I. Go—good thing you are here. Can pull rank, yes?"

"Stop that!" Lucian guarded his cane and stood on one leg as if the fiend was a spider. "You think I need to pack weapons?"

"No. Too skinny. You should eat more souls. Suicide was way fatter."

"Well, now she's a skinny vampire bitch, so..." Lucian shrugged.

"Mmm... no good, no good. You haven't eaten any of your souls this century, have you? No wonder you look like a chicken in a suit. Never be able to command respect so skinny."

"Can we … not … talk about how hungry I always am? How about you? You are so tall! What are you… four feet now?"

"Five-three… thank you." Fed smiled with grease-stained teeth and breath that smelled like delicious fried chicken. "I've been eating loads. Been a good steward I have. Done everything the Church has told me." He nodded thrice.

Lucian noticed Unification Helldivers and soldiers looking over at him, chuckling for some reason. It took a moment to realize that he had trailed toilet paper out of the chamber on his heel. Lucian just shrugged and winked back, and magically, they all found something to busy their hands with, lest his evil eye shine upon them.

Fed began eagerly pointing up. "Today is a busy day. The soldiers have been out gathering sacrifices for the ritual, and they caught a BIG catch. A girl!" He jumped. "A girl who is untainted by blood in this world and powerful of soul and magic. Oh! Also, two souls escaped through your exit just a bit ago. One killed by Suicide and both descendants of Lazarus. They offered me a job if I could fatten up the gods."

Have minor demons always been this glib? Why couldn't I be assigned an arch demon? Lady Fate gets to consort with fallen angels, and I get... He just reached out and patted the loyal little chap. "What would I ever do without you? Know your power, Fed?"

Fed shook his head.

"You're an adorable idiot who everyone else takes for granted. Who would want to eat the heart of some pitiable creature like yours? Let me ask you a little secret question then." Lucian knelt. "You said I got here early. When did everyone expect my arrival?"

"New moon! On the new moon."

"Is that when everyone is going to start the sacrifices to begin the assault then? You are saying I have a fortnight before I've actually got to work!" It was the best news he'd heard in ages.

"Uhhhh…." Fed wasn't sure how to respond, so the demon just paused and wriggled its gangly fingers.

"Perfect!" Lucian rose and went back into his chamber. "I'm going for a walk then! A good commander always gets to know the battlefield first, right?" He dipped his straw hat and magically commanded the pulley to start raising him back to the lands of the living.

"Good idea, sir. I'll make sure everything continues as scheduled, and I'll make sure your throne is polished!"

"You do that!" Lucian waved enthusiastically back down with a wide grin that faded the second he was out of view. He left so fast, Lucian never even stepped more than ten feet into the church's prison... even if he was secretly curious who they imprisoned there. *So, the enemy is already marshalling forces, eh? Well... lucky for them I'm already here. Let's go find these descendants.* He flipped the mask of coins in his hand and balanced on the back of his hand before donning it. "Cinderella time."

Strolling through his own stomping grounds was as gleeful for Lucian as a child imagining a stick was really Excalibur. Every time his shoes stepped in indescribable muck or pans of discarded food, he enjoyed the sickening squishing sensation. New Orleans was no longer ruled over by a tourist association or had any governing bodies to slap CONDEMNED signs for improper food handling. Police, fire firefighters, and medics were no longer a state-sponsored and public-funded source. Since the fall, corporations mostly ran the show, and that meant they only put up the basic fronts where profits could be found—and that certainly wasn't here.

No, Lucian knew where the true treasures were to be found—the small family-owned or community-supported businesses. Their exteriors weren't fancy or grand to look at, marred in anti-magic graffiti or with a single neon sign, yet inside smelled of true spicy food with an aroma of homegrown vegetables and fresh seafood. Far better than

the NutrientGoo™ that was peddled by Barghest Burgers and cleaned off his shoe in a puddle. This very dichotomy played out in every country on the world. The communities that banded together found a way to survive. The rest had to survive on the charity of their corporate overlords.

Lucian breathed the deep fresh smell in while pulling off his mask and marveling at the restaurant. It was tucked underneath a small flat of apartments, and whoever ran it, clearly ran a tight ship. Every counter inside was clean, and the teenagers who worked hustled as if their lives depended on it. Nobody on the street seemed to notice Lucian's appearance fade back into a walking mottled zombie with torn shoes and a skeleton free. This wasn't surprising to Lucian given that most of the street was already filled with ghosts and other supernaturals for some festival a few blocks over.

The small ring of a bell echoed as Lucian opened the door, and he stepped over a small circle of salt meant to keep out ghosts.

"You ungrateful little ragut!" A shout echoed from the back followed by the sound of a harsh slap and echo of pots clashing against the ground. The teenagers working widened their eyes and cleaned harder in the empty restaurant.

Lucian whistled. "Guess I walkin' in on sunshine." He shuffled over to the counter and peeked through the cooking window. A small teenage girl with greenish crocodile scales lining her face popped up from the ground holding her face and glaring at a man so round, Lucian thought he swallowed other men whole.

"I *will* kill you all if you don't let us go. We are *done* here." The spitfire in a leather jacket and torn jeans had a fire in her eyes Lucian knew all too well.

"Ya know what..." The man grabbed a spray can of Angel-Be-Gone and started spraying her as if she were a misbehaving cat.

The unholy growl that came out of the small girl made Lucian get smaller on the barstool as her jacket tore and she grew in size. Bones began to snap in place, black talons grew from her fingers, and her

jaw bloodily ripped open before snapping back in place—this time as an alligator snout. Hunched at ten feet tall, the alligator shapeshifter gazed down on the man, who grabbed a silver knife while screaming for help. Several pounding footsteps echoed from above.

Lucian just placed his mask on the countertop. "I'll come back another time. You two have fun. I think…" He turned to the frightened teenagers. "You cats don't need to worry about returning that if you use it. It alllllways finds itsss way back to me," he said, walking outside. He did not look back at the carnage that would soon unfold but instead up at the black sun tucked under his rain clouds. "Fine! I'll go do my job!" He spat on the ground and turned to the large crowd a few blocks up. *No Lucian, you can't just pause and smell the lobsters that you can't eat. You have to kill all humans to fix the world.*

At least finding two souls that escaped from his labyrinth was easier. All eyes on the festival had turned to gasps of horror, and anyone near the French Quarter was straining to get a glimpse of a tragedy. Lucian easily moved through the crowd like it was water. Subconsciously, people always ignored the dead and doubly so in his case. Even vampires and sorcerers would twist their heads away at just the right angle for the flesh-rotted beggar to slip between the cracks until he saw what everyone gawked at: an entire street filled with mangled bodies from all walks of life, enough that it made stones in Lucian's stomach physically turn. Each body had their limbs bent in the wrong directions, and it reminded him of a hundred dead spiders littering the ground.

Church of Lazarus priests kept the crowds away while necromancers hiding beyond the veil reaped the souls of the murdered. The priests offered calming prayers mixed with fiery speeches ranting over the perils of magical abuse… while at the very same time their companions physically ripped the souls from the eyes of the dead. Surprised and confused souls screamed in terror as necromancer spells bound them into service. Lucian wasn't surprised that those on the side of the living nodded their heads in agreement with the

priests while children and ghosts covered their mouths in horror at the necromancers. The few vampires, shifters, or other types in the spectator crowd that had actually consumed a heart—their reactions were individualistic. Some were angry, some smirking. "Welcome to church, ladies and gentlemen," Lucian mumbled as his unblinking eye searched for his quarry. "They show you one thing... while real power does the dirty work."

His mind trailed back to ancient memories of the earliest elite brotherhoods sharing the blood of fiends for the power to shape the modern world, but his reminiscence was cut short by a very angry-looking ghost.

Two rather.

Mike and Jane Auburn were both marked by Death Lords even if they didn't know it. Jane by Fate, and to Lucian's surprise... Mike currently fell under him. The manifestation of their souls in the real world were less faded than the typical ghost—they actually had feet, a sign that they had marched out of Purgatory, and with the power that resided in his own withered heart, Lucian could see their markings clearly. Granted, markings of a Death Lord on a ghost were subject to debate between the politics of liches. It happened naturally when someone died, and any Death Lord with a mask could view who belonged to whom—in that moment. In most cases, nobody challenged a claim. If someone died by starvation, they were clearly meant for Famine's ranks... but if they were destined to die of hunger because they led a great protest to change fate, the lines got a little blurry. Divine magic wasn't an exact science, and it certainly kept the council on their toes. *Well, ain't that a little somethin' somethin'. Two good ol' humans from a long-guarded bloodline standing in my own little city and up to no good.*

Scooting through edges of the crowd, Lucian chuckled slightly while tiptoeing up behind them. At any moment, the duo looked ready to leap into action against the necromancers performing binding.

"How come all of you are just standing there?!" Mike shouted to nearby ghosts. "Fuck these guys! There are legions of us and only six of them!"

"Calm, child." A priest raised his hand. "These poor souls have been murdered, and this transition is always painful. Yet rest assured we have caught the one responsible, and the Church of Lazarus will mete out proper justice."

"Bah." Jane flicked the priest off. "Stuff it, twinkletits. We've seen what—"

"BOO!" Lucian jumped up between them and grabbed their shoulders with his bony hands.

Mike and Jane *actually* turned white in shock, which was impressive to the Lord of Misfortune. The boy one was tall and looked like a lucky son-of-a-cobbler by trade, and the girl was vastly too pretty, even when making scrunched faces with her lips and several stab wounds and bruises. Since they were both dead, they had a slight translucence to them. Ever since the dead crawled back from Purgatory though, the myth of floating invisible ghosts sorta got busted. Now they had feet.

"Why don't you two kids come with me before anyone realizes who you are…?" He chattered his teeth in Mike's ear. "You're famous after all, no?" With a simple shove, both Mike and Jane slipped back deeper into the crowd before their wits came back about them.

"Aren't you a bit forward for a zombie?" Jane finally peeled his fingers off her chest.

"Eh, ain't nothin' I haven't felt before. You're just a giant squishy chew toy for me. Don't think much on it." *I'll pull you by your ears like children if I must.* For a someone made of more bone than meat, Lucian had no problem moving the ghostly duo back off the main street into a cranny of a red-bricked building despite their struggles and kicks. "Behave in five… four… three…"

"Okay, stop counting!" Mike finally held up his hands before tugging his shirt back into place. "What the hell, old man? You see what's going on."

"That's your question?" Lucian made a *hrmph* sound and flicked his forehead. "Not curious why you can't do shit to stop me?"

Mike's look of pain stemmed from both confusion and a flicked forehead.

"We're new... so... can't." Jane folded her arms.

"You clearly died more recently..." Lucian still flicked her forehead in turn. "But you're right. Been out of dead-jail for what... a few hours? Already causing trouble. Just what do you kids think you're going to do against skilled necromancers? You can't even lift a po'boy yet to your lips."

"Uuuggghh... I hate starting over." Mike knocked his head against the brick. "So, what are you—our great zombie mother here to sprinkle dust on us?"

"Something like that." Lucian slapped his knee while he laughed. "You two are something special, you know? You fucked up the Unification's plans and got a world to start munchin' on demons' hearts, and you peddled those products until you had a cage match with Suicide. Good job." He gave two bones up.

"So... how do we stop that?" Jane scrunched her nose and jutted her head over to the slew of corpses littering the New Orleans street and their souls being shackled.

"You don't." Lucian shrugged. "They were murdered. So, they fall under that Death Lord. They'll either go to Purgatory and wander around lost for eternity or be forged into chains, weapons, or who knows... maybe some necromancer's ashtray. You two, though..." Lucian pinched Mike's cheek like an old aunt. "Weren't. An old favor for Lady Fate is the only reason I'm not turning you two in right now. Instead, I'm pulling your blonde ass out of it." He poked Jane in the shoulder. *It's pretty rare to find souls marked by Lady Fate, and it would be a shame for another Death Lord to recognize them before her.*

"Would. You. Stop. With. The. Poking."

"Ahh, I can't help it. It's just kinda funny that you are still walking around. Frankly, I don't know what the hell I should do with you now.

Wanna roll a dice for it?" He pulled out a small six-sided dice carved from chicken bones and placed it in Mike's hand. "You roll a 6, I'll tell ya a secret. Roll a 1, and I'll go back to my diner and pick up what's mine from a very shocked alligator and a pile of corpses."

Mike rolled the dice in his hand as he sized Lucian up. "You're a curious one. What's your angle here...?"

Lucian lowered his one eye to the dice. "I mean... you *could* find out. Unless you're chicken. You like holding peoples' fates in your hand, right?"

"This seems a bit personal. Do you two know each other?" Jane shot daggers between the two.

"Oh, not in the slightest. I promise!" Lucian stepped back to give room for a die roll. "All you people are special people. I'm just a zombie who is always looking for a way out. You two think your connection to Purgatory makes you some sort of chosen one or something. Ain't that special, so just roll away. Because..." Lucian pointed up the street.

A pack of motorcycles rode along a sidewalk, and on each sat members of the Sons and Daughters equipped with enough anti-freak gear to tango with a pack of werewolves and come out unscathed. The lead biker, a very determined purple-haired girl dressed in skin-tight black leather and armored shin-guards, expertly navigated through every crack in the crowd without hitting a single person.

"I like to avoid being at the center of conflict. So, secret... or..."

Mike tossed the die back to Lucian with a beaming smile. "Nah. I'm not playing that game, stranger. Even if you've got an alligator."

Lucian went deadpan. *Disappointing. Sigh... Can't tell people how to kill me if they don't roll.* "Bye."

Just as fast as Lucian pulled them out of the crowd, he faded back into it as the sound of bikes grew louder. The necromancers' work had already been completed, and the priests were already laying grave clothes upon the dead. Lucian was half tempted to end the spell the necromancers cast to strengthen the veil to hide their actions, but

doing so would only reveal the growing army to everyone's eyes. *Panic before the end never goes well.*

He simply shook his head and rolled the chicken die as he walked back to the café. A single 1 was visible before rainwater washed it down a gutter.

"Today isn't going to be a great day for anyone, it seems."

CHAPTER 8

"So, there I was sleeping in my apartment, and the witching hour comes. My alarm goes off, and I grab a can of Angel-Be-Gone like we all do, right? Sure enough, a Slenderman is standing in the corner of my bedroom looking all sassy with that suit and several tentacles... and it was the best night of my life."

–Interview "I got railed by Slenderman"

"**W**eirdo." Mike shook his head as he watched the gambling zombie shamble off into the crowd. A mixed crowd filled with living, dead, the scared and the bold—yet all with eyes fixed on the crime scene as if a live accident just happened. To be fair, Mike couldn't honestly believe that the scene playing out before his eyes was supposed to be natural. Watching souls get reaped and assigned to their respective prisons in Purgatory was apparently something that had happened for centuries, only nobody else really saw it before. Even now, most of the living in the crowd paid more attention to the priests than the necromancers for some reason—and the screams of the ghosts cut into the fabric of his being. From the twisted expression of pain on the face of any other escaped ghost, Mike wasn't alone in that feeling.

He made the motion to crack his knuckles, without the satisfying pop that usually followed (on account of being dead), and performed the mental gymnastics of trying to fight Unification necromancers. *Being outnumbered isn't a problem, but not being able to kick them in the nuts ... is. But we do have backup.*

"Come on, Mike," Jane said, tugging his sleeve with her head down. Escaped strands of blonde hair blocked her green eyes that she kept pointed down. "The zombie is right. We'd just end up getting caught. Can't fight every battle, can we?"

"No, we can't. At some point..." he allowed Jane's tug to pull him in the direction of the oncoming bikes, "people need to fight for themselves."

"Yeah, yeah, you're just a giant ball of revolution tag lines, aren't you?" Her grip tightened, yanking Mike in front of her and then pushing him from behind with two hands nestled firmly under his shoulders.

"Okay!" *I'm totally more than pretty speeches. Thank. You. Very. Much.* His lips pursed. In his gut, Mike knew damn well he was an adrenaline junkie who just wanted to prove he was alive—even if that meant facing death. Unfortunately, the metric he used to determine "living" had shifted on a scale further than he ever imagined. Yet the sight of old friends did put a giant shit-eating grin on his face.

The Sons and Daughters slowed on their bikes, waddling them through the crowd with the occasional engine rev and several sharp jabs to scoot oblivious people out of the way. Phoebe, the point runner for the group, readied a sawed-off shotgun on her handlebars in case the Unification soldiers got a little feisty as she pulled up next to Mike and Jane.

"Undead Uber, at your service..." Phoebe winked at the duo. "Get on, so we can get out before..." She nodded at a priest who was already pointing at them.

Another helldiver a few bikes back with a white cloak, two battle axes, and a lantern dangling off her handlebars growled at Mike while

pointing her finger at him. "You and I are going to have words, you little fucker. Get. On. Before I stake you to a wall."

Mike quickly grabbed Phoebe's waist and hopped on the back of her bike. "Go before Lucy kills me. Should... should I crawl back into my grave?"

Phoebe chuckled. "That might be wise."

In just a matter of minutes, the entire group raced through narrow alleyways at high speeds. The soft orange glow of lanterns provided illumination against the neon-lit signs that decorated thoroughfares of New Orleans. The violet-hued moon and a night sky filled with a vast array of stars was beautiful to Mike. Purgatory was muted in colors and more often than not a perpetual landscape of balefire green. It hadn't been more than a few hours since he'd escaped, and he'd honestly forgotten just how *pretty* the world could be. The cool breeze washing over him as Phoebe zigged through and the pine smell of her dark, dyed hair reminded him just a smidge of being alive.

The sensations and rules of being a returned spirit were still unclear to him. Clearly, he was able to ride on the back of a crotch rocket. His hair still blew in the wind. He still felt the curves of Phoebe and the cool sensation of leather around her waist. Yet when the bike jostled or she took a sharp corner, his forearm would slip inside her. Mike was thankful he didn't feel organs. Sneaking a look back, he saw Jane being equally as curious, if a bit bolder. She was outright sticking her hand through the chest of Doc Daneka and wiggling it around while he batted at her arm like an annoyed cat.

Once they hit the 610 highway, all semblance of caution was thrown out the window. The entire group gunned it across the Lake Pontchartrain Causeway at easily over 120 miles per hour. Zipping across the lake so fast was a terrifying experience. Outside of the moonlit sky, the lake itself appeared obsidian black and nearly a solid surface to Mike. The causeway was nothing more than a stick-straight narrow road anchored by concrete pylons that stretched down into oblivion from his eyes. Moreover, warships, ghost ships, and galleons

anchored closer to the city proper within the lake. Mike swore he could see ghostly figures walking on the surface of the lake, but they raced by so fast it was difficult to make out.

Only once the lights of the city had faded out of view, and the Fontainbleau mainland came closer, did Phoebe start signaling which way to go, leading everyone safely off an exit to what appeared to be their makeshift headquarters.

The Waffle House of I-90.

"Annnnd home!" Phoebe parked her bike as the others pulled up, kicking the stand down. "You can stop with the death grip, and if you touch my spleen again, Lucy is the least of your worries."

"A Waffle House?" Mike peeled himself off Phoebe and stretched near the bike. Surrounded by dead trees and yet still covered in vines, the Waffle House was indeed open for business. Even during the apocalypse. A Moo Moo's Frozen Custard stand and Drive Thru Crawfish were also open nearby. The custard stand had a large sign outside advertising the sale of Fairy Dust Custard with limited supply.

Doc Daneka practically chucked a giggling Jane on her bum before fetching a thin set of wire-frame glasses from a case. "You've got something against waffles now, Mikey?"

Mike flailed both arms frantically at the tilted open sign. "Can't we afford a better headquarters?! Where the hell is boss?! How did we go from the Drake Hotel to..."

Akira balanced the balls of her feet on top of her bike while crouching. Her hair was still multi-colored, and black-blue beetles occasionally crawled along her neck like a moving necklace. Unlike everyone else, Akira did not hide her fangs, gleefully licking them as her rainbow-hued eyes studied both Mike and Jane. "I voted for Moo Moo's."

"Right!? At least they sell Fairy Dust Custard. I wanna try that..." Mike looked forlorn.

"You're dead, asshole." Lucy grabbed the back of Mike's head with ink-coated fingers and bunched his hair, yanking him down to her height and dragging him inside.

The sudden sharp pain of her iron grip hurt Mike. Try as he might, her grip was inescapable, and Lucy used his face to open the door with a soft thud. Mike wished he understood, but when Lucy was dragging him, he was suddenly *very* real to every object in between him and her. His only solace was the soft impact of a booth he was chucked into.

"Coffee?" An old man with a bright yellow apron asked, holding up a pitcher of Midwinter Black coffee. "It's coffee that can raise the dead, so you can drink it, Mikey." The old man wore an old cabby hat, black slacks, and blue suit coat under that apron and had a ring on every finger—each could be used for knocking out someone's teeth. Mike recognized the ticking time piece attached to his belt.

"Thank heavens. Boss is here... someone with hos-spi-tality." He glared at Lucy.

Jane seemed to be spared the worst of the dragging, but Doc did navigate her into the same booth by the scruff of her neck despite her pleas.

"You two are a real pain in the ass," Edward Morris said from the counter while grinding down a cigarette into a waffle before picking up a glass of fresh blood. "The world doesn't revolve around you two. Instead of having the decency to escape Purgatory in CHICAGO, you two just HAD to drag us down to this hellhole. Right in the middle of Lazarus country. Next time, walk the extra miles, you lazy bastards." The well-dressed, skinny vampire downed his glass like a shot and crossed his legs.

You'd think that returning from the dead would fetch a more heartfelt welcome party. Mike's expression pleaded with Doc for some mercy. Surely his best friend would come to his assistance. Doc was more interested in cleaning his houndstooth jacket and found the entire scenario rather amusing. *Ooooh... it's a hazing. Ha... real funny, guys.*

Mike relaxed slightly and finally looked around the diner. It was filled with Sons and Daughters members, each engaged in conversation over a late night brinner. The majority of tables had some sort of weaponry either on or nearby. The waitstaff paid no mind to any instrument of violence and made every custom dish without missing a beat. In some cases, they used supernatural powers to expedite the process.

The old man poured the black-blood of undead-branded caffeine into a cup before Mike and Jane and silenced everyone with a wave of his hand. The core leaders of the Sons and Daughters—Akira, Doc, Lucy, Phoebe, and Morris—all stayed closer to Mike and Jane, as everyone in the diner set their forks down.

"It's been a few years and a tough road for all of us. In the case of these two fallen soldiers, even more so. Mike enjoyed the fine kiss of Warlock Vryce's lightning outside of the Twin Cities, and Jane gave her life to save this country from the Death Lord of Suicide." Boss gave each of them a slow nod of appreciation. "Yet they aren't the only ones of us who've died. I know each of you secretly wishes we could fetch every fallen soldier from Purgatory. With so many ghosts returned, it must be simple, right? There are millions of souls in the lands of the dead, and millions more that have crossed over. We are but needles in the celestial haystack. The return of these two was a mix of fate, sheer luck, and a lot of hard work by these five who stand before you."

Akira was short, so she jumped to be seen and waved to the diner. Doc looked surprised at the sudden recognition and quickly sat down in the booth next to Mike. Morris lit up another smoke while Phoebe collected three vials of mercury from Lucy for some unspoken bet.

Boss raised a glass of blood with the entire diner each raising a glass of their own chosen beverage. "As my predecessor once told me, keep the speeches short, the blood of gods flowing, and everyone is happy. So, here's our toast, to teaching the world about the folly of man, and may you all forget we've ever met."

Several cheers and salutes in different languages echoed around Mike. With each glass being bottomed up, a twinge of desire to drink blood again railed in his soul. He recalled the sweet taste of peach and cinnamon from demons and even the liquid metallic taste of human blood. Unfortunately, he had to settle for bitter black coffee... that really did seem to have enough kick to energize the dead.

Mike stuck his stomach forward out of curiosity to see if the liquid black would race through him and was pleased to find it naturally absorbed itself into... whatever the plasma that comprised him was called. "So, why the hell are you so pissed at me if you're happy I'm back?" He looked at Lucy.

Lucy glowered at Doc, who quickly shifted farther in to make room while the Boss just whistled and folded his hands. "Because," she grabbed his chin and pulled Mike's nose closer to hers, "I helldived for a *year* trying to find you. When I *did* find you... what did you do?"

Oh shit. Mike gulped. Gazing into her deep amber eyes, the heavy black ash eyeliner was a pretty sight, but beyond them lay only death. It had been so long ago; their fleeting encounter had almost slipped his mind. He was hot on the trail of locating the prison where gods were held, and all he had time to do was throw her his coat before diving farther down through a portal before it closed without explanation. "I ... gave you my coat."

"Mmmhrm. Your ... coat. Apparently, a magical item strong enough to keep an arch demon's strength imbued in it. So, you disarmed yourself and threw it at me as some ... paltry memento that you were still alive. Rather than keeping it before going deeper into hell on whatever mission you had up your ass. Do you think I'm an idiot?!" Her forehead was now pressed against his... and her fist was a tiny ball yanking his shirt closer.

"No... but... that's... why... you're?" As the gears clicked in his brain, he became aware of everyone's glares.

"Do you think that I *wouldn't* understand if you couldn't follow me back out after a year? You were onto something. You found

something. Instead of taking the *one* object that would have allowed you to solve the mother-fucking-problem right then and there, you got all sentimental and wanted everyone to know you were alive. So, what did you find Mike? What … did you *find*?"

Jane held up her fingers and tried to tap Lucy's shoulder. "Look, if I may… I um… did kind of use that coat to kill the Lord of Suicide? You know, super strength and all…"

Lucy practically hissed like a cat. "Shush, princess. You aren't off the hook yet either. You *also* died and left the coat behind. Since you're siblings, you would naturally find each other in Purgatory. Phoebe's vision was all about Mike having the coat, to do something *in* Purgatory, and then we could win. Yet here we are…"

"Here we are." Mike nodded, pushing Lucy's shoulders away.

"Here we are," she added again. "Both of you, OUT of Purgatory. No coat… and an army of Unification soldiers swarming over this city for round fucking two."

Mike and Jane looked at each other, back to Lucy, and both glanced at Akira simultaneously. "Where the fuck is our coat?" they said in unison.

Akira had settled into mid-meal on a cryptid heart for a late-night snack and held a papillary muscle on a fork just between her lips. "That thing is huge and baggy. You're a big guy, Mike. It was oversized on Jane and makes me feel like I'm twelve years old." Akira shrugged and nommed down with a smile and a dribble of orange blood down her chin. "It's hanging in the freezer."

Jane rolled her eyes and elbowed Akira in the ribs.

Mike clutched his non-existent heart in relief. *Imma be honest, there was a fifty percent chance Akira traded it for a Playstation.* "Well, Lucy, simple. I grab my chilled coat, Phoebe drives me back across that terrifying bridge, and I jump back down into the same entrance I came from. Beat up everyone inside that prison… and free Paul Bunyan."

"Am I just a TV dinner then?" Jane sharply elbowed Akira for the second time, who swatted her back with a fork before taking her

late night meal out of the booth and jumping up to the bar near the booth where everyone sat.

"Paul Bunyan..." Morris pulled out a small black notebook and jotted it down. "Now we are talking. It hasn't been so long since Boss and I were Unification fixers that we aren't aware of some plans. Is that what you found? A single legend? Or..."

"Multiple..." Jane added before Mike could cut in. "A bunch of old gods it seemed. Including one crazy entity named Balor with massive beams of cold-iron imprisoning him. There was this whole friggin' labyrinth down there!"

Lucy flicked Mike's forehead but finally let him go. Mike wondered if her salty anger with him dissipated entirely, or if this would be an ongoing feature of their newfound relationship. "What she said. We had to run because the place was swarming with both demons and the Unification. They were farming it... for the same blood you gave me, Boss."

The old man started cleaning off the table. "Well, it's not my proudest moment, but I did have a hand in capturing old legends once. You don't become a Worshipful Master within the Unification by delivering nothing. Blood is power, after all, and godly competition isn't exactly good for the ruling party. North America's gods had to be stored somewhere. I'd bag 'em; they'd harvest them." He wiped his hands clean and tossed the towel over his shoulder. "Even the heavens need a janitor."

"I remember those days." Morris let smoke swirl just beyond his red lips and savored the moment.

"Boom, and just like that, the power nabbin' team is in action." Mike went to hi-five Doc, who left him hanging. *Ouch.* "Awkward... okay... so we are back. Phoebe's prophecy found us, coat's in the freezer. We bust in, free the gods, and then enjoy immortality? Right?" Mike knew full well that wasn't the case, but he found it a little harder to be as cynical when he was already dead.

Doc slurped his coffee and finally spoke. "Waffles are the epitome of late-night breakfast dinner combinations. Jane's from Texas, so she's familiar with the prevalence and survivability of the Waffle House institution. But you being a Chicago boy have never enjoyed such pleasures. I know you've a penchant for racing ahead, and right now, I imagine you are trying to pretend that you aren't ... an actual ghost. In the simplest terms, you are correct... which you've an eerie tendency of actually being. At some point, we smash a prison. But right now, enjoy the smell of waffles. Watch the news. Let it sink in."

"Pancakes are superior." Mike readied his fightin' words as Jane quickly distanced herself from her suicidal brother. "But let what sink in?"

"That you both have been dead for over a year, and the world has moved on without you. We are sitting in a Waffle House, talking about imprisoned gods with two ghosts, while overpriced gasoline is being pumped across the street. An actual devil is vying for leadership of the U.S. government now. Wolves of Wall Street trade crypto currencies across every nation and siphon off power from every transaction. Dystopia has become a hellscape of automation and given rise to a new silicon-based lifeform since Jane last saw it, and the Society of Deus was just voted one of the best micro-nations in the US to raise children and live by *Homes & Garden* magazine." Daneka set down his fork. "It's not the same fight as when you each died. People did what people do... survive."

Jane filled her cheeks and let out a puff of air as she slinked out of the booth and climbed up next to Akira on the bar, threatening to elbow jab the wary vampire.

Mike leaned back and let Doc's statement sink in. The words were both true and also stung. When he was last here, everyone still had a normal, albeit oblivious life. Now he had to wonder. With magic returned, was everyone still just as oblivious... or had they won at least a little bit? *At least tell me reality TV shows died in the apocalypse. I can dream for one wish, right?*

Jane kissed Akira on the cheek and cleaned the blood off the gutter punk. "Hey, least not everything changed though. Some people still are the same... just stronger."

Akira raised two fingers. "Oh! I won an E-sports tournament."

Jane ruffled Akira's hair. "See?"

CHAPTER 9

"Don't let fear paralyze you. The global supply chain may have collapsed, but thanks to new improvements from our territories in Texas—all your favorite goods are available! From diced unicorn to root beer, all your old favorites can be delivered next day anywhere in North America with our premier subscription package. Upload your personal data to our mainframe and unlock access to exclusive weaponry as well!"

–Triumvirate Email

"So, besides the tournament, what's new with you, sugar?" Jane wiggled her feet near a coffee-stained stool, letting her left pass through every third swing. It felt gross. Like she was looking at a picture of a lotus flower with a thousand eyeballs kind of gross. Even though she'd asked a question in Akira's direction, the perched vampire didn't respond but rather gave Jane the quiet to explore her newfound foot freedom. Every time Jane's foot swung through, Akira looked equally as queasy.

The chatter in the Waffle House continued in the background, fading away into a lively, warm, and sad reunion at the same time. Jane watched Mike bond with his best friend Daneka over the time-honored tradition of friendly debate. Phoebe danced between tables and

other members of the Sons and Daughters, absentmindedly refilling drinks as she did so. Yet at each table, Jane saw only strangers. Lucy and this Edward Morris fellow seemed more concerned with their endless work and glared over a map of the United States. Morris burned out his smoke on D.C. with a frustrated snarl. Even the boss had quickly faded from memory to somewhere in the back of the house. Jane wasn't even sure he was really here to begin with. *He was right? That has got to be the most annoying power for anyone to have.* Jane's eye twitched.

Akira shoulder-bumped her. "You really sure you wanna ask about me, twinkle toes?"

"CATS!" Jane shot stick straight and pinched Akira's ear. "You. Fed. My. Cats. Right?"

Akira flailed helplessly, with a look of horrified confusion about how this ghost was pinching her ear, and thwapped defensively at Jane. "Geez, yes! I can assure you that your cats were not absorbed into the machine hive mind. Probably the best fed felines in all of Texas."

Jane's nose touched Akira's cheek as her green eye remained wide and unblinking. The gaze of heavenly judgement brought upon Akira to weigh her very soul. "I'll accept this answer." The pinch faded with a heavy sigh from Jane where she tried to puff up a rogue lock of hair. Yet with no actual breath, her blonde hair remained parked just over her nose. "Being dead sucks." *I'm not stuck forever like this, right? I went out like a champ but...*

"There it is..." Akira gave head pats to Jane. "Technically, you should be talking to Doc Daneka about this. They call it the drop. That sudden realization you are no longer a pretty speck of stardust filled with life and are instead a wandering fragment of consciousness that refuses to let go. You're like ... glitter. People can see you; they know you are there, but no matter how much they swat at you—you won't go away."

Oww! What the hell? Jane looked horrified at Akira and clasped her chest. To lay it out so plainly was one thing, but glitter was a step too far. "Excuse ... me?"

Oblivious, Akira continued, "I know! It's entirely a problem. I mean, think about how I feel? Here I am, badass professional assassin of supernatural creatures. Before the fall, when I killed a bastard, they stayed dead. I didn't have to hear them or ever see them again. Now," Akira threw up her hands, "bitches be returning. Wandering 'round all confused and shit about who sliced their throat or decapitated them. I tell ya, if I wasn't so good at remaining speedy and hidden like a ninja, your home slice would have a legion of ghosts all giving me the evil eye when I'm in my jammy jams."

"Okay. Wait. I've just died. Spent probably a year wandering 'round Purgatory. Found a prison of dead gods. Escaped a labyrinth. Returned from the dead. And I'm sitting in a Waffle House with a bug-obsessed vampire who thinks of me as glitter," Jane deadpanned. "This is my eternity now. This is hell."

"Cheer up!" Akira swatted through her. "Think about how many jump scares you can get on people now by poking your head through the wall. Or even better, hide inside refrigerators and pop out at people at 3 a.m.! I bet with enough practice you can actually get a bloke to shit themselves." Akira hopped off her stool and produced a single smoke from a pack. "I'm just messin' with ya, Jane. You're the kind of glitter that can stick to me all day, but I'm also not going to kick the pig. I can't. You're dead, and it sucks marshmallows. I can't make you feel better, but I can make you a promise." Akira grabbed both of Jane's cheeks and squished them together. "If anyone bullies you for being dead, I'll cut their heads off and make them a ghost-ie-woastie so you can bitch slap them, okay?"

Akira winked and gave Jane a forehead smooch before skipping outside the doors with a soft clatter of a bell.

I have no idea how the rules of this world work. Jane watched the short killer step out into the night, and the soft features of a

flame kissed her cheeks through the reflection. Jane's own reflection remained ghastly. Once pretty features were ruined by battle scars, her left arm looked mangled, and Jane knew she looked like a drugged-out deadbeat. Mike, however, looked like he did the day he died—instead of a lightning-fried crispy critter. Mike was probably oblivious over something that'd happened a few times now, but it kept scratching in the back of Jane's mind. Sometimes they could interact physically—pinch an ear, get their cheeks squished—and other times, they were as intangible as a fart in the wind.

"I need answers," Jane muttered and swung herself around to the back of house. Truth be told, she knew that most of the Sons and Daughters were good at helldiving and killing—and not much else. Hopefully, the one who kept disappearing would be a little more help, and that asshole owed her anyway. For it was he who arranged the winning lottery ticket which set her down a path of fame and glory. *Here you go, Jane! Winning lottery ticket out of your hellhole as a waitress in the Devil's Steakhouse. Get super speed, sell vacuum cleaners, die a martyr. Jerkface.*

Jane didn't waste her life. It had purpose and meaning, she told herself as she slipped through the back kitchen, not really wanting to know how the waffles were made these days. Or why the eggs were red. Past the manager's office and a small janitorial closet, she found the back door propped open with a jar of maple syrup. Poking her head out, she saw her target stooped over a small freshwater turtle. An old man meeting another at strange crossroads.

"Hey... um... excuse me?" Jane asked, shuffling closer.

Boss regarded her with a raise of a bushy eyebrow and not much else before making a kissing noise at the turtle. Something about his posture felt ... welcoming to Jane. Harmless and like home. The smell of cedar mixing with vanilla pipe-tobacco didn't hurt the old man's inviting image either. Jane found herself next to him, looking up at his wrinkled cheeks and old man brow, but with blue eyes as vibrant and colorful as a newborn.

"Listen. I'm feeling a bit lost here, man. It would really help if you gave me some answers." Jane nervously twitched her fingers. "So, like, Mike and I are siblings... but for starters, he's not all jacked up as a ghost like I am? Why is that? Also, does anything we do actually matter? I mean we spent all this time trying to kill Fredrick the Lord of Suicide, but if I come back from the dead... why doesn't he? Everyone inside is already readying themselves to go after the next target. Hell, thirty minutes ago, so was I. Creepy shit down there with that blood farm. Yet what's the point? I mean... you've been at this for a while. You've gotta have the answers, right?" Jane's eyes nearly sparkled with tears that weren't there.

The old man crouched down and petted the turtle, a turtle that didn't flinch back inside its shell at the touch. He chewed on her questions for a moment before packing a pipe with more tobacco. "Going to need another one of these, suppose." Several dry puffs later and small rings of smoke faded into the night sky in silence. A silence that made Jane's nerves quiet down with each passing ring. He handed her the pipe.

"I ... can't? I'm dead," Jane refused, but after a second nod from him, she reached out to try. To her surprise, the wooden pipe felt solid, smooth, and most importantly, warm in her hand. With caution, she pressed the flute to her lips and inhaled. Fire filled her chest, and a rush of flavors danced through mouth. *Whoa.* She felt her pupils dilate, and the rush of pure nicotine calmed her brain. "How?" *You know what? Don't care how... That was potent.*

"Memory." The old man winked. "Memories are magic. Not in the cliché sense either. You think your body is wrecked and destroyed. I don't see it that way. Unlike your brother, you aren't living in denial. You carry your memories with you and embraced your fate. Before Mike died, he was a vampire who consumed the heart of Golgoroth. One giant hellspawn of war. So, Mike views himself as an undying vampire still. Mike traded away what made him human to be eternally

static, forever unchanging. His soul is forever trapped in the state it resides in. You never ate a heart, did you?" he asked knowingly.

"Just injected my ass with enough chemical cocktails to rival all of Mardi Gras," Jane realized and choked on her own swear word. "Sorry, sir." *The fuck? When do I censor?*

"So, unlike Mike, you can still change. Evolve. You can be reborn, pass on, change, and more. Or you could... if the world worked. Purgatory has been broken for centuries. Souls of the dead were supposed to resolve their lingering life memories and then return back to the cycle. The Unification had a plan to fix it... but let's just say that involved a little tyranny that didn't sit well with the heavenly host."

Jane was still catching up to her own self-censoring. Honestly, she'd never really spent much time in the old bartender's presence before. She felt like a small kitten being emotionally petted by a kind deity—and any protest she gave would be a small mew. Jane had been around demons, cryptids, faeries, and more... but the more she thought on it—she never knew just *what* the Boss really was.

"Your actions matter, Jane. They always have. For you humans represent the power of the world. It's a message you'll hear time and again in different ways. Vampires, Death Lords, Werewolves..." He scoffed. "They've got material power. Left unchecked, they can, and did, absolutely rule the world. But when you kill them... all that power is useless on the other side."

"So why don't they just come back? I mean..." She pinched her cheek.

"That's a pickle." He whistled. "It used to be impossible. A simple divine law put in place ages ago. Tasting the fruit of the divine or using their blood was allowed to shape creation. Magic as a gift. Eating the heart." He tutted. "Eating the heart was made forbidden. So, your soul was forever altered. Removing you from the wheel. Of *course,* with enough determination and power—some found a way to break that restriction. Now we are in uncharted waters, dear."

The old man reached down and picked up the turtle, carrying it over to a small stream out of harm's way. "This creature is a reptile. It survives on the heat of the sun. A sun that rises black each morning, Jane, and yet... this turtle still survives. Is it the blood of demons that run in the water that keeps it alive?"

"Hey, vampire turtle is a ba—" She paused. "Blamazing turtle, okay, but don't get all cryptic on me." *Wait, that turtle isn't a vampire turtle, is it? I mean, it is out at night.*

"Apologies. We all have rules that we live by. I ... try my best to be a guiding hand but never too direct. Sometimes it works; other times it causes the sun to rise black. Let me ask you a question then." Suddenly, he towered over Jane, and Boss's hands held each of her shoulders. "If nothing you did matters, why are you still here? What memory are you hanging onto?"

Jane choked. "Bloofernutters'-n-hell, y'all dropping that kinda bomb on me?" Suddenly, Jane felt very shallow inside as a wash of memories bubbled up. The thrill of the fight, adrenaline racing through her, flying through the air, and even facing death head on were exhilarating. A feeling she never wanted to let go of. Her entire life might as well have been a dead, zombified existence when compared to the badass feeling of fighting for *something* she had during the final year. What didn't sit right was the kernel of truth that Jane didn't care which side she was fighting for—only that she had the power to *fight*.

Her deflected gaze said all it needed to for the old man.

"That's the point right there. Everyone has been asleep for quite some time, dear. Magic, for better or worse, has returned, and the world is going to evolve in new ways. Sure, Fredrick might claw his way back out of the underworld. Lazarus might martial armies and stamp out anything left alive. But it's a big fucking world, lass—and you kids have only seen just a fraction if it. I'm just an old dinosaur watching an age turn. I've done my god killing, and perhaps I was too good at my job. My outlook is a little longer than most, and this isn't

the first Ragnarök I've seen... but I will say it's certainly the most fun. Aren't you the least bit curious as to why the Church of Lazarus is buzzing over New Orleans like Black Friday shoppers descending on a Walmart? If I was a betting man... I'd bet the Sons and Daughters are blowing things up and ruining well-laid plans by nightfall tomorrow." He ruffled Jane's hair and snatched back his pipe. "That should answer your questions, no?"

The old man was already chuckling as he walked back inside—leaving a very confused Jane outside.

"Wait a minute!? No, no that doesn't answer anything! And I heard you say fucker! I'm never censoring myself again around you!"

The door closed.

"You ... left me ... alone? Out here?!" Jane screamed back inside. "What if the vampire turtle comes for my throat!" With folded arms, she scowled at the Waffle House. The old man was as cryptic as they came, but she did feel at least a little better. *If the old rules that ran the show have been shattered, then there is hope after all. Maybe I don't need to stay a ghost? Which honestly, why didn't I think of that before? I mean, hell, I spent most of my boring life wishing I was dead just to escape. Now I'm dead! Mike's fucked, though. He's stuck being a vampire turtle.*

If nothing else, she did feel a little smug and very curious as to why the Church of Lazarus was guarding lower New Orleans and ignoring the rest of Louisiana. An unchecked yawn forced her jaw to pop. All those times Jane had seen ghosts floating aimlessly finally made sense—the dead slept standing up, which was only a little bit creepy, but she decided that was probably a wise course of action as she faded back into the restaurant. With a soft smirk on her face, Jane chose to cozy up inside the refrigerator.

Akira sometimes has good ideas.

CHAPTER 10

"Dystopia offers you the illusion of safety. Your favorite magic products on every store shelf. Toilet paper that always grants the perfect wipe. Even robotic limbs to replace and mend the broken. Yet at the core of their technology lies magic. Why purchase and sign your life away when you can learn those very secrets for yourself? The Society of Deus academy's ten-year program will mold you into a master of the arcane in a field of your choosing."

–Brochure from the Twin Cities found
in an empty local library

The iron taste of blood caused Vryce to jolt against restraints. His small hands were clamped by cold iron manacles with a wooden brace that circled his neck, holding him hunched over. As his eyes first opened, the ringing sound between his ears furthered the migraine pounding through his skull like an angel bringing fury upon a devil. Nerves slowly came awake through the rest of him—and everything ached. His left thigh throbbed from where he was shot, and whomever issued first aid had tied some cloth around it so tightly that his toes were turning purple. With a soft lick, Vryce tasted the

dried blood that was dripping down the right side of his face, and he let out a long groan of acquiescence.

This again. If I have to restart my life again, I swear I'm going to bind every one of these pricks' souls to a tree on the edge of oblivion. With a soft puff, he blew the long brown hair away from his face and took in his surroundings finally. The soldiers had stripped him down, leaving him with only underwear and a tie around his thigh. Vryce had some wiggle room in the manacles only because they weren't exactly designed for a teenage girl. Immediately around him was a ten-foot-wide circle filled with thaumaturgical runes etched into a white marble floor. Two steel rivets formed straight lines outward in a V position that Vryce's gaze followed—each ending in another circle with another person bound in the same fashion. *Really?* Anyone in the chamber could have heard his eye roll. The Church of Lazarus was using a summoning ritual via the Ten Sephirot of the Tree of Life. In this chamber, there would be a total of nine people, each in a Kabbalistic circle with the exception of Tif'eret, the sixth circle. *Sixth is adorned, glorious, delightful throne of glory, the house of the world to come.* The thought flowed naturally to him. For in the sixth circle, whoever was doing the summoning would bind their would-be-servant as if they were king.

Vryce knew this ritual better than anyone—he invented it.

Like a veteran craftsman, his eyes focused less on the other poor souls bound in the chamber and more upon the works of ritual laid into the ground. None of the circles were up to his standards. A symbol a few centimeters off to the left, a rivet line curved slightly in the stone, or even a prisoner's feet dangling too close to the edge—all minor imperfections that could spell disaster for a ritual as complex as this. Yet each imperfection offered the tiniest bit of hope and caused his lip to curl in a wicked smile. *At least they believe me worthy for the sphere of Keter, the topmost of the sephirot and crown. Blessed be his name and his people. Whether they know it or not... they picked right on that at least. I am, indeed, godly. Just... currently a bound godly being.*

Damien closed his eyes and recited a meditative prayer to push the migraine and pain away. There was nothing magical about it, but centuries of honing his will left him with a few tricks. He was *hoping* that they were going to practice a basic satanic ritual for summoning and just use bloodletting. Maybe sacrifice a few goats or perhaps several chickens—then Vryce could simply bargain with the summoned entity for his freedom. Alas, this ritual would require his head to be ceremoniously parted from his shoulders during the casting. It allowed for a deeper reach... not into hell but into the Room of Guf itself. A chance to reach into the heavens and perhaps summon forth an angel—or even a divine vision about fate itself.

"Somebody needs a champion for something important, eh?" Vryce whispered to himself while testing the wiggle room within his restraint to no early success.

"H-help?" A soft voice echoed from the person bound in the sphere next to him. She craned her head over and looked at him through bloodied eyes. Like him, she was stripped to her underwear, but she was older, easily in her late twenties with jet black hair and running makeup.

When their eyes met, the rest of the room finally dawned on Vryce. The wide chamber with marble floor must be in some sort of grand mausoleum. Catholic trappings adorned the walls with wooden plaques filled with names of the dead. At the far end of the chamber, a massive stained glass window with depictions of Jesus Christ looked upon them with pity. *Don't give me that look.*

Vryce swished his mouth and spat in defiance before replying. "Sorry. We are each going to help ourselves. Our own errors led us to this room. I've made mine, and clearly, you've made yours."

"Wow. You are a little cunt, aren't you?" the stranger said in scared disbelief.

"No. I'm just lacking sympathy. You live in a world of magic now, and you wouldn't be here if you had any power. So, what's your talent? Other than being the person whose head is about to be chopped off

before mine? I figure you can probably buy me six... seven seconds based on how much you scream." Vryce winked. *I don't need you to help. I need you to panic.*

"Head... they are going to chop off my head!" She suddenly started flailing against her restraints. The shrill panic in her voice woke the two next to her, and thanks to her frantic screams about losing her head, they instantly began to panic and stress as well. Each captive daisy-chained to the next until the volume of the chamber was filled with nothing but cries and the rattling of chains.

Vryce's gaze focused on the prisoner three full spheres away in the Hod position. The Church of Lazarus had pinned one man a little too close to the edge. His athleticism also marked him as the biggest person in the room—and perhaps Vryce could coach him in wiggling just an *inch* to unwittingly break a circle.

The warm glow of lantern light cast over Vryce from behind as the door opened suddenly. A single Lazarean priest with rose-colored robes and a black skull strolled into the mausoleum and held her lantern up. Out of the corner of his eye, Vryce could see the deathly pallor in her complexion. Porcelain skin, sultry red lips, and dead eyes gave away her vampiric nature.

"Oh, calm down." She spoke calmly with a voice that silenced the weak-willed instantly. "This is but a transition in your life. The gates of heaven shall be open to you, and your suffering will soon be brought to an end."

Her honeyed words backed by a power of vampiric hypnotism calmed nearly everyone in the room instantly—even in the face of their demise.

"Good evening, Katrina," Vryce said once silence befell the room. "Still sucking the bony toes of the Lord of Murder, are we?"

Of all the things a vampire committing sacrifice would expect to hear, a scrawny teenager addressing her like an old friend did not make the checklist. She walked over and lifted up Vryce's chin to gaze into his heterochromia eyes.

"I do not know you..." she said with a look of amused curiosity. "But whoever you are, you've probably had better nights."

"Many. I've had the misfortune of being caught in the wrong fishermen's net, it seems. As I told your soldiers, I'm not exactly sacrifice material."

She pursed her lips and purred, wiping away the half-dried blood on the side of Vryce's cheeks. "I don't know. Seems like you add a certain charm to this ritual. Everyone else is weak willed enough to be culled... but you... you've dabbled with magic—and insulted my lord. Perhaps you are right where you are meant to be."

"That depends on what you are trying to summon. You, a vampire, consumer of demon hearts, and only seven decades old... are going to attempt a ritual to reach into heaven? Doesn't that seem like it's going to burn?"

Katrina crouched, pulling back Vryce's hair and inspecting his neck for some marking or tattoo that would betray his identity. "Where is your witch mark? I'll give you extra credit in school for recognizing this ritual. It's only been attempted a handful of times. It *was* highly guarded until a few years ago... but I guess now you can download it. I hate the internet," she said sarcastically.

"You'll find no markings on me," Vryce lied. His eyes were his marking, and his left-handed nature was equally as obvious and oblivious to those who dabbled. "I'm an agent for the Lady of Fate. Everyone knows she imparts wisdom on her agents beyond their years... all to deliver a single message at the exact moment. This could be *your* moment, Katrina. You open that portal, and the *very* real sun of the Morning Star will burn you to cinders. The black sun of Anthelios that you can walk under now does not exist in the heavens."

She paused for a moment and looked back at the circles. Vryce clocked a slight flicker of doubt in her brow. Katrina was a vampire far down the totem pole within the Unification, and he remembered when she was granted her first heart in the seventies. The bloodline of sorcerers she came from were always treated poorly by the Unification,

but they stayed true to the Church to climb the proverbial ranks, a slow process given the turnover of immortal creatures. *That's right. You were sold up the river.*

"I ... could ... be of assistance." Vryce sweetened his voice. "New Orleans has plenty of people still who haven't drunk blood or eaten a heart. It *would* be a shame to make an error... or several errors on a ritual this important, no?"

She folded her arms while stepping back with a wide-fanged smile. "You alllmost had me. Well done! You certainly are a cheeky one. I'll admit, I am most certainly curious about you... but this ritual isn't mine to lead. Merely tend and shepherd the dead murdered as such. The one leading this ritual ... is him." She nodded behind Vryce. "I'm just the janitor who's going to grind up your souls as gruel for some gods. You might make a fine soup for Molly Pitcher. She's getting a bit thin since the revolutionary war."

"Making friends already?" The raspy voice and chuckle of laughter behind Vryce caused his ass to clench.

"The room is all yours, my lord." Katrina curtsied and gave a soft finger wave to Vryce. "I'll see you on the other side, deary," she said while walking past, pausing to whisper one more thing in Vryce's ear. "I suck nobody's toe."

Petrified, Vryce felt all hope fade away from his chances of survival. Truth was, Vryce had no idea what would happen to him if he perished in this body. It took years of planning to create children that were genetically similar to his original form, and his soul was stretched across many items. The children grown were the only receptacles that could house all of his shards when he was ready to unite them—and the ability to make more wasn't exactly on the table. Without a full soul stitched... would his consciousness merely inhabit an object? Would he fade from existence? Or would he be given a chance to roam the astral realm by willpower alone until he could find a way to possess? *This isn't exactly a scenario you get to practice! Why is there a Death Lord here! Out of all the Death Lords... it had to be...*

"Lucian…" Vryce let his head flop.

"I'd say you are about to get fucked, but honestly, culture has moved beyond that, and you are a teenage girl these days. Very fashionable, Damien Vryce…" Lucian skipped into the middle of the room. Vryce noticed that one boot was broken at the heel and flopped around the Death Lord's bright yellow sock. Mottled and torn khaki pants and an atrocious Hawaiian shirt with a wide straw hat looked worse on him than the skeletal nature of the Lord of Misfortune.

"Well, at least I've decided for an upgrade. You couldn't even be bothered to cast your illusion of a handsome Frenchman, could you?"

"Katrina finds me rather dashing."

"Is it just me, or isn't having your ritual second, a vampire named Katrina, a *little* too on the nose for New Orleans?"

"When fate hands us a lemon, let's make lemon drops and toast to the apocalypse." Lucian cleaned up Vryce's hair and tied it back into a ponytail. "Do you have *any* idea how wanted you are? Hell, you *invented* this ritual and broke the world with it. I mean… I, for one, am a big fan. The look on other Death Lords' faces when all you little warlocks pulled a fast one on the big ritual?" He fist bumped the air. "Fucking priceless, *bel fanm*."

"Oh, I can only imagine the irony here. Me, being sacrificed to my own ritual that was meant to bring back Lazarus. Sue me for taking back what's mine. How's that Lazarus working out for you? Is he being a good little god?"

Lucian pried some gunk from under a nail. "Oh, a mix of this, a mix of that. You know how powerful popes are—filled with the insane dreams of world conquest and unification of faith to become god. Not gonna work out so well for most of you, though."

"Same as always then. Got it." Vryce bit his bottom lip as a question formed. *Just what the hell are you of all people doing here? You gave up your crown and seat how many times now? Hell, your warlock Sydney DuWinter was the first one to join me.* "You … helped Sydney betray the council and return the legends of old back to the British Isles. So…"

<*Let you go?*> Vryce heard Lucian's voice in his head. <*I enjoy a good laugh now and then, and DuWinter is still holding out in Cambridge... but even I can't deny fate.*>

"Yes!" Vryce flailed out his hands the best he could. "Let me the hell go, you gloriously insane bastard. You aren't..."

A bony finger pressed into Vryce's lips. "Shhhhh..." Lucian stepped back and waggled the finger. "Some tidal waves can't be stopped. You are a cunning and ruthless bastard. Calculating to the core... with all your plans and schemes. But I've been around FAR longer than you, and it's time to rev the engine of this apocalypse, eh?"

"Fine... just tell me then: what exactly are you doing with my ritual here in New Orleans?"

Lucian held up a bone six-sided dice. "Tell you what... evens or odds?"

"Odds."

A soft clatter rolled just under Vryce, and three little dots appeared.

"Lucky day. I always enjoy that you've got the guts to gamble with me. I'm not going to let you go, but I will tell you." Lucian leaned on the wooden brace over Vryce's shoulders and gestured grandly to the room. "While I was gone, the Lord of Murder was diligent in killing a bunch of American folklore legends above my fancy seat of tears. Yet some are so far forgotten they are erased from memory. Now they are but pure forces of the abyss and oblivion. You Americans have all your fancy tech, sorcery, and big fucking guns. Lazarus wants me to obliterate your continent... so I'm going to half cast your ritual and rip open a portal to oblivion. Then just sit back and watch the chaos ensue until everyone is dead." He nodded thrice.

<*Wait... That ... won't... You're insane.*>

<*I am indeed, sir.*>

"Once you start this ritual... everyone in this state will be made aware. Even *my* people. Do you think you'll even finish?"

"Eh... maybe?" He shrugged. "I'll be honest. You are the best of us when it comes to magic. They gave me an army of fanatics to

jumpstart this shit show. If there are fireworks, then so be it. Just try and keep your head on your shoulders if you can. I'd *loathe* for you to fade into Purgatory before you see my great works. It will be your future prison once the angelic host gets their paws on you. Plus... I'm curious what chaos a sacrifice like you will bring. Who knows? Everything could go tits up."

"I want you to know I hate you."

Lucian backpedaled down to the middle of the room. "Feeling is mutual. But for the rest of you!" He clapped his hands and rubbed them together. "Let's have a fun and wholesome meeting with nameless horrors that exist between realms, shall we? I'll buy drinks for the rest of you in my afterlife. Really, the lot of you fall under my domain, and my beggars ... actually enjoy being dead because we get the cosmic joke."

Lucian paused with arms out wide, tilting his head down so shadows covered his face under the wide hat. "We've always been fucked." The half-skeletal zombified grin was nothing short of diabolical.

Chapter 11

"The sun turned black, the whole moon turned violet purple, and the stars in the sky fell to the earth. Vampires prayed for the black sun. The cryptids knelt for their Lilith Moon. But what of the stars? They were the dead trapped in Purgatory, yearning to taste life yet again. With all three, our Kingdom of Heaven... the very soil we walk upon no longer has room for the meek human. Soon, we will all be forced to crawl on our knees."

–Lazarus

Lucian feigned joy in the cries of anguish that echoed in the room. It was easy to wear a smile, stretch out his arms, and force dusty air from his lungs in a semblance of laughter—harder to lie to himself. Vryce's ritual he was about to commit a blasphemy upon would condemn most of New Orleans to certain death and soon the rest of the country. It took warlocks centuries to *perfect* the ritual for its intended purpose—lowering the veil between the living and dead so a soul could cross over. The Unification's master plan to pull *a single* god back from the dead was all so they could fix the mess left by the last god, who became a bit of an absentee landlord in Lucian's mind.

They were never supposed to be here... The dead, vampires, demons, and more walking among mortals so openly was hilarious to Lucian. Sure, they'd *always* existed. *Like cockroaches who are always in the corner of a clean house. Just when you think you've scrubbed the place—boom! Roach.* But Lucian knew the original plan was to fix the cosmos, not make it worse. It's why he signed on. Of course he called the warlocks' betrayal, but nobody ever wanted to listen to the insane beggar lord. Just like clockwork, Vryce and the other warlords kept a card in a back pocket and played it at the right moment. They opened the portal to the heavens and hell—and then broke the key. So now Lucian was going to do the same and let even more crap into the world.

He would rather be fishing.

"I bet you all think I'm a giant monster," he said to the room while breaking the wings of a dove over a golden bowl. "See... the thing is, I'm actually the good guy here." *Mostly.* Lucian leveled a blood-drenched bony finger at Vryce. "That one there broke the world all so the master of possession could have its soul back. A free lich? *Bah.* Little girl, the very angels and devils made us liches and chained us with divine purpose. You don't have the luxury of running free."

Ten gold coins, each from a different continent, plopped in the bowl of dove's blood. *A little thaumaturgy to represent the larger world. A small coin from a priest... each of a different faith to grant our ritual guidance.*

"As for the rest of you? Stop lying to yourself about your innocence. Scream and cry all you want, but *I* know that everyone in this room is a murderer at the least... some rapists, and at least two people guilty of using magic to curse others. Bit cowardly those ones. Cursing never goes well. Always comes back to bite you."

As if it were a Tuesday stroll, Lucian walked over to man chained in the circle of Hod and placed his decayed skeletal hand on his face. With but a touch and a fragment of his power, the man's entire body aged into the nineties within seconds—teeth clattering to the floor.

"How about you *don't* stick your dick in anybody you can drug in next life, eh? Can you do that?" He held the man's chin up and gave him a glare with his one good eye. "I don't want you fucking up the good name my souls have in the underworld. Not that it will matter. Little willy is all shriveled now." Lucian leaned down to pluck a tooth and drop it in the bowl, giving a small wave to Vryce who was trying to kill him with a glare. *Now is that a look of disappointment I see? A dash of hope perhaps?*

A white-blue fire began to spread around the etched circle within the crypt, and before Lucian was back in place, a pillar of light erupted in a perfect cylinder from Hod that shattered through the ceiling and eventually kissed the clouds.

Lucian ducked and hustled faster back to Tif'eret in the middle. "Holy angel tits! I was expecting a candle! Not Santa Claus's cock!"

The teenage girl that was Vryce, perhaps the most dangerous person in the world, let loose a chuckle. "I take it ... you've only read my *Arcanum Arcanimisum*, all powerful lich? You've been around for what, three thousand years... and never *once* tried to open a gateway between worlds?"

"NO!" Lucian laughed at the absurd thought. "I'm not insane! Why the hell anyone worships the shit God kicked out is beyond me."

"Amateur." The girl scoffed.

"Oh, excuse me for doing my actual job instead of spending six hundred years sulking and trying to find a way to stitch back together my soul. It isn't *that* important." *Well, they are handy for bartering with devils, but I mean really... was being a warlock that bad?*

"I don't know what's more insulting," Vryce continued. "The idea you have no appreciation for my craft, or that you are purposely going to botch my ritual. You don't even have the fuel to make it past the third circle without a furnace of souls to continue, and you are killing everyone all wrong. Ours was global... took centuries to prepare. You've got a fragmented city and an army of necromancers. How

are you going to survive the coming assault when every demon in the area is drawn like a moth to us?"

Oh, you poor child. Lucian shuffled away from Vryce to the Netzah circle, as he withered a woman guilty of slavery unceremoniously. The etched lines in concrete between Hod and Netzah were set ablaze in a warm candle glow of black flame before a pillar of dark eldritch green light exploded to the sky, peeling away the roof of the church like shards of a broken mirror getting kicked inward. Divine magic poured openly into the room, electrifying the air and melting the concrete walls into a dripping gray slag that flowed upward. Broken glass, candelabras, and several severed fingers floated in the air in defiance of gravity.

"See, you might have a problem with demons and angels over there... I won't have such. I didn't break divine law. I ... have an official seat as a Death Lord." Lucian winked and tapped the mask on his shoestring belt. *And what do I care if Murder's agents finally must prove their worth? I'm not here to fight Murder's war. If Lazarus is going to make me wipe out a nation... I'm doing it with my own army. And my misfortunate souls need a guiding light. It's not exactly like they have Verizon.*

<You know I can still read your mind right?> Vryce's voice echoed in Lucian's head.

<Oh shit, forgot to turn that off. Your head's still coming off, belle. >

Mike pointed at the French Quarter in the horizon. "Plan A is simple," he said. "We kick down the door and bust some legends out of prison. Paul ... fucking ... Bunyon and Johnny Appleseed are down there."

A pillar of blue-white light erupted at the top of Mike's finger in the distance. He maintained his best smug look and simply blew on his index finger like a gun. "Booyah."

Jane punched him. "You are banned from that phrase. Only the king of demonic vacuums can say 'booyah.' They really, and I'm not joking, actually get cat hair out of a couch."

Everyone else nearby collectively gave the most *what-the-hell* look possible.

Akira palmed Jane's face. "Excusing the fact that a certain blonde someone scared actual poop out of a vampire earlier today by hiding in a fridge, that's a feat worth ten points—why not just *eat* the legends' hearts?"

Mike tapped his chin. "Still part of plan A-point-one then. Plan A is really kick down the door."

Lucy just flipped an ax into her belt and hopped on her Ducati crotch rocket. "For once, I agree with both of you insane bastards. Because unless Mike suddenly developed powers of the world's best vacuum, someone else is kicking down a door. So, plan A-point-two is get there before the door is open."

By the time the Sons and Daughters were halfway across the bridge stretching the lake, a second column of green fire touched the sky. Panic spread through the region as people prepared for an apocalyptic onslaught, but some dared to stay, lured by their curiosity, like moths to a bug zapper. Some of them, now on plan A-point-seven.

Lucian dropped the semblance of banter as he focused on the third circle Jesod, directly across from Vryce, but still connected at an angle to the pillars of fire that were once Hod and Nezah. Jesod, the foundation of the world and material power, and according to Vryce's stupid book he wrote, that sphere represented the current ball of rock everyone's feet were currently stapled to, and botching the cast would mean the feedback and ramifications would hit here the hardest. Chained within Jesod, there was a punter who had spent her

life embezzling money, and once she had learned enough magic to change her appearance, she continued her cons. The minor sorceress was of no importance, but it was a step closer to an act Lucian was not looking forward to.

The girl in the fourth circle, farthest away from Vryce was none other than Lumine—a completely innocent girl Lucian had helped earlier. *She shouldn't technically even be here, considering she has eaten a heart. But you can't break a ritual with the exact components. One always has to poison the well.* Vryce was correct; a ritual such as this required fuel. When it was globally attempted, the Unification convinced demons to pour legions of souls into furnaces. Lucian didn't have access to a place like Chicago to fuel his ritual, or rather, he didn't have the commanding presence required to organize such a feat.

"I'm more of a ... go with the flow kinda skeleton," he muttered aloud as he withered the con-woman, aging her body to the point where it almost turned to ash. His torn boot allowed the pus and blood from her eyes to seep into his sock as he hurried back to his post—dodging the pillar of earthly brown flame erupting behind him.

With three gates open, Lucian could finally see between the realms. Below him, the floor faded away directly into *his* Seat of Gilded Crowns. Some may have called it hell or even the beggar's dream in life. A mountain of forgotten trinkets, washed from across the universe, collected themselves in impossibly deep pits like trash heaps of missed opportunities. Wedding rings, lost patents never invented, and even used condoms of royal importance comprised his beloved trash heap. Each item represented a fortune that was never had or a missed circumstance that led to starvation. Upon their death, his souls should have had the chance to find that which caused their twist of fate. Yet ironically, the destined souls never ended up under Lucian's rule. Most were murdered or died of starvation or burned by heaven's wrath... leaving his armies the weakest among every Lord of Death.

Above him, the gates of the heavens were shimmering. At least, the heavens as imagined by those who resided in this region—an eclectic mix of spirits and nature rather than the pearly gates imagined by most Catholics. Spirits were more concerned with moving the forces of nature than ever really paying attention to mortals. They made the wind blow or the flowers bloom—or even laid curses upon the deserving. It was Christianity that gave them attributes and names, but these spirits were far older and far less concerned with what name someone called them by. A large quantity of humans within New Orleans both worshiped them in secret... or simply played along with whatever name they were assigned during their white assimilation in the *"good lord's* name." If anyone would survive the coming wrath in the city, Lucian knew it would be those who still practiced Vodou.

Yet it was the in-between that Lucian was concerned with. The fractured tethers of that stitched reality together. Reality was defined by humans, who were ultimately the real drivers of divine will. Outside of known creation slept unspeakable creatures that were never born. Like shadows upon the world, an abyss in the darkness that was endless. Fragmented aberrations seethed at even the slightest light, for they were never allowed to even *exist.*

Lucian knew their power, for they did not need faith or worship to give them form, but he hoped their message would summon his army. He never had the heart to send his collected artifacts into oblivion. Holding onto some vain hope that his misfortunate souls would discover what tethered them to the afterlife eventually and enter the cycle of reincarnation to try again in the next. The creatures between realities didn't have such illusions. They desired only the end of all existence. *If Lazarus is real, then he can turn back this clock and reset the world. If not, we all deserve to finally rest.*

Lucian grabbed a single shadow... and tugged on its thread from between the light of the fires. Just a thread. A fragment of oblivion into the world. A fragment that he could release among the treasures of the forgotten... hoping his legions would come to save their

forgotten treasures before it was too late. A small worm could only eat so much, so fast.

Jane marveled at how organized fleeing civies were while clutching her arms into Doc's houndstooth suit coat as they ripped through streets toward the beacon. She assumed that when shit began hitting the fan, people caught in the zone would be nothing but panic. Not without good reason either, as Jane had seen plenty of supernatural warfare. In the time since she was dead, clearly people had gotten more acquainted with the absurd. *That, or New Orleans really has had a lot of practice.*

Civilians moved as a single unit, organized and calm with a prepped evacuation that began instantly upon the first pillar of light. Hobbled together or hastily repaired boats were quickly positioned along the waterways. Volunteers used flare guns to provide guidance for growing crowds of people regardless of car, foot, or the occasional medical helicopter flying directly across the lake. The crowds themselves, even ones made primarily of dead souls, all had important belongings ready to go at an instant's notice. The living with bug-out bags, and the dead—significant mementos.

Altogether, downtown New Orleans was drained of individuals who didn't want to be there almost as fast as the Sons and Daughters (and others) who wanted to get in. Jane smiled as she snuggled her cheek up to Doc's back and closed her eyes to enjoy the sensation of wind flowing through her. *It's been ages since I can be so close. Doc was a creeper when I first met him, but... he's a good hoss through-and-through. I don't regret taking the actions that led to my death, but it doesn't mean I can't miss this smell! Also, Doc is a scrawny bastard. The hell has his mama been feeding him?* Jane squeezed his ribs the best she could

without feeling his liver. Doc tapped her forearm with one hand as if he sensed her curiosity before following the crew down the exit ramp.

A slow grin crept on Jane's face… one she let fold into a full pearly white smile in anticipation of what was to come next. Everyone disinterested had left, but the soldiers from the Church of Lazarus were certainly buzzing around the cemetery. A wrought-iron gateway with the broken letters for Lafayette Cemetery was guarded by several helldivers and their Barghest demon hounds. The pillars of light erupting from deeper within cast an ominous shadow upon each helldiver who readied themselves for a sortie. Motorcycles weren't exactly the stealthiest of approach vehicles. *Revenge from the graves, fuckers.*

Jane was quick as ever, hopping off the bike and blowing a kiss Doc's way with a wink as she skipped backward to the soldiers.

"Evening." Jane gave her dearest smile possible given her ghostly tattered state. "Rather, afternoon? Hard to tell with the ball-o-darkness for a sun."

"Jane," Lucy said while hopping off her own. "Heh… Jane, you idiot."

"What?! Can't we say hello and ask nicely first? It's only polite."

One of the helldivers looked to her friend and just chuckled, pulling out a femur bone that was dipped in iron with several bent nails sticking out of it. "I mean, it *is* polite, dear ghost. Manners have meaning."

"Jane, you are a ghost," Lucy said deadpan. "Like that idiot over there…" She thumbed back to Mike.

"Fuck you too."

"You haven't exactly had *training*." Lucy thwapped one arm forward into Akira's chest before the gutter-punk assassin started beheading people. "She's gotta learn sometime, I suppose."

Jane waved the unbelievers off and turned back to the helldiver holding the bone. The pale vampire had stark white hair and wore tight black clothing with an adorned rapier to her side. *Shit, she's actually kinda gorgeous.* Slightly flustered, Jane sauntered forward with her

hand extended. "Ma'am. Nice beat stick... love those boots. So, how about you, me, and your companions here all go fetch something to drink? Let these experienced problem solvers behind me go fix..." Jane looked behind the vampire as her thought trailed. "Whoever is summoning the god of juicy fruit or whatever that is before it attracts some larger devil."

Katrina gave a small curtsy and tilted the heel of her boot. "Thank you, dear. Found them in DC. Great bargain. Brook & Talbots. They even have little pockets hidden..."

"Ugh, POCKETS! Right? Skintight uniforms never give us enough space." Jane tugged at her torn, ghostly purple jumpsuit filled with worn corporate logos—the last bit of clothes she had on before she died.

"Dammit. We could probably be friends." The vampire sighed before swinging the femur bone with accelerated speed right at Jane.

Either assuming she couldn't be hurt, or because she had been so used to having super speed herself... Jane didn't dodge. *That will just pass thr-*

Even Lucy winced when Jane was sent like a baseball far to the right, flying *through* several bikes and leaving ectoplasm behind like a snail's trail.

Jane landed flat on her back and skid along a mix of gravel and grass and winced at the killer headache. *I just got swatted like a bug! That bitch!* When she tried to stand though, her ghostly form disobeyed her, and only her head tilted up to see Lucy's know-it-all frown. *Don't you dare say I told you so.*

"Mike, get your sister. Go see what's happening inside. We'll deal with our dance partners." Lucy flipped her handax at the same moment Akira produced two deadly looking sickles and let her fangs grow. "As is, you two are useless in a fight. Can't hurt them..."

"But we can certainly hurt you..." Katrina finished the sentence while drawing her rapier. The sound of guns being readied filled the air as squads in each crew readied for a drawn out fight.

A third pillar of earthly brown energy erupted from the middle of the cemetery.

Lucian held the wriggling mass of abyssal energy and surveyed it with amused curiosity. *How's it feel, little one, to know that the worst thing you can inflict upon me is freedom from my misfortune?* The small slithering worm held insignificant power at the moment. It was, after all, nothing but a fragmented essence of something that never had been allowed to exist. Lucian didn't expect such a tiny, poor, unnoticed entity to change the tide of any war. It did, however, ignite a sliver of hope within his withered heart that given time—it could unite the world. The secret, he figured, was not trying to claim it. Centuries of being stepped on by egotistical fools who sought power taught him better than that.

Mages had dabbled with such creatures for centuries. They gave them form and purpose whenever one slithered its way into the world through whatever crack it could find. *Even you, Vryce, stitched your souls together with strands of such shadow. How's that working out for you?* Lucian allowed himself the momentary pause to look across the chamber into Vryce's eyes. Not the small brown-haired lass that made up his current body, but the lich's very soul—a tattered and soul-stitched abomination that appeared as very determined (albeit strikingly handsome with pointed features) rebel who wasn't the least bit scared. "Judging me for being a copycat? Here's where we differ..." Lucian let his skeletal fingers open and dropped the sliver down directly into Purgatory amongst all the lost treasures that comprised his Seat of Golden Crowns. *I couldn't help but notice, little one, there are a few imprisoned gods down there. Who knows what trouble you'll get into in time?*

With the matter settled, Lucian dusted off his hands and fished for a fat, half-burned cigar out of his Hawaiian shirt pocket. He surveyed the results of his ritual while tapping off the burnt end. "Well, looks like I done fucked this up, didn't I? Three gates open, check. Three pillars of light, check, and not enough fuel to open a fourth." The warm light from an old oil-fueled Zippo danced along his rotten and bone-exposed face. Smoke flowed from nostrils without a nose, cavernous in his skull as he sauntered over to Lumine and lifted her chin up with two fingers.

"By all rights, you should be dead," he said.

"I already was. I can rest easy now, ghost... but..." Her crocodilian eyes became lidded at his touch, like a kitten warming up to its owner. "I like not being able to see past this day. But I owe a debt to that girl opposite me... so kill me instead of her."

"You owe a debt to more than that creature... You have something of mine, don't you? Something that led you into here? It's curious to think that bad luck can often lead to new encounters, no?" Lucian reached forth and the cold-iron chains that shackled her down aged quickly into rust before crumbling away entirely.

Lumine rubbed her wrists and flopped to her knees, bare soiled feet peeking out from behind her. She was malnourished, Lucian noted, kept hungry and farmed for her blood like a cow by cowards who were afraid to eat a heart themselves. *Nobody needs to eat a heart to survive. It's that fear of death that keeps people fighting... but this poor girl has lost everything that made her human.*

"You can keep the mask if you like. I'm not particularly fond of it, no matter how much it keeps me alive. Keep trying to get rid of it, but..." He coughed on the cigar. "It's like herpes for me. I just can't shake it."

Lumine traced a finger around the long string around her neck before pulling up the golden mask made of coins that dangled around her wrist. Two large cracks traced down the mask under each eye and one more in the center, but it still held together and refused to break

no matter how much Lumine worked it in her hands. Her yellow eyes almost appeared hungry at the desire to simply put it on, but she cautiously looked across the room at the other girl staring back.

"I shouldn't. It doesn't belong to me... I just found it." She offered it up to the Lord of Misfortune.

"Once I take it, belle, everything is going to go haywire here. No tellin' what is going to happen. You might die."

"It's not right for me to take someone's power. I've had that happen to me more than I care to admit... so please. Just take what's yours back. Even if that means I can see my future again."

"You can't see your future with the mask because Misfortune doesn't play by the rules..." Lucian tapped a coin on the mask. "Each king had a soothsayer who foretold their fate... and their empires still crumbled. You can keep it. If you are paralyzed by visions of the future, then sometimes that silence is helpful to take action." He lowered himself and whispered in her ear, "Like murder your captors."

Her breath cut sharply. The sounds of muffled gunfire echoed outside while she struggled between choices, and Lucian calmly twisted the lit cigar out at the edge of her circle, breaking the ritual line.

Lumine chucked the mask like a burning hot pot over Lucian's hand as her cheeks flushed. As realization over the source of the gift, and what she had done, washed over her, she began to panic and retreat to the best of her ability. Her bones suddenly snapped and twisted as green scales grew from under her skin, and her face distorted into a crocodilian jaw. Still in the midst of shifting, she lunged forward clumsily, falling over and slipping on blood while desperately trying to cross the crypt to the other side.

Vryce had shown little signs of fear until the sight of a growing fifteen-foot monstrous half-girl half-crocodile was tumbling and sliding out of control through a sacred ritual meant to merge worlds—right at him. Lucian didn't need to read his thoughts to begin cackling in genuine laughter. *That poor sap doesn't want to be crushed by some random girl... how fucking fitting. Killed by the very one who wants to save you.*

The arcane energies within the room, once carefully laced, began to reverberate out of control at the sudden chaos. Ley lines between worlds were being crashed between with abandon, and even Lucian could feel the energy starting to shake his ribs as heavens and hells began to crash.

"This is like lich bowling! Come on! Give daddy a strike!" He motioned at Lumine like she was a ball he rolled down the alley with the mask never leaving his grip.

Lumine's tail suddenly crashed into the concrete, vaulting her upward over Vryce and body slamming her into the doors right behind him with a loud shatter. The energies in the crypt exploded outward, blasting stained glass window and concrete wall out—even throwing Lucian halfway out the large glass window, spilling his rotten intestines while he scrambled to keep hold of his hat.

Everyone's ears were ringing, and even Lucian needed a moment, dangling halfway out of the stained glass window. His spine bent backward with a crack, and he spied the battle going on outside. *Vampire on vampire action. Oh, that always... Wait, the Sons and Daughters! Ha! I love them. Ooooh... Katrina is going to fucking hate me after this. She's going to have to stab that Akira so many times her poor arm is going to tire out.* "Well, better get back to it." His wounds stitched and healed with loud pops as he pulled himself from the broken glass.

Two familiar-looking ghosts were standing with their mouths open, unaffected by the explosion just outside the doors. Mike and Jane recognized him, but certainly not the shape changer knocked out in the hallway that just revealed their presence.

"Evenin.'" Lucian nodded. "Looks like I dun messed up here. Hey... hey!" He snapped fingers. "Any of you sacrifices have a secret stockpile of souls we can grind up to finish whatever it is we started? I mean, otherwise all your heads are coming off without a purpose." His gaze fell on Vryce, hoping that the explosion killed the body-hopping abomination, but no, the unholy bastard was still alive. *Blow up*

a church and the teenage girl lives, ugh, typical. "How many souls did you stitch together inside that frame again?"

"Team distraction?" Mike looked to Jane, thumbing over at Lucian.

"Fuck it. You tackle Mr. Bony fingers. I'll ... free?" Jane's eyebrow rose as she circled a finger while counting the prisoners.

Mike's boots impacted the floor within the crypt as if they were solid. The barrier between the worlds was thin, granting him a fraction of his old strength and the same tangibility he had in Purgatory.

Lucian danced a jig and raised his fists in the old bellicose style. A side of his lips stretched what little smile they could muster. Here he was, watching two dead heroes try and save the world once again while their squads battled outside against the Church's first fiddle squad. Yet nobody, not even the gods, Lucian figured, noticed the small sliver of abyss he dropped... or the Cherubim which had grown curious about the folly of mortals, peering its goat head from beyond the pillar of eldritch green light. The four-headed, four-winged angel would only need gaze upon Vryce to become enraged... and shatter the remaining barriers to rip the heathen apart.

A brick suddenly knocked off Lucian's hat.

"Don't smirk," Mike said as he grabbed Lucian's bony arm and planted a boot right between Lucian's thighs.

Buckling over, Lucian *would* have felt his balls crunch. If he had any. Before his jaw could open to fire off a retort, Mike tossed scooped up shards of broken glass into his one good eye, blinding him. Connerie *motherfucker. Cheap.* Lucian soon felt his back slam into the ground and the wind flow through the hole in his boot. "Aaaaah... ooooowww... oooooh..." he sarcastically cooed.

Letting undeath flow through him, his eyes suddenly glowed red. The world came back into view as his true power flickered alive in the chaos of battle. Centuries of boredom had kept it down. Mike was fully visible, as was everyone. A tint of red colored each person, but Lucian could see more than his sight allowed. He saw them, and their strands of fate tying everyone together like dominoes. Jane freeing

Vryce from his shackles was out of sight, but he could see the reflections in the strands flowing from Vryce. Lucian could see how a loose brick nearby would cause the entire crypt to collapse... or even how blowing on a dandelion would cause a prisoner to sneeze and distract the Cherubim from ever laying eyes on Vryce. The one thing Lucian hated about his power more than any other... he never saw anything positive. It was always *what could go wrong*. This time, Lucian saw an interesting chain reaction that required *many* dominos.

Lucian effortlessly grabbed Mike by the throat and floated back vertically standing, dangling the six-foot-one ironworker like a children's toy. "Do you wanna find out what happens when we die?" Lucian suddenly spun Mike around, holding him as a hostage and a body shield.

The second Vryce's fingers touched blood, Lucian saw an opportunity and blew his kiss at the unshackled lich.

Vryce rose from the edge of his circle, muttering words in Latin as forces of weather heeded his command. His hair now flowing free, Vryce's toes lifted off the ground as he stepped forward, a frenzied look in his eyes. Blood ripped itself out of the other prisoners' bodies in a violent torrent before Jane could free them and swirled around Vryce in a shield. With his arm stretched stick straight and fingers splayed— his viola talisman was telekinetically summoned to its master's hand.

Lucian knew Vryce was pissed when there wasn't even dialogue. No thoughts to read. No facial emotions—just cold eyes that arched with white fury of lightning hidden behind the unassuming frame of a possessed teenage girl.

Mike grasped at Lucian's trousers. "Fuck man... not again."

"Yup. Again." Lucian sighed.

Seventeen lightning bolts burned through the heavens and struck Lucian and his companion like a thunderous tidal wave of energy. In an instant, only the charred remains of Lucian's ectoplasm covered boot remained with a small wisp of smoke trailing up through the shattered window.

CHAPTER 12

"Their blood gives you strength. It heals wounds. It can fucking cure cancer, and they have kept it from us! This is your chance to rise. They are trying to summon more of these in secret to force us into another lie, and they messed it up worse than every oil spill that's ever happened. You have this one chance. One chance in your life to change your lot."

–Mike Auburn, at the Dawn of the Apocalypse

Mike had never once, in his life, his unlife, or his actually dead life, sat with imaginative thoughts about what it would feel like to be boiled alive. Sure, Mike reasoned, he often pushed himself to the brink of death just to *feel* alive, but he wasn't actually out there sticking his hands inside live electrical currents. At best, he was known for walking on I-beams without a safety harness or perhaps the occasional jump down in an *almost* suicidal fall. Back when he was human, brushes with his own death had a habit of allowing him to glimpse into Purgatory, the greenish, decaying hellscape that lay just over the real world and infinitely far down would reveal itself the closer he got. Back then, it was the perfect balance for him. He'd come close to death only to escape its narrow crutches, and in doing so—prove that he was very much alive. It turns out, dying was not

nearly as fun or insightful. Particularly when it was feeling his insides liquify and the memory of eyeballs melting before exploding out of his face. *Ugh... let's remember this one fact of life, Mike. Just... accept this as surely as the laws of attraction. No matter how much you are struck by lightning, it will never, and I mean fucking never, hurt less.*

The fact that there was a thought in his head, in his own voice, caused his eyes to creak open and his nose to wrinkle shortly after. He smelled like burnt marshmallows, and he was crumpled in the corner of a room, lying upon a glittering pile of pointed gold and brass objects. Cutlery, earrings, wedding bands, tiaras, crowns, and... Mike couldn't even make out half of the trash. More importantly, the ringing in his ears and head-splitting migraine dominated any sensation as he came to. *Being ... a ghost ... should mean I don't hurt, right? Why is God an asshole who keeps our memory of pain?* He groaned as he peeled himself up and plucked earring needles out of his blackened hand. *Please tell me I'm not permanently stuck like the Stay Puft Marshmallow Man.* Before Mike could further investigate the nature of his ghostly wounds, another string of curses, not from him, cut through the ringing.

"It's always the feet," Lucian groaned in a raspy tone. Mike spied the blurry form of the smoky skeleton crawling through the golden sea several piles away. "I never seem to die with my fucking feet attached, and the cost of boots today... Shit ass inflation can choke on my ear."

And ... I'm still fighting. Right. Mike secretly longed for a pint of demon blood, or hell, even human blood to instantly heal his wounds as he pried himself up to a standing position. *Being a vampire was much easier.* He was pretty sure his left eye was either still missing or just wouldn't open but forced himself to stumble forward. A tee-ball baseball trophy for second place lodged its bat right in the soft squishy part of his foot, causing Mike to inhale through his teeth before tumbling back down in a clatter of pointy treasures. A witty thought about dragons tried to form, but Mike just lay on his back at the base of the mound and focused on deep breaths to calm the pain.

Moving was currently a worse torture than driving behind a tiny girl in an oversized luxury SUV while she yapped on the phone.

"Oh, I feel that." The zombie patted his leg as he crawled past. "Let's call a truce for a moment okay, Bonzai? Getting disincorporated ain't common. Leaves a mark on ya, and *ti gason,* you've already got several."

"What in the name of all things does *ti gason* even mean, you miserable twat waffle?" Mike touched his chest and felt the raised scars from the burns but kept picking at the edges. When he realized that it didn't hurt as much, he began to peel off the scabs. *You know, I'm just going to let mystery go. Wanna know why? Because this fucker is BOUND to monologue about ghosts needing to scab but recover.*

"In the language of creole, boy. In my humble opinion, the most determined survivors to ever grace this ball of rock invented that language. You should try getting out more." Lucian pulled himself up onto a throne made entirely of crowns that sat within the middle of the massive chamber. Crowns of bone, gold, silver, jade, and every other type a ruler would fashion heralded their importance. Many of the crowns were so faded, they almost looked as if they were hewn from stone. With a long sigh of pleasure, like he was sinking into a warm bath, Lucian let the stress melt from his body as his bones and tendons popped and his feet regrew into their skeletal form.

With one eye, Mike watched with a sneer. *Missed my chance, didn't I?*

The zombie's toes twitched and stretched, fanning themselves out like he was about to get a pedicure. Mumbling to himself, Lucian ferreted around in small leather sacks tied to the side of the throne for a few minutes, occasionally chucking a random object or voodoo charm out to the side, before finally widening his eyes and pulling out a pack of brown cigarettes, a Zippo, and a small purple tube.

If anything got Mike to sit up, it was the sight of smokes in Purgatory. Suddenly, the tiny amount of fight he had in him was

enough for him to sit upright and pluck a wedding band from the pile. "I'll trade you someone's beloved treasure for a single smoke there?"

In the piercing focus of Lucian's narrowed gaze, the weight of a Lord of Death descended upon Mike. Lucian's limbs gracefully intertwined as a pristine white suit materialized, and with a solitary blink, the once-zombified figure transformed into a resplendent Frenchman. Adorned with azure eyes and lustrous, straight blonde locks, he sat regally, akin to a sovereign on his throne. "All the sorrows of the world can be cradled in the palm of your hand," intoned Lucian, his voice carrying the weight of ages. "It only demands the sacrifice of your soulmate, to watch them exist but remain forever beyond your grasp. No matter how fervently you seek, or how ardently your descendants continue the quest, reunion will forever elude you. Thus, you cling to the solitary memory, an indelible imprint carried through the fragility of your existence until even your bones succumb to dust. Yet, the alloy of memory persists, enduring the eons like an unyielding metal, a testament to the relentless ache within your soul."

Mike blinked while calmly placing the ring down. The gravity and reality of the situation finally settled. Damien Vryce, regardless of form, was imposing and terrifying with his endless machinations and honeyed words, but this Lucian figure represented one of the highest seats within the Unification. One, Mike recalled, who probably had a hand in the very creation of Vryce. *The price of evil is unknown, and tragic fates await all of us, but I ate my demon with open eyes, buddy.* Mike found the temerity to stand on his own pile in front of the Lord and refused to bow. "I've already lived a life of tragedy, and the world has been broken. Poetic words aside, you broke the world to build a god, so what do you ache for?"

Lucian's lips pressed into a long grin of thin as he leaned forward, deftly grabbing the small purple cylinder. "Death, my Purgatory-bound companion. Fate has eluded me ever since I dared to defy starvation by stealing bread from another dying belle. She died, so I may live. I hold no secrets or mysteries, Mr. Auburn." He spoke sharply

and pressed the cylinder to his lips. A small blue light on the end lent a cool light to the chamber of treasures, and a puff of smoke exhaled from the Lord.

It was in this moment that Mike knew beyond a shadow of a doubt, he stood face-to-face with the absolute scum of the earth. "You. Truly deserve. To smell only the finest carne asada corn tortillas tacos with a hint of cilantro, cooked by the tamale legend of Chicago's own hand, delivered in a red cooler—and have not a single five-dollar bill upon your person."

Lucian grasped his chest and feigned a deep pain. "Oh, you poor thing, you wound me so, not denial of food... that I haven't been able to taste since before that dish was invented!"

"No wonder all you Unification cultists are so bitter. The last time you enjoyed life was when you had to wipe your ass with twigs." Mike crouched, elbows resting on his knees as his ghostly bones cracked with a slight bounce. "So, what is your master plan this time? Piss off the American South? Despite the world ending... do you know how *long* most Americans have prayed for a foreign invasion?"

Lucian cackled. Loud raspy chokes as his hand slapped the throne filled the chamber of treasures for an awkward minute until his legs crossed, and he looked at Mike as if he were a curious child meant to be toyed with. "The Unification, eh? Yeah, I suppose that was a name." A long drag on the e-cig bought Lucian time to pontificate. "That organization might as well be an empty wasp nest these days. The Church of Lazarus is the new trend. Haven't you heard?"

Considering I'm the one who killed Lazarus... just a tad. Mike's eye twitched. "Changing names doesn't count as a plan, bone boy. Come on... what threat am I to you here? In 'your' domain. Ain't you all powerful here? This is where you monologue and tell me all the wonderful plans before you turn me into someone's wedding ring or some other bauble, right?"

That earned Mike at least three taps from Lucian's fingers on the throne. "You really are a peach but a damn impatient one. There's a

lot to unpack here, so let's rewind. Get comfy." He gestured for Mike to sit back. "First off," one finger rose, "you most certainly are a threat. You are a descendent of Lazarus. Most ghosts in Purgatory can't see, hear, smell, or anything. They wander, trapped in their own dreams. Even worse, you once consumed the heart of a demon that gave you an absolutely wild amount of strength. Since you've been wandering down here for some time, answer me: How many dead vampires have you seen here?"

Mike bit the bottom of his lip and actually thought about it. Demons, creatures of myth, and recently a few trapped gods were certainly on the radar, but he couldn't recall any vampires, psychics, or anyone else who imbibed the blood. *That does make me wonder why there are actual gods and legends in chains though. Completely unrelated.* "Alright, I'll bite. No, I haven't. What's the deal with that? How can you have Paul Bunyan trapped and chained but no dead vampires?"

"You are smarter than that... Come on, Mikey! Let's jump to some conclusions."

Mike held up his hands. "Sorry, bones. I'm not exactly someone who attended Catholic school."

Lucian grabbed the pack of smokes and gave it a rap. "First ones free if you actually try?" He slid a single smoke out.

"Fine. Purgatory is for the innocent. Not innocent in the 'I've been a good person' kind, but you haven't eaten or drunk any sort of monster goo."

With a soft flip, the smoke flung over to Mike, tumbling in the air before falling down perfectly between a crack in the mound of treasures. *Son of a!* Mike kicked, sending chains and rings scattering over the throne, but his eyes gleaned the butt of his prize. *Annnnd... it's broken in half. Fuck it. Beggars can't be choosers.*

Mike didn't have a lighter.

"Bingo! So, you sir, are an anomaly. Your sister is an anomaly. Marked as it were. No matter what you do in life, this is your limbo.

Just like Lazarus. Killed, raised from the dead, and killed again later," he rolled his eyes, "and probably repeated that cycle a few more times somewhere in history. Either way, people like you just *end up* going here. If you don't drink any celestial blood, I'm sure you will get recycled like everyone else. Then again that's the problem, isn't it? People stopped getting recycled when god died."

"Which god? The flying spaghetti monster? The god of Give-Mike-A-Lighter?" Mike motioned for a light.

"Suppose it doesn't matter really," Lucian acquiesced and chucked over a lighter. "All the other gods put down here were pretty much hunted for one reason or another over the years. Their blood, after all, grants humans that secret sauce for magic. Most of them were put here by..." Lucian's brow furrowed, and he actually seemed, annoyed by something.

"Ra-amen." Mike caught the light and... at long last... finally felt a rush of dopamine wash over him as he reveled in the memory of a smoke. *The ultimate social pause. Fuck, I've missed you.* "Most of them were put here by...?"

"I ... can't remember their name. That ... is troubling. That ... person owes me money and..."

"It's like having a song stuck in the back of your head that you know but you can't remember?"

"EXACTLY!"

"Real bitch that is." *Heh. Nice one, Boss.* "So anyway, master plan. Let's not let that attention deficit disorder of yours sway things too far."

"I'm feeling real called out here," Lucian growled. "I don't even know what that is, but I, good sir, am not a fan." He fretted with his suit coat in protest. "Well, I suppose the long and short of it is—we are going to kill every human left in the world except the ones who worship Lazarus."

Despite the million fundamental flaws Mike instantly saw with such a stupid plan, he somehow knew the Lord of Misfortune was telling the truth. *Even my plan was better! I suck at making plans!* Mike

simply took a drag and let the smoke wash against the roof of his mouth. *Man, those are stale... ugh.* "Alright... so your plan is to murder everyone? How exactly is that going to help and why would anyone... oooooh..." A thought suddenly clicked in Mike's mind.

"Exactly. At least exactly if your brain just realized that giving every human a choice of dying or worshiping means most choose worship. When that scale of belief tips until Lazarus is unanimously worshipped, then he might as well be god. Then all of this can be reset as if it never happened—"

"Hold the fuck on. What about the other gods?"

Lucian pointed to an unseen room as if it was a stupid question.

"What about other cultures? Japan? China? Hell, the damn Kiwis? You saying that they are just going to... poof, fall in line?"

"Oh, not at all. In fact, those will probably be the hardest places. Did you know that some places are actually thriving with the return of magic? Funny how the first world countries get hit the worst. Won't matter in the end though."

"Because of Murder."

"Because of Murder... and Pestilence... and Fate... and what the hell am I? Cat shit?!" Lucian sprung up and paced closer. "Liches like us are shackled with divine purpose. Angels and demons would smite the hell out of us and chain us in Purgatory if we broke our reign. Ergo, we command the legions of dead, right? All so we can get them back into the wheel. Unfortunately, the wheel's broke." He tapped his two fingers together like a kid in trouble. "So, we've gotta fix it all. Over mountains and mountains and mountains of bodies. Blood as far as the eye can see," Lucian said while trying to put an arm around Mike and pan his arm out over the horizon.

Mike pushed him back. "You know we want to kill you, right? That shouldn't be a surprise." *When Doc says people need therapy, he ain't fucking kidding.*

"Not a bit, but I'm also not one for murder. But I'll leave that to... well, Murder. That's his army up there in New Orleans. Turns out

people enjoy murdering each other a lot over the years, so technically, he's got the best army. My people are just unlucky."

"I'm surprised I'm not one of yours," Mike groused.

"Same! But that's Fate for you. She's a peach," Lucian said uneasily.

"So, what do I have to do with your little master plan if I'm such a threat?"

"My little feisty friend, you are what us gamblers call a hedge bet. Officially, you are my prisoner of war. A good luck charm. Something I can string along to show the world that I, Lucian Montague, have brought to heel the great Mike Auburn." Lucian put his arm around Mike this time fully, his grip like a grandfather's bony grasp he couldn't shake. "I report in I caught you; I buy myself a little freedom. Plus, someone has to teach you. You aren't *Morte-vivant* anymore, and I'm sure you've been wondering just how and why you crave that smoke and heal quickly."

I KNEW he would finally get to that. Despite calling the cards of Lucian's desire to ramble, Mike had no intention of remaining a prisoner or really playing along. Unfortunately, he'd also been fried twice by someone vastly more powerful than him, and Mike was at least picking up the pecking order of the power hierarchy—and he knew he needed more. *If I'm a threat, I just need to figure out how to BE a threat. Someone has to level the playing field.* "It's not like I have a choice in the matter." Mike grunted.

"Of course you do! I'm always willing to gamble for your freedom. You just don't have anything worth betting right now, but when you have something finally worth risking—you can pick the game. Until then, you and I are going to be best friends. Maybe even lovers..." Lucian suddenly nipped Mike's ear.

"ENOUGH!" Mike roared, shoving Lucian with a power that sent him tumbling headlong into a pile of glittering treasure. Lucian's agonized groan reverberated throughout the cavern, followed by his soft whimpers as he painfully picked himself up, bones clacking back into place.

"For as hard as you hit me, I can take it and more," Lucian spat through gritted teeth. "The sweet release of death hasn't been in the cards for me yet. Call it my unfortunate luck."

"Then perhaps there's hope for us yet..." Mike grinned slyly as he stuffed the rest of Lucian's cigarettes in his pocket. "We should get going though, shouldn't we? Don't you have some babysitting to do? Before... you know, they are all destroyed?"

"Oh... we have plenty of time for that. As long as I'm here, nothing above will ever go according to plan." Lucian started sauntering to an exit, and Mike found himself compelled forward as if there was an invisible leash tugging on his soul to follow.

I am going to hate this.

CHAPTER 13

"Communication is your survival. Yet who maintains a global network these days? Veriton Cellular Networks has never faltered in providing global communications in the darkest of days, and these troubling times have affected us all. With our new will-o-wisp peer-to-peer network, arm yourself with vital cellular service when the satellites fail. Even better, we now accept payment in Dystopian Bitcoin, cryptid organs, and your bricked useless phones. Let us enchant your devices with magic that will never fail. Let Veriton guard you."

Jane froze. Lightning flashed seventeen times in the same location with only a fraction of a second in between each bolt. A second prior, her brother stood with that skeletal Death Lord. A second prior, she was trying to unshackle a civilian from the wooden pillory. When the blood ripped itself through the pores of everyone still shackled, Jane knew it wasn't going to be good. That today was going to be one of *those* days. But even in her worst days of life, she wasn't expecting a category five hurricane to be summoned with a snap of a finger and lightning to slam down so quickly.

With a single blink, both the Death Lord and Mike were gone.

It took six more blinks before her brain finally rebooted itself. *Wha? What ... do I do?* Her hands trembled next to the exsanguinated

corpse as she looked up to the floating girl—and the massive goat-headed four-winged angel still staring directly into the room. The floating girl, roughly her own size and height, sported tailored brown and leather traveler clothes and wild hair that whipped in the wind currents. Her eyes bristled with electrified energy as she tapped a viola three times with an elaborate cedar bow before the sharp crescendo of music blasted out from her.

The gathering storm above New Orleans moved in sympatico with the symphony now being orchestrated as she continued walking forward. The symphony channeled the sorcerer's pure unbridled rage at seemingly anyone, or anything, it deemed a threat. Jane felt the music incite her soul into action. Its growing tempo and heralding of calamity reminded her of listening to badass fight music while working out. Still, it took one look at the crazy angel to knew she better get into gear herself. *If she hasn't killed me yet, maybe I should hide in this eye of a storm?*

The goat-lion-bird-ox angel opened four maws as its hands and talons shredded the invisible barrier of innocence between heaven and earth. Jane half expected to hear a monstrous roar from it as it stepped into reality—there was but utter silence. She raced forward to the epic witch without a clue of what she should do. *Fuck around and find out?* The silence was deafening. As if the very celestial chorus of the universe itself had suddenly been muted. As Jane jumped out of the shattered crypt into the storm, she plucked Mike's boot off the ground and sprinted through the whipping winds toward his murderer.

It was when her gaze fell on the Sons and Daughters clashing swords and fang with the Church of Lazarus forces that every-thing *finally* clicked for Jane. *THAT IS A CHERUBIM! I know those fuckers! You pluck their feathers for pillows, but they take armies to kill. Sleep tight with Cherub Blankies. They only made like... two.* Why a random commercial from her past popped into her brain, Jane inwardly blamed on the heavy doses of drugs she put herself

through. Luckily, in her scrambled ADHD brain, rational realizations did form. Slightly.

The silence radiating from the Cherubim had stopped all fighting from her allies. Allies that a very furious and arcane frenzying teenage girl was marching directly toward—on account of the Lazarean soldiers from the faction of Murder. Katrina with her amazing leather boots had skewered Akira from the chin through the forehead, but the gutter-punk assassin had her bare feet wrapped around Katrina's throat—with her toe in the vampire's mouth.

Both had paused, staring at what was headed their way.

They stopped fighting.

They both ran.

Now jogging along under the musical witch, Jane marveled at the dichotomy between the girl's power and the heavenly power. Only in proximity did Jane hear any sound, the violent and angry symphony. Lagging a single step silenced the universe, as it did when Jane stepped or skipped to the left or right. And so, Jane reasoned, her best course of action was simply to follow along with the viola-wielding weather bitch. *From behind. Frooom behind.*

Unfortunately for the Church of Lazarus soldiers and nearly every demon, cryptid, and minor celestial in proximity to Lucian's ritual—heaven's wrath was not pretty. The soldiers who didn't instantly flee began bleeding from their ears before their skin started to slough off their bones and liquify as the gaze of the Cherubim fell upon them. Most of the Sons and Daughters took to hiding or fleeing at the same time Akira did, but several that Jane didn't know met the same fate. For others, currents of wind or lightning from the witch annihilated them into cinders one minute, or she ripped the blood from any demon—storing it in floating orbs around her.

The Cherub can't melt this girl while she plays... but playing this song requires blood. Jane kept walking with her back to the girl, who continued to float forward at a steady walking pace a few feet off the ground, and Jane inspected the Cherub in closer detail. Trying to

kill it wasn't for lack of effort on everyone's behalf. Spells, lightning, and gunfire all *attempted* to scathe it, but nothing ever got close. Jane was trapped in the eye of a violent storm, and for better or worse, her fate seemed momentarily tied to one very angry teenager hell-bent on playing her instrument. An instrument that Jane was sure should make noise, but either the Cherub or the witch made every-thing non-magical deafeningly quiet. The silence seemed to mute any-thing of earthly creation. *How... did they make pillows of that thing again?* Jane knew there was SOME trick to beating it, but it hung in the back of her head like a song she couldn't remember the lyrics to.

The worst part to her was—she felt useless. All she could do was jog or pace behind the violinist. Leaving the sphere would likely see her get caught in the crossfire, and she couldn't exactly juice up with drugs and super speed fight the Cherubim with magical chains as a ghost. Her fate was tied to someone killing the angelic freight train of death, or there not being enough creatures filled with divine blood to keep the hovering orbs nice and topped off. *Well, so much for Plan A?* She hugged Mike's boot before tying it to her waist. *As a ghost... do you think he'll have new boots? Or will this boot fade away? It's a ghostly boot after all, right?* The thought made her nose wrinkle in frustration. "We really broke the world, didn't we?"

The witch didn't respond.

An hour later, Jane had followed the violinist from the cemetery all the way into the heart of New Orlean's Garden District. It was some time ago that Church of Lazarus soldiers had given up fighting the Cherubim. Jane figured that the heart, while powerful, wasn't worth the cost when you were already a vampire or shapeshifter—and it could melt you with a look. Similarly, the Sons and Daughters were concerned with the ritual and pillars of light now far off in the

distance. A gateway had been opened between worlds, and as hell-divers, they could both profit from plunging the depths—but also were best equipped to close it.

Yet the skeletal lord really did set the duo on an interesting path of destruction. Every neighborhood they strolled through, the hurricane flowed with them—ripping off anything that wasn't reinforced. By now, Jane had realized that the girl wasn't talking because she was unfriendly—but because she was focused. A single lapse in playing her viola, and the Cherubim lumbering about fifty feet behind them would liquefy her flesh. Yet anything that was living within eyesight needed to die to fuel the spell. Jane figured that she was only "alive" because she didn't have any blood, or she had just stayed close enough. *The urge I have to just chat away and have a polite conversation to cut the tension here... UGH! It's so nerve wracking.* Jane fidgeted.

The Garden District wasn't exactly *loaded* with monsters or people. Just the opposite. The duo strolled along trolley tracks lined with twelve-foot-tall wrought-iron poles that were gas lit. At least until the intense winds knocked out any flames. Flanking the road stood dead, leafless trees, long withered under the black sun. It reminded Jane of a creepy Samhain forest walk, and she waited for a masked werewolf to jump out at any moment. With the heavy cloud cover and rain-infused wind forming a mile wide wall around them, it was practically the dead of night inside the eye of the storm with the Cherubim only becoming illuminated with the occasional strike or flash of lightning that had become less frequent of late. Jane spotted there was only a single swirl of floating vitae around the warlock.

She didn't know what was worse, Mike dying instantly or marching slowly to her own inevitable second death. It felt like being trapped in a room that filled endlessly with water and knowing you were going to drown eventually. *Do I just make a break for it and hope for the best?* She eyed the elaborate French-Southern white mansions that lined the road. *Maybe only the bird head can see in the dark? The cow... surely not. Cows are dumb.* The less the lightning attempted

feeble and useless incineration strikes, the more the thought rose in the back of her brain as the swirl of vitae withered into a small thin ribbon.

"Why can't I remember? I HATE THIS!" Jane pulled at her hair. She *knew* that angels had a weakness, but she couldn't remember the commercial. "Hey! Girl! You just going to be stupid and keep walking to your death!? Aren't you some super powerful fucker who should know how to beat them?" Jane tugged at her trousers. "Lady, we gotta do something different here, okay? Listen. I know you are angry and REALLY into playing that harp or whatever, but if you haven't noticed yet—there's nothing here! There are no demons, no angels, no cryptids... Hell, even your storms are barely scratching the houses now! You're like the big bad wolf trying to blow down the houses of rich people who can afford Angel-Be..."

Fuck me sideways and don't call me back cutie because I'm a fucking genius.

Jane pointed her finger up to the sky and danced it along as she sang a catchy melody that only had a smidge of dark humor.

> *"Angel-Be-Gone, a spray so divine,*
> *Keep those angels in a celestial line.*
> *Pricey and potent, for the elite's care,*
> *Spritz away the worries, breathe the unholy air!"*

They may have devastated and killed huge swaths of New Orleans, but their journey had taken them to the neighborhood of the rich. The kind of rich people who probably abandoned ship long ago or left at first sign of trouble. Jane pinched her cheek for not remembering it sooner: Angel-Be-Gone and its lecherous inventor she could never forget. She shivered as she recalled the way his eyes undressed her when she was working behind the bar. Regardless of how horny that piece of corporate scum was, his product apparently worked— because the Cherubim never took one step near a house.

Jane frantically tugged on the floating leg. "Hey! HEY! Turn into a house."

The witch kept marching, focusing purely on the spell that warded them together.

"Listen. Smooth-brain!" Jane raced to her front and held up her hands (It didn't work. Jane still had to backpedal). "Okay, Pushy McPush. TURN RIGHT!" She tried navigating like a tarmac airport attendee. "No? No... not going to listen?" She raked her hands down her face in frustration.

The girl's eyes, filled with less lightning than before, one gold and one green, finally looked down upon Jane with a *flicker* of sentience behind the rage. "I can't."

"What do you mean you can't? Okay. Fine. You don't like right turns. I get it. Some witches can't walk in houses without being invited. Totally okay. Totally okay." She flung her arms and spun around. "Here me out. Turn left then! It's genius. I know, but you'll owe me for saving your life."

"I can't enter these houses or cross the threshold. I'm a warlock," she said without ever stopping, looking behind her, and never letting a note be missed.

"Let's pretend for a minute, that I KNOW WHAT THE FUCK THAT MEANS!"

"Half angel. Half demon. Zero human."

"Didn't they call you a lich?"

She narrowed her eyes. "That's why it won't stop. I broke divine law."

"Not the time for that shit. What the hell do you want me to do then 'she-who-hates-the-ground'?" Jane folded her arms and widened her eyes while wiggling her pupils out of a growing desperation at the mere droplets of blood left in the stream.

"You didn't break a law. So run."

Oh shit, you're right. Jane didn't hesitate and sprinted with everything she had toward the nearest house, grabbing onto the

wrought-iron gate and vaulting herself over it with her feet wiggling in the air and kipping off the top for extra measure. She landed with a gasp of air as her shoulder hit the ground, tumbled through, and braced herself for the feeling of ick that was about to come. Emptying her brain of thoughts, she faceplanted into the wooden doors like a belly flop on a still pool and ghosted herself through the entry.

It felt like her kidneys got stuck on the doorknob.

Shaking it off, Jane quickly took in her surroundings. An eclectic mix of armor, ancient weapons, and masonic paintings decorated the foyer. Even with a quick glance, Jane spotted several robes on coat hooks with the sigils for the Church of Lazarus. *Of course, I pick the culty home. They better not be having a sex party.* She didn't have time to care, so she quickly set about burglarizing the home for bottles of Angel-Be-Gone. Winter clothes were chucked out of cabinets, garage baskets were ripped down, and Jane thrust her head into just about every cabinet she could find to peek in.

She fretted that she'd come up empty-handed, but she also *knew* that she was right. Standing on the third stair she recalibrated her bearings as her foot tapped impatiently. *If I were a super-rich cultist who would host monsters for dinner, where would I keep an emergency bottle of magic-shit-killing juice?* The snap of her fingers happened passively, and before Jane knew it, she was standing in front of the liquor cabinet. One smashed glass window later, and Jane opened the wide double doors to the holy glow of small ever-burning ghostly flames and a full wall of booze that would never be made again.

On the upper left shelf, three bottles of Dystopian brew Angel-Be-Gone with black-licorice bottle stoppers stood proudly.

"Let's hope you don't have an expiration date." Jane clutched the bottles tightly to her chest and grabbed one bottle of Ol' Rip Van Winkle 25 reserve. *Backup plan. If this fails, I'm fucking drinking this just to waste something precious before I go.*

A smarter person, Jane reasoned, would have just taken the lich's advice and run off, but she had never been one to shy away from

danger. *Besides, I've got a soft spot for that kind of music.* As she kicked open the front doors, she tried to bury the memory of a time when she tried to give up and went on a drug-induced spree straight to oblivion—but heard someone playing a string instrument, and then everyone around her was dead.

"I know that was you, bitch. You ruined my vacation and gave my life meaning, so this is your fucking payback. Next time, just let an angry chick die and don't make them take a damn exploding train into the heart of corporate America and kill every CEO that was minting magic out of revenge." *Maybe I need therapy?*

Jane huffed and her eye twitched as she stormed out to the trolley tracks to the sounds of the viola clashing against the muted celestial silence. The girl was no longer floating, but now kneeling upon the stone with three smashed vials of bottled blood held in reserve. The fragile-looking teenager frantically strung her bow across the strings with bloodied fingers as her brown hair now clung to her cheeks from sweat and rain.

She reminded Jane of an angry, wet cat.

Arcane power no longer attacked the Cherubim directly, but with each drop of blood, a lash of lightning would parry a claw or blind the gaze of the cow. It was only a matter of time before the girl herself was drained dry of any supernatural blood. Jane didn't have the means to know that the witch *only* had external blood in that form. Or that she only had seven notes left before her soul was shackled to the edge of Purgatory for eternity.

Jane crouched at the nearest twisted tree and broke the seal off the first bottle. With a quick whiff, she recoiled and batted at the air in disgust at the odor—a sharp distinct spike of crude oil and cat piss assaulted her mind. *What the hell is in this shit?* Apparently, Jane realized, Angel-Be-Gone had nearly the same ingredients as energy drinks with a healthy splash of crude oil and creatures of shadow. She chuckled at the thought that the serving size was 480 calories.

The viola's melody pierced the air like a blade of ice as the witch played with determination and an intense glare that sent shivers through Jane's body. The shadows seemed to move in time with the music—and every so often raging blades of divine fire sliced through the dark ambience, ricocheting off burning sparks of red-and-black lightning that threatened to consume anything within reach of the small girl.

Jane knew she had only moments before their fate was sealed. With a scream, she grasped the first vial in her fists and hurled it toward the angelic Cherubim with all her might. It sailed through the air, tauntingly slow, until the creature lifted one flaming sword and effortlessly batted it away, shattering it over a nearby iron lamp pole.

A thick cloud of smoke spewed from the vial, engulfing the right side of the street in a murky darkness. Sharp flecks of gold sparkled within the gas as if alive, before the mysterious substance began to writhe and wriggle on its own accord, coating every surface near Jane and the lamppost. The earth quaked beneath her feet as all four heads of the terrifying Cherubim snapped toward her direction at once, causing her to yelp in terror as it lunged across the street with malicious intent.

Jane scrambled to retrieve the other two vials next to the tree, moving with such panic she struggled to keep her balance. She could only hope that the other two bottles wouldn't be as disgusting as the first one because there was no way she could handle throwing up on top of everything else that was going on. *If ghosts even CAN throw up.* She frantically tore off the black-licorice bottle stopper and tilted the bottle back, bracing herself for the taste.

A lash of sound and lightning kissed her lips as the witch wasted a note to prevent her drinking. Jane focused on a lock of her hair still smoking from how close that lightning raced between her face. "Fine! YOU DRINK IT!" She yeeted the vial at the kneeling girl,

setting free another cloud of shadow yards away from the witch—who quickly tumbled forward to hide behind the cloud after taking a deep breath.

The Cherubim's charge toward Jane was petrifying. A nearly thirty-foot-tall four-headed celestial wielding four swords and with breaths of fire and screams of utter silence was bearing down upon her. Spotting an opening, Jane quickly grabbed the last two bottles and fired her legs like pistons, diving forward under the Cherubim before its swords were brought down. She regretted not drinking the whiskey prior, certain that a flaming death soon awaited her.

It never came.

The Angel-Be-Gone from the first vial followed in her wake as she ran. The Cherubim, despite its size, refused to touch anything with the substance. As Jane ran beneath its legs, its four wings flapped to banish the gas to no avail, but it leapt to reposition itself.

From where the first vial had exploded to the second where the witch was now standing, a triangle was forming. The lamppost, the witch, and Jane now stood at three points with the Cherubim in the middle—frantically breathing fire and attempting to avoid the shadows.

The witch rose, and with the last of the blood kept playing... filling the air with magical sounds to prevent the Cherubim's silent screams from ending them.

Jane quickly smashed the third vial at her feet, completing the triangle and trapping it in. At least until it decided to fly away. She remembered how Mike defeated the arch demon Golgoroth and claimed his heart, realizing that this might be her chance. A chance to defeat something legendary.

Unlike her brother, there was nobody around to witness this. Their march through New Orleans had killed anyone their paths crossed.

She dipped her hands in the black gas, coating them with golden flecks. *It's fucking glitter?! The most evil of substances. I am never getting this shit off... and neither are you.*

The witch was equally barred from the triangle, being part angel as she said earlier, and Jane reasoned the angel would simply fly after them if they ran. Plus, Jane didn't know what would happen if the Cherubim's silent gaze fell upon them when the music stopped.

"It's time I claim a heart."

Jane approached the trapped beast with fingers curled into claws. She knew this was her moment, her chance to prove to herself she was more than a misfit with a chip on her shoulder. Her chance to claim something that could turn the tide of war against the Vatican. The heat radiating from the Cherubim's body was intense, and its size certainly made her planned move risky. With each step closer, Jane watched its shoulders and elbows... waiting for the strike.

The wild strike came as the four heads thrashed like a cornered animal—sweeping down its swords to cleave Jane in half.

She was already running and leaping when they came. A forward somersault to run up the left arm and catapult herself into the intense heat of the angel's chest. Her fingers melted through the chest cavity like hot butter, and she felt the pulsing source of power surrounded by the walls of bone. With both feet planted firmly into its chest, Jane ripped her prize free.

The Cherubim immediately looked down upon her with sadness. Not for itself, but out of genuine concern for her future as its form melted into ash. Jane fell to the ground, clutching the bone-encased heart to her chest like a kitten.

It took her a minute, staring up at the clouded swirling sky before she realized the viola had stopped playing. She looked over and realized that the witch was standing outside of the triangle, studying her with a look of curiosity—that or the lich was pushed to the brink and about to pass out. Either way, within this triangle, Jane was safe and had put two apples together. *Wields lightning, is a powerful lich, and I've seen that magic before. I bet that's Primus Vryce.*

"You killed my brother," Jane said flatly.

"He was in the way."

"You're a dick."

Both of them sat in the quiet silence of the soft wind and toxic smell of Angel-Be-Gone for several minutes before Jane held the basketball-sized heart up for inspection. "So, do I just eat this? It's like a pineapple with a shell."

"That would be a waste, child. Ignorance, it seems, runs in your family."

This jerkface needs to come with me, and I'm SO looking forward to it. "I am going to hate this." Jane sighed.

CHAPTER 14

Journeymen of the Golden Dawn. Mastery of the divine is more than imbibing a philosopher's stone. The reagents and components for immortality have been held in secret since Heka of Egypt performed their first Ka, and with good reason. The power to shape our world with will alone is a dangerous tool when wielded like a sledgehammer. Within our Society of Deus, it is our duty to guide our new world. To educate the sledgehammers on what true magic looks like. Otherwise, the corporations will strip it of its wonder.

Vryce inspected his broken golden-rimmed spectacles with dismay. He *liked* those glasses, and after a day of misfortune and adventure—they were fractured and bent. Hardly appropriate tools. The long sought-after vacation he'd been planning barely lasted an evening before he'd been swept back up in the politics of the Unification, the Church of Lazarus, and meddling Death Lords once again. *And of course, it had to be the Lord of Misfortune.* He clicked his tongue in dismay while secretly wishing it was only Murder or Pestilence that would be the conquerors. The fact that Lazarus had dispatched Misfortune meant that he was desperate and viewed the world as broken. Not unlike the bent pair of spectacles being held up over a barrier of Angel-Be-Gone. *A small microcosm indeed.*

Within the triangle, Jane Auburn clutched the heart of an archangel on a street lined with trolley tracks and elaborate mansions. Watching her was impressive, and she certainly reminded Vryce of her older brother. Chaotic balls of determination and clever application of modern tools. The means may be unrefined, but the outcome was the same. *It seems, my children, I've found myself in debt to the dead after all.* Against the Praenomen and Gabriel's wishes, Vryce had taken his journey to New Orleans incognito, and that meant only a limited supply of the Society's artifacts and tools. Defeating a Cherubim wasn't in the cards while *also* in the middle of a white-hot arcane frenzy. As much as he didn't want to admit it, Lucian got under his skin. He lost control and much of the past hour was truly just a blur until the sassy ghost finally snapped him out of it. By then, his supply of blood was too little, and the Cherubim was already within striking distance.

He, unfortunately, owed Jane his current life. *Although considering her brother rudely obliterated my original form, perhaps we can call it even?* It was right then that Jane reminded him he blew up Mike with lightning. Honestly, when she first mentioned it, all Vryce could remember was that Mike was in the way of Lucian. It wasn't out of hatred or revenge that Vryce used eighteen and a half lightning bolts to annihilate that section of the crypt. *I was just ensuring a job well done.*

He sighed.

No matter which way he tried to balance the scales of debt, he wasn't getting out of this. He may be a centuries' old creature who violated divine law, but he'd never let himself violate the very rules he set in his own society. A boon is a boon. When someone does you a favor, even if they are a vile enemy, you must show them hospitality and repay the debt in equal measure. *Ergo, little girl, I must save your life in turn. Given how quickly you leap into battle... I wager this won't take long.*

Vryce put the broken glasses in his pocket and tried his best to tie up the wet brown hair in a ponytail... before realizing that this "scrunchie" component given to him by Gabriel was missing. Vryce cursed Lucian under his breath and let it go, shouldering his viola—an artifact that would not be leaving his side again so soon.

Jane had risen and dusted herself off while he collected his own thoughts. She remained within her triangle of safety, reminding Vryce of a political prisoner, with the cocky demeanor of being safe behind guarded walls, not realizing the very barriers trapped her. He didn't even need to read her thoughts to see the plans unfolding in her mind. First, she would inquire about why she shouldn't eat the heart, and then assuming that Vryce was defenseless, she'd make him go back with her to the Sons and Daughters—and help them enact whatever psychotic plan they'd hatched to battle another Death Lord.

He had to admit, however, they did succeed last time. *Only with the intervention of the Society, my Praenomen, and even myself. You certainly weren't ready for a fight when I found you in that Second City hotel high on drugs, Jane.* Vryce knew it was better to not mention that last part. In his experience, most people never reacted well to finding out that their puppet strings were pulled by many hands. Including himself.

"I spend centuries freeing myself from the Unification, only to end up right back into a global war with them..." He looked at Jane. "You going to pace in there all day, or are you going to ask your questions? I'd rather avoid a second fight with the Church of Lazarus right now, and your wielded prize makes you a target for anyone hungry enough to snatch it from you."

She paced along the triangle line. "Dude, there are so many. Like... fifty of 'em. Why shouldn't I eat this? What the hell are you exactly? What's going to happen with that big portal? Why can ghosts leave behind shoes? Why are you so weak yet so strong? How the fuck am I older than you? You were in my hotel, weren't you? Back in that fight, the necromancer with the slick leather had a stick that swatted

me like a bug—what was th—" Her speech increased in speed as the questions began to pour out like waterfall. Vryce had to interrupt.

"You shall never address me as Dude. Let's establish that rule right now. You can refer to me as elder, mentor, or Lord Vryce. If you are to be my student, decorum is required. The Society of Deus has rank, and only those with the status can speak so informally. You may think these rules are cumbersome or annoying, but this decorum is the only thing that keeps vampires and creatures of the night like us—from devouring each other like food."

Jane had the *look* of trouble. A glint in her eye fought against her mouth to blurt out in rebellion. Inwardly, Vryce approved of the rebellious spirit but never let it show.

"So, you're the Society's big daddy." Her eyebrows waggled. "Is that cutie Dragosani still one of your generals?"

Vryce's eye twitched. *Angel-Be-Gone, a crass concoction of abyssal magic and spirits of those-who-wait-beyond, glitter, oil, and taurine. Only one of the components is needed to harm an angel, but it doesn't bottle well or look pretty without the others. She should be thankful for this ward.* "Dragosani is indeed. Promoted ever since the battle of St. Louis. I recall that on the screens, you and he looked as a couple. Lovers?" Vryce smirked.

Jane's cheeks turned a deeper shade of green, and she looked away. "I have a date with the vampire, okay? Sue me. Since you're his boss... any chance you could..."

"No. You called me 'daddy.' I am not your father. My lineage no longer has mortal descendants."

"Oh, you sweet summer child. All big and filled with bluster, but... you never learned modern lingo." She shook her head. "Okay, seriously though, you," her hands framed Vryce's height and waist, "are a teenage girl. What's up with the Lord title? Also, questions... start answering, Primus. You are the one who is on a ticking clock here until someone notices us."

"Thank you." He nodded to being appropriately acknowledged. "Bodies are simply vessels. I had this one made to be as close to my original. Unfortunately, your crew of anarchists and a demon named Bollard destroyed the orphanage. I've many enemies and thus mastered possession to enact my will. Your brother notoriously refused my offer, and for better or worse—I no longer have a body. This one, I am fond of for the moment." He tugged at his brown hair. "I should trim this, however."

Jane breathed in through her teeth. "My lord, you are *really* going to hate that body in a year if it hasn't happened already. You picked wrong being a girl. Welcome to a lifetime of pain and misery."

Vryce honestly didn't know how to respond at first. He knew *exactly* what Jane was talking about, and it wasn't like he hadn't possessed female forms countless times in the past during unfortunate windows. "I disagree. That pain threshold you spend a lifetime dealing with makes these bodies vastly more durable for internal endurance. Handy when you need to push your spellcraft to the limits. That's why witches were the first to discover death curses—and to wield them properly."

"Huh." Jane seemed momentarily impressed.

"As for why you shouldn't eat the heart? Simple. You warded yourself in a circle of shadow magic and possess no ability to fly. Consuming the heart would see you trapped within a triangle of your own making for who knows how long. The second reason is you're a descendent of Lazarus and a natural fit to explore the depths of Purgatory better than any helldiver. Angelic beings often grant powers of higher mental sorcery, psychic abilities, or command over singular elements like fire or wind. What you seek is a demonic heart, cryptid, or a named creature. Don't lessen yourself for settling on the first meal that comes your way. Use the heart as barter for a favor and earn something worth your legend, Miss Auburn." Vryce gestured farther down the road where they had originally come from. "Shall

we walk and talk at least? I'm assuming you will escort me back to your Sons and Daughters, no?"

Jane looked at the shadow-stuff forming the thin line between them while clutching the heart closer before relaxing slightly and turning around just a smidge—before suddenly swinging and slapping Vryce across the face.

Instantly, he felt a bloodthirsty rage rise within him and bit his lip, focusing on a deep breath as the red imprint throbbed inside his left cheek. *Do not gut the ones with promise... Do not boil ... the ones with promise.*

"You fucking killed my brother. Let's get one thing straight: This isn't some casual stroll. You are simply too much of an asset for me to bury right here. Right now. Now pack it up, sister, and follow." She stormed off in the opposite direction.

"Creatures like he and Lucian do not die so easily... but I'll allow that this one time, child. We creatures of the night aren't exactly known for controlling our hunger."

Damien Vryce followed Jane's brisk walk back the way they had come. For a mile in all directions, the city of New Orleans was leveled from the intense storm magic brought forth during arcane frenzy. He wondered if Jane thought he would perhaps feel some remorse for his actions by choosing a path through shattered homes, exsanguinated people, and charred cryptids. Unfortunately, it wouldn't work. He'd long given up any pretense of humanity. *It's tricky to relate to creatures that have the life span of cats.* Unlike other immortals, though, Vryce did still believe himself a shepherd of those who had potential. He wasn't as old as say, Alexandria of Ur, who had descended entirely into selfish pleasure and petty amusement simply to pass the time.

From time-to-time, Jane would inquire what he meant about Mike and Lucian, on the prospect of them still being alive. She was never satisfied with his answers while she grasped for hope. The best he could offer her was that it certainly wasn't the first time Lucian had been ripped to shreds by another member of the Unification, and Mike was a ghost. Without the usage of the necromantic arts or devouring his soul... he was probably lost in the ether of Purgatory for an unknown amount of time.

That only made her walk faster.

"I'm certain he's annoying enough to crawl his way back again," Vryce muttered and picked up the pace with shorter legs that were beginning to frustrate him. *I am used to being at least over 5'8" as a British man.*

The site of Lucian's ritual had long been evacuated—with ample signs of helldiver activity. Small chalk outlines, oil lanterns, and ropes dangling brazenly into Purgatory dotted the cemetery, yet no members of the anarchists remained. Vryce noted they had some classic witchcraft sense from former Unification members to ward the tears with the best of their ability. *With any luck, those tears will fade in time, but it might require a stronger witch.* It was then Vryce recalled that this location might as well have been the Lord of Misfortune's private domain and swiftly made a mental note to contact Gabriel at the Society to dispatch some acolytes.

After seeing the cemetery grounds, Jane's cheeks puffed out like a fish, and once again she began marching. This time over an impossibly long bridge that spanned the river. Splashing through the puddles of blood was easy with the Doc Martin's Vryce was recommended. *Not a single leak. Why is there blood?*

"Wait." Vryce stopped Jane briefly as he stared at the horizon.

Just outside of downtown New Orleans, where over a hundred thousand people had taken refuge on small boats to cross away from Lucian's impromptu ritual, sat ghostly battleships from the Church of Lazarus, each flying the banners for the Lord of Murder, and they

teemed with soldiers and killers alike. They peered over their bows and looked at the rubble of ships below while occasionally dropping soul-binding chains down into the water to pull out a freshly dead soul from its corpse prior to its descent into Purgatory.

"That is what the necromantic arts look like. Soul Binding." Vryce did not sound amused. "If I'm not mistaken, it looks like the Church of Lazarus just 'recruited' the city of New Orleans by killing everyone who fled."

"Do you think they have Mike?"

"Probably. This perplexes me. Unless the council is at war with each other, forcing recruitment has not been their charge. Most churches *want* their followers alive and filled with faith."

Jane slowly craned her head and narrowed her eyes at him. "Have you *met* someone called a Death Lord? Fredrick made *everyone* in Austin commit suicide."

Vryce slowly nodded, eyes never leaving the bay as he kept walking. "Of course I have. They made me, and that didn't make sense either. Something is amiss, and I do not like being ill-informed." *I need divine blood for a few spells. Delilah, my dear apprentice, what do you know about this?*

Two hours later, Vryce stood in front of a Waffle House with everything in this human body burning from exhaustion and hunger, except his feet. The vampires and helldivers that made up the motley crew of the Sons and Daughters were largely repairing their traveling gear and resupplying. Other than the one Vryce knew they called Akira, nobody paid him special attention. Akira, however, perched like a raptor on top of a picnic table and stared directly into Vryce's eyes, never even twitching as colorful beetles crawled over her arms.

Jane and Vryce almost made it to the front door before Lucy cut off their path. The click and clack of every shotgun, pistol, and crossbow bolt rattled off like a row of dominos. Vryce sighed. He didn't even need to turn around to know that everything was pointed in his direction.

Vryce leaned his viola along his thigh, shaking out his arms. "A little help here, Jane?"

Jane moved the angel's heart to her side and held out her hands. "Lucy! Cutie... Buddy... Can you not point the flamethrowers at the super pyscho?"

Lucy just flipped a handax casually. "We can. We won't."

"Want me to hold that, Jane?" Vryce reached out for the angel's heart, changing his voice to be more casual. Jane, for her part, reacted as instinctively as Vryce predicted when defending another—and accepted the help. It was only after it left her palm did she seem to realize the grave mistake she had made.

"Kneel." Vryce simply spoke a word as blood flowed out from the Cherubim's heart and spiraled along his arm. Every vampire, mortal, sorcerer, and shape changer outside slowly began to kneel—instantly under his mental control. All except Lucy and Akira, who possessed that annoying resistance to casual mental commands for some reason. *Proximity to Golgoroth's heart is my theory.*

The screen door opened, and Edward Morris stepped out, adjusting his cabby hat and lighting up a fresh smoke. "Typically, Primus... Oh sorry, you aren't in charge anymore. Damien Vryce, mental commands are my coffee cup around the new recruits." He took a long drag and let the smoke hang in the air with the tension.

"And typically, I wager you are alone and make eye contact. Vampiric mind control is ... so last year for me. I've upgraded." Vryce grinned.

"So, the rumors are true—you have discovered humor." Morris curtseyed. "Let's speak a language you understand. You are in our territory, and as the second in command, sparking a war here will spread through both our organizations."

"Only if they ever find out." Vryce flicked a finger and lifted Jane off the ground, releasing her from the kneel. She would certainly slap him later. "With a prize like this, your army can now be my army."

A voice spoke, one he didn't even see or notice even after the angelic blood restored his sorcery. "Except it's not your prize, is it?" The old man had been standing side-by-side with Vryce for who knows how long, and neither Jane nor he ever paid attention to him until he spoke. *Where do I... I know you...*

It clawed at the back of Vryce's brain like an itchy squid writhing its tentacles. He *knew* he knew the old man's name but could not for the unlife of him recall it. Yet the person was an old friend, a mentor, a colleague, and perhaps a best friend—yet entirely forgotten. The itch disarmed his current threat. "I was about to say, this one was victorious, and we brought it back." *This one is old. That's all I know. Older than I... and familiar.*

The old man looked at Jane and winked. "Good job, birdie. Want some advice?" He pulled out a toothpick and gestured to everyone who was now kneeling and pointing guns at the three of them.

Jane nodded thrice.

"You, uh, you can make this all go away. Trade it." He nodded to the heart.

"Yeah, trade it to this bitter warlock," he raised a finger, "sorry, free lich now. For his service. He owes you a boon already for saving his life, and if you gift the heart to his Society... it's worth what, Damien my boy? One war? Two? A Cherubim is highly ranked..."

Damien clicked his tongue. "A bit one-sided, old prince. You know the dance better than most but hardly worth two. Unlike the old days, we are vastly more equipped to gather divine blood and the occasional heart. How else do you make a sorcerer?"

Jane grew a wry smile. "But I *did* save your life AND you did kill one of ours. So, you let us kill your... Gabriel? And we can let you off with one war. Otherwise... your tiny violin self is serving us for at least two battles. Plan A and Plan B."

I... miss this. Vryce bowed. "If it is war, then my protégé will require his own payment. I'll accept two battles, and all debts cleared. You'll have my mentorship and arcane assistance, Miss Auburn, but

you alone. For it is your prize and debt. The rest of the Sons and Daughters can merely consider me a consultant. Now then, since you and the old man have probably been talking secretly this whole time while we walked across the bridge—what is Plan A?"

The release of tension left everyone sitting outside (except Akira, she was always ready for murder).

"Simple." Jane smiled. "We dive into Purgatory where that portal was cracked open—and eat the hearts of gods that the Church of Lazarus has kept hidden. Do it before they do it."

Vryce choked. *The... What?! Gods... the old ones? Are they crazy? Absolutely not.* "Forgive me for a moment... but allow me to say, absolutely the fuck not."

CHAPTER 15

"We truly stand in the Dark Ages, longing for a gaze at the prideful morning star and its golden warmth. You've thought Purgatory was a myth, ignorant of magic behind your veil of innocence. And lo, persecutors and betrayers of the righteous will have half their body set on fire, cursed to wander a dark pit while their entrails are eaten by worms that never sleep. The earth is our dark pit, the betrayers—those who consumed divine hearts—and the fire will be Heaven's Wrath. No matter your creed from East to West, the Church of Lazarus welcomes the pure.

But the heathens will burn."

–Broadcast in Vitaly, France

Within the hallowed halls of Raphael's Rooms, nestled within the walls of Vatican City, John Daneka limped slowly through the frescoed Stanze that comprised the four rooms with purpose. The rooms themselves were living architecture in John's mind's eye, a place where artistry intertwines with the divine, each room unveiling an ancient symphony of celestial grandeur. Frescoes of angels and demons danced upon the vaulted ceilings, their ethereal forms

155

captured in the masterful strokes of Renaissance genius. Meanwhile, pillars adorned with intricate carvings whispered secrets of the centuries, pronouncements of the dead just beyond John's mortal ears.

Ever since the crusade began, John had felt the murmurs of power crawling behind his eyes. At first, when France was defiled by Pestilence, his skin ceased its constant agony of pulsing blisters. When Murder began the war against the warlock Rasputin and his menagerie of monsters, John's sense of smell returned. The more the world perished, the more his flesh restored itself. *Yet there is so much more to do. We've barely scratched the surface. Senator McCarthy would roll over in his grave to see his plan in action. Godhood, through populism. No matter what god you wish to be, it's not a particularly lofty goal when you truly break it down. Control the masses, eliminate the rest, and be the only human worshipped.* "Of course, non-believers will need purging, even if I'm the only human left."

He stopped within Sala di Constatino, the Hall of Constantine, and admired the works. *No wonder ancient times gave birth to so many gods.* A harsh cough of phlegm, and John was pretty sure a piece of his left lung spurted out onto his gray clothes. "I'm pretty sure Joe Camel was an iconic god in the '50s. The amount I smoked then—" The lung cancer took over, causing John to nearly collapse in a coughing fit for several minutes. *I ... can't ... let ... them...* "See me as such." Fear was the reason he stood, rather than determination. Fear that if he was even so much as spotted by an attendee, they would see that gods can bleed. *But gods are infallible. Which is why Lazarus... I am here.*

The four Raphael Rooms were nothing more than reception rooms within the Apostolic Palace. It was here Lazarus had agreed to meet with two Lords of Death and one ... demon. They had formal petitions for the Lord of Heaven's Wrath, and well, Lazarus had an agenda of his own. Besides the demon, the Lord of Murder and the Lady of Suicide were his most loyal allies. As for the demon, Lazarus admitted he had no fucking clue what such a creature could

want—or how it even got here. *Something that powerful best be heard and put to use.*

There was the pecking order Lazarus had to weigh. The reception rooms were each individual, and he would speak with each privately—but the others would have to wait hours. The old psychologist in John knew the Lord of Murder to be a narcissist, and he would take the greatest offense to waiting. *Perhaps, leaving him waiting until last will make him desire my favor the most.* The Lady of Suicide, being the newest to hold a seat, might be the most desperate. *Yet she is perhaps the freest of us—not yet a lich. The black sun allows magic to exist freely and without constraint, but for vampires, I imagine it is the most freeing of experiences. To not fear instant immolation like before.* The demon, however, was entirely unknown other than his name. Hal Morgan. A mortal pseudonym. Entirely unknown by every intelligence organization still left on the Vatican's payroll.

Lazarus stepped into Stanza di Elidoro, the room of Heliodorus, choosing the Lady of Suicide first. Alexandria of Ur wore black, an impossibly short, black fishnet skirt with a dog collar around her neck and nothing for a top except two black pieces of tape while sitting in front of a tea set and two chairs. In John's mind, she was dressed as a whore appropriate for nearly every decade of debauchery since the dawn of time, and yet her impossible beauty and poise added an air of danger to her presence. Easily slipping into the mindset of Lazarus the moment the door opened, John found it easy to roleplay and lie about disinterest—focusing his attention on her mask—a mask made out cut skin, dried and adorned with peacock's feathers.

Alexandria of Ur gestured to her assistants, who set forth bottles of angelic and demonic vitae from the 13th century on the table and poured two teacups before waving them off. *No garish display of vampirism by having them open their wrists? I'm disappointed.*

Both waited for them to be alone before Lazarus gestured for the vampire to speak.

"Oh, have a seat, darling." Using her heel, she moved the heavy chair with ease, its scrape echoing within the room. "You and I aren't even friends yet. You're too new here," she purred. "And I'm curious."

Lazarus refused the seat but rested his hand upon its back to ease the pain in his joints. "You wasted an offering of such ancient blood out of curiosity? Private meetings are not cheap, even for one such as you."

"Waste is a matter of perspective. From where I sit, you are a mystery, Lord of Heaven's Wrath. Launching your little crusade against the world, purging the world of humans, but leaving the creatures of the night who pay their tithe? I'd almost say you were courting my favor."

"Come, neither of us, nor the old bastions of the Unification, wish for such secrets to be in the hands of the masses. Stymie those who have yet to imbibe before they do so. We both know this age will wither and die without them."

"The religious rhetoric is as boring as your masquerade. You and I both know you couldn't care less about restoring the world. You hide it about as well as you hide the eye twitch that can't stop looking down." Alexandria slid a finger up her fishnets. "So why don't we try something unheard of among this new Church of Lazarus?" She slammed a shot of demonic vitae, or rather, an entire wine glass. "A little honesty."

John Daneka almost fractured behind his persona. *Did the grave clothes and mantle of Heaven's Wrath not provide protection against mind reading? Does she know?* He closed his eyes. Such a feat was impossible. *It's my mannerisms, or she knew the original.*

"Purgatory has a way of changing your perspective," he lied. "What does being honest with you get me?"

She smiled. "If you answer but one question for me honestly, then I'll answer one for you in turn. If you ever want another question..." She tapped the half-empty demon bottle. "I'm a cheap date."

Lazarus weighed his options before nodding. "You first."

"Dr. John. C. Daneka, Lord of Heaven's Wrath that led the Unification with an insane plan by some stupid politician to control the world by spreading fear and using the radio. He rose through the Unification's ranks quickly, taking to a secret society like ice to water, easily usurping command of our ten warlocks and cutting off the creation of two more before they could be made." She rattled off John's history as if she followed him everywhere. "Disappears into the Sistine Chapter on December 12th, and Lazarus steps out—charred and naked. It was I who delivered to Lazarus the grave clothes recovered from the Society of Deus, hidden inside Purgatory."

"I'm not hearing a question."

"The pretense sets the mood. It's foreplay." She leaned forward with elbows on her knees and studied him before finally asking, "Will you allow me to prevent you from committing suicide? I want to see where this goes." She paused. "John."

Lazarus smiled, burnt lips bleeding as the blisters cracked and his lidless eyes widened under the cloth. "No."

The sudden rebuke broke her façade. It was not what Alexandria expected. Perhaps, John reasoned, she had expected him to fold like a meek human. Yet when it came to the supernatural, even before his machinations behind the façade of Lazarus, John C. Daneka was still the Lord of Heaven's Wrath—and his purity gave him an incalculable edge against the whims of supernatural creatures. *Some might even call it power.* Before she could recover, John quickly walked over to her, leaned down, and whispered into her ear.

"My turn. Alexandria of Uruk, a stunning beauty of Mesopotamia who charmed the Lilim to grant her powers of immortality. One of the oldest walking vampires who resisted getting so bored, you've avoided walking into the sun's rays just to end your torment. Now with the rise of the black sun, you are forever a prisoner in this world until your head is removed from your shoulders. You play with us like an amused cat staring at ants, devoid of loyalty and conviction. You yourself stood in the room with Damien Vryce on the eve of

his ascension and only ran when you saw the power of a young man remove the warlock's head through sheer determination. In that exact moment—you saw the future. You knew that with so many new players in the world, your control was slipping."

Long thin fangs grew reflexively out of anger. *Vampires, with their short tempers, are easier than most to bend.*

"I'm not hearing a question, Heaven," she said behind a veneer of calm.

"Foreplay sets the mood, as you said." Lazarus hooked his finger through the collar on her neck and lifted her off her seat. "Will you kneel before a god?"

The sensualist in Alexandria *almost* bit her lip. "No." She rose, looking the Lord of Heaven's Wrath right in the eye with curiosity. "I've outlived most gods, and they tend to be a passing fantasy. Most end up chained under Fate and Misfortune anyway... so not really my kink."

"Then like proper Lords of Death, we have harmony. I'd expect nothing less." Lazarus gave a soft nod. "Still, I think there can be some merit in us continuing this game. I'd like to play it further. Would you?"

Her black lips curled over her fangs with curiosity. "I'm listening."

"I'm officially giving you authority to create something we'll call the Sanctum. Unless you have a penchant for government names, in which case, call it Division 7. Draw promising young recruits who are misfits or outcasts from every other Death Lord's ranks, use them to garner honest information from what they see, and have them carry out select missions on our behest. Once a week, we will meet here over a single bottle and ask each other one question." He refilled her glass and handed it to her.

"That," she seemed confused, "is eerily similar to... what I was going to offer you? To catch the snakes. Perhaps it is the boredom of centuries, but I do wish to see where this goes..."

"Either way I'm sure," Lazarus said while leaving. "Regardless, we meet next week." John closed the door and let his bones relax. *Immortals.*

Alexandria would be a problem for John; he knew that much. For starters, she was ancient, and he was mortal. They weren't even comparable in manifested power. She danced with societies of the night; hell, John reasoned, she was AT the Society of Deus the day the sun rose black. Furthermore, her vampiric gifts were so refined she could make a city kneel and lick the boots of her latest fashioned trend. He focused on a deep breath before continuing down the corridor. *Easy there. In this end, you are her superior. She can use blood to command and entrance a crowd; you used a radio to twist a nation. That's why I became a figurehead of the Unification.*

John reasoned he would need to approach an alliance with caution, but it was no different than putting up with anyone else's bullshit. Whether it be boredom, fanaticism, or love, creatures like Alexandria enjoyed an activity to pass the time, and he already knew his Lazarus gamble was a fascinating splash of entertainment to her. A performance that would quickly become reality if everything played out as he planned, and since anyone who sipped divine blood or ate a heart lost a portion of their soul—his purity would hopefully tip the imbalanced scales of power. *Just stick to the plan, John.*

John wasn't sure what to expect when opening the door to Stanza della Segnatura. The Room of Signatura was the first of Raphael's fresco, studying the library of Julias II and, in theory, brought about the harmony of Greek philosophy with Christian ideals. It was his least favorite of the four rooms, perhaps, in part, because it housed a demon.

Hal Morgan looked every bit like the devil in black: a tanned, fifty-year-old man dressed in a Brioni suit, bespoke and custom tailored in black and red with a pair of cheap sunglasses. That he wore indoors, of course. Hal turned instantly, removing headphones from an old Walkman CD player, decades out of fashion, and strode quickly across the room as if to shake the hand of Lazarus himself.

"Lazzy boy," his hand extended, "Hal Morgan, at your service. You don't know me, but I'm your biggest fan. Fantastic work you've done with the place. I'm a particular fan of you mostly purging this place of any semblance of actual faith, and of course, Catholics."

Lazarus looked down at the extended hand and noticed the fingertips charred with blackened gunpowder. "I don't meet with jailers often. Speak, demon."

"Yeah, I didn't think that would work." Hal chuckled and pulled out a pack of Camel cigarettes and a bronze Zippo with a slogan about P.O.W.'s. "You're a former smoker. Want one? No? You all end up in Purgatory anyway so..."

Lazarus had barely even made it into the room before he was practically cornered by this wiry demon. *Do I just have him killed now?*

"No, no, that won't work, see... you, buddy, summoned me."

"Wait?" *He can hear my thoughts?*

"Yeah, that's what happens when you summon a demon. Backdoor into your brain. Don't worry, Lazarus, secrets safe. Like I said, I'm your biggest fan."

"You have my attention, but I didn't summon you."

Hal snapped his fingers. "Aha! But you totally did. I get it. You don't know *who* or *what* I am, buuuut... I do you..." Hal casually strolled up the mural on the side of the wall, ignoring gravity as he paced and talked like normal. "Let's cut to the chase. Your time is very important. I'm an Arch Demon of Unity." Hal twirled his fingers as if to lead Lazarus on.

Despite John's charade as Lazarus, he'd still served, and led, within the Unification for decades and had plenty of time to study

demonology. One couldn't claim divinity without a deep understanding of how the forces of the divine worked. Angels governed cosmic forces, barely even noticing mortals; demons, however, governed higher principalities of human concepts by testing them—hence their usual bad reputation. Loyalty, for example, proved loyalty's existence by seeding betrayal. Once betrayed, a mortal would understand the concept of loyalty. It was a basic principle of reinforcement.

"So, you're a demon of war."

"Arch. Demon. Recently promoted. Golgoroth had his fame with the Nazis, but his fat ass got his heart eaten, and that left an open spot. So, since everyone *else* is leaving Purgatory, I'd figure I'd take a break and journey up here on account of your little crusade."

Lazarus took a moment of silence to circle around the demon standing on the ceiling and studied him closer, paying attention to every detail. The Zippo with a P.O.W. symbol was probably a holdover from the 1970s, and if John had to guess, it said "P.O.W.'s never have a nice day" on the other side. Hal's CD player and corded headphones were from the late 80's, but when John first walked in, Hal was listening to Black Sabbath. In particular the song "Wizard," released in 1970s as a debut single in France. France, a territory the Church of Unification had silenced as of yesterday. The cocky display of power by walking into sanctified holy ground, much less putting shoes on the ceiling—was not a ploy for attention. *Former Vietnam soldier, U.S., and you don't care if I deal with you at all.*

Hal pouted. "I wouldn't put it THAT bluntly, but yes." He dropped to the ground with a flip, rose, and patted Lazarus's shoulder. "Deal or no, I get to watch the fireworks."

"So, what do you want?" John said, even more curiously.

"Did you ever notice that almost every god that..." He paused and snapped his fingers like he couldn't remember a name. "Your unification assassin. The one who killed a shit ton of gods for you WAY before you were born. Always had them go to Fate or Misfortune?"

Lazarus narrowed his eyes. "A little before my time. God was dead when I was born."

"Because you can't murder a god, bucko. Once you get there, you can only... ever... be... unmade." Hal tapped Lazarus's chest with each pause.

It hurt.

"Gods have a destiny, so it makes sense they are jailed with those two."

"Bingo." Hal stopped and produced a Susan B. Anthony coin from behind John's ear like a children's magician. "Now I want you to picture something. What would make a *demon* actually afraid? Is it having our heart ripped out and eaten? Maybe... okay, BESIDES that... Bollard and Golgoroth kinda had it coming though. But angels, demons, cryptids, gods... What would be the *one* thing that would make us all afraid?"

"Being forgotten." Lazarus felt in his gut where this was going but pushed down any conscious thought.

"I knew you were smart. They told me so. When I was down there ... *waiting*. Being... you know, forgotten. Sitting there minding my own business on the edge of the abyss, where let me tell you—there is shit out there that was never even *conceived*. And those shadows, they really hate all of us."

Lazarus saw an opportunity. He strolled over to the one chair in the room, sat down, and calmly folded his hands. *Murder will have to wait much longer.* "It sounds like you need me more than I need you then."

"Oh, do I ever..." Hal leaned back on the wall, taking a long drag before grinding out his smoke on the marble wall.

CHAPTER 16

If you can hear my voice, there is still a chance for hope. They have tried to tear down the towers, silence the internet, and scramble the satellite transmissions in order to keep us from giving you this message. Do not turn off your radio; do not look away. If you are. hearing my words now, then it means that our Church of Lazarus has found a way to reconstruct one of our towers near you. Find them. Seek refuge from the magical pandemonium that surrounds us."

–Paid for by the Church of Lazarus

Lucian and Katrina strolled through the prison of Purgatory while taking inventory. The first phase of Lucian's haphazard plan had been put into motion—the Church of Lazarus had been announced. Now, it was just a matter of letting the Lord of Murder's worst general prosper for herself across the rest of North America. The Lord of Misfortune didn't *dislike* Katrina; rather, it was more hatred for what she represented. Katrina was a younger vampire by most standards but a fantastically skilled necromancer. Just enough to be on Murder's radar but young enough that the skeletal asshole could pull her every string. *The amount of overtime he makes his minions work is absurd. Murder doesn't even pay well.*

Katrina rattled off statistics and numbers that Lucian had long ago tuned out. His focus was on the streams of orange lights and eldritch greens that flowed like blood through the amethyst walls that comprised the prison for folklore legends and people that *almost* became gods. Rip Van Winkle, Sal of the Erie Canal, and even a wind spirit that was *almost* given a name for causing strange weather phenomenon off of Lake Michigan were a fraction of what was imprisoned here. Each of them was locked away in a unique fashion for containment and turned into a blood farm to fuel the Unification when magic had turned thin. To Lucian, each of them served as a personal reminder that even legends end up in a shitty place. All it took was one bad day.

Not unlike the sourpuss he had chained behind him was having. Mike Auburn had earned enough fame and been at the center of so many important events, the unlucky chap could have *possibly* been a legend, and nearly every day since his most recent death, the little bastard tried to escape, much to Lucian's amusement. *I'm not cruel. I'm just reality.* He craned his head back and watched Mike glower behind his perplexed looks into each cell, each time trying to work out who was imprisoned or how.

"Am I boring?" Katrina cut in. "I'm trying to lay out the split of soul royalties on who will join your armies and who falls under Murder's, and you've had the attention span of a squirrel chasing nuts. Accounting is important." She closed a small notebook of hand-scribbled notes and tucked it into her satchel.

"You, belle? Noooooo, not boring at all," Lucian deadpanned. "Clad in black, pale beyond belief, stark white hair, armed with a luxurious rapier forged from dead souls—you should be on the cover of your own novel." He tugged the chains around Mike's wrists. "Come, come. Time to go up soon."

Mike was too busy looking at why there was a mule named Sal of Eerie hooked up with a muzzle bag in a cell of hay to notice the tug

and tripped forward. "Hey, cinnamon roll, you could at least explain that first."

Katrina rolled her eyes. "You really think having…" She stopped herself, answering her own question with a look. "I'll report these numbers to the Lord of Murder, and we can sail out then, yes?"

Ah yes. Numbers. Kill my city and all of them will go to Murder. "Katrina, let me put something in perspective. See that mule?"

"The donkey?" Both she and Mike pointed at the same time into the cell of the only beast of burden that somehow was considered divine.

"Sal is famous. More famous than you or I." Lucian pulled out a small imp heart from outside the cell and chucked it in. "Anyone ever sing songs about you? No? Thought not. Fifteen years on the Erie canal and countless folk songs about her, she represents the mule barges that built America in the 1800s. Legend said their kicks would send you across the borders into Buffalo. But a mule's a mule, and eventually, they are still used to make glue. So, despite every worker making their entire life around a good ol' gal like her—she was still sent to the factories. I call that a bit unlucky. She had no control over her destiny at any stage. Eventually, rail and steam phased the mule barges out of existence and… what is she good for now?"

"I don't fucking know? Children's rides?" Katrina shrugged.

"I mean, possibly. I don't have a clue myself, but she's still stuck here in this place getting farmed for the fraction of power her blood would provide. When times were thin in the '80s, her blood was considered passing for basic spells."

"Can we not talk about the bloody mule? We have an entire nation to kill. Just … sign here." She pulled out her small notebook again and pressed it into Lucian's chest.

With one look, Lucian was glad he ignored her earlier. The sum of souls to be added to the beggar lord's rank … was zero. He changed the goose egg to a single "1" and then signed it. "I'm taking one." He gave a head nod back to Mike. "He's my mule."

"Fuck off" was the reply.

"Yeah, whatever." Katrina stamped it with Murder's seal and promptly hid it. "Look, I get this is unfair. I'm not blind, buddy. But technically, everyone who died was indeed murdered by that crazy weather kid and our soldiers. All you did—"

"Was set everything in motion," both said simultaneously.

Lucian suddenly hugged the leather-clad vampire. "Jinx! You owe me a Coke!"

Katrina, arms held stick straight by the Death Lord, looked at Mike. "You sure you don't want to be counted as Murder?"

"Oh no, I'm good. He's a moron so my chances are better here." Mike nodded.

"Can't disagree," she said while attempting to pry herself away from the zombie. "We ... have ... one more," she resorted to kneeing Lucian in the crotch to earn her freedom, "order of business. Next location."

"Vegas." Lucian adjusted himself and led them to the elevator doors. "I've always had my best luck in Vegas."

"You want to sail or march fresh legions of the dead through the borders of Dystopia or around Mexico into the demon city of Vegas? Absolutely not. We wait until our ranks have snowballed and march westward. We solidify the east coast first. New York City is tactically our move. The shipping ports alone..."

Everyone loaded themselves into the rickety wooden elevator still driven by manual hemp rope that would lead them back into the real world. Their bodies scrunched against each other in the cramped space that was designed for a single person, and Lucian began slowly raising them up. *New York. That would be substantial power for Lazarus and Murder. Those wolves barely need to touch the blood to be ruthless, and capitalists are scary enough without power.*

Lucian paused the elevator and looked up to Katrina. "Upon deep consideration, and as your current general, I've decided my answer is no. New York actually has guns, humans, and worst of all, atheists."

Katrina smooshed her nose right onto Lucian's. "After deep consideration, and as the leader of your only army, I've decided your fear is bullshit. All three things you named are exactly why they need to go."

Lucian raised on his tip toes, pushing Katrina up and letting his wide brim hat tangle into her locks of white hair. "And upon deeper consideration, and as a way better necromancer than you, I've decided that plan is stupid, and we should go to Reno!"

Katrina pressed her chest into his Hawaiian shirt, choking back the smell of a creole who never bathed, and poked his neck. "After an impossibly deep consideration of your stupid plan, and as a better swordsman, I've decided you only want to slack off and recruit some souls who have bad luck and kill themselves. But. It. Won't. Work. Because Suicide will take them." Her finger squished with each poke.

"Well, if I consider this any deeper, I'll be considering what the inside of your ass looks like as I shove my head up there, and frankly, I don't want to see what Murder's hand looks like so far up there." Lucian climbed up over the taller vampire and peered down over at Mike. "Boy. Fix this." *Because honestly, I'm curious.*

Mike was, without a question, the largest person in the elevator, and like a big dog trying to hide on a crowded couch, he just looked squished in the corner. "Um... I think you two should quit working for Lazarus and just get a hotel room?"

"Not helping," both said in unison.

"Jynx!" Katrina blurted out. "Fucker, Coke debt is nullified."

Lucian glared at Mike. "I trusted you."

"How about you gamble for it?" Mike raised a brow. "You're a dice-loving dead thing, no? Gimmie the bones, and I'll roll for you. High roll, Katrina and you move out to New York; low roll, you both head out to Reno?"

Love it. Lucian put his knee on Katrina's shoulder and started pulling the ropes again. "What happens if it's a three?"

"Then I pick." Mike smiled.

Katrina kicked him in the knee. "Absolutely not."

"Fine, then you split. The army goes one way; Lucian goes another."

"You mean I can be free of him?"

Mike kicked her back. "I want to point out that you both are trying to decide the fate of people you are about to *murder* in a fucking elevator over a dice roll. Are there any actual adults in your secret society, or is this pretty much par for the course?"

Lucian laughed and kept his hands at work, lifting the trio up. "It's more honest than how most leaders do it. Kyoto avoided nuclear bombs because Truman liked to vacation there."

Katrina wormed herself out from under Lucian. "I'm going to ask one more time: we can count you as murdered. Lazarus would very much like to meet someone who can see in Purgatory as a ghost."

Absolutely not. Lucian snapped his fingers and channeled his ability to manipulate the lands of the dead. The elevator doors suddenly opened into the lobby of an empty Saint Hotel within the heart of New Orleans. "You're right, Katrina. Elevator is no place for a dice roll. We are back."

Lucian had never seen anyone free themselves from an elevator so fast before. He sniffed his armpits to make sure he wasn't being awkward with his odor and was pleased to find he only smelled like a waterlogged corpse. *Better than most days?*

Katrina sped through the lobby, smashed open the door to a small gift shop, and quickly rifled through the children's games until she found a fresh die. Lucian could hear her chatting on the radio with her soldiers to reveal their location as she did so, now that there was reception. Lucian and Mike just waited by the concierge desk for her to finish, recompose herself, and eventually stroll back out.

"First, I'm not using your rigged-ass misfortune dice. Second, we have one order of business whichever way this rolls and the delivery is on the way." She tossed a white Monopoly die to Mike. "Table is yours."

Lucian couldn't help but feel genuine excitement for the possibilities. Even with his entropic sight, he could not predict this outcome.

Fate and Misfortune were two sides of the same coin, and with beings like Mike, it was always tricky to see which side they landed on—even if Lucian knew Mike was prone to bad luck. What Katrina had overlooked in this entire scenario was that Lucian had never actually *claimed* Mike as his single soul. Rubbing his hands with glee, Lucian practically giggled over the dice. *What will it be, ol' bones? Watching Lazarus's army swell by letting murder rampage through New York, or a nice vacation filled with weeks of nothing on the way to Vegas? Effective military application or lazy easy rivers.*

Mike held the dice, and for someone who was Lucian's prisoner, played the role of dealer well by showcasing that the dice had all six numbers before letting it tumble out of his fist. It clattered onto the glass counter anticlimactically with a soft patter and only two flips.

"Three." Mike shrugged. "Shame I don't get to pick."

"Well, Katrina," Lucian offered his hand, "good luck in New York. We'll rendezvous when you are done earning stripes for your master, I suppose."

She seemed honestly confused and a bit nervous that she would be leaving without the power of a Death Lord behind her this time. Lucian watched the anxiety spread through her pale features as reality set in. Out of five possible numbers, only one of them would have her stand alone on the battlefield. *Oh Kat, I'm sorry. You are going to have to please Murder all on your lonesome. Don't fuck it up.*

"I can do this." She coughed. "Well. Very well then." She stood awkwardly. "Yup. That's ... a thing. New York. Humans... guns... atheists. Demons, cryptics... vampires... money." She rocked to-and-fro as she fidgeted with her gemmed rapier and ran the math in her head.

Lucian knew full well that Katrina had a very good chance at extreme success if she moved slowly, refilling their ranks with the dead souls they claimed first. But an impatient Church of Lazarus and pride could also be her downfall. It was the arrival of a Jeep with two Lazarean soldiers and a prisoner that snapped Katrina out of her worry.

"Right. I'll contact you with updates then, Lucian. I suppose this is farewell for a little while. New Orleans, as promised, is yours, even if there is barely anyone left. We did find this one survivor, though, under some rubble in the crypt." She held open the door. "I believe she's one of yours."

Lucian was surprised when the small girl walked in and had a black sack ripped off her head. The small starved shape changer who had refused his mask. "Lumine?"

Their eyes were locked so thoroughly that Lucian barely even noticed boring Katrina leave with her soldiers. Every focus was on the girl who had every bit of bad luck as Lucian did and still somehow survived. *She's going to be my one soul.*

The tragedy of her eventual death made him equally sad and overly protective of a rare recruit to his ranks.

CHAPTER 17

A shaky camera from cellphone video zooms in on Mike Auburn and Primus Vryce standing on the 21st floor during a party three years ago. "You know what? Fuck all of you. I'm not your endorsement. You want a message to carry on? Here is one. Gods can fucking die." Mike's fists clenched and began to smoke from a supernatural power before chaos filled the room as helldivers and Sons and Daughters assaulted the party attendees. The viewer dropped the phone to run for their safety with the camera catching a glimpse of Vryce's dead eyes.

"You must be the laziest Death Lord." Mike kicked his boots against the graffiti-laden brick wall while watching Lucian and Lumine play a game of Go in an empty park. A week had passed since the Church of Lazarus dropped off the underfed teenage monster girl like some foster kid. *If Katrina's plan was to give Lucian some sort of toy so he would stay out of her way, that certainly worked.* Every hour since, Mike was dragged across a nearly empty, rotting, city on some sort of tour for days on end. Lumine ate at five-star restaurants before the food went sour, joined Lucian in burning down a few buildings they found annoying, and then played mini-golf on graves.

Downtown New Orleans was entirely theirs. *The apocalypse comes three years after, it seems. A skeleton, a ghost, and a werecreature walk into a bar... the last on earth.* "Can we at least play something three player? I'm a motherfucking pro at rock-paper-scissors." He lay back on the half wall, staring into the black sun dangling overhead while practicing his toss.

"Bah, quit the bantering. I'm focused!" Lucian cackled and tried to loom over Lumine in a vain attempt to scare her into making a wrong move.

"Give it up, Grandpa." Lumine finished him. "You will lose every game against me." She stuck her tongue out and dusted off her shoulders. "I'm just that good."

Mike rolled off and tussled her hair. "Or a soothsayer versus the unluckiest person in the world is the biggest rigged game I've ever watched."

"Buzzkill, let her have this!" Lucian seemed aghast but quickly slipped on his wooden sandals and adjusted the belt on his khakis around his skeletal hips before beginning to stroll down a random side street.

Mike noticed that Lucian often preferred to appear as a flashy skeleton or zombie ninety percent of the time. It was only when angered or nervous did he cast an illusion to appear as the pretty Frenchman. As for Lumine, after a week of being properly fed, she finally pulled her own style together—a squirrel crossed with a magpie. Lumine, left to absolute freedom, put feathers, beads and random trinkets from discovered dead bodies into her messy braids. From behind, her brown hair reminded Mike of a squirrel's nest. The rest of her was a patchwork dress she fashioned out of both fancy Italian fabrics and blue jean fabric stolen from empty stores, complete with a set of knee-high brown boots that refused to match anything else on her persona.

"Do you think he's going to ever do anything?" Mike asked Lumine as they strolled. Mike never had any ill-intent toward Lumine, for in his mind, she was just as captive as him.

As they followed the skipping Lord of Misfortune (who could only walk about ten feet without getting distracted by a shiny), Lumine observed him like he was an object. "No." She shrugged. "I don't think doing things is his style. He's not *evil*, Mike. He's just..."

"Scummy? Genocidal? Insane?" Mike pressed a smoke into his lips and lit it up. "There is a reason this city is empty, Lumine, and that reason begins with him."

"Death comes for everything eventually. Entropy has a purpose. Something about him gives me the impression it doesn't come from cruelty, more... hopelessness? I think that's the right word." She nodded.

Mike silently agreed. Unlike everyone else he'd met, Lucian didn't seem to have an agenda. At least, one that he could predict. *Then again, he probably plays games that last a few thousand years, and I'm looking at thirty seconds.*

Suddenly, a small stone went through Mike's head, passing right through from behind but knocking the cigarette out of his lips. *The fuck?* Annoyed, Mike peered around for the crackshot. Nobody was seen at first, but from around the mossy brick at the alley's end, he caught a glimmer of Akira peeking around the corner.

"Heylookatmelookatmelookatme," Akira mimicked a small bird horribly.

Lumine and Lucian were distracted by a find in a nearby dumpster, something to do with a set of faerie wings covered in condoms.

Fucking FINALLY. Mike scooted to the alley's edge so he was still in sight of his jailer but close enough to whisper around the corner. "Where the hell have you all been?"

"The. Cow. Kicks. The. Candle. At. Six." Akira leaned on her toes and whispered around the corner. Mike struggled to not chuckle at her outfit. Akira was wearing secret agent sunglasses, a fedora, and a brown trench coat but was still barefoot with tattered jean shorts.

"Well tell the cow to kick faster. The city is empty. Only demons down below."

Akira shook her head and pressed a set of fingerless gloves with a tag on them into Mike's paw like a drug dealer. "A gift from across the river. The cow moves at six. Plan A. Be ready."

Mike spotted Akira popping up the coat collar and strolling away like the worst secret agent in history. *Stealth is relative, I suppose. Can't fail when nobody can see you. God, I love them.*

Judging from the black sun's position, Mike probably had about four hours before the cow would kick, so he dusted off his cigarette and decided to join Lucian and Lumine in this discovery. A discovery that turned into a small memorial service as they buried a faerie who had been used and discarded.

Mike, Lucian, and Lumine were in a costume shop, playing dress up as vampires. This time, it was Mike's idea. He figured keeping Lucian out of Purgatory was a smart call for Plan A, and if they needed to sport outdated Halloween costumes, then so be it. Mike had to admit that Lumine did look adorable when she wore an inflatable T-rex costume, but then shapechanged into her alligator form and gave soft "rawrs" as she hunted the aisles.

"I think I'm going to name this region Samhain," Lucian said with a tinge of remorse in his voice as he ran his bony fingers over a cheap plastic skull. "Eventually, it will fill up again when my souls find it. There aren't many, but this will be a good home for them to be free of worry and just do what they wish."

"That's a mood shift," Mike said while holding up a pair of assless chaps. *I wonder if Gabriel owns a pair?* Mike secretly imagined Primus Vryce's lackey Gabriel DeAngelo strutting around with smug look and cheeks clapping in the wind.

"It's official. No longer New Orleans. It's Samhain."

"I like that name." Lumine tackled a model in the background. "Samhain is safe."

For how long? Just as the thought crossed his mind, the storefront glass shattered, impacted with lightning that came from clear skies. Doc, Akira, Phoebe, and Lucy raced in, each from a different direction. Doc and Phoebe appeared from the sides wielding shotguns and not wasting a second before pulling triggers at Lucian. Akira and Lucy rappelled down from the second story with ropes, flipping into the room with sickles and axes coated in chemicals, both racing to Mike. Phoebe, who must have crawled on the sidewalk, popped her head up and lunged in to grab Lumine.

Lucian wasn't even trying to dodge; he simply dropped the skull when the glass shattered and bent down to pick it up as the shotgun blasts obliterated the countertop and cash registers behind him. Because the store was unkempt, Mike watched Akira and Lucy land but quickly fall on Mardi gras beads with loud cracks. Phoebe's shirt got stuck on the broken glass, and when trying to free herself, the entire front tore right off. She ducked back down the moment skin was revealed.

"Did you guys hear?" Lucian said to the room. "We call this place Samhain. Welcome to my empire of dirt." Without a care in the world, the Death Lord stepped over Akira and casually placed a severed Halloween finger in the barrel of Doc's shotgun. "Do me a favor," Lucian rasped a laugh while softly tapping a finger on Doc's shoulder. "Tell the very frustrated lich standing down the street he might want to stay in the middle of the street."

Everyone heard the sizzle and pop of a power transformer exploding, followed by the overhead snap of electrical cables crashing down onto the sidewalk. Mike swore he heard someone shout "Not the hair, Jane!" in panic.

"Hrm." Lucian sniffed the air. "Too late. Come, children. Our night continues."

Mike felt a tug in the center of his chest, like an invisible chain tied around his heart lurching him forward. He tried to grab onto Lucy's hand, but just as their fingers touched—Lucian had pulled the three of them across the barrier into Purgatory.

Samhain didn't look much different in Purgatory than normal when you weren't below ground. The sky was perpetually cloudy and green, and the buildings looked just as rundown and burnt. Instead of cellophane-wrapped Halloween costumes, the store was filled with rusted silver cutlery from the 17th century. A building long-since destroyed but perpetuated in the memory of local residents was out of sight but never forgotten.

Mike knew the Sons and Daughters could helldive across the barrier of Innocence, but by the time their ritual completed—they would be long gone. Mike had never met anyone besides Lucian who could tug people across or through the barrier with such ease.

So much for the cow kicking the candle.

Mike was pulled through ancient (nearly) empty streets like a sub upon his master's leash, and he was horribly conflicted. On one hand, he knew his and Lucian's relationship was toxic; consent wasn't exactly given in his ability to make a choice. On the other hand, it did cement home a perspective for the vast difference between their levels of power. *Jane KILLED one of these donuts? I seriously need to give her props.* Mike wasn't jealous. Not in the slightest, for he actually beamed internally with pride over her accomplishments. But he couldn't help but wonder why Lucian seemed to be afraid of Vryce when Mike had so clearly killed him at the pinnacle of his power. *Little good that did, idiot. He's still up and kicking.*

Lucian and Lumine strolled happily several paces in front of Mike, with Lucian casually remarking about bits of Louisiana history

as they strolled, completely ignoring the recent assault. Lucian would pause them in front of a burnt building and explain why the memory of a burnt-out hotel survived on one side of the shroud of innocence but never appeared in the real world. After the third stop, Mike was already tired of the word "memory."

"Alright," Mike sat down in protest in a puddle, "I give up," he lied. "You two can keep bonding, but I'm sitting here 'til my friends come across."

Lucian and Lumine stopped talking and almost looked hurt at his sudden non-silent protest. Lucian went to speak first, but Lumine thrust a finger in front of what remained of the zombie's lips.

"You don't get it, do you?" She came over and sat down in front of Mike, joining him in the puddle and wiggling her toes in the water with childish amusement. "You think you don't have a choice to be here, but that isn't true. Most ghosts on this side are blind and dumb. You can go both ways. If you really want, just leave." She patronized his hands with a pat.

"Rrrrrriiiighhht," Mike narrowed his eyes, "because you can just walk away."

Lucian held up a bony finger to protest but continued to be cut off.

"You know as well as I do that you could gamble for your freedom. You didn't. Not because you are afraid, but because you know following along is your only chance to learn how to defeat him." As Lumine spoke, her tone carried a wisdom betrayed by her age.

So, so not... almost... right? Mike tilted his head. "Heh. You and Akira would get along, you know that right? I've been through some shit, but... it did make me stronger."

"Exactly. Even when Edward Morris locked you in a barrel and taught you to fear the sun, you learned your lesson. Forged your bond with your friends and chose to keep fighting. You aren't the kind to give up by any measure—no matter how much pain you endure. So why would you quit now?"

Lucian tried to cut in again, clattering his jaw and creeping closer.

"How the fuck did you know about that?" Mike leaned in.

"It's my job to keep memories. Soothsaying, at least." She moved her brown hair behind an ear. "I was trained," she bit her lip and fidgeted with the dirt under her nails, "before eating the heart and forced into labor, that the past is more important than the future. The future hasn't been written yet. The past, though, is filled with lessons. So, I don't look into people's future when I read them. I look at their past and predict. Same thing with that angry teenage girl." Lumine fought back some tears as she looked up at the sky, pushing the emotions of her own past back down into the stormy void of her own turmoil. "He's scared. Always has been scared. Scared someone will take away something important to him again. Not unlike you." She reached out with a finger and booped his nose with a small, cute sound. "So, knock it off. Your only hope for change is coming along because clearly, punching isn't working."

Mike's teeth ground as he muttered under his breath. "You know I do more than punch things, right? I point out the flaws in the system and actually help. Also, hold the fuck on. Forced heart eating? Labor? Let's rewind—"

Lucian tossed his hands up and finally just grabbed both of them on the head. "KIDDOS! Look, I'm all for a moment of self-reflection and bonding, but you are both ... semi-right."

"How?" they both asked. Mike flinched under the sudden grab while Lumine leaned into Lucian's paw like a cat—thankful for the interruption.

"Three things. Number one, Mike, hate to break it to you, buddy... but nobody sees the flaws in the system better than I—it's my curse. Number two, Lumine, if the past was a perfect guide, then all of history could be prophesied, but it can't. Number three, I'm out of vape juice, and that will make me cranky—so we are making a pit stop."

Mike's eye visibly twitched. "Here is where I can choose to leave, right?"

"Nope. Because you haven't learned a new trick yet." Lucian chuckled and gave a tug upon an invisible leash.

The neon sign for the Puff N Fun Smoke shop was broken, much to Mike's happiness when they crossed over to the current world. Mike reasoned they had to be down the street but at least a few blocks over as he watched Lucian struggle to break into an empty store.

"I'll get you in, but you need to answer a question." Mike walked to the door and faded between the thin glass as a proper ghost and waved from the other side. "If only someone could walk through walls..."

Lucian adjusted his hat. "I, good sir, am a beacon of information."

"How is it you can snap your fingers and swap between Purgatory and the current world like it's a barrier that's still real? Ghosts like us can crawl out. Magic is back. The black sun is *right* fucking there. And yet... you dance between a world I had to nearly kill myself just to see."

Lumine peered up at the skeleton out of curiosity while Lucian slowly clapped. "A REAL question. Finally." If the zombie could smile, Mike swore he saw his cheeks stretch into a grin. "Magic is back, m'boy, the dead hath returned, and the entire world is descending into oblivion. Welcome to the apocalypse." He bowed.

"That's not an answer." Mike looked at a counter filled with cherry vape juice and kicked it, toppling it over and sending plastic bottles flying against the wall. When a single bottle rolled under his boot, Mike threatened to step upon it. "I'm waiting."

"Okay! I wasn't holding out." Lucian tapped the glass with bony knuckles. "Necromancy. It's a magical art that all Death Lords are proficient in. We can command the dead, sort them, pull them, raise them, and even make places. For a long time, poltergeists were how we dealt with enemies of the Unification. We'd lower the shroud of Innocence to let them wreak havoc and then raise it to hide our involvement. Everyone would think the living survivors were crazy. I'm," Lucian sheepishly rubbed the back of his head, "the best at it. There isn't a Lord who can match my skill at the barrier because I've always been banished."

So, what you are saying is when it's gone, you lose your best trait?

"Nope."

Mike's eyes widened.

"Yeah... boy... um... in order to become a lich, you kinda need to eat a demon heart and an angel heart, which will tear your soul into shreds—killing you unless it's removed from the inside out. If you are unlucky enough to survive that, you are a warlock." He poked his two skeletal fingers together. "That already makes you absurdly powerful with training and unlocks so many divine and infernal magical secrets, but you still have no soul. Ergo... you need to get it back."

Lumine muttered something about who needs one of those under her breath while she casually stacked discarded trash into something of a snowman, just made out of garbage.

"That's a whole different can of anchovies. So in short, yes, I can read your thoughts, I can heal like a vampire, and I can command your soul. We each have a specialty though, but one thing is true of all Death Lords and liches..." Mike spied Lucian glancing down the street. "We are gods in a small bubble of our own reality. Mine is being fucking unlucky. Now open the goddamn door before I shatter this glass and melt your cute face off that soul of yours."

Mike hastily opened the door.

Lucian and Lumine strolled in, but not without Lucian tapping an empty vape and taking a dry puff that made him choke.

Mike couldn't resist and fished out a pack of vanilla tobacco from the broken glass he kicked. "You know, this does the job with vastly more style. Just get a pipe."

"Oh, heh." Lucian was already inspecting vials and cheap lithium pens. "I'm not doing this because I have any interest in actual nicotine. I'm dead. I'm here because this *really* rubs you the wrong way, Mikey. Are you afraid of change?"

"You call bad taste change?" Mike looked at Lumine, who simply shrugged.

"It was the wave of the future, Mikey; your sister was in *a bunch* of ads."

"First off, stop calling me Mikey; second, you leave Jane out of this."

"Oooh!" Lucian's eyes flashed red. "You protective? But you haven't been alive for a while. Didn't you know what became of Dystopia? What became of your sister's victory over the Lord of Suicide?"

One less of you fuckers. Mike stood proudly and placed his hands upon his hips. "Yeah, she killed the fucker and discovered your secret god lair with me."

Lucian barreled over in laughter and then fell on his back, cackling on the floor. He continued cracking up in his own insanity, causing Mike and Lumine to actually check in on his health. None of them noticed Akira, Lucy, Doc, and Jane all sneaking in behind them.

"No, no, you can't... you didn't know... okay... okay..." Lucian lay between the shelf of cannabis vapes and giant dildo-shaped bongs, gazing up at Mike and Lumine with glassy eyes. "Okay, so, after Jane killed Fredrick, who was a sweet soul by the way, all of Texas became some sort of soulless abomination of silicon robots. Their so-called artificial intelligence started ripping magical creatures apart in the name of profit and making the entire global problem worse. Then, a few months ago, Alexandria of Ur just simply took up the mantle of Suicide. So, you swapped a child killed in Jonestown for a vampire older than dirt."

Mike heard a female voice scoff and then another mutter, "He's smart, fuck off."

It looked to Mike like a cascade of absolute calamity as he saw Jane peering over a shelf with Akira to her right. Their combined weight tipped over the shelf, which ran into the next one, and the next one, and so forth until the entire store's shelves were dominoed down. Lucy, who had snuck around to get a free shot on Lucian, was left standing with her ax over the Death Lord who was looking right up at her. Doc Daneka, standing at Lucian's feet, just sighed and cracked open his shotgun. "Yup, dead rounds."

Lucy rolled her eyes. "This is never going to work on you, is it?"

Lucian smiled. "Random assassination attempts? I'm praying it does someday, but you lot don't have the right divine juice. So unfortunately, no. I'll be honest, I'm not even trying to stop you. I keep putting myself in the right spot for you."

"Any chance you could just stop working for them? You don't fit the mold," Doc asked while furiously nodding at Mike to get the fuck out.

Mike didn't hesitate and started scrambling over shelves of ceramic dildos toward his sister and Akira... but only made it halfway before the invisible chain around his neck tightened.

"I think not." Lucian rose as if he was possessed, through sheer telekinetic force. "I've no ill will against any of you. For each of you are already dead. The world's battle is over; your fate is sealed. So, you l'enfants are just passengers in the universe's most famous car crash." He looked right at Jane and raised his bony fingers to bind her soul.

Everyone moved to protect her. Doc raised his shotgun's hilt to attack but slipped on a vial of apple. Lucy brought her ax down only to have the wooden handle snap as it hit the Lord's bony hip. Akira used her speed to lift up the tipped over shelf, hoping to block line of sight, but a ceiling light fell upon her head at the worst moment.

Mike, however, saw the flaw in Purgatory. The flaw was clear as day in Lucian and Lumine's eyes. They didn't *want* to capture Jane. In the real world, Lucian looked every bit the skeletal death lord of malevolence, but behind the shroud of innocence, Mike saw a lonely and sad lord move slowly. As if he was begging for the future to change. *I'm already dead, so what's the worst that can happen?* Mike stepped sideways in front of the spell and felt it hit his chest and the burn of yet another chain binding around his heart. "Pick her or me, buddy. We don't play well together. She likes Chinese food, and I will die to defend tacos." Mike grimaced as he felt his chance of escape slip away.

Lucian tipped his wide-brimmed hat. "Magnifique." He glanced at Lucy. "Clever bitch. I'm sorry, my lost souls, but our dates tonight

are at an end." His rotten fingers snapped, leaving bits of thumbnail upon Doc's cheek as Lucian effortlessly returned them to Purgatory.

A Purgatory that was under assault by the rest of the Sons and Daughters.

Mike could only watch helplessly as the assault upon the Seat of Golden Tears was foiled. He was a prisoner behind his own eyes as the Sons and Daughters, Boss, Edward Morris, and even a face he'd never expect in Vryce's latest possession puppet, took to assaulting the Church of Lazarus's prison of gods. Then easily defeated by a simple placement of a toothpick in an elevator rope. It was particularly heart-breaking that hardass veterans of the Unification like Edward Morris were so easily sidelined. Morris was the functional right hand of the boss and a powerful vampire in his own right who could walk into any organization and find himself drinking at the big kid's table in an hour. The fact that Morris had only been able to recruit the core group and a few stragglers showed either just how far their influence had fallen or that Morris was more of a hardass than Mike imagined and viewed the whole NOLA operation as a scouting mission. *Guy goes from pulling the strings of Chicago to loading up biker gangs with shotguns on the front lines like he's living out a Capone fantasy. For a consigliere to Boss, he really didn't pull in the big favors.*

The realm of Purgatory may have overlayed the real world, but it also descended far deeper. The Sons and Daughters were using the assault to free Mike as a distraction for their real goal—his plan A: free the gods. Unfortunately, it required the usage of helldiving and ropes to descend deeper into the lands of the dead, and it appeared to Mike that once they entered Lucian's domain, there was no escape.

Demonic jailers screeched as they were fried by Vryce's magic and the gunfire barrage of the Chicago crew. Each drop of blood spilled

only fueled further magics in a beautiful exponential cascading light-show of destruction. Yet once Lucian peered in from above, he only needed to place a single toothpick into a hemp rope to send the entire assault into a chaotic failure.

The wooden elevator crashed down, causing Vryce to look up just briefly—his, *or her?* (Mike had to admit, he never actually knew Vryce's true history)—single delay allowed a Barghest to race past both Boss and Morris and tackle the teenage girl.

What happened next, even Mike wasn't ready for. Samhain was nearly empty above. They had wandered for days on end without encountering a soul. Yet down below, hundreds of ghosts came out of the very golden walls themselves to tackle and wrestle the Sons and Daughters back. They weren't the same souls killed by the Lord of Murder but seemed to be fighting for the very treasures at stake. Their desperation to protect their treasures of misfortune, forgotten gods, and even their own rest reminded Mike of scorned workers who were never paid—for they fought with the ferocity of a nation being invaded.

Just as Mike, bound helplessly in a rickety elevator shaft next to Lumine and Lucian, thought he'd watch the very same Boss who once made him a vampire perish, Lucian shouted, "Wait!"

Everyone stopped.

Lucian leaned over the edge and shouted, "Yeah, um, dumbasses. You … kinda … don't want to fuck with that one." He pointed to Boss. "Or that one." He shifted over to Morris. "Or really any of them," he said, flailing his hands comically at the lot. "Just let them go. Hey, Ol' Man! Been a while! Didn't think you'd come back to visit your prisoners so soon, but you know the rules. If you want them free… gotta bet me or Fate." Lucian put his chin on his folded arms and kicked his legs up in the air behind him. He reminded Mike of a kid excited to prove to a grandparent how far he'd come. "Since you two broke up, I don't think that's likely. So why don't you go back to your Second City and wait for the world to turn, Ol' Man?"

Mike raised an eyebrow. When Morris was assigned the task of bringing Mike into the fold, the group all worked for the Unification and under the Death Lord of Fate. Sure, Mike probably fucked a fair bit of that up by starting the revolution, yet *they* all went along with it. *I guess that explains why the crew seems a lot less official these days. The Chicago outfit was cut out for not toeing the party line.*

Morris looked up and reloaded his submachine gun before quickly downing a potion of demon vitae. "Boss, we need to go. It's here."

The old man gazed up and took off his cabbie hat, revealing the gray balding hair and winked at Mike. "Lucian, you are still singing the song of the ol' guard. I suppose our bet will have to be finished later then. You promise to let me use the usual door?"

Oh, everyone fucking knows everyone. Mike's eye twitched. *It's like watching the Godfather only with apocalyptic dead men. I gotta remember to punch Morris in the gut at some point for not letting us know earlier there was a V-fucking-IP entrance.*

Lucian's rotting boots tapped with glee as he lay over the edge like a school girl, and Mike could only picture the zombie twirling around a phone cord while trying to set up a date. "But of course! How could I forget your aura? Your name is easy to forget—you change it so often. *Mi casa su casa*, except right now with Lazarus here. You should just sit back and watch. Let the kiddos determine what happens. Maybe... you could do me one favor?"

"And what's that?" The old man started walking through fields of ghosts and demons who parted ways to the exit.

Yeah, Boss. What deal you cutting with the Death Lord we are meant to kill, eh? How about quit working for them and switch sides? We have dental. Worked on me. Mike shrugged.

"Let the lich stay here? It doesn't belong in your ranks."

Mike watched the teenage girl levitate the bodies of shattered demons and rip the blood out of them. Sparks of energy flowed between her fingertips, often arcing off any metal buckle or latch on her Brook & Talbots bag, but Mike also spotted something else at

her feet. Purgatory didn't *truly* exist at her feet. Not in the same way. Seven shadows instead wove fragments of the girl's reality, preventing Lucian's rampant misfortune from creeping closer. It appeared to Mike that Vryce was summoning forth subconscious memories of English cobblestone while inching backward against an ever-growing horde.

Boss, a few steps ahead, nodded to Morris to grab the girl. Morris slinked over, leveling his gun, and whispered into her ear. Suddenly, she looked up, her heterochromatic eyes landing on Mike before darting over to Lucian. Sheer icy hatred was all Mike felt.

"Aren't you always the one to say you are unlucky?" the old man shouted. "So unfortunately, he gets to use my door today."

"Tsk," Lucian clicked his tongue. "Not even that one teensy, tiny favor. You know he's broken the rules. Why does he get to be the one free of judgement?"

"And you are not the judge of such rules. Our god left us. We only pick up the shambles." The old man, and everyone in his retinue, was suddenly gone in Mike's eyes, like they'd never been there. And yet, Lucian peered endlessly at their exit to the left, toward a simple arched gateway that Mike had been dragged through dozens of times.

We are so fucked. Mike felt his stomach sink. *Unless...* Mike's idea was a jumbled mess of thoughts, but as he looked at the fear and curiosity behind Lucian's eyes, his brain raced all the way from plan B through to plan L. Beyond plan L, however, Mike had nothing. Regardless, as Lumine had said—he wasn't giving up. He only needed to find the right crack in Lucian's armor, and he was starting to see a few tiny chinks. Most importantly was how Mike could save Jane from being bound. *Someone,* he thought, *doesn't have his heart in the game.*

As soon as Mike thought of it as a game, he hated himself. He was becoming more than a person caught up in the byzantine schemes of immortals; officially, he was one of them.

CHAPTER 18

Every ghost deserves to be glamorous. Don't let a small case of death deter you from slaying at the latest gala. They say ectoplasmic hair never cuts, never dyes, and is prone to split ends—we say no more. Gooette hair and dye products are tailor-made to make your radiance shine through, even on your worst days. Now, the WILDEST colors you can imagine are in the palm of your hand, and even a poltergeist's stick-straight hair can be permed to perfection.

Gooette hair products guarantees that only the most humane collection of faerie blood is utilized in our products.

The dented blue- and rust-colored van sailed airborne over the I-10W while swerving wildly between abandoned cars or cutting someone off on the wrong side of the road.

"DRIVE FASTER, SLOTH FACE!" Jane flicked off her latest victim and slammed on the gas pedal right as everyone else inside bounced violently. Several were holding on for dear life, but Doc Daneka casually feigned a nap in the passenger seat.

"Raise your hand if you are surprised Jane has anger issues," he remarked with his eyes closed.

Akira, Morris, Lucy, and Vryce, notably, did not raise their hands in the back of the van as they clutched shoddy wooden shelves.

"It's not anger." Jane perked up. "It. Is. Calm. Valid. Urgency."

"I want you to know, Lucy," Vryce said, "if I die, I'm permanently going to possess your body."

"Jane, Houston is only five hours away," Lucy replied.

"Five hours too far. We need firepower *yesterday*." Jane looked back at everyone and gave a two-fingered salute. Their escape from Lucian's lair left Jane feeling like a cat sprayed with the no-no juice. *That undead cocky... smarmy... little shit. OOoohhh, I wanna punch that smug face so bad.* "So, let's stop playing around with these little pea shooters and get some real toys. Wars are won with morale, money, and artillery."

"EYES ON THE ROAD!" everyone shouted and tried to scramble forward to grab Jane's wheel.

Jane jerked right, sending them tumbling. "Oh no. Mama's driving. You just leave this to good ol' Jane. I'll be getting us right round to Dystopia in record time. This bucket of rust has enough gas to make it and two spare tires I stole from that beamer back in Baton Rouge."

Doc sighed. "You are aware that we didn't have a *choice* in your driving, so as far as I'm concerned, the sooner we get there, the better."

"See, Doc believes me." Jane beamed with pride. "I always knew you were the smartest, hon."

Akira chimed in. "I feel like this is the moment where I need to make an obligatory swordfish joke about Doc's true motives here. I'll refrain for everyone's sanity because I'm really more curious on what happens to us when this hole in the floor keeps expanding."

"Hole?" Doc shot up.

"Oh, they just be back there doing the worry warts." Jane spied back to see Akira poking at a spot of rust beneath her bare feet. "Don't pick at it, you nit wad! If you go zipping through the floor, and I speed bump you, it's your fault!"

"EYES ON THE ROAD!"

Jane swerved left into oncoming traffic for the next ten miles, cackling as she leaned over the steering wheel with intense focus, swears, curses, and zigs as she avoided the lucky New Orleans evacuees stuck in gridlock closer to Houston.

Four hours later, Jane learned exactly how pale three vampires, a wight, and a sorcerer could really appear.

The only member of the Sons and Daughters crew who fared well was Phoebe—who bopped along to French-metal under her bike headphones and tailed the van on her motorcycle with ease.

The Triumvirate States was visible from as far away as Beaumont, dozens of miles away. Huge concrete walls seventy-five feet tall spanned from the sea, leading all the way around three major Texan cities—Austin, Houston, and Dallas. Jane knew the walled garden of Dystopia all too well, and those walls were the first thing constructed when shit hit the fan. Until she left that concrete bosom, she never realized those walls weren't for protection from demons and monsters, but to guard the natural resources of those who lived within. Let too many outsiders in, and then you've got rations on food and water. The last time Jane was here, she was very much alive. *And I sort of threw several stakeholders off skyscrapers. Hopefully, they don't hold a grudge?*

"Anger issues," Doc remarked as if he knew what she was thinking. "Not quite intermittent explosive disorder, but Stress Inoculation is certainly in your future when I get you in my office."

"It's rude to read my thoughts." Jane slammed on the brakes.

"Meh, I'll live with the scorn. You are feast of emotions." The balding emotional vampire smiled, fangs bared, and looked the most rejuvenated out of any creature in the van.

"Is that why you sat in front?" Jane pointed to the listless group in the back whose adrenaline had long since crashed after three hours of near-death driving.

"If you are offering a buffet?" Doc shrugged and opened the van door, stepping out to stretch.

"And they thought I was ruthless."

Leading up to the concrete walls were massive tent cities that had been in place for three years now. Twilight cast its eerie glow over the sprawling tent city that conquered every square inch of territory in the shadow of the Triumvirate's impossible skyscrapers. As the sun set, the clouded sky had beautiful violet haze, as under the black sun Anthelios, warm oranges and deep reds were a distant memory in Texas. Any natural light from Anthelios perverted the color spectrum even more when it set each night as the pale gray would paint the sky with greens, blues, and occasionally streaks of jet black. The moon at least had the courtesy to stay consistent in this warped world; Lillith's Moon was always a deep royal purple or red. When the barriers between worlds was shattered and the celestial bodies changed, Jane at least was happy that nights got a whole lot prettier.

Her hometown's beautification was entirely subjective, however. The skyline of Dystopia loomed in the background as a testament to humanity's defiance against a world where rules of nature had been shattered. Unfortunately, the city was a poor monument that promised safety for those who adhered to its rigid rules. The flickering lights of makeshift shelters blended with the harsh neon of corporate logos, each promising some new magical product or golden lottery ticket into the city. It wasn't everyone's cocktail of choice, but Jane still felt some hope was better than none. Plus, she still was proud that a few of the billboards featured her.

On foot was their only path forward, and Jane led the way effortlessly through the mélange of cultures and languages that echoed through the narrow alleyways crafted in an almost mazelike structure. Worn-out denizens, most of them still human, navigated the streets easily, often huddling around generators powering makeshift tech hubs, where scavenged electronics were meticulously repaired and repurposed (and always near the smell of freshly cooked spiced meats). Akira was endlessly distracted by the glow of holographic graffiti, both political and artistic, as if she was a bug drawing to a

zapper, and on more than one occasion, everyone needed to split up to locate the gutter punk wandering off.

Eventually, Jane was able to keep everyone on track enough to make it to gate number 15B. An automated black box with a small red light scanned barcodes tattooed on people's arms as they entered through washdown barricades before being granted entry. Meanwhile those exiting sported the classic dead-behind-the-eyes look that the nine-to-ten office day tended to warrant.

"Immortals of the world, I present to you technomagic in all its glory," Vryce snarked and buttoned up her peacoat.

"Hush you, I'll have none of that. Without the glory of tech-nomagical Angel-Be-Gone, your skinny legs would be chicken bones for an angelic cow right now." Jane rose on her tiptoes looking for the *right* entrance. *It's gotta be around here somewhere. Where is the little...* "Phoebe?"

Phoebe had been the quietest one of the bunch the entire walk over. Jane never really knew Phoebe too well. She was hot. Even if Jane wasn't into girls that way, she could still certainly admire a girl with the confidence to pull off leather, and Phoebe was also the group's prophet. Visions were already rare for a vampire, but Jane had heard the others mention that Phoebe pretended to be vampiric to fit in, and that she really ate the heart of a faerie, not a demon. It made some sense to Jane since succubi and incubi fell under a nebulous classifica-tion. Either way, when the prophet shut up and just followed along, it didn't bode well for Jane.

Phoebe popped a stick of gum in her mouth right when Jane called her name. "Mmm?"

"You, uh, you see another door marked 'residents' round here?"

Phoebe's gaze quickly darted around to the same visual of crowded lines being ushered in automatic scanning robots that they could all see. She pointed a single finger at the long line. "The um... cashier-less check-out line for cheap labor?"

"Aww, come on. Use that right-place-right-time prophet thingy."

"Sorry, love." She shrugged. "To my eyes, this is just one big empty place."

Worth a shot. Jane tapped her lips and then smiled before sidling up to the first person in line. "Hi. Hi, excuse me. I know you've been waiting in line for..."

"Three days."

"Three days." Jane nodded. "I know this is a BIG ask, but could we perhaps cut? I'll give you an autograph?"

The tired-looking man with incredibly striking blue eyes, as if they were soft LED lights, just smiled. "Yeah, have at it. No need for the autograph. It's not worth anything."

Jane blinked. She wasn't sure if she should be offended or thankful, but rather than protest, she bowed with a smile. Tugging Vryce's coat, she quickly pulled her group into line standing at the front. Once she came up to the small box, she gave a soft cough and leaned forward. "Dear Skynet. It is I, resident JK-47. I have returned! Now open the gates!"

Akira's facepalm was audible.

The red light on the box flashed three times and scanned Jane. Much to everyone's surprise—the steel doors opened for all of them.

Dystopia was a paradise. Artificial grow lights and waterfalls kept lush greenery alive in nearly every corner of the well-lit streets. Walkways between skyscrapers spiderwebbed above them with moving directional signs to highlighting the purpose of each level. Jane couldn't see above level thirteen from the ground floor. Even if there was a night sky, or a black sun, from here—the sky was neon.

The smells of cooking, cramped sweat, and makeshift diesel generators gave way to the freshest air they had smelled. A bouquet of lavender and fresh, mountain spring-filtered water calmed their senses

and added a tranquil air to the atmosphere—despite the otherwise busy pedestrian traffic. Since Jane had last been here, the entire city was renovated for localized living, and even the riches of the upper echelon penthouses had since flowed down. *Why is it every place gets better when you leave? It's like when you graduate high school, and then they install a Starbucks.*

Getting inside was easier than Jane had expected, but figuring out where to go took far longer. All the helpful you-are-here signs meant little to them when room 303 could be inside any building, and even if Jane remembered which building was the headquarters she was looking for—the city was constantly shifting and upgrading itself. Six albeit beautiful corporate lobbies and several miles of walking later, the entire crew sat down in protest. Even Doc's beaming energy had drained out of him.

"This place," he remarked, "is absolutely soul crushing."

"I think it's become rather pretty," Jane said, frustrated but still charmed. "Jack did a good job."

Doc craned his head back her way as he took off his dress shoe and wormed his toe through a hole in his sock. "Jane, since we have been here, we haven't talked to a single person. It's been lobby after lobby, all of them, mind you, with free offerings of home-baked chocolate chip cookies that *nobody* touches, one after another. What twisted hell have we entered where people pass up free cookies?"

Jane narrowed her eyes. "You didn't have any."

"I'm a vampire..." He waved his hand in front of his face. "Even Akira passed out from boredom."

Akira was lying underwater in a nearby fountain. She also didn't need to breathe. With the amount of hearts Akira was addicted to eating, it was anyone's guess what the bug-laden shapeshifter was, and honestly, Jane had given up trying to guess since she'd seen Akira in life. *Vampire, shape changer, bug whisperer, video game expert, and apparently mermaid. Know what? Fuck it. Go you.*

Vryce looked at the group. "Everyone inside the walls is different. They aren't people; they are objects. Walking golems and gargoyles, it feels like."

Phoebe finally threw her hands in the air. "I told you I can't see anyone here! But NOOO, you thought I was just being Phoebe and cryptic. This place is dead. Like, literally, and not in the purgatory sense, dead."

Doc put his hand on Jane's shoulder. "Look, we are sorry, but this isn't a valid lead. You know what happened with the Lord of Suicide better than everyone. This place is just a machine that makes things for the sake of making them. It's like someone programmed artificial intelligence to generate product lines so it could sell them to itself."

Frustrated, Jane punched Doc in the chest. "Could you just fucking trust me!" she shouted. "That god of unluck or whatever fucks with probability. Well, he can't fuck with a bomb, can he!? Or a missile! I don't care if this place is soulless or whatever—what they do have is weapons. Weapons and people—which we fucking need right now because the Church of Lazarus has a fuck ton of gods. They killed *everyone*. They are going to kill more, *again*. They have MIKE! Your boss is back there licking his wounds with every other anarchist you brought down." Jane grabbed Phoebe's leather jacket without even looking. "Phoebe thought you were there to kill a Death Lord. Turns out it's a whole goddamn armada. I've been on their front lines before, remember? They are just going to keep going from village to city, killing everyone, and raising an impossibly large army that a few tornadoes won't solve shit. We need. To buy. Nukes." The quiver in Jane's voice was a bit of emotion she wished she could take back. *I just need people to believe in this. It's all I can think of.*

Edward Morris had been with the group the entire time. Dressed casually with a cabbie hat that his messy sandy blond hair curled out of, five o'clock shadow, and a brown trench coat, he had followed along from behind with a cup of warm black coffee and quietly pretended to sip. Ever since the van, he'd been quiet and observational,

a trait Jane figured he picked up from his boss given how closely they worked, but his presence still made Jane feel as if she needed to be competent. Morris was always higher up in the ranks of the enemy in the past, and he didn't have the aura of calming mentorship that Boss did. Yet, after her outburst, he finally spoke, lending gravitas to her words. "She ain't wrong." He sipped the coffee and gave a quick spit before rising. "If you want to buy weapons, you are going about it the wrong way. Trust me, I'm an expert at arms deals." He winked and walked down the cobblestone street, chucking the coffee cup on the ground.

Jane sidled up to his side. "We've been to six different companies and haven't even made it past the help desk. What's your secret?"

"We aren't speaking the right language. I'm surprised you haven't realized it yet, given you are this place's star. I mean hell..." Morris pointed up to a vid screen that showcased an animated version of Jane battling in a media retelling of her story. "Your autograph doesn't mean a damn thing here, and nobody is jumping out to greet you—but you are still a part of their entertainment."

Jane looked at the animation and down at her own chest. *No fucking way. I'd break my back with those.* "So where to?"

"The bank." Morris pointed to the nearest self-service terminal. "You need money. This entire place relies upon money. Every lobby we've been in had a sign to pay for custom consultation. Everyone's time is worth something here." Morris grabbed Jane's head and held her eye to the retinal scanner on the bank's terminal.

"Please hold. Welcome to Tri-City Bank. JK-47, would you like to hear your balance?"

Jane's face was squished against the glass. *Huh. They remember me.* "Uh, yes."

"We are terribly sorry for the inconvenience." Mr. Anonymous, warlock of Dystopia, and penultimate ruler of the so-called Triumvirate States poured a glass of archangel blood into a crystal goblet for Doc Daneka. Fifty-seven floors later, Jane and everyone else found themselves in a penthouse suite, hand-waited upon by the silicon lifeform of the world's premier technomancer.

Mr. Anonymous wore a cracked Guy Fawkes mask, reminiscent of the hacker collective but had long blue silicon weaves that flowed down to his mid-back for hair. Easily six foot nine and dressed in a custom-tailored green and blue suit—personal style wasn't in short supply for the warlock. "Our paradise is an evolution of time management, but there are still bugs in the system. We didn't realize that our beloved JK-47 returned to us until she activated her bank account." Mr. Anonymous placed a black-gloved hand on Jane's shoulder. "We trust you are satisfied with the results of our investment strategy and royalty payments?"

Jane nearly spat the delicious demon-infused cocktail meant for ghosts across his elaborate onyx-marble desk. She caught herself in the nick of time and ended up with a dribble down her chin. "Uh, I'm fucking rich. Not rich like 'oh, you can buy a cute house' rich. I'm— what did you say, Morris?"

"You functionally have the national GDP of several smaller nations."

"Yeah, that!" She pointed. "So, I'm satisfied. More of this, please..." She tapped the glass.

Mr. Anonymous gladly refilled her and added a small umbrella for décor.

"Unfortunately, we can't do anything about your condition of being dead. Metallic Jack tried to warn and upload you prior to the ... evolution of our society," he intoned. "The best we can do is facilitate some equitable transactions." Jane could feel him staring at Akira, who was following the silicon lifeform from three paces away with an unblinking gaze. "Can you tell your S-class vampire assassin that killing this body will do nothing to damage the mainframe?"

"Akira…" Jane scolded. "Pete—I mean, Mr. Anonymous is a friend. We kinda killed the Lord of Suicide together." *Albeit smothering and ripping me to shreds in the process.*

"Where are the cats?" Akira asked. "I haven't seen. Any. Not a one."

Mr. Anonymous shook his head. "Living creatures with red blood attract the hungry. Both for meat, blood, and magic. We found that all mammalian human companions are unnecessary within these walls. Thus, we sold them. All."

Jane felt a moment of heartbreak over the fate of her apartment of cats and wondered just who would steal her scrunchies.

"Monster." Akira leaned closer.

"I've been called many things by punks and anarchists. Monster is one of my favorites." Anonymous clinked a metal glass filled with liquid glass against Akira's cocktail. "Every time one of our facilities gets blown up or someone takes down a distribution center, our profits go up. But," he set his drink down and clasped his hands, "let's talk business, shall we? Time is of the essence."

Jane spied Vryce leaning forward *just* a fraction. Ever since they took the elevator, Vryce had not made a single peep. Even his eyes were both glamoured to appear regular brown.

"We need you to bomb New Orleans," Jane said bluntly. "Missiles will work. There is nobody left *in* the city but the Lord of Misfortune."

"Lucian Montague," Anonymous intoned. "Lazarus brought him out of retirement, did he now?" He clicked his tongue and lifted the mask, revealing a handsome black man with neat eyeliner and clear blue eyes that glowed. He sipped the liquid in his glass, which traced geometric lines in the unnatural veins along his cheeks before fading. "The Church of Lazarus has many ambitions. Killing our satellites and blacking out global communications is one of their unending usages of magic. We would very much like to annihilate another of his Death Lords, but there is a problem with the maneuver."

Morris folded his leg over another and lit up a smoke, and let everyone find a seat either at the opulent table or chairs lining the

large glass windows. "A problem money can't solve, I assume. So, let's talk the old currency. Information and power... what solves the problem, bub?"

Anonymous winked at Jane. "I like this one. The problem is that if we unload enough of our arsenal to kill a Death Lord, then the Archive, Ravenous, or the Society of Deus will see an opportunity to attack us. Our co-existence on this continent is plagued with inherent ideological differences with only the Church of Lazarus as a unifying front. Ironic that they were once called the Unification, we are aware."

"What if—" Jane slammed her drink. "What if I could leave you a prize at the end of the rainbow that might unify everyone?" She could *feel* Vryce boring a hole through the back of her head.

"We are always ready to listen to our star."

Jane rose and paced. "Okay, so beneath Purgatory there, they have a bunch of these ol' chained up gods, right? Well, not REAL gods, kinda like mascot gods, I think. I dunno, Paul Bunyan must have been someone important, but I'd take Mothman any day."

"Yes, their blood farm." Anon tilted his glass for her to continue.

"Right. That. So, you have all these new companies that, really, is anyone buying from? I mean, don't you just ship everything out and it gets looted anyway?"

"It's a long-term investment. If everyone dies, there is no market," he acquiesced.

"So, what if your companies help free the gods and get them rebranded and reset into modern day instead of ancient history? Then, you'll have ambassadors, good ones, that can brand products and go into all those places that don't want your tech. I mean, I'm sure there is a god of magic buried down there, and it could go a long way to being friends with the Society if ya put on a little friendlier smile."

Vryce's eye twitched.

Jane had slowly begun picking up on an ever-growing list of things that caused Vryce's eye to twitch and added binding gods to contracts to her mental checklist. Although, she wasn't sure if it was

the act of binding, or more than he wasn't in charge of the contract. *Does he simply want to be in charge, or is it a magic thingy with him? Like, I figure someone with his reputation has probably bound some creatures into his service against their will.*

"There will have to be contracts." Anonymous didn't say no.

"Entirely. Contracts." Jane's ponytail bobbed as she smiled, extending a hand. "And missiles."

"The Second City and Sons and Daughters will have to introduce any new ambassadors on our behalf to others. Your lot is ... more welcome." He pulled off a black glove.

"If you pay us for our services, of course," Jane wasn't going to give in that easy, "at a fee to be negotiated later. I'll also need my old chains back. Those runic badboys are somewhere here in a vault, I wager?"

Cautiously, Anon circled Jane. "Yes... they are. There is an inherent risk. These ... gods ... upon being freed could be unwilling. Integration is never smooth. We feel they would look at our citizens as nothing more than walking rocks or objects. You'll take no issue with the use of binding magic?"

Jane removed her hand. "I'm not selling prisoners from one place into another. I'm giving you a seat at the table to talk to them, buddy. Miss out, and I'll just have to march to the Society and see if their army is willing to come down..." Jane rocked back and forth on the balls of her feet.

"Very well. We can accept these terms. Even if the freed deities seek employment elsewhere, we are certain that our offerings will be pleasing." He extended his hand formally.

And just like that. We've got bombs. Jane shook on it, grinning from ear to ear.

CHAPTER 19

The magical lamp is simply an oil-burning lamp with a wick used in more archaic times to illuminate an area of work at night. Yet the old papyrus texts show-case the Hermetic tradition of the lamp being used for divination. You may have seen helldivers carrying oil lanterns before a descent into Purgatory. Oils, incense, and intent can allow a wielder to utilize light for both illumination and protection with one caveat—never paint your lantern red. Brass lamps with red ochre is the liturgical color of Set-Typhon, a divine force to be avoided by magicians of antiquity.

—Society of Deus class notes

Vryce played by every rule while inside Dystopia. He never spoke. He never channeled. He even refused entry into several buildings. Yet when he sat across from Peter Culmen, aka Mr. Anonymous, he bled slightly—from biting his tongue. Before they left, he was studious enough to ensure he left not a single hair or object anywhere within the city, for doing so would be a certain invitation to scrying magic.

No matter how glamorous or elaborate the construction of Peter's cities were—they were empty shells. Vryce was torn between

mourning a fellow colleague and general contempt for how much a once-great warlock had fallen. Peter was the youngest of the ten warlocks created by the Unification and, in his naïveté, was one of three warlocks who never joined Vryce's rebellion. Peter's refusal wasn't out of loyalty to the Unification, but out of firm belief that his fusion of Sacred Geometry with these computers could usher humanity into a new age—and the societies of the Unification were willing to bankroll it. *I wonder if his soul resides somewhere on the edge of oblivion, waiting to be pulled back and stitched to the frame of Mr. Anonymous.*

Unfortunately, it was a question that Vryce didn't have time to explore. For starters, Mr. Anonymous' silicon-based lifeforms were a perfect sentry, and Vryce had to admit they were better than his gargoyles. But also, the opportunist was about to have first access to the Church of Lazarus's vault of local gods, and as Vryce power walked through the exit, he was already planning the end of his vacation. *I brought magic back so WE could be the gods, not restore a bunch of failures. But if I can get my hands on them and stitch them into gargoyles... or new blades... Power always has purpose.*

He barely paid attention to Jane or the rest of her lackeys during his warpath march back to the van, and as soon as he got to the rusted death bucket, his backpack, viola, and coat were instantly chucked into the back as he rolled up his sleeves in front of their vehicle all the way past the Dystopian slums and just past the official border that marked Mr. Anonymous' domain.

"Dagger," he commanded.

Everyone seemed pretty unsure of who he was talking to.

His eyes rolled. "I would like one of you kids to hand me a dagger or knife, please. I need to contact my children."

Lucy flipped an ax out of her thigh belt and glowered behind her heavy black eye shadow. "Is this where you betray us?"

If only you were worth such an honor. Vryce untied his ponytail and grabbed the ax with haste. "Unfortunately, no, but you hired the wrong army."

Jane smirked but was more interested in hugging a black attaché case with band stickers like it was a special prize. Even Vryce had to admit it was. *Magical chains that once bound Odin's wolves? Those will come in handy.*

Phoebe just flopped on her bike. "Oh, here we go, the big boy pissing match is about to begin. My ArMy iS bEtTeR tHaN tHeIr ArMy."

"Actually," Vryce sliced the backside of his hand, dripping several droplets of his blood in a reinforced water bottle from his pack, "not so. Dystopia's army most likely exceeds any military force except the Ravenous remnants of the U.S. It's a matter of application. What exactly do you think is going to happen when you allow them to sign contracts with gods and legends?"

Jane replied while she opened the case, clutching the glowing violet chains as if they were old friends, and nearly instantly commanding them to her will with a simple flick of the wrist. "They make some gods very happy and rich, and we kill a Death Lord."

"Incorrect." Vryce flicked his fingers, summoned a flame under his bottle, and set it down inside the van to boil. "You kill a Death Lord and make Dystopia the world's greatest enemy. Anyone without a god now needs one. You set Lazarus's sights squarely upon the Americas with the full fury of the remaining twelve Lords—and *hope* that everyone is strong enough to resist."

Doc Daneka and Akira both curiously peered into the simmering water bottle as Vryce shooed them back. Doc though, always eager for a debate, tugged at his neck skin and stood across from Vryce. "Throughout history, due to the two oceans that surround the continental United States, a military invasion is extremely difficult. What also says we won't be taking the fight to the Church of Lazarus? Plus, if anyone has a chance to restore global communications so we can garner allies—it's the technocats."

"Technocrats," Jane corrected.

Vryce wrapped up his hand and began violently shivering from the cold air setting into his small frame. *Nighttime is never pleasant.* He was the only one present whose glasses fogged up from breathing, and that was still an odd sensation to him. Possessing bodies was natural, but two years of being *forced* to breathe for existence paled in comparison to the several hundred being immortal. The one problem he had yet to overcome was *thinking* like a human and not an undead creature. Half the time, he forgot to blink until the annoying sting happened to remind him that yes, his eyeballs did need liquid. It was tedious. "I'm not saying ... impossible. I'm ... saying ... incendiary. Ergo... we ... let ... everyone ... else know."

Phoebe couldn't help but feel sympathy, grabbed a pink sweater from her rucksack, and offered it over. "I still can't believe that you are some heathen warlock who broke the world and became a lich, and yet here you sit, a shivering teenager ill-equipped for road travel."

Vryce glared as he snatched the sweater and folded his arms up within. "Thank ... you. I suppose, everyone can b-b-be a surprise." He warmed his hands over the boiling water and then suddenly knelt over it, draping the sweater over his head while beginning a small chant in Latin. The spell he cast was simple but highly practical: whisper to those of his blood. Given his age, Vryce often wondered if someday he'd whisper into the wind and hear a response from a descendent several lines away, but today, he knew at least two would hear it. *Gabriel D'Angelo and Delilah Dumont. Ruthless to the core and currently holding my Swords of Deus, which I rather desperately need at the minute.*

When Vryce spoke, it was almost at a whisper, but he knew that wouldn't stop anyone from eavesdropping. "I hope this Lilith Moon finds your endeavors tonight fortunate. Our reunion, unfortunately, must be hastened. The Death Lord Lucian Montague, Lord of Misfortune, along with the Church of Lazarus's armies from the Lord of Murder have arrived within New Orleans. The army has dispatched elsewhere. The Sons and Daughters, yes, including Mike and Jane

Auburn, have taken up the fight—but also granted Mr. Anonymous first crack at the well of gods for their artillery support. I trust… I'll see you both soon, but please do not kill each other en route with your respective armies. Now isn't the time for an otherwise healthy rivalry."

As soon as Vryce finished, he rose and looked out at the motley crew. "Alright. You've bought my services with the heart of the Cherubim. But you." He pointed right at Jane. "You need training in the magic available only to ghosts. Purgatory Manipulation. Because of this, you are banned from driving while you are in lessons with me. You lot, you need to practice fighting from the disadvantage of misfortune. Everything that can go wrong will go wrong. The only way to win is to ensure that every loss is also a victory, and that means playing the field."

Akira scooted closer with her eyes widening even farther. "Teach me how to kill faster, Daddy."

Ahem? Vryce recoiled. "I … am not your father? So please, Elder to you. Still, I'm feeling generous. Here's what I see. Akira, you are a vampire with a plague demon heart. Shapechanging and speed are your primary skills, but you are impulsive and act with haste. You should hide and wait. Lucy, you are clearly a tactical helldiver, practically a wight with solid command over basic rituals, but you feel the need to rescue everyone around you rather than make sacrifices. Stop that. Doctor Daneka, you're an emotional vampire who feasts upon both pain and happiness, a rare talent that allows you to survive as an immortal in nearly any society without tipping your hand. Learn how to blend in. Phoebe, your prophecy and insight are powerful fate magic. You need to actually enroll in divination classes to master that talent but compared to the power of your companions in battle—you offer nothing. Fashion gargoyles to guard you so you can focus on reading a fight while it's live and unfolding around you rather than attempting to be useful. It's like watching a kitten paw an elephant."

Edward Morris casually flicked a Zippo open and shut while leaning on the side of the van. "Forget about me?"

"Not at all." Vryce grabbed Jane by her collar and dragged her into the back of the van. "You and your boss are already playing the game. You wait, you stay in the shadows, and you mind control where it's appropriate. Mental manipulation and memory altering is a valuable asset—but it only works on those weaker than you. So frankly, survive another three hundred years."

Jane squealed as Vryce pulled her in, but everyone else sighed that Jane wasn't driving anymore. Once seated, Vryce claimed a spot in the back-body directly opposite of Jane on the small bench and leaned in. "Tell me the exact minute these bombs are supposed to drop upon Samhain."

"Tomorrow at 9:03." She counted and nodded. "So, what am I learning until then?"

Only everything I can teach you in the span of one day. Vryce pulled forth some papyrus and Hermetic Myrrh ink with a few droplets of angelic vitae from the heart. The formula of celestial language he intoned nobody understood around him as his smile grew wicked and wide. He ignored everything around him while writing out a lesson plan upon the papyrus before rolling it up and sticking it within his boiled water thermos and handing it to Jane. "This water was taken from seven different springs, cleansed, boiled, and now enchanted. Drink a cup every night on an empty stomach for the next seven days, but only when the moon is rising to the east. When it's done, you'll know the basics of Purgatory Manipulation."

Janes nose scrunched. "You want me to drink your blood?"

"If only I was still vampiric. Back then it was a prize." He sighed. "I don't have five years to teach you the basic formula and thesis behind manipulating the barrier between world or warping Purgatory to your whim, so... we are taking a shortcut. I hate shortcuts. When this is over," he held her hands, "I promise you this, Jane Auburn: I will erase your memory. Knowledge is a power earned, not given. Enjoy it while it lasts, but when it's over—you will have to learn the old-fashioned way." Vryce could feel his smile grow and a fire warm his belly. He

actually enjoyed teaching, even if he was known to be harsh. "Now that we have settled that matter, let's begin. What do you know about the history of Purgatory?"

Lucy and Akira jumped in the van's back seat as Morris and Doc took the front. The door slammed shut, and the rusted death bucket shook itself to life with a violent lurch and the smell of gasoline and exhaust mixing through the rusted cracks Akira picked at on their way here.

Vryce enjoyed watching Jane gulp as eyes were suddenly upon her, and he leaned back onto a wooden slat.

"Um. History? Of... Purgatory." Jane's ponytail bobbed as she nodded. "Right. Okay. So, you see. Persephone and Hades wanted to shag, and pomegranates were a part of this, so they made fruit juice that allowed you to cross between the realms. People who experience death or near-death experiences often see into their realm, but ever since Persephone's Pomegranates, that you can buy for $9.99, a single bite allows you to peer across and wave to your grandma." Her eyes had become saucers as she knew damn well her answer was wildly off.

It was a long, perfectly calm van ride for Jane.

"So let me get this straight," Jane said while fixing the knowledge-bottle to a backpack as she jumped out onto the pavement. "Humans created Purgatory because we don't know what to do?"

They had parked along the Mississippi River between a cargo control facility and the Pitstop Saloon a few miles outside of the city proper. Several rusted shipping containers were piled sloppily along the riverbank, and despite the orange lantern glow from the Saloon, the suburban neighborhood was a ghost town. Yet by climbing a few containers, everyone could observe the explosions downstream from a safe distance, and still be close enough to race in.

The black sun had just peeked over the horizon, its distorted rays causing shadows to spring to life, flickering violently as the silent peace of nighttime was banished by the rise of an abomination that spread darkness across the land. Jane admired Vryce against the grayed rays of morning. Despite their travels, and no change of clothes available, the hand-stitched peacoat he wore was still perfectly tailored, and as he cleaned his glasses off, he carried himself with an air of command. If it wasn't for the neatly tied ponytail and otherwise obvious feminine features in his youthful angular face—Jane would never have assumed that Vryce was anything *but* an ancient vampire. It only added to his mystique that he was the only person standing in the middle of the road that had seven shadows, and not a single one matched his current frame. *Girl. Stop it. You have a date with a vampire. You are just wishing you could command a room with the same poise. That's all.*

"In summary. They," Vryce palmed out to the world at large, "create their own gods and prisons. The creator above long ago abdicated the throne, and creatures like us are merely passengers with the power to shape the world." He smirked. "Well, creatures like you anyway." Vryce closed his eyes and inhaled deeply, relishing the morning air.

Lucy tapped Phoebe off her bike and straddled the crotch rocket before flipping open a chained silver pocket watch. "So, we've got fifteen hours. I'm going to cross to the other side and mobilize everyone else. Remember, if there is an opening, with him here," she nodded to Vryce, "this side is basically its own army. So, take the shot. If shit goes tits up, then we fall back to the tent city outside Houston. It's closest and safe. Hopefully, we will meet in the middle."

"Lucy, wait!" Jane ran over and fiddled with the helldiver's hoodie, tucking in her auburn-red hair and pulling up the collar on her leather as she leaned closer. "Listen, I'm pretty sure this is a crazy plan. But I want you to make sure of something for me at the Waffle House, okay?"

Lucy appeared unamused. "You're going to tell me to leave the magical fucking coat behind, aren't you?"

"Whaaa, noooo." *Jeesh, way to call it, woman.* "Okay, yes. Look, Vryce said something about turning losses into victories. If things go haywire, Mike is still there in the city. If we pull out and take his coat with us, he really won't have any chance in hell."

"I'm all for being a pessimist, Jane, trust me, out of all of us here—that's this bitch. But, call me crazy, I actually think this plan of yours has merit. It's a solid plan, and who knew you are not only rich enough to buy several batteries, but also had the connections? JK." Lucy fist bumped. "You did well on this one. Now go learn some magic. If it really does go haywire, I'll leave it in the freezer."

That's going to make me all sappy now. Jane gave a small wave as Lucy peeled away before turning her attention back to Vryce. Meanwhile, the others were gathering lawn chairs and hunting for small imps to make beverages from. "So, we've got the time. Should we, you know, get started?" she asked politely.

Vryce looked up at Jane and folded his arms. "Fine. Sit." He pointed down right in the middle of the road.

"Now?" Jane looked over to Akira for clarification. She was no help as she eagerly snapped open a lawn chair on top of a shipping container. *Ah, screw it. What's the worst that can happen? I get hit by ONE car in New Orleans.* She sat down.

"Now that you know the history, and you also know that you can see within the lands of the dead when others can't, here's your secret." Vryce sharply grabbed her head and twisted her view to face New Orleans. "You don't need blood to manipulate, view, or alter Purgatory. In fact, celestial blood makes it harder. For people who brush with death enough, first master the ability to see into it at will. Then cross over at will. Then alter its landscape at will. You've got a natural leg up by your lineage, but that doesn't make you special. You're just likely to have near death experiences your whole life." Vryce walked out of the road, brushed off a spot of pavement, and sat upon his viola case. "Ergo, you need to get hit by a car."

"Nani?!" Jane looked down the road and back. "Buddy, I don't think you got the memo, but most people have evacuated and also a little warning! What if I go sploosh! Or... or..." She didn't really know what to say.

"The idea that it's empty is exactly what you want to tell yourself, Jane. Didn't you see a bunch of cars still leaving?" Vryce cracked open a vial of vitae. "Look again, and remember the panic of how people drive when running from something."

Jane recalled the traffic they saw miles closer to Dystopia and still didn't believe Vryce was going to summon a vehicle just to hit her, but when she looked back, a yellow Mini Cooper filled with luggage zipped out from behind the Saloon and hit the gas. The driver clearly saw Jane but had zero problems accelerating through a ghost and refused to swerve. *MOTHER FUCK!* Jane jumped, but it was too late.

Seconds before impact, the view of Purgatory flooded into Jane's view, revealing the historic carnage from a hurricane that devastated the neighborhood years ago. She winced, bracing for an impact that never came. When her eyes opened, the world had returned to normal, and both Doc and Morris were now sitting next to Vryce.

"I'd like to think," Vryce said with a tinge of pride, "I could even teach these two a thing about mental manipulation. Even if you disbelieve me with every ounce of that pretty little heart of yours... I can make you believe nearly anything." Vryce snapped, and Jane relived the past moment. Again. And again. For hours.

By the time nightfall set in, Doc and Morris had nearly filled up a notebook each on different tricks, but they argued over application. Jane was certain her hair had to be white by the end of it, or at the very least, her skin had to be as pale as a banshee.

"Hey, sparkle eyes!" Akira shouted. "I think it's starting!" Akira and Phoebe both waved from atop their pile of containers and furiously pointed at the sky.

Oh, thank Walmart. I need a break... Jane raced out of the road, hopping over a wooden railing that only existed in Purgatory, and

scaled the containers. Sure enough, the western horizon was filled with balls of light trailing through the sky in neat horizontal lines, leaving behind trails of billowing smoke as they burned toward their destination.

Everyone seemed to hold their breath and silently cheer as they congregated above the Mississippi bank. Jane needed this to work. "Come on, Anon, don't let mama down. Let's go beauties..." She continued praying and bouncing as they watched the missile barrage encroach closer to the city. The ruins of Samhain showed no mysterious or ghostly signs of a counterattack in Jane's eyes. Beautiful, aged buildings from yesteryear superseding over the modern-but-weathered modern structures of the skyline wielded no anti-air defenses or crazy cultists casting spells of defense.

"Is it too soon to be hopeful?" Akira asked, tugging on Jane's sleeve.

"Can you count them? How many are there?" Phoebe tried rattling off what they could see... "Ten... twenty... hundred?"

"Impressive," Vryce mused. "Redundant." He pointed to the second and third waves coming into view.

"THAT'S WHAT I'M TALKING ABOUT!" Jane cheered and started punching the air in excitement. "EAT FIREBALL, FUCKERS!"

The first explosions shattered the modern skyline of New Orleans in a cascade of thunder. The clear night sky was filled with embers of orange and hot-blue flames that melted concrete of the tallest buildings. Jane watched as several buildings instantly exploded into concrete dust from the modern world and became apocalyptic pillars of history within Purgatory right before her very eyes. *All my years peeking into Purgatory, I don't think I've ever watched buildings cross over in real time. It's so friggin' cool! I mean, except for the loss of buildings in the real world, I suppose. Then again...new jobs?*

The rockets of the second barrage suddenly turned green in color and exploded into hundreds of swerving mini missiles that crossed the barrier into Purgatory and hammered into the very lands of the

dead. This time, Jane heard screams of demons, cryptids, and as much as she tried to avoid it—anyone remaining above in Samhain.

"Spirit bombs..." Vryce judged.

"They are cracking open a portal to the prison," Phoebe said. "I can feel it... in my fuzzy brain part." She shot her gaze up with wonder at the third wave. Her bright purple hair reflected the dancing flames of the burning city behind her. "This is needed for events."

Vryce took a few steps to the left near the edge of the container. "Yet this is where it ends."

The ground beneath them shook as metal violently clashed with shrapnel from a nearby explosion. The deafening explosion of the Saloon caused Jane's ears to ring as she was showered in dust. The hanging lantern on the door, now broken, clattered at her feet. Looking up, Jane saw the third wave of rockets had gone haywire, like a swarm of buzzing wasps that flew wildly in every possible direction.

A red light washed over all of them, right as Jane watched an Avalon Arms Bunker Buster explode fifty feet above them. All she could do was cover her head and listen to the sound of a thousand balls of shrapnel pepper the containers around them—yet none touched her.

There was a massive shadow standing over Jane. Looking up, she saw the largest black creature made from pure onyx with a twelve-foot wingspan shielding everyone. To the left, Vryce was privately guarded by a winged creature carved from jet-black obsidian, and to the right, a jade feminine monster guarded Akira.

From the red door that opened suddenly at the edge of the container, a figure wearing a porcelain white mask, a black trench that went down to her heels, and a small black sword wielded by pristine white gloves with arcane markets strolled forward. Jane knew the figure all too well. A ghost from her past stepped forth from thin air, bringing guardians and death. *Oh shit.* "It's the Praenomen," she whispered to herself.

"Yes, and Gabriel." The black gargoyle shielding her from shrapnel looked down, and Jane realized that his winter blue eyes were perhaps the only human feature on the massive creature whose voice sounded deep and baritone. "You are lucky," he comforted and gave Jane a squeeze on her shoulder that certainly did not match the tone of his voice. Jane felt it was to prevent her from starting a fight. *Body guards and bouncers all have the same attitude. Remain calm, but I'll throw you if I have to.* She huffed.

"Master," the curt British female accent came from behind the mask, "I think it's time for a tactical retreat, no?" She was already walking back into her portal, taking the hand of a bright-blond sorcerer with a calvary saber strapped to his back on the other side. Jane didn't know where that other location was, but it certainly wasn't under a stream of hellfire.

"Wait." Vryce calmly held up a finger while picking up his viola case. "Phoebe. What do you see?"

The look on Phoebe's face screamed panic, that she wanted to run, but she was frozen between the gargoyles who never once winced at the pain from heated shrapnel and concrete ricocheting off their wings. "That we need to go, NOW!"

"Tell me your vision. Now." When Vryce spoke, it was a command. Phoebe obeyed.

"The only way we win is if you take a knee before Daneka's champion. And trust me, I'm just as confused about how Daneka has a champion!" She gestured over to Doc with tears welling up in her eyes.

"I see." Vryce's lips pressed thin. "Perhaps Phoebe, that's not the Daneka your vision refers to." Vryce circled his finger. Every gargoyle took flight and retreated through the red door except the one made of liquid shadow personally guarding the teenage frame of its master. "You can all *stay* if you so wish, but I would suggest that you move."

Jane and everyone ran through the red door as the world around them became flame kissed. Where the door took them, Jane knew it was near Texas, but it was only a passing thought as she saw Doc

suddenly clutching his mouth, and Morris grabbing Akira by the waist. Everyone was looking behind Jane through the red door.

What? No. Fuck no... don't say it. Jane looked behind her and saw Phoebe standing there at the edge of the container—frozen in fear. Tears streamed down her cheeks, and Phoebe held two fingers up as her hand quivered in a peace-out sign. "PHOEBE!" Jane shrieked.

The Praenomen waved the door out of existence before anyone brave enough raced back or the flames that washed over Pheobe would consume the rest of them. "Unfortunate."

Akira was frenzying and flailing with bloody tears streaming down her face. She clawed at the air where the door was and battled those attempting to hold her in place, shapechanging constantly from giant insect to normal human as everyone nearby scrambled to keep Akira from bounding back in.

Jane fell to her knees against the backdrop of Akira's howls. Vryce put his hand upon her shoulder. "A prophet's final words are their most important. We have a path to victory."

His words carried only the slightest hint of sorrow.

CHAPTER 20

"Fear not, I am the first and the last, 12 and the living one. I died, and behold I am alive forevermore, and I have the keys to Death and Hades. Know thus, the events played out before the eyes of innocents, and the events to come for the blasphemers will be washed away upon this forsaken land. Together, we will journey into the Kingdom of Heaven and feast upon the Tree of Life and drink from the Tree of Knowledge. With your faith, we banish interlopers upon our world, and to do so—we need only your peaceful repose."

Church of Lazarus Sermon –The Vatican

Lucian watched the loose brick fall unceremoniously and dent his golden throne. *Et tu, Ceiling? I hath not harmed thee!* He scurried through the maze of forgotten treasures like an expert hoarder, navigating precarious paths without delay, leading Mike and Lumine deeper into his sanctum. "Bombs? Why didn't you warn me they had bombs, Michael? I take you in, show you the wonders of Samhain, and BOOM. Your friends try and blow us up. They must not like you."

The ceiling shook violently, causing larger blocks to crash down, displacing the mountains of jewelry and oddities, and ruining Lucian's chaotic organization system. Explosions continued to annihilate the

216

surface at an increasing pace, a firework show of violence pummeling the real world into oblivion. An oblivion Lucian happened to very much enjoy. The reek of Samhain leaked into Purgatory as the spirit bombs dropped, hanging like a hot summer day three years ago. Steam rose from the sewer gates above to release pressure as gaping holes into Purgatory itself brought the city above to the below. Corpses left behind by the Church of Lazarus rained down like methane-filled husks into Lucian's world. A world he desperately wanted his misfortunate souls to find someday.

Crawling onto his throne, Lucian tipped the entire thing backward into a sea of crowns as the sewer lines busted above him in the physical world but flowed down freely into a completely exposed Purgatory. Lying on his back, staring up at the night sky, Lucian opened the buttons on his ripped-up suit coat and wiggled his toes within his worn sandals. He gazed into the fractured night sky under Lilith's Moon and began to giggle, as for the first time in his existence—his world was revealed. His very soul felt on fire, and he writhed in pain and tears as each bomb exploded a bit of his history. Giggles gave way to tears as treasures were crushed and long loyal demonic jailers were incinerated. Lucian laughed and wildly looked at Mike and Lumine as death was marching for them all at last.

The madness and beast of survival railed on his bones, but death was finally coming. *I have wanted you for so long. Take my hand, lover.* Lucian lay there, gaining insight on the purpose of this upcoming death with his hand outstretched as if he could pluck the very missiles from the air. *Will this be the end of Samhain's young life? How will the souls here transition to what lies ahead? Is this all I was ever meant to build?*

His lips peeled back as he snarled. "But what of Dystopia? Perhaps it is they who wish death, and they are clearly showing fear of death... right?" he asked nobody in particular. "They continue the cycle of violence for their own survival. Oh, Lady Fate, let us end this. I've thrived in misery for so long. I am wiser and older now than when I was a young boy. I've woken up. Is this where I sleep?"

Lucian slid on his hated friend, the Mask of Misfortune, and peered through the ancient coins coldly pressing against his withered skin and gazed at the threads of fate. The Seat of Golden Tears became a tapestry of strands reaching out across the world—each treasure tied to a lost soul. Some alive, some dead, but it mattered not to the Death Lord. "Be free, my children." With a single twist, he grasped an invisible strand from a missile arcing down and led it into the next. The chain reaction of misfortune unfolded. With a cackle, Lucian scrambled blindly to every strand of fate he could see from above. For every strand he grasped, a treasure withered and died from pile, and Lucian felt one of his lost souls be set free somewhere in the world. *You are free to die at last. I'm sorry you never found salvation, children.* The tears continued to flow as Lucian channeled every fragment of energy he could to twist Dystopia's well-laid plans into a ball of unsortable chaos.

Tears that wished one missile would strike true. Perhaps Lucian wondered, that here on his throne, covered in sewage, that Peter Culmen's science could be the end of Misfortune. *If everything has a place, then remove the bug in your code, technomancer.*

No such missile came.

The world was quiet. Not even Mike and Lumine made a peep as Lucian watched the embers of fire kiss the sky as he mourned for every lost soul. Thousands of treasures were reduced to ash in this war that Lazarus commanded, and Lucian grappled with feelings of rage, sorrow, and laughter at the absurdity of it all. *Of COURSE I DON'T DIE!* "Is this what you want, world? You want me to end your pain?" His hand flopped to his side. "Maybe Heaven's Wrath is right," he said quietly.

Minutes passed as buildings continued to collapse in the physical world, with some fading into Purgatory as a hollowed fragment of their former selves. Lucian heard the clatter of coins as Mike and Lumine each came into his vision above him. Mike scratched his stubble and looked up at one of many gaping holes. "Ya know, I

probably know some workers who could fix that right up for you." He extended a hand down. "I've got bad news for you: you aren't dead."

Lumine choked on dust and peeked out of the mountain of debris she hid herself on, only popping the top of her head out to verify that she wasn't the only one still moving. "I'm not dead either," she whispered meekly.

Lucian wiped a tear from behind the mask and looked into Mike's brown eyes that carried the same spark of curiosity and wonder about the world as a golden retriever pup. *Not taking the cheap shot?* It was probably for the best. Once the strands of fate were jumbled, nothing ever went a person's way. Lucian accepted the hand and was pulled halfway up, before Mike's other fingerless glove plowed into his face, smashing him back down.

"Coward." Mike grabbed Lucian's shirt and ripped him off the ground. Lucian's boots dangled in the air. "All you had to do was nothing."

Lucian's left ear had an annoying ring as his vision came back into focus. "OWW! What gives?!" He looked down at Mike, the black bandanna he wore was covered in dust, and the stocky ghost had no problems rattling Lucian back and forth like a bag of bones.

"What was that, eh? Heaven's Wrath was right? Is that what I heard you say?" Mike punched him again, knocking dust out of Lucian's lungs with a heavy cough. *That ... really hurt.* Through the pain, Lucian realized he didn't see a single strand of fate upon the ghost. In the chaos of his magic, Lucian must have grabbed everything nearby and tangled it all up—or even severed them. *Okay. That's a new one.*

"Listen, buddy," Lucian went limp in Mike's hands, dangling like a drying shirt, "hit me. Stab me. Kiss me. Fuck me. Use me. I'm worthless."

The leather of Mike's gloves creaked as his grip tightened in frustration before he shook Lucian violently and threw him to the side with a scream. "Motherfucker." Mike grabbed Lucian's Zippo and

fished out a half-smoked cigar as Lucian lay there. "How are you worthless?" He lit it up out of annoyance and plopped down into the wet treasure heap that was now a mix of ash.

Lucian lay there, letting the sting of jewelry clamps poke into his bones. "Lords of Death have but one job. Guard our souls until they move on. My army, the beggars and paupers of the world, the unlucky kings or forgotten children ... is the smallest. Their downfall is immortalized here at my Seat. I keep their treasures until they discover them—or let them go. Then they move on to peace." Lucian saw a small jade ring and plucked it from a pile of ash that remained from several others around it. He looked through the center where an inscription said *half-my-soul* upon it and cleaned out the grime. "My curse, I bear, to free others. When I tamper with fate on such a grand scale, I burn their memories as fuel. I've never once freed them in such a way. Now, they will fade into the abyss. An abyss jealous of creation itself, for it was never made. An abyss teetering on the edges of our universe, wishing only its noisy neighbor would turn off the lights." Lucian flicked the ring elsewhere, passively wondering if the sliver of abyss he summoned into this world was somewhere below, feasting.

"Alright fuck stick, how does killing everyone help you guard their souls?" Mike's hands twirled. "Walk me through this grand plan of yours. It's not like you've got somewhere to be, right?"

Lucian sat up, only to be shocked by Lumine with her trinket-filled hair in braids sitting cross-legged right in front of him. She nodded at the request. *Ugh, fine.* Lucian fiddled with sewage slick coating his fingers and sighed. *At least the smell isn't so bad.*

"The purpose of misfortune was always to make the fortunate moments stand out. Demons," Lucian gestured to the prison in the distance, "test happiness by bringing sorrow, for example. When we were a young council of Unification, we discovered divine secrets that could usurp the seats of arch-devils and wield their power. Unlike demons and devils which endlessly, per their very nature, test and meddle with mortals—our guidance could usher souls back into the

cycle. We thought ourselves as shepherds and gods of the afterlife. Each seeking what salvation looked like for the billions of souls that die over the ages. Then we fucked up."

"What did you do?" Mike called him out.

"Bit on the nose, no?" Lucian clutched his heart. "Fair though. Then *I* fucked up. I broke the world by playing fair. Little things. Letting an old hermetic lose a spell book here, or letting a djinn grant wishes, and so forth. As centuries went on, I would cause small misfortune leaks of divine secrets, the Unification's secrets into the world. When I was young, I thought, 'Gee Lucian, it sure doesn't make sense that all magic is in the hands of these lucky few.' So, I spread it around a little."

Mike's mood shifted, and even his gaze fell to his shit-covered boots. "Yeah. I get that."

"So of course, the secret societies grew and just recruited everyone else. Century by century until the world was controlled in secret by mortals high on power. God, whichever one you want to pray to, fought back in their own way... but even they fell in time. Ergo, a madman in the fifties came up with a perfect plan to seal the deal—bring back Lazarus as God. One of their own into an empty world. Now of course," Lucian punched Mike's shoulder, "I laughed my ass off at this and let it unfold. Sure, why the fuck not! What could go wrong?!" Lucian flailed his arms at their broken surroundings.

Mike glared. "You could have stopped it? Really?"

"Not a fucking chance. From my eyes, I didn't need to. It was never going to work. Lazarus wasn't going to come back, and the entire thing was doomed to fail from the start." He shrugged. "Then of course, the fucker comes back."

"Mmm, what if... he didn't?" Mike fiddled with the Zippo, opening and closing it in time with drips of water splattering down near them.

"Doesn't matter if it's real or not, buddy. Divinity is belief. So, thus, Heaven's Wrath is right. The only way to set things back to normal is to end everyone and reset the wheel." Lucian stood up. "Which means we've got a lot of world to burn."

"You fucking zealots." Mike rose to match him and stepped inches away from Lucian. "Grand plans for little gain. You need some demons' blood to cast a fly spell? Bitch, we made jets. Angels' blood to send a message across a nation? We have cell phones. You didn't break shit in the world. We did. We let you guys run the show and keep us satiated with sex, TV, and body dysmorphia. Now when we have a chance to build the world we want, what does your scared little Church want but to put everything back in a bottle? Nah, it isn't you who is going to fix this world. It's us. Because it's our world. You're just outsiders with dog leashes on our necks."

Lumine, feeling left out, put on a cute angry face and joined the duo. "You have the power to help us survive, so use it!"

Lucian couldn't help but feel charmed. It always seemed to him that the best people were those who suffered. They had the best perspectives on life—it sucked, but at least there was cheese. *I miss cheese.* He clicked his teeth for a minute and plotted his next move. Mike and Lumine did have several valid points, but they were misplaced. There was no stopping an eternally growing army from Lazarus and the rest of the council. Not without the power of gods.

Lucian snapped.

"Alright, kiddies, hear me out here. Samhain no longer has a hat, and that's a crime. A crime against good fashion everywhere. All these little gods here are going to catch a cold. If you really want to prevent the cycle, we DO need to kill. If we don't, then someone will swoop right down here and go *nibble nibble* on deified booty. So, let's blow up Chicago." Lucian tried to start skipping away but didn't make it more than an arm's reach away before Mike tugged him back.

"Chicago. No." Mike dangled Lucian again with one arm.

"You were nicer when I had you bound," Lucian choked. *I need to eat more. I'm just bones! Not fair.*

"Yeah well, guess you got unlucky. Why Chicago?"

"Why not?" Lucian shrugged. "Look *le pote*, the Second City has a whole gigantic thriving underworld, one of the hottest purgatories

out there. I'll just move my seat there, and then we have a hat again, the gods and treasures are safe, and *wooosh*, just like that—your bony homey did his job of keeping souls safe."

"How about we set them free and see what they have to say?" Mike began walking with Lucian out in front like a lantern.

"You *really* do not want to let vindicated gods go. It's not exactly a recipe for a happy world. They have SO many rules. We did kill them for a reason you know?"

"Maybe, but when your lot took over, things also got worse, no?"

"EXACTLY!" Lucian laughed. "It doesn't matter what we do. Everything is always fucked!" He stretched his neck just to smile at Mike. "And dinner isn't even included."

Lumine kipped up and followed along, occasionally trying to get a word in as the two argued but could only trail along like a mutt hoping to help.

Mike used Lucian as a doorknob to open the gate into the Unification's prison. Lucian breathed a sigh of relief as he saw the wards on every prison still held. There was no longer a shroud of innocence hiding its presence anymore, but everyone was still in their cages. With significantly fewer jailers around them.

"So, do I just shake you to free them? I'm not going to age, and it turns out ghosts really don't get tired physically, so I can sit here and shake you for a few hundred years if you want."

"You really don't want to free them." Lucian folded his arms. "It's a stupid plan. Do you know how many gods there are in the world? How many forgotten ones? This is just ONE folklore prison. Uno. Une. If you let these ones out free, then unchallenged, they become the new de facto pantheon. What are people going to do? Pray for harvest from Johnny Appleseed?" Lucian snorted. *Oh, please grant me apples, mister.*

"Nah mate, we eat them. Cut 'em up, cook 'em, and deliver them to the masses. It's like *Soylent Green,* god edition."

Lucian looked horrified at Mike. "You aren't serious, are you? Can you imagine what someone like Vryce would do with that power?

Hell, even Lazarus. Last time that happened, we got the Greek pantheon and look how that turned out. A hodgepodge of mythology that everyone bastardized."

"All you are doing is selling me. Why shouldn't we eat them before Lazarus? Maybe that's his real goal."

Lumine muttered something about trying to talk to everyone, but neither seemed interested in paying attention to what she said.

"Mike," Lucian rubbed his mask and gave it a soft tap. *This thing working? Or has Mike's unluck reached a point of no return,* "Lazarus refuses to touch them. Death Lords don't need them. Most of the Church uses their blood regularly to fuel their magic. The only people who can benefit from wielding their talents—are those without. If you give everyone else hope, then all that will happen is a more devastating heartbreak when everything ends. You remove any possibility of these gods ever being reborn from belief naturally. You literally end their cycle."

Mike growled, "Omelets need eggs." A frustrated sigh heaved his shoulders as he dropped Lucian. "Fine. Go ahead. Give up then. Serve Lazarus like a good little slave and kill the Second City. Let Katrina fill Murder's ranks, while you, me, and Lumine sit in an empty city on a mountain of forgotten ash and gold like old cranky dragons for another thousand years. Will that satisfy your masochism?"

It wouldn't. Mike is an idiot, but a correct one in this case. The war was going to escalate, and it was only a matter of time before the old gods, ones even stronger than these, were released back into the world. Lazarus's entire gamble was to murder the world first before their return—and reseal all magic beyond the barrier. Lucian chewed on his lingering thoughts for a few minutes longer before settling on a course of action.

"Fine. It won't. So, help me with one thing then you might agree with. I'll be rewarded for doing my job, and you'll stop these weaker gods from falling into the wrong hands. Come with me to the Society of Deus. There is no other magical force in this country who would

covet these legends as much as they. If you are hellbent on watching the world burn, at least let me balance the scales. In the Society's hands, every one of these legends would be forged into a ceremonial blade or used for Vryce's agenda. The most dangerous creature on the planet."

"You know I killed his real body, right? That bastard has more bodies than a cosplayers wardrobe."

"And do you think that someone with his arcane potential would usher in anything less than a dictatorship?"

"No no, I agree, he'd go full Doctor Doom."

"So, you'll come with me?" Lucian extended a hand as a symbol of peace.

Mike mulled it over before shaking. "Fine."

"Good." Lucian winked. "You didn't have much of a choice anyway. I would have dragged you there regardless. But at least now I don't have to re-leash you." He walked down to the prisons, casting French spells to reinforce any damaged wards in preparation for leaving. *Worst case scenario, I die. Best case scenario, Katrina and the rest of the army get involved and everyone kills each other!*

"I'm SOOOO glad you two are done with your lover's quarrel," Lumine finally shouted. "Hello! I exist! Your friendly neighborhood shape changer! The peanut gallery behind here would like to remind you that we are just trying to survive. I betcha the gods have the same mindset. Maybe... don't eat them?"

"Sorry, lass." Lucian shrugged. "Thick bones an' all sometimes. Don't feel bad for the prisoners. Seriously. If they were lucky or strong enough, they wouldn't be here."

She crossed her arms. "That's a shitty reason, and you know it."

"People spent a long time lockin' em up for a reason, child. Gods have a run, and then they go. If nobody decided to be the hand of entropy, the world would have never changed. Granted eating them is basically what we've been doing for a eons, but magic gotta magic..." he muttered under his breath.

"Let it go for now, Lumie. We ain't making progress on this fight. Hypocrisy boils under the skin of every organization, no matter how noble." Mike flicked one of her beads. "It's why gasoline and pipe bombs were invented."

Lucian stopped in front of John Chapman's prison. The mortal hung upside down with wrought-cold-iron clamps on his ankles and tree-sap drains hammered into his flesh in several places. Johnny Appleseed was only days away from becoming a god of Fertility when the Unification issued the hit on the old man, nearly eighty years old at the time. His death was sudden and peaceful to the living world, and he was fondly remembered for his antics, becoming an Indiana icon for decades after. To Lucian, he represented a bit of wonder stolen from the world so the Unification could fuel their great ritual. "Sorry, buddy, looks like your streak of bad luck isn't ending anytime soon."

There was no spark of life or sanity in the once shrewd eyes of the budding god. All that remained was a husk of latent blood ripe for drinking. Blood which made Lucian's world continue to fester. "Just ... hang there and enjoy the end of the world. The next domino needs a little push before it tumbles."

Lucian climbed through new rubble and scorched buildings, through the layers of Purgatory, constantly cursing about having to learn new pathways before crawling back into downtown New Orleans—the barrier of innocence completely shattered. The pitfalls down to the depths of Purgatory were as common as potholes, and on street level, it was hard to tell what was an old French building that weathered the ages or what belonged in the land of the dead.

That Samhain name is really stickin' if I don't say so myself. Now, how to get north?

CHAPTER 21

"I'm Mike. Nice to meet you." The cellphone watches a pale Mike Auburn kick a Chicago cabbie clear across a warehouse, shattering into several crates. "Mind if I bum one? I just had the worst day of my life," he asked the cellphone holder.

"Akira. Charmed. Sure thing, Boss." A wiry arm flicks a smoke from behind the phone. "I ain't too keen on being on your bad side, seeing as you just put that guy's head up his ass. So, if you let me eat a heart, you can be Boss."

—Akira667's Twitch channel

Mike refused to turn the volume down as he slammed on the gas, forcing Lucian to clutch his straw hat and refuse to blink as he panicked for unlife. Any time the bony hand reached to turn off Metallica, Mike either swatted or gave Lucian another burn with an old car cigarette lighter. *They don't even put these in cars anymore. Talk about retro.* He casually inspected the small glowing metal circles, marveling before reloading it in the dashboard of the old 1980 Dart Coupe de Lux. The car was a pea-and-vomit green chunk of

metal with roll-down windows, a cassette player, and to Mikes particular amusement—three surround-sound speakers.

"Before we hit the expressway, since I'm the only one who can drive, I pick the pit stops," Mike was already pulling into gas station that sold unleaded at absurd prices. At least, he thought so, considering a BTC with a lot of zeros had no meaning to him. "Lumine, you are on snack duty. Lucian..." Mike thrust the nozzle into his hand. "Don't blow us up. I need to go hit that Waffle House across the street, pick up something, and hit the can."

Lucian tilted his head. "Did ... you die with a full bladder?"

Lumine crawled through the window and swiftly yanked the flammable nozzle out of Lucian's hand. "Let's not let Lucky here play with gasoline. We've got plenty of gas, Mike, so I'll just go steal some water. Go get your special item." She winked.

Thanks, shorty. Mike jogged across the street to the Waffle House and instantly began searching for any signs of the Sons and Daughters. There were no motorbikes or large trucks anywhere in the parking lot, and the insides were picked clean. *Well, that means that they are alive.*

Mike spied a bullet casing sitting upright on a waitress notepad near the coffee machine.

Children, don't look for answers behind this bar, for it's run dry. We've gone helldiving to get reinforcements, so don't wait up for us. I'll find you when the time is right.

—Boss.

"Dry bar, my ass, old man." Mike vaulted over and hunted through old bottles of demon blood until he found a small flask taped to the underside. He smiled, took a swig, and shivered as the taste of peaches and spice infused his ghostly being with a real jolt. As he pocketed the flask, he couldn't help but notice that Boss had scratched the recipe

for Demon Juice on the side, and apparently, Japanese Plum Wine was an added ingredient. "Right, now for the real thing."

The freezers in the back held Mike's prize, the patch-covered green trench coat. It took some fiddling to open the freezer door. His first instinct was simply to reach through and grab the coat, but he realized he couldn't pull the coat *through* the door. *Right, it's like driving the car. Just focus.* He cracked his knuckles and tried again. Grabbing the door felt like trying to pull open a handle made of water, but he managed. The coat, however, was as tangible as the demon blood in the flask. *Meh, magic coat be magic.* He shook it off with a loud clank from the variety of pins that adorned it and slid it on. It still fit perfectly, and he certainly felt energized. Almost unstoppable. *I can't believe I slayed Golgoroth in this. I bet getting drenched in that demon's blood gave it life.* Struck by an idea, Mike coated his gloves in demon juice as he shouldered his way out the front door—no longer able to fade through it.

Mike soon discovered his idea was, in fact, a brilliant idea as he could drive the car without intense focus... and that meant faster. There weren't any windows, at all, so driving over ninety mph felt like blasting himself through a wind tunnel, and Lumine would occasionally choke on a winged maggot beelining into her throat. But unfortunately for Lucian and Lumine, Mike was their only way north. *Lucian's got a ... not unreasonable fear of flying and can't drive, and Lumine never learned. Does this make me the responsible one for once?* He tapped the roof and ground his boots as he sang along to "Battery" for the thousandth time.

It felt good to be in the driver's seat for once. It felt good to finally have a plan. Mike had been led by the scruff for weeks now, and thanks to someone's ballistic plan—he finally had leverage. Lucian was so old, he was the kind of creature who walked everywhere and had absolutely no knowledge of how to make the old car function. It only took Mike an hour hunting through garages on the outskirts of town to find something usable. Once they were on the road for a few

hours, Mike really began to cut loose and drive for fun rather than practicality.

Would I really care if he snapped and magicked my ass into the trunk? Nope. We'd all end up back in good-ol' Purgatory and must start all over again. Mike smiled at Lucian knowingly, blowing a soft kiss as he jerked the wheel right, dodging a semi-truck carrying Dystopian aid. Lucian didn't exactly have a skin tone to showcase his emotions; to Mike, he looked like a skeletal Halloween decoration propped up in a car with his jaw open screaming. With a quick glance, Mike spotted Lumine had at least discovered the concept of a seat belt. She had rolled herself up in it and lay down in the back seat.

Mike figured they would have hours and several stops left to drive before hitting the Twin Cities. He didn't even need a map to navigate I-55. The Stevenson ran straight from Chicago right down to where they were, and then it was a simple pop left up to the shimmering magical-fuckery of Unification monsters. To say he was thrilled was an understatement. *Let's just drive the Lord of Misfortune right into a city who, as far as I can tell, served him two years ago.* Mike contemplated taking them off a bridge and into a lake. *Do we reset if we are just ... buried?*

As they drove past the outskirts of Memphis, Mike saw the illuminated farms of cryptids behind tall wire fences with spotlights. Large bucks with human faces grazed like cattle under the watchful guns of AmazCo. Entire industries of summoning, farming, harvesting, and bottling the very concept of magic sprawled as far as the eye can see. Mike saw the people as a mix of shape changers, dead and ghostly, or obvious blood drinkers. Perhaps one of the truckers was living, but to Mike's unique vision, not alive for much longer judging by how his soul was twisted in knots around his heart.

There wasn't even a second hesitation about slowing down as Mike took the ol' beater between double-wide trailers, riding the shoulder at times, and in Mike's later defense—choosing to get rid of the review mirrors rather than cutting it close. Nobody was keen on

ending up on a corporate farm that had swapped turkeys and chickens for creatures that thrived under the black sun. It was a collective sigh of relief they made it past the worst of it before the Dart's terrible gas mileage finally came into play, and six full plays of the *Master of Puppets* cassette later, it was finally quiet.

Lucian cheered when Mike turned off the engine. "Oh, Lucifer's beautiful golden buttocks, please explain to me why you gave knowledge to the humans."

"Quit your whining. You're immortal and unkillable, right?" Mike got out and picked up a gas pump in an open station under the white flickering lights. It was quiet. There was only an occasional truck or small car driving down the road, and nobody seemed to work inside. They did have demon dogs and pizza though.

"You are really putting that to the test. I thought *I* was annoying." Lucian crawled out of his dented door before helping Lumine through the window. "Think of our daughter, Mike. Why would you show her such horrid parts of culture?"

Mike plugged in the gas. "*Master of Puppets* is a rather poignant commentary on culture that, apparently, is well ahead of the times, given our apocalypse here."

"Not the music! The music was great. I loved that shit. The giant steel containers containing devils. The stags being farmed. Hell, didn't you notice that we passed at least three succubus brothels?"

Mike scratched his head while he tried to figure out how the small black box affixed to the gas pump was meant to accept payment and what the hell a BTC was. "Huh. Yeah. Succubus brothel. Wouldn't ... that be a one-way trip?" Mike was more interested in getting gas.

Lumine freed herself from Lucian's earmuffs and raided the unmanned gas station for hotdogs, drinks, pizza, and more. Mike was jealous. *I really... really want to taste all of that again.*

"Do you know how to pay?" Mike asked Lucian.

The Lord of Misfortune came over, and both stood at the pump, lost men who didn't know where to begin. "What's the district number?" Mike asked.

"District is easy. We are district one. But why can't I put coins in? ACCEPT MY BARTER!" Lucian then paused. "What do we need to pay for anyway?"

"Without gas, we are walkin.'"

"Never mind. You are on your own there, ghosty tits."

"If we walk from here to the Society, I'm pretty sure the war here will be over before we get there."

"Great!" Lucian sat on the hood of the car. "Katrina will be happy and get promoted. Lazarus will look lovely in white."

"Or the Society gets all the gods and uses your skull as a ping-pong ball."

Lumine returned with steaming-hot pepperoni- and cheese-stuffed crust manufactured pizza that was anything but hand-made, yet it smelled delicious. She tapped a card on the black box and opened the car door, crawling behind a seat that leaned forward and reclaiming her spot. "It's crypto. Station is run by zombies. Automated," she munched. "We goin' or sitting out here all night?"

"Well, fuck me, I guess..." Mike laughed as he filled up the Dart.

Heading home to Chicago and ditching Lucian wasn't in the cards for Mike. St. Louis forced a detour on account of a stationed army of militia and soldiers closing down any road from the south. The long trip up the I-55 corridor was losing its charm for everyone in the car. Mike had spent most of his entire life in Chicago's concrete embrace, rarely even making a road trip to the armpit of America he considered Indiana, but driving through now was a verifiable recipe for depression. Most vegetation, national forests, or other scenic elements had

long since withered under the black sun. *It's like driving through a Tim Burton movie.* Then, if there was a farm powered by grow-lights or a cultivation of fruit which glowed, it was heavily guarded by local fiefdoms.

The culture of rural America had certainly changed since magic returned to the world. With no federal government or global manufacturing services and an ever-present threat of *actual* monsters—survivalists had free reign to live out their post-apocalyptic fetishes. Granting the local "badass" the supernatural strength of vampires or the powers of cryptids only enhanced village isolationism in Mike's eyes. They'd passed countless flags or had to speed through suburban streets to avoid patrols. The Silver Foxes ran Jefferson with their werewolf Harley riders, and three miles later, they were in Light Bringer territory with an insane Catholic preacher and his army of devils. The farther they got from Dystopia, the more diverse each pocket of people became. Mike found himself daydreaming of building his own little community during long stretches through the miles-and-miles of miles-and-miles. *If I was still a vampire... oof... our city would be so unique. I mean, fuck, I'm a damn iron worker. I could build some shit...*

Mike slapped himself. "Get the fuck out of your head, boy. You aren't a libertarian moron. Not some massive, beautiful cake made with a teaspoon of shit."

The sudden slap only got a passive reaction from Lucian, who tipped his head away from his own silent musings long enough to pat Mike's thigh. "There there, least it's not a theocracy." With a huff, Lucian returned to his window and stared out into the empty dirt fields of Iowa.

I bet everyone runs into the same problems. Good idea for communal survival, but how would they stop an army like Lazarus? What about greater manufacturing? Advancement of science and medicine? Is that all gone now? Mike tapped the wheel. *I mean, I am dead, I guess. Do I really need dental?* It was a struggle for Mike to grapple with the reality. Individualism, communal societies, and mutual aid

had benefits for sure but could easily fall into tribalism, tyrannical rule, and more. Hell, Mike figured, even before the apocalypse, Nazis marched in Skokie, Illinois, every year, and he shuddered to imagine what they'd do with the power to control minds. *Hopefully, they all became lunch for Akira while I was dead, and she was left unchecked.*

Crossing into Minnesota didn't feel like entering another small town, however. It felt like entering a different country entirely. Fields of wheat, sugar canes, exotic palm trees, coffee plants, and more began to exist—in a part of the world they never should. Even more than mere existing, they flourished in an intertwined, chaotic mess on either side of their expressway. Lumine and Lucian both sat up and excitedly started playing a game to call out what they saw. If it wasn't for the cruel fact that Mike was driving them into the Society of Deus as an act of war, this very moment might have otherwise been wholesome and heartwarming to him.

Unlike the Dystopian farms they saw closer to Texas or early on their trip, the Society's farms were chaotic, uncontrolled, and exotic. A rolling mass of impossible vegetation was powered by an irrigation system that, in circles and geometrically acute angles, formed wards and spell patterns. At one point while driving through, they watched a sprinkler system come alive, showering blood across the canopy of herbs and fruits while animated homunculi rose from clay soil and began harvesting.

The soulless humanoid clay creatures paid the sickly green Dart vehicle, with three very curious faces peering out, absolutely no heed.

It wasn't long, however, before the Society of Deus came into view. Mike remembered it very well, and driving from a different angle didn't change what he saw back when he started a revolution within its borders.

A massive, inverted pyramid the size of St. Paul hung impossibly in the sky with its tip a hundred meters above the white skyscraper for Walsh Tower. Chains as thick as rail cars streamed down in seven directions from the impossible floating structure and bolted

themselves through every main artery or road leading into the city. As they drove closer, they could feel the arcane energy vibrating off the chains and empowering countless wards that were carved into prismatic-hued walls that surrounded the city. Nothing in their eyes was normal about a city that was bold enough to declare itself above the laws of gravity. Mike saw only one difference between his arrival this time and three years ago. *This time, that pyramid isn't in Purgatory. Everyone can see it, not just me.*

Before they arrived at the walls, Mike pulled the car over. "Well... here we are." He rapped the wheel. "Is this where you step out of the car and destroy the ones smart enough to grow coffee?"

Lucian fashioned and dusted off his hat before stepping out to stretch, his bones cracking like popcorn. "Something like that, boy. This city has a debt due, and I'm simply here to collect a divine tax."

Mike killed the engine and petted the green baby. *Good car. You stay safe here.* Once his boot touched the pavement, however, he felt a shock of energy race through his ghostly form, invigorating and empowering him. Even his mouth tasted like he just drank melted wire, and when he put his hand on the door for balance... his hand was fully solid. He didn't need to focus as hard just to interact or not phase through. It was exactly like standing in the crypt when Lucian had opened a portal between multiple worlds—but without the celestial violence.

"Whoa" was all he said.

Lumine was similarly stunned when she reflexively shapeshifted into her half alligator form and was now towering down over the car.

"Welcome, my *la petits*, to the Society of Deus. The focal point of Unification's blood, finances, and magical energy for centuries. A city grandly chaperoned by Primus Vryce, warlock of the seventh circle, apprentice to a master, master to an apprentice. If this city had collaborated with its Chicago sister as designed, then the world would be none the wiser about our existence, and Lazarus's return would have been seen as miraculous, infusing the world with enough faith to keep

the engine turning." Lucian took off his hat and bowed, giving the city a moment of silence out of honor. "Instead, out of spite, greed, or just simply being a bastard, Vryce convinced the eight warlocks to open gates to not just Purgatory, but all celestial spheres, and flood the world with magic." Lucian's toothy grin and crazy wide eye look back at Mike made him seem magical in the moment. "But then you convinced the world to eat that magic and take it. How's it feel to return to the scene of the crime?"

Mike inhaled from a fresh smoke, this time enjoying the throat hit and the countless other sensations that came from a rush of chemicals tickling the brain. "I think that your version of history might be a bit distorted. One thing." Mike began walking to the city walls. "You never once asked why I really agreed to bring you here, did you?"

Lucian and Lumine began to stroll down the empty six-car-wide expressway past the humming chains with Mike. "No, because it's obvious." Lucian twirled his fingers and summoned forth a cane of bone with one hand and slipped on the Mask of Misfortune with a simple wave of his hand, simultaneously masking his zombie nature and letting his pretty human form come to the front. Even if his tropical pelican-dotted shirt still smelled of grave dirt. He looked dangerous. "You either win here, or you win here, Mr. Auburn. It's fate, either way. She may have marked you lot first, but you'll be mine when this is through. I'll either finish what you started and topple this city. Or this place has the arcane knowhow to kill me."

Lucian shrugged and looked up Lumine, who now fully looked like someone crossed a werewolf with an alligator and then decorated it with dreamcatchers, small trinkets, and pale blue crystals. "If I die, you know the mask is yours, right?"

"When that happensss," she hissed, with a surprisingly young and feminine voice given her new size, "then I'll gladly wear it. Until then..." Her long claw pointed forward into the city.

Mike chewed on a thought as they walked closer. Last time they entered the city, they didn't even make it a night before the Society

hunters were on them. "So, what exactly is the plan? I know some of the people in charge here and..."

Lucian tapped Mike's ass with the cane and pushed him across the threshold into the city behind the magical barriers. "There is no plan, kid. Everything that can go wrong here ... will. So, enjoy the show. Find something tasty to eat while we wait." His gaze drew upward to the floating pyramid. "Things always have a way of crashing down."

Good was all Mike thought as he readied himself. *This is where I end you, just like him.*

"Don't threaten me with a good time." Lucian grinned as he spun to walk backward and bow at Mike's wayward thoughts. The Death Lord was incorrigible.

CHAPTER 22

"Unicorns are assholes. For centuries, they were revered as pure spirits of nature, but nothing could be further from the truth. Luckily, we here at Avalon Enterprises have found the perfect use for these pests. Get ready for the journey of a lifetime with our new sports drink UniCron! We use only the purest of Unicorn Puree, hunted right here in the Dakotas. One drink, and you won't sleep for days."

– Gas station auto-play advert

Your bombs were shit!" Jane pounded the table in the middle of the boardroom. "Honestly. You truly are a Texan failure. So much so I can't even believe I came back here for help." Jane flicked off the CEO Peter Culmen in the heart of the Dystopian boardroom, not giving the slightest of fucks. "Let me paint a picture for you silicon bitches. We," she gestured behind to the cabal of ghosts and vampires that made up the motley crew of rebels against Lazarus's stupid Church of Unification in her mind, "literally gave you the location for their newest Death Lord, and you only sent 667 missiles? That's it!"

Doc Daneka tried to calm Jane by putting his hands on top of hers to no avail. She was as prickly as a cactus. Still, he attempted. "Jane, Phoebe... they tried. We are all—"

Oh, don't you even try. You again stand with the Praenomen. Jane batted her hand through his inconsequentially as a powerless ghost and hated herself even more for it. She longed to rip out fangs and smash circuit boards but was bound to be nothing more than a cute smile and a remnant. "What about *your* boss, bitch?" she snarled at Daneka. "Where are the rest of the Sons and Daughters, huh? Blown up like her? Standing there with a moment of hope only to burn in the inferno of superheated plasma that couldn't even hit ONE skeleton?" *I swear if one more person tells me I'm out of line.*

"JK-47," the current sitting voice of Dystopia intoned, "you of all our talented stars know we wished to end this war with a swift strike." Peter tried to appeal for the ninth time to no avail. "Killing a Death Lord is like trying to smash a diamond. It's an experiment, and now we know one more fact about Lucian. His power is reflexive. You were just a child when I studied under Fredrick, the Lord of Suicide, and all of Mexico felt its wrath because of my lack of progressive foresight. Unfortunately for all within this room, magic has been around far longer than reason."

Mr. Anonymous reclined in his soft leather chair, his face inscrutable behind the masked persona of a smirking Guy Fawkes mask. The only sign of his indifferent annoyance was the slight twitch of the long silicon blue locks that brushed against his tailored black suit. With a soft flick of his white gloves, he summoned several small, winged sprites of electricity to stir and reheat the tea of everyone in the thirty-seventh-floor boardroom of Triumvirate Enterprises. Several humanoid-shaped silicon entities representing the heads of multiple corporations sat closest to Mr. Anonymous. The only marker to identify them was the occasional floating corporate logo that bounced around their crystalline body like a windows screensaver. *Some people*

take "Live for the company" a little too seriously, Jane thought, crossing her arms.

Her allies in the room weren't much help either. The Praenomen was afforded a seat at the table and apparently took her fashion sense *from* Mr. Anonymous. She wore a porcelain mask that sported a wide smile and black lines vertically slashing through the eyes. Jane knew the black trench coat she wore held more witchy spell shit components than the cupboards of every kitchen witch in Arizona. It was a marvel, considering the diminutive and delicate frame of the Praenomen. *She probably figured being entirely androgynous would get her more little minions. Might as well be a seventeen-year-old girl trying to look menacing.* Jane silently chuckled at her own thought, considering that the actual terrifying warlock was *indeed* a centuries-old vampire and currently sat in the stiff chairs tucked at the far edge of the room with the rest of the Sons and Daughters but one: Doc Daneka, who, Jane figured, was only sat next to her because she needed to be "not hysterical." *Recognition is half of status, Vryce... You gotta work on your marking, babe. And fuck you, Avalon, for calling me hysterical. It's perfectly acceptable to be a raging bitch when bombs kill the wrong people.*

Over the past hour of analyzing the situation, nothing important had been accomplished. Unless, that is, someone counted discovering that Doc was highly protective of his tea, a critical discovery as he futilely tried to shoo the sprite away.

Jane knew Peter, or rather Mr. Anonymous, had insight. After all, he *made* her the hero she had become, but nothing pissed her off more than being told to wait. She had just found her brother and just found a path back out of Purgatory only to have it stolen away by yet another creepy cult. Honestly, she almost preferred that the creepy inventor for Angel-Be-Gone had never entered her bar in the first place. At least then... *Shut up, girl. Without him, you never would have made it. You going to give up now?* She sighed, clenching her fists futilely. "Fine." She suddenly put on a fake smile with her ghostly red

lips and feigned a perky pose. "You want to give up and call it Mission Accomplished, I'll go along, sweetie. Hunkie Dorie Dooh-Dah."

Mr. Anonymous held the same masked face as they always did in the boardroom, that of an inhuman masked grin that Jane just felt like punching. The Guy Fawkes mask was *so* outdated. "You know we would never give up, but casualties are a calculated risk in war. Furthermore, war does breed progress, including opening up a pathway for discussion. Are you anarchists ready to sit at the table?" Mr. Anonymous picked up his cup and tilted his head as the small faerie crawled into the overheated tea and boiled itself. "And you, dear Praenomen of the Archive?"

Oh, fuck me sideways and call me Susie. DEAR Praenomen? Jane's eye twitched.

"I thought you'd never ask," the Praenomen said, their voice a mix of male and feminine. "You've had the guest entourage waiting outside those warded doors for thirty-six minutes now. I understand letting someone's boiled blood leave their system." As if to hammer home the threat, the Praenomen took off their black leather gloves one finger at a time and tossed them on the marble conference room.

With a quick snatch, Jane grabbed the electric sprite and squished it between her fingers. "What part of Hunkie. Dorie. Dooh. Dah. Was unclear, dear Peter?" *Ever hear of Ghost in the Shell, you uploaded cyborgs? I can't slap you, but any ghost can fry circuits.*

Doc leaned over and whispered into Jane's ear. "You, uh, do know, that at least two, if not far more, people in this room can either read your aura or listen to your thoughts, right?"

Several people in the room chuckled. Even Vryce's lip curled slightly.

At that particular moment, Jane despised existence. *I'm just going to crawl back into Purgatory. Fuck it,* she thought with the biggest and happiest smile her waitress self could muster.

The large doors opened behind Jane, and the sounds of several footsteps echoed in stereo around her, with at least one pair in high

heels, as the envoy from the Church of Lazarus entered the room. Three necromancers in priestly outfits with collars sat opposite the Sons and Daughters to Jane's right while a gorgeous tall lanky vampire with white hair sauntered over to an empty seat across from the Praenomen. Before sitting, Katrina pulled off the ceremonial Italian rapier and leaned it against the conference table.

"Oh, tea." She seemed confused briefly as she stared at the cup of liquid and the soft struggling pair of sprites that pushed it closer. "Interesting." The lady bit her bottom lip with a fang as if she wanted to say more but instead looked at all within the boardroom. "The Lord of Murder wishes to thank all of you on behalf of Lazarus for this emergency meeting. The Lord himself is still occupied elsewhere, but as one of his swords, I, Katrina, can speak on matters relating to North America. The Lord of Misfortune tends to err on the side of being a one-skeleton show and isn't really the type to discuss policy."

Jane faceplanted her head into the table with a loud groan before sitting straight and folding her hands politely. "Greetings kind, not at all murderous, vampire who represents the large body of secret societies who single-handedly broke the sun, turned it black, and now suddenly turned religious. By the way, nice boots." She pointed at Katrina without lifting her head.

Katrina's thick eyeliner only added to her beauty as she smiled back. "Well, we all have our messy hair days, don't we? I'd say the view outside is vastly more pleasant and thank you! I bought them from Brook & Talbots." She turned to look out... and saw only the darkened landscape of steel and concrete enterprises mixed with neon lights and nearly constant rain. "Well, nicer on some days, that is. I'd recommend a few stores for footwear since some of you," she nodded at Akira, "seem averse to hygiene." As Katrina got settled, she rinsed out her mouth with water as if recalling a past experience, but the entire time, her pale-blue eyes constantly flickered over in the direction of Vryce.

"I invited everyone here," Mr. Anonymous set his tea down and rose, "because of the recent tragedy in New Orleans. An entire city was blown into Purgatory, shattering what remained of the veil of innocence in the region. All on account of the Church of Lazarus's mobilization of another Death Lord. Accounts, which according to the intelligence provided by the Praenomen, are happening across the globe. As warlocks, created for the purpose of Lazarus's resurrection, our reward was to be our dominion and freedom. Rather than turn the rest of America into cinders... let us negotiate." His honeyed deep voice silenced any chatter in the room.

Jane bit her inner cheek and mulled on the idea. Everyone in this room probably knew the Church of Lazarus was harvesting the blood of myths and legends to fuel their magic, and she had to admit a bit of curiosity to herself. *Was blowing open the chambers in New Orleans the catalyst for Katrina to show up?*

"You, and your anonymous legions, are correct, sir." Katrina leaned forward, folding her hands and letting her pale vampiric frame pour out of the black dress. The pale blue lights of the conference room only enhanced her natural contrast between flesh and fabric. "Your reward is indeed dominion, but I believe you misunderstand the goals behind our mobilization." She nodded to her necromancers. "Ladies."

The three priests rose, fished out a large amethyst crystal orb from a leather satchel, and set it in the center of a table. Each took position around the room while intoning a Latin chat, causing the orb to swirl with images. Nobody else in the room seemed fussed about the display of magic to Jane, so she figured a show was about to begin. *Propaganda video in three... two...*

The high walls and glass of the conference room faded from view, replaced with a scene showcasing good ol' Big Ben, a three-hundred-foot-tall gothic clock tower. To everyone in the room, it appeared as if they were sitting at a table right on Parliament Street looking up. Surrounding them, full plate mail classic soldiers bearing shields and banners raced toward the clock tower, where a massive reddish

black dragon coiled around the top, spewing hundred-foot gouts of fire. Jane could smell the metallic shells being welded to the flesh of the soldiers caught in the inferno, and her eyes watered from the black smoke that billowed to the sky above. Sensing them somehow, the dragon's glowing neon-red eyes pivoted to their conference table with a bone rattling roar. A jet stream of fire streaked to their location, causing Jane to jump down under the table as the heat washed harmlessly over the room before the vision ended. It took a second for Jane to realize that it was just some sort of immersive vision and that she wasn't, in fact, burned alive. *Shittletits. These guys need to get into the theme-ride business.*

She sat back down and tried to pretend that she simply needed to tie her boots up. Luckily, before any chuckles, the vision shifted. This time, the iconic White House lawn served as the center. Massive tattered American flags draped down each wing, and nearly every pillar was coated with magical runes, each pulsing with green energy with wisps of soul-flames flickering along their edges. In the garden, suited humans knelt before a devil. Jane's eyes widened. *Oh, hell yes.* The devil wasn't a gigantic, oversized, fat hideous thing. Rather, this devil was perhaps just over six feet with a floating golden-white crown that hovered between proud curled horns. His golden eyes looked down upon the bowed followers, and Jane marveled at the bright golden lines that delicately spiraled, etched into his chiseled face and trailing down along his exposed char-black skin. The gaze alone made Jane's thighs tighten, but it was the skintight leather pants and twelve-foot-long bat wings that made her swoon. She ignored the fact he wielded a claymore larger than her and stood atop several bodies that were probably ritually sacrificed.

"Rest, children. No longer shall you be ruled by the impotent." The creature spoke, not to just the kneeling followers, but directly to those viewing the scene. The devil gave a coy smirk as the vision faded.

"We are going to D.C., right?" Jane said. "Fuck it, I'm just saying what half of us are thinking. Look at Katrina! Even she blushed!"

"That's enough." Katrina waved her necromancers away and quickly licked a dollop of blood from her bottom lip where she'd bitten it. "Our point in showing you these scenes is to highlight some events unfolding. In a desperate attempt to solidify power, inexperienced humans are summoning creatures that have no business walking this earth. Our world is turning into fractional kingdoms ruled by those who have power—but soon will be ruled by arch-devils, dragons, and demigods at this rate. The Church of Lazarus holds the largest body of sorcerers, vampires, faeries, and witches across this globe. Together, we've used magic responsibly for thousands of years. Our intervention is only to protect those humans who haven't yet tasted the blood of the divine or are too weak to stand as individuals."

"A protection that comes at the cost of kissing Lazarus's scorched ring," the Praenomen cut in. "Your army grows the more death there is. Left unchecked, your god is no different than the ravenous arch-devil of Pride in D.C. Even worse, lest you forget, killing an entity such as Pride will remove the very *concept* of pride from the fabric of creation. Or do you intend to chain it up and lap up its blood like a mewling kitten?"

Katrina tsked. "Oh, come now, you would gladly drink Pride's blood. Hell, you'd probably *beg* for it. Besides, the old Unification had several demonic agents. J.J. Bollard was one of our finest field operatives before he suspiciously went missing in the Society of Deus, no?" She tapped her black-painted nails alongside the otherwise untouched teacup. "Prison, my friends, is where these creatures belong. Demons make the best jailers. It is their purpose, after all." Katrina's voice lifted an octave as she turned to the silicon lifeforms of the other corporate seats. "You manufacture products based on magical goods in this new economy. Currently, you invest a *substantial* amount of resources into the hunting and acquisition of each cryptid. The Church of Lazarus has no qualms about lowering your bottom line. After all, we certainly enjoy sugar-infused unicorn blood

as much as the next consumer. Even if... putting sugar with unicorn blood is a little concentrated."

Several silicon board members turned to Mr. Anonymous, who remained silent as if listening to a secret conversation. "The legions of Dystopia are ... interested. What would the price of such a boon be?" He spoke at last.

"Neutrality," Katrina said. "We don't care if you have products branded after Miss Auburn here or sell to the Society of Deus. Profit is profit, after all. Just keep your weapons and your," she flicked her fingers in the direction of Avalon's silhouette, "uploads officially neutral. It's bad economics to ignore the shifting world trends. Haven't you heard? Purity is the new gay. Personally, I'd recommend expanding your ghostly product line."

Don't fuck with the money, Jane. Never fuck with the money! "Fuck the money," Jane blurted. "You, you of ALL people should know this is bullshit, Peter. Don't you regret Mexico? Isn't that why you forged ahead to evolve humans with your technomagic? Isn't this place supposed to be a sheltered utopia for everyone if you work hard enough?!"

Mr. Anonymous swiveled in his chair while contemplating (or conferring) the offer. "I do indeed, JK-47. However, I am not one person any longer. We are the collective minds of the greater whole, and our outlook is meant for the stars, not just the present. I understand us backing down from this fight and assuming neutrality would anger you, but it also means we do not fight for the Church either. Our weapons flow equally to both sides."

Katrina began to smile before she suddenly froze.

Without warning, both the Praenomen and Vryce rose simultaneously in perfect harmony. "Perhaps," their voices combined perfectly, as if their souls were joined as each spoke, "the legion needs a stark reminder of what is at stake."

Mr. Anonymous sprung to his feet with an outstretched hand. "Do not seek violence within this vaulted hall of Elysia, lest all upon

your side be cut down. Remember sorcerers, you are within my sanctum, and my will is law."

The twin-entities of Vryce and Praenomen chuckled. With each step, shadows twisted around them, and lightning danced perfectly between their fingertips. "That is exactly our lesson, young Peter Culmen. A lesson taught to me by a simple bartender. You should know to never invite another warlock into your house... much less one who actually has their soul. Do you know why the Death Lords fear an unchained lich?" Vryce and Praenomen each raised their right hand, threatening to snap their fingers and unleash chaos. Each stood flanking Jane, who suddenly felt very small—and as if she was about to be in the middle of a threesome she'd rather avoid.

Mr. Anonymous and the silicon board members gestured in the air as if something was supposed to happen.

Nothing did.

Peter closed his eyes behind the mask with a heavy sigh. "So, this is your choice then, Lich. You waste your one trick with the Praenomen to prove your point. I can see your secret now. You split your soul into several containers. If you had asked sooner, I could have shown you why my method is superior, but I suppose you've always been afraid of the future. My technomagic never had a true place at your table, now did it?"

Vryce tilted his head back, gazing up at the ceiling with a wild grin.

Jane could feel the energy radiating off of the teenage girl. *He's ENJOYING the challenge? Damn, man.* To her right, the Praenomen's mirrored movements felt exactly the same to Jane. *But also, are you ... both people? Did you fucking boil my blood and then save my ass? This conversation isn't over.* She rose from her chair and stepped back, addressing the board. "You mentioned shifting tides. I don't think you'll get a chance to see what shores those tides wash up on, hon, but before you die, can you PLEASE tell me where you got that dress?"

Katrina bit her lip and tied her white hair up in a ponytail. "Brook & Talbots, dear," she passively commented as she adjusted her chest

and moved the teacup to the side. "Well, ladies, it's been a pleasure." Suddenly, her eyes shifted from pale blue to dead-white, and her body collapsed like a sack of wet sand on the floor.

"Reality, Mr. Culmen," Vryce and Praenomen spoke, "is controlled by those of us with a human soul. That is the foundation of magic, no? As Above. So below. You forsook yours entirely. So, remain neutral and kneel before the gods that rule when the dust settles." The duo snapped their fingers, and a loud crunching sound echoed within the room as the board members and necromancers imploded on themselves—telekinetically crushed from every direction.

Mr. Anonymous's silicon frame was ripped asunder, and the blue-blooded body quickly dissolved and melted. Nobody else in the room had a chance to react before their untimely demise or the sudden magical attack that discorporated their mortal frames. Even Katrina's throat and neck twisted until her eyes went white, and she was only able to whisper a single phrase in Latin before her body collapsed like a puppet with its strings cut. The only ones left unharmed were those who walked in the room with Vryce.

Jane cringed when flecks of internal organs from the necromancers landed in Doc's tea.

Doc, for his part, had remained silent up until that point. He finally jumped out of his seat and flailed his arms around at the bloody boardroom. "Who the hell serves tea when nobody drinks it!"

Jane opened the doors to leave. "Who the hell invites everyone to negotiate terms after the first volley? Let's... go figure out what's next." Out of the corner of her eye, she clocked Akira sneaking over to Katrina's body with her fangs out. "Akira! Nooooo... nooo... bad bug. You step away from the corpse right now."

Akira's eyes looked like big round saucers pleading to enjoy a tasty meal to no avail as she obeyed the group—albeit with a string of protests about the free meal.

One hour later, sentience entered Katrina's white eyes, and she jolted up. The boardroom was entirely empty except for the broken bodies and splattered organs that painted the walls. She forced air into her lungs for a deep breath and tried to stop her hands from trembling. It was an old necromantic spell, and she honestly had no idea it would work. All it did was turn her into an actual dead corpse for a brief period, but she was completely helpless. If the lich had done anything like fire or lightning, she would be a pile of ash. The whole ramble by the creature was far beyond her knowledge of the occult, and she was damn sure such a low-ranking spell didn't escape his notice. *Maybe it was the dress?*

She offered a small prayer to Lady Fate for the sudden bout of luck.

The prayer was cut short when a video screen cut on above Mr. Anonymous's chair. "Lady Katrina, we think it's time to negotiate terms. However, Dystopia is going to need some assurances around our ability to brand demigods into suitable products. Given the recent string of events, we are going to need a little more than supply. We want to shape the future."

A lump formed in Katrina's throat. She was only sent here as the Lord of Murder's sword to assist Lucian. Now she was front and center for negotiations on behalf of the entire Church, and she knew damn well her Lord would flay her undead ass. *Sorry, Lady of Fate. I meant the Lord of Misfortune. Fuck you, Lucian.*

CHAPTER 23

...rules of magic, p73, Arcanum Arcanimisum. "...to the uninitiated, the performance of magic may seem miraculous. A thaumaturgist is nothing more than a conduit between the divine and the material plane, channeling the flow of energy from other planes into our own. Talent, practice, and components are the hallmarks of a practiced magi. Yet willpower and determination are the hallmarks of a legendary magi. For without strong will, the conduit is weak and can only channel droplets."

Vryce casually twirled a small glass vial tied to a twine rope as they strolled along the side of Highway 45 outside of Dystopia. A small campfire burned about a hundred paces ahead, and he could already make out Onyx's massive black wings slowly twitching as the gargoyle roasted some fresh catch over the fires. Several of Vryce's personal gargoyles and Gabriel D'Angelo needed to wait exactly six inches outside of Dystopia's borders because Vryce knew showing up with them would give an entirely different perception. *Gabriel never had the stomach to sit through a board meeting. Regardless, I'm starting to feel a bit like the Pied Piper.* Following in his footsteps was a decently long trail of misfits from the Sons and Daughters with the Praenomen at the rear. Ever since leaving the skyscraper, the usual

witty banter and scathing sarcasm had been muted—behavior Vryce had seen time over for centuries when plans suddenly pivot. For his part, the sudden shifting winds of war only ignited a fire in his soul. *I meant to enjoy the era of magic that I fought so hard for.* "To think I'd kneel before Daneka's champion," he muttered.

Vryce could picture the Lord of Heaven's Wrath easily in his mind: a handsome American-Italian from the Midwest with clever brown eyes behind thick wire-frame glasses and sporting the 5 o'clock shadow. When he operated in the 1940s, John C. Daneka's agenda for the Unification was the practical application of control. The doctor ran several experiments with media to make some magic easier and require less blood due to the dwindling supply, and with Senator McCarthy's witch hunts on communism, he struck gold. The propaganda's success proved that the long shot theory to revive a god was possible. For better or worse, Vryce fondly recalled, warlocks had been training for a ritual that was entirely based on his own treatises of magic in the *Arcanum Arcanimisum* he'd authored a few hundred years prior. *And so, the pencil-neck psychologist got promoted to the Lord of Heaven's Wrath until his champion Lazarus took over. I wonder where the little human scurried off to...*

"You all look cheery," Gabriel remarked, snapping Vryce out of his reverie. "I'm assuming it went fantastic judging by the amount of free swag you brought back?" Gabriel wore his smirk to perfection with those bright blue eyes. It was even cockier considering he was dressed in a ripped-up white hoodie, blue jeans, and shoes that helped him sneak. It was exactly that smug *knowing* look Vryce had come to expect from his hand-picked replacement. An Italian prodigy in the arcane arts, Gabriel had a knack for counter magic few in this world, except for Vryce of course, would ever master—and he knew it. Thus, he intentionally never seemed to wear the iconic clothes and blue coats found within the military ranks of the Society of Deus. It was exactly because of his competence, and perhaps a bit of long-term nepotism, that Gabriel was one of the few souls on the planet who

could get away with breaches of etiquette or even outright disrespect. This often led to Gabriel constantly trying to, in his words, "modernize" his mentor. Apparently, that meant learning to "keep his chill" or *something something dating app.* Luckily for Gabriel, Damien had long grown tired of sycophants found within the Unification seeking to curry his favor.

Ergo, Gabriel already knew Vryce most likely exploded.

Vryce hadn't given a single thought to his recent display of power. "Oh," he glanced back at Jane, "it was pleasant. It's always charming when the young warlocks believe they've mastered their magic. So, let's just say we gave Peter Culmen a little homework to do. Right, Jane?"

The Praenomen kept marching forward and cut Jane off with a stiff arm across her chest before thrusting a porcelain mask into Vryce's arms. Underneath the mask with her hood down, Delilah Dumont maintained her impeccable appearance. Stick-straight, light brown hair framed her thin angular face neatly—only tussling when she pulled a runed-etched short sword out of its sheath and threw it point first between Vryce's feet. Vryce raised an eyebrow and looked at his granddaughters' sharp eyes that flung daggers in his direction. Since she'd been in service, both her eyes had changed remarkably as her left eye was scarred over and replaced with Bollard's red demon eye, and her right had become a multi-hued amalgamation of violets and gold ever since she'd consumed Bollard's heart.

"He did the thing, Gabriel." She sat down on the log next to the cocky blonde sorcerer. "I hate being possessed."

And yet you carry nails, child. Vryce clutched the Blade of Deus and felt his soul stitch itself back with one of its phylacteries. "Yet possession has served you well, Delilah. As has my mastery of blood magic. The price you pay for wielding my power is that, at times, it is still *my* power."

"Bullshit." Gabriel patted Delilah's knee. "Almighty Primus Vryce doesn't need to bend fucking reality all the time. Last time you pulled that shit, I punched your ass, and I'll do it again." He smiled as he

threatened. "You've got puppets to possess, and you know the rule." He nodded at the short sword. "The more phylacteries you hold on you, the more attention you draw from the divine. So, aren't we playing it a little risky? Viola? Mask? AND a Deus Blade? Please tell me you don't have the nails on you. Ouroboros amulet?"

Akira, Jane, Lucy, and Daneka had all stood a few feet back watching the family argue. Lucy chimed in. "So, you are telling me you really aren't just a tiny teenage girl? D'aww."

Vryce's cheeks reddened as he handed the blade over to Gabriel. "I would prefer it if you kept the rest of them a little more secret in company."

"Don't worry, the VHS tapes are safely hidden." Gabriel flipped the short sword with expert dexterity and sheathed it behind the second blade strapped to his back. "What do you care anyway? Just mind wipe 'em." He nodded to the anarchists.

"Need us to kill them?" Onyx said between bites of roasted jackalope. "Jade, kill 'em."

The nearly naked female gargoyle of pure jade sipped on a packet of medical blood like a Capri-Sun pack and cocked an eyebrow. "Boss hasn't given the order." She shrugged and folded her legs a different way in defiance. For a creature that was an amalgamation of vampiric flesh, crystals, and a human soul all stitched together to be the perfect loyal guardian for a mage, Jade's defiance was exactly what Vryce had built her for. Unlike traditional gargoyles, built from several vampires in an arcane ritual, adding a fresh human soul made his creations more sentient than the usual fare of a frenzying watchdog the size of a large van. Yet somehow, it still felt like they were becoming too independent, alongside Gabriel.

Vryce pressed the bridge of his nose between two fingers in annoyance. *I used to command fear and respect before I even entered a room. Do all females face this level of ... dismissive sass?* "We will not be mindwiping them or altering their memories to suit our needs. In the absence of leadership from the Second City forces... our two

groups are temporary allies." Vryce glared at Jane through his fingers. "Despite Mike Auburn's destruction of my original body, his sister has proven to be an extremely determined individual with untapped potential. Potential which we have a current use for."

"Excuse me, what?" She held up her hand. "I have been through a fuck ton of shit in the past week alone. Who the hell knows if Boss and the crew are even alive? Phoebe is blasted into Purgatory, and we JUST listened to corporate America functionally sell our pale dead asses to the lowest bidder." She stormed over the fire and got right in Delilah's face. "...and we haven't even settled this bitch's involvement. That bloody black sun will be three shades lighter if you lot think we are on the same side."

Delilah wore the most unimpressed British look. "Agreed. Our side actually gets results," she remarked while opening a small journal and crossing items off a checklist.

The fires of youth. May it never burn out. Vryce took a second to study the auras surrounding the Sons and Daughters. Lucy's was pale and deadened, a mix of gray and egg-shell white. She was emotionally sealed off, and probably had been, for a very long time. *Ruthless commander then.* Doc's aura was a kaleidoscope of emotions, and it even took Vryce untangling the threads of emotions that were actually his versus his recent set of emotional lunch. *Psychic vampires. We always hated them in our courts for this very reason.* Under all the layers, however, was grief and regret. His guilt ran deep, which Vryce surmised kept him moving forward, and he was perhaps ... close to Phoebe. *Her death was the most useful she had ever been. Get over it.* The last, Akira, was worth a chuckle. Akira perched on the edge of a highway guardrail and watched everyone with unblinking eyes as a cigarette dangled from her mouth. Her aura was pure black without a single hint of another color. Either she had consumed more demon hearts than any other entity Vryce encountered in a hundred years, or she was perfectly meditative and calm. Either way, the only true threat

among the three of them was Akira. *I'll have to see if I can forge that one into a gargoyle later...*

"Jane," Vryce said at last while starting to undress his outer layers, "you are a descendant of Lazarus, like it or not. Why else do you think you possess the ability to see and move in Purgatory when every other ghost wanders blind? Typically, when someone who has wielded divine blood dies... there is no return. Do you truly think that every ghost walking around the skinlands these days was once a magician? You have power. With training, you can bend the lands of the dead to your will... and just where do you think you will learn this talent?" Vryce threw his peacoat over to Delilah.

Jane caught the coat before it reached its destination.

"Stubborn." Gabriel fucking smiled and pulled out a bag of potato chips. "Jade, did you bring the popcorn?"

"Always," Jade replied.

"Fuck off." Jane waved the coat back as she ranted about the past week. The tirade spawned everything from dead gods to the inability to locate scrunchies and a hatred over being stuck in the same outfit and wearing the same bra for weeks. Only near the end did it dawn on her she was holding Vryce's coat and waving it around like it was real. "Cowgirl goes moo?" She looked so confused.

"Ghosts," Vryce explained as he put on the Praenomen's trench coat after swapping outfits with Delilah, "are far from useless in the real world. Poltergeists have long been a known quantity, and something that even most human cultures are aware of. Even when they chose *not* to believe in magic. Possession, telekinetic force, machine control, dream watching, dream control, environmental manipulation, and immutable forms are inherently easier for any ghost than any vampire or sorcerer. Try as he might, Gabriel would need to master several schools of magic before possessing his beloved VHS box. Lazarus will only ever train his most loyal ghosts such tricks, and if we are to face a legion of necromancers." He nodded at the coat.

"It is in the Society's best interest to at least impart some tricks to the Second City helldivers."

"So how can I suddenly hold your coat?"

"It's enchanted. Just like your brother's."

"Wait... I can work with magic gear?"

"Ghosts only pass through mundane objects with no connection to either Purgatory or magic imbuement. The sanctified walls of a church would be as real to you as that coat, but Akira's guardrail you could kick right through. Your subconscious also plays a role. You are standing on the ground, yes? You've ridden a motorcycle? Perhaps... accidentally opened a door without realizing it?" Vryce focused on tying up the impossibly long combat boots that Delilah wore as the Praenomen. They fit perfectly, and he supposed, that was the point of their deceptive duality, but he wished she picked something a tad more practical.

"We know lots of ghosts, right? Chicago's full of the bastards, right, Lucy?"

The redhead nodded. "I mean... nobody ever asked me, but what makes everyone think I'm not? I've been with Boss since the 1920s. I just assumed that it came with age," she muttered under her breath about drinking a few pints of blood.

Their boss was always so coy with information. Not surprising. Vryce shook his head to clear the fog. Every time he tried to recall his own lessons during that era, it was like a mental haze blocked any of the fine details. Pushing the thoughts down, he tied his hair up and removed his glasses before donning the mask and becoming the Praenomen. "There is no rule that ghosts cannot drink the blood or learn sorcery. They can also eat a heart." He reached down and picked up the satchel containing the Cherubim's heart. "Ergo, I've elected to teach you the basics."

Lucy raised an eyebrow at the glasses being removed. "Just out of curiosity, but don't people typically need those to see? What good are

you in battle if you blur the lines between friend and foe? I'd consider that tactically basic."

"Mind control." Vryce dangled the glasses in his gloved hands. "I wear these not to see, but because pushing them up your nose or tapping them subconsciously makes people look at your eyes. A mask has the same effect."

Lucy pondered the retort as a slow smile crept along her pale face. "I ... appreciate that. I'm assuming since you've outgrown the need for material trappings or eye contact, you do so out of reflex and old habits, making any mind control you perform habit. I'll see about adding that tactic to our ranks in the future."

Delilah tapped her glasses with a pen and coughed to get everyone's attention. "Before you run off to sully my Archive's reputation, Primus Gabriel of the Society, and myself... the lowly bureaucratic ghoul, have some orders of business."

"Ah, forgive me, children. The plan. Sorry, I get rather excited when dabbling with magics I rarely get to play with." *My wish was granted, but if Lazarus is going to threaten my world, I'm not going to sit idly by.* "Jane?" Vryce held out his hand. "You and your lot are a part of this plan. I will only ask you once for your willing participation."

Jane looked terrified. The new appearance Vryce donned caused the blonde ghost to take a step back, and her head shook side-to-side. Vryce could easily see the indigo and brown colors of fear and indecisiveness swirling wildly around her crown. She needed a push.

"The Praenomen was created as a persona. A persona meant to be wielded and vilified by the world when needed. It is nothing more than a tool utilized when controversial actions must be taken. This mask," he tapped, "shields the wearer from any scrying, aura reading, or other means of magical detection. Every spell I cast as a lich leaves a mark upon the world, a signature that can be traced. Until the heavens and hells are brought under control of the masses, I am as bound to this earth as you to Purgatory. This is as much for my safety as yours.

So, find your villains elsewhere. I will only kill you if you betray me. Loyalty begets only the reward of knowledge."

Jane gulped. "I..." She looked to her friends.

They are passive sheep and useful but need to be led. Claim your spot.

"I," her fists clenched, "will assist you." She nodded with determination. "We need contracts, however. I'm not a cheap talent. My fame and past commercial work speak for themselves after all. I can have my agent draw up paperwork for you after we discuss terms."

Akira leapt up and slid next to Jane. "That's uh, me. I'm her agent now." The gutter punk elbowed Jane in the side. She nodded.

"Cute," Delilah cut in. "Still, the plan. I'll handle contract terms and negotiations with Akira and have the paperwork drawn up for the use of JK-47's talents along with the appropriate copyright and trademark applications with the office of who-gives-a-fuck. What. Exactly. Are we doing? My checklist is empty." She held up a blank page with only one line:

- Acquire African Dark-Chocolate Mocha with Caramel and Barghest Blood.

"A tragedy." Vryce nodded. "The plan, as most complex schemes are, is fluid. You, Delilah, will go to the Vatican, begin conversations with the societies, and get a feel for the politics at play. Take Roger and Whisper with you. Gabriel and the Gargoyles will go back to the Society of Deus and rally our own army. As for the Sons and Daughters, their forces are fractured, but Jane knows the way through the Purgatory prison in New Orleans where they have hidden several myths and legends for harvesting. I believe this is what Gabriel calls ... a heist?"

Gabriel was staring off into the nearby tree line and snapped back after he heard his name. "Huh? Sorry, yeah. Again, with the complex plans. Just invite everyone into a room and burn them all. Simple. Done."

"Where is the fun in that, Gabriel?" Vryce smiled under the mask. "We've got centuries to enjoy. If we kill everyone, then Alexandria of Ur and I will be stuck having to date, and I'd rather not."

"So instead, you want to bring a bunch of has-been-gods back from the dead?" Gabriel rose and chucked his chip bag to the side. "Isn't that against your morals? They failed, so why do they get a second chance?"

"Who, my apprentice, ever said a thing about giving them a second chance? After Jane and the Sons and Daughters free them, they will be bound, chained, and devoured. The Church of Lazarus is only using their blood for petty magic. We can do..." dreams flashed in Vryce's mind of a world where humans once again wielded power over the gods, "so much more."

"So, what does the Society of Deus get out of this? After all, Boss... you uh, kinda gave me the throne. Just in case you forgot that little detail?"

Vryce opened his gloved palm to Jane. "That depends on your skill at negotiating the contract. A bank heist has more than one asset to divide. As long as we get the freed demigods to the ritual chambers beneath the Society, we can forge blades, and we can bind souls together. And I'm sure several of the bygones have a litany of secrets and lost magic. The risk is evident. We must face the Lord of Misfortune head-on, and it will escalate the war. We bring gods; Lazarus will send more Death Lords. We will usher in a war of forgotten magic versus faith. This time, I have no intention of losing."

Jane took a step closer and looked Vryce in the eye proudly as her aura shifted to one of righteous revenge. She shook on the deal. "I officially consent to this Plan B. You are going to teach me to be effective again. And I'm still going to use Dystopia tech. I want my rocket boots back."

"Jade," Vryce tilted his head, "will you fly on over to Dystopia and make a purchase for this ground-born ghost? I will begin training immediately while the rest of you negotiate terms of contract."

"Ugh... fine, but I'm picking up a new Mk22 Mod 0 sniper rifle on your tab." The gargoyle dusted herself off. "What size shoe and any particular color?"

"Purple. Size 9. Not the Avalon tech knockoffs either. LexCo. Original brand."

Vryce gave his consent and led Jane by the hand into the woods. "Then let us begin," he said, completely unaware of any social awkwardness from pulling a girl alone into the woods alongside a Texan highway.

CHAPTER 24

*"And the fourth angel poured out his vial upon the sun,
and power was given unto him to scorch men with fire.
Yet in these days, the sun shall be eclipsed, its light a
mere memory, and the shadows will claw at the land.
The defilers of faith, who consort with sorcery, shall
be marked by boils and blisters, their skin charred by
Heaven's righteous flame. The streets will run red with
the blood of the unrepentant, and the pure shall stand
unscathed. The Church of Lazarus stands as the bastion of the virtuous while heretics will only know the
searing embrace of divine retribution."*

*–Church of Lazarus broadcast in
New Bethlehem, Washington*

Within the haunting silence of the Basilica di San Clemente,
John C. Daneka, known to the world as Lazarus, found
solace in the shadows. The layers of history embedded in the ancient
walls whispered to him, their secrets intertwining with his own. He
imagined that the real Lazarus would have hated these chambers,
filled with elaborate murals and wealth of the Catholic church. *So
much decadence for a pope's private residence.* John limped through
the dimly lit nave, his footsteps echoing against the marble floor, each

step a testament to his relentless pursuit of power and survival in a world gone insane.

His body still recovered from the Greek fire years ago when he poured the flames over himself to sear Lazarus's grave clothes into his skin—a grotesque canvas of his suffering and rebirth. Charred skin cracked and bled, yet the pain was a constant reminder of his transformation. Each wound, each blister, was a mark of his divinity in the making. The more the world perished, the more his flesh restored itself. With every calamity, his power grew, his skin healed, and his mind grew sharper. Yet the struggle was far from over.

John paused at the ancient frescoes depicting the life of Saint Clement, the vibrant colors faded yet still potent with the stories of old. His gaze lingered on the scenes of martyrdom and sacrifice, finding a twisted kinship in the suffering of saints. *I wonder what my legacy will be.* The air was thick with the scent of incense and the weight of centuries of faith, but John allowed himself a pained and deep breath. Here, in this sacred place, he felt the pulse of ancient power coursing through his veins.

Divine Righteousness.

Not a power stolen from the blood of demons and angels or a whispered forbidden secret in a witch's spell book. But actual, true, creation-infused power. The ability to create reality, not merely bend it to one's will like a chained lich. Already John knew that feeble spells would wash over him like rainwater.

As he moved deeper into the basilica, descending into the subterranean levels, the air grew colder. The whispers of history grew louder, mingling with the murmurs of his thoughts. He was in pursuit, not just of survival, but of something greater, dominion over the world of men and gods alike. Yet the recent news weighed heavily on his mind.

The city of Dystopia had dropped bombs on New Orleans, a desperate attempt to eliminate the Lord of Misfortune. The effort had failed, and now Misfortune was off the grid, a dangerous variable in his grand plan. He'd truly hoped that Misfortune would have been

removed from the chessboard by the usurper Vryce at this point, and Dystopia's involvement left many questions. Yet somehow, one of Alexandria's newest picks for entry into the Sanctum, Katrina, had begun negotiations with Dystopia? *Perhaps this will be my question for Alexandria today.*

John's breath came in ragged gasps as he reached the lowest level, the Mithraeum. The subterranean chamber, dedicated to the god Mithras, was a place of ancient rites and secret ceremonies. Here, surrounded by the relics of forgotten faiths, he would hold today's meetings with the errant Lords and Ladies that comprised important members within the Church of Lazarus. John hoped the relics of past gods would put his guests at ease. For they, too, had been worshipped and then cast aside. *In truth, the Unification bound them and slowly drained what elixir ran through their veins, but let's not look a gift horse in the mouth, no?*

He fell to his knees before the altar, a violent cough racking his body. Blood and phlegm spewed forth, staining the ancient stones. His body was not healing fast enough. Resisting the divine blood and lure to have magic heal his injuries or become a vampire was costing him dearly. Nor could he afford the basics of modern medicine and still keep his secret. *Get it together before they arrive, John.*

His eyes, lidless and burning with fevered intensity, gazed upon the ancient symbols carved into the stone. His trembling fingers traced over each line in a meditative ritual meant to calm his failing body—even if his nerve endings were so singed, nothing was felt. The world above was in chaos, but here, in the depths of the eternal city, Lazarus could at least be honest.

"I'm going to die before the work is done."

A sultry female voice echoed behind him. John, in his stumble and bodily revolt, never noticed. "You know I could fix that, my dear," Alexandria of Ur said as she rubbed his charred back with cold hands calmly. "Just think, let me give you the kiss of ecstasy. To slowly taste you and imbibe your life into mine and grant you eternal life. Your

struggles would be over, and you could marvel at the historic turns of the new era."

To what end. A thousand years of darkness? To admit my thesis was wrong? I'd take a prison in Purgatory. "Sadly," John rose, "I have little desire to remain immortal as a charred and phlem-ridden cripple. My mobility is returning because the plan is *working.*"

"Oh, John, and here I thought we were establishing honesty with each other." She pivoted and sat on the altar in front of him, crossing her legs. Alexandria wore a purple dress that split along her thigh and left nothing to the imagination, although this time, she was bereft of accessories except the flayed-skin mask with peacock feathers. "Do you have any idea how difficult war is? For centuries, we colonizers looked down upon Africa, for example. We thought it was a place we needed to bring civilization to, and our gunpowder allowed us easy access to the riches beneath its soil." Her voice was musical as she mused. "Now imagine just how powerful that continent would be if suddenly, all their gifts and magic returned to them? Perhaps it is we who should be bowing to their thousand spirits and gods. Not just the Egyptian ones either."

"Then luckily for us, we aren't after their gods." John used her thighs as leverage as he lowered himself to sit next to her on the altar. "They will remove themselves from the global war in their own way. They do not need violence from us. Russia, however..."

"Old magics there, indeed," she reminisced. "Some would say that humans never really ruled there. A lesson many warlords learned throughout history all through Ukraine, Siberia, Russia proper..." Her tone trailed off each note to make a point.

A point that John was insane.

"If I could raise an eyebrow at you, I would. I'm not blind to history despite my ... youth in present company. Unlike past crusades, we seek neither territory nor resources. Our armies do not need to hold territory and lord over it. There are no diamonds to line our pockets with. Merely, my dear, war." Lazarus held aloft his trembling hand

with tattered grave cloths dangling into the shadows. "The mere act of fighting forces the faithful to our cause and pushes the defilers to consume hearts for power. People, Alexandria, are morons. Making them vampires, warlocks, witches, werewolves and who knows what else gives morons power. Material power. Earthly power." *And it utterly destroys their inherent divinity in time.*

Alexandria shook Lazarus with a sisterly hug. "See, I knew I liked you for all the best reasons. Fredrick had his role as Lord of Suicide all wrong. All I need to do is wait... because in two hundred years, over half of these new immortals will be worshipping at my feet *begging* for the sweet release of endless boredom."

Ow. Lazarus gnawed his inner cheek from the shake and let the daggers of hatred behind his eyes melt away before speaking again. "Speaking of ensuring you don't get bored, here's my question for this meeting."

"I'm all ears," she purred.

"The Sanctum. You've been recruiting members from every faction and training them. How is it then, within less than a month, one of your recruits, Katrina Millner, is entering negotiations with Warlock Peter Culmen?" Lazarus handed her a blooded handwritten scroll. "A field report from two weeks ago. Murder's backup forces to Misfortune continue their conquest of Florida and the southeast. Yet Katrina and her guard left for Dystopia *before* the bombs dropped. How did you know?"

"D'aww..." She rose and sauntered into the center of the basement as she contemplated. "Busted I suppose. We did agree to honesty." She folded her hands and bowed. "Forgive me, Lord of Heaven's Wrath, for I consult with the enemy. There is one known as Delilah Dumont, a former member of the Unification with impeccable results, who agrees to trade information for the right price. There is another, you shouldn't be concerned with his name, from the Second City who always has the juiciest gossip. Like how our own Lord of Misfortune is on a road trip across the country with the very famous Mike Auburn.

Rumor has it, they are headed directly into the heart of the Society of Deus." She tapped her lips to keep the secret. "Katrina is new, and I have my own spy, one of those hideous Nosferatu-esque vampires, skulking amongst the general ranks of the Sons and Daughters. My mind-controlling agent tells me *everything* about their movements," she looked down sharply, "and also tells their boss *everything* about ours," she muttered.

John was amused. This level of duplicity and overly complicated scheming was typical for vampires. They viewed the world as a chessboard and often loathed to see other long-lived creatures removed off the board—vastly preferring games of tit-for-tat. *Still, what do you gain from confessing? That I will cleanse you of your sins? Save you when the sun returns?*

"I see," he stated. "So, business as usual then? Tell me more of this mind-controller and Delilah. Mr. Auburn, I'm very familiar with."

"Well, Delilah Dumont is the former D.C. political lobbyist for the Unification responsible for the coordination of ritual site 6 within the Twin Cities. She, of course—"

John waved his hand. "*Where* is she? I know the basics."

Alexandria smiled. "In Rome. Lobbying."

"And the double agent? His name?"

"Just an informant. In their organization, goes by Edward Morris; in ours, he once held the ranking of a captain in the legion of drowning. I'm not exactly sure who turned him into a vampire, but they made sure he certainly wasn't kind upon the eyes before doing so. He's been traveling with a group from the Second City since before the black sun and is something of their boss's right hand. Currently, they are trapped in Georgia on account of the bombs and our own forces in Florida. Their boss is a constant enigma and apparently asked him to reach out to me with a message."

"So, this Morris isn't *your* informant, you prideful bitch. He's *his*." John couldn't even speak the name he knew so well but could never remember. He spat phlegm, and it pooled beneath his feet. "If you

encounter this Morris, sever his head. I'm sorry your pawn will have to be removed, but I suppose, what is this message?"

"John, I'd wager to say the Second City pisses you off more than Damien Vryce. Cuurrriiiousss..." She grinned. "The message was, and I quote: 'Tell the Lord of Heaven's Wrath that I've locked up more fallen gods in Purgatory than anyone else. It was good work. Well-paying work. That contract expired.'" She tapped her cheek with a long fingernail. "I'm not sure if that means they are looking for work?"

No, it means the gates to Seat of Golden Tears are open, and it's a warning of what is to come. What have you allowed to transpire, Lucian? Thank the world that the All Father and his get aren't in North America. He studied Alexandria. By all accounts, her meddling was an act of suicide, which oddly might only strengthen her position—and she knew that. This information exchange was an easy secret for them to keep between each other, but there were too many variables in North America to let it sit. "Set up a meeting with Delilah and myself next time."

"Easily. Now, John, for my question."

"Go on."

"What is stopping me from simply killing you here? What trick do you have up your sleeve?"

"Nothing," John replied honestly.

John hoped her laughter was fulfilling for her because it was an answer she already knew.

"Perhaps someday you'll give a different response. I wonder if I'll be less amused then." She began her slow walk out of the chambers. "By the way, I couldn't help but notice you've recently taken up smoking. I'd be careful with that. Cancer is a hell of a way to die."

Smoking? John watched her leave, confused about her observation. At least, until he spotted a silver Zippo sitting tucked in a nook within the altar next to a pack of Lucky Strike cigarettes.

"I thought she'd never leave." Hal suddenly appeared and grabbed his smokes. "Although, for a little bit I thought you two were about to

make some hardcore porn." He lit up and drew in deeply. "I ... LOVE ... watching you." He exhaled several smoke rings from his lips and lowered his sunglasses to peek at Lazarus. "It's always the frail ones that get the most done in war. I think you need a little acceleration though for your plan to work."

So much for solitude.

"Please, we both know you want to spread her thighs. We just need to get you back into fighting shape, so I'm going to offer a little suggestion. You might not have heard of this invention. It's a magical thing but entirely foreign to you since you haven't fucking used them."

"Bombs." John lowered his head into his hands. "Why is the answer always bombs?"

"Because the answer is always fucking bombs. You need to kill a shit ton of people really fast. Blow them up. The end. Quick. Simple. They even make them now with fancy atomic logos if you didn't know. If you don't, you'll be in a cold war, or someone else will have the cajónes to use 'em."

"Mr. Morgan, need I remind you that we represent the Church of Lazarus? We do not deploy thermonuclear warfare. We deploy legions of the dead and faith. We peddle salvation for the masses, not nuclear winter."

Hal packed his cigarettes. "Eh, worth a shot. So listen, I know we are booked for our meeting, and I arrived early—"

"—and uninvited."

"But buddy, I want to pick your ear about Pride in D.C. and Dystopia... This could be a fortuitous opportunity of making America armed again."

"You are as dimensional, Mr. Morgan, as a sheet of paper." John was finished with the conversation and began to shuffle himself back out, all the while listening to Hal's insane plans surrounding D.C. Both of them knew it was just noise to each other. Hal already knew his inner thoughts and Lazarus's real goal, so the conversational foreplay was just to wear John down into agreeing to a small concession.

This meeting's concession was allowing the trade deal to go through with Dystopia—on the one rule that no regular humans within Church-controlled territories were allowed to use any of the goods. The soldiers and necromancers? Sure. Human civilians, however, absolutely forbidden.

"Purity must be maintained" was the final demand from Lazarus. Lucian Montague wasn't even worth a conversation. *Let America devour itself. Just stay over there and never return.*

Chapter 25

"The mortal mind is fascinating. You can bend a world to your will by giving them an enemy. In our case, communism and Catholics. Let the reds go nuclear and let J.F.K. be president. In time, they will be martyrs and tyrants, and we will be free to shape the world in the shadows with more weapons than heaven's army."

–The Daneka Doctrine (1944)

Lucian hummed a song about decapitation to himself as he worked. *The space between your molar and your jaw, this caliper, no cause for fear. No no, it doesn't hurt. It only helps me measure the layer of fat.* His hands ran along the corpse laid flat on plastic Home Depot containers as wisps of black threads animated dead sinew and tissue. The corpse violently shuddered, its dead eyes opened wide, and a soft groan whispered from its mouth from the first gasp of air it took since, well, Lucian didn't quite know. "What's this one's cause of death?"

"Ass cancer," Mike idly responded from across the suburban yard as he struggled to close the doors to the large C-Container. The zombies kept trying to stick their hands out, which caused Mike to swear and bat them back in.

"We've been at this for two full weeks," Lucian remarked as the most recent creation rose up and followed his command to go stand

and get hosed down by Lumine's gardenhose before shambling into the next container. "Does everyone in Minnesota die of heart attack or cancer? Haven't you mortals solved that yet?"

Both Mike and Lumine responded, "No."

"Horrifying." Lucian held his hat and deftly picked up the next corpse and slammed it down on the crates in the garage. The next in a routine desecration of some families' pagan ritual involving evergreen trees with blinky lights on them. *Another soul from the chains.* Lucian need only raise his hand to and make a small wish. The great chains that ran over this suburban neighborhood were forged from Purgatorian Steel, the same mystical shackles used to bind angels, gods, or humans who stepped out of line. Over the centuries, it had taken on many names: demon steel, hellforged, shadow steel, and more, but it all was functionally the same. With each stroke of a hammer, a smith in Purgatory would forge a soul into shape to create something inherently magical. The Society of Deus, in all Vryce's infinite wisdom, used it to hold a massive golden pyramid up in the sky.

Lucian figured it made sense when the pyramid was *in* Purgatory, and for the unlife of him, the Death Lord had absolutely no idea about its purpose. *Fucking hermetic warlocks. I swear they masturbate to Trismegistus.*

The soul heeded the necromancer's call, and the blackened wisp freed itself from a link eighty feet up in the air and flew down, only for Lucian to bind it into the next body while humming. The zombie rose and shambled over to Lumine who sprayed it down with a look of sheer boredom, and Mike would lock them up. Over, and over, and over again. After two weeks, only Lucian was still merely humming along in their deserted suburb.

"Graveyards for breakfast," he sang, "necromancy for lunch, calamity for supper, makes the trio as snug as a pupper!"

Mike kicked a container after a button on the arm of his coat got lost inside. "ARRRGHHH..." He kicked and dented the container

in several more times. "Can't you tell these zombies to move to the back? I liked that button."

"I can." Lucian shrugged and adjusted his sleeves farther up his arm before walking over to the wheelbarrow that held two more bodies from this morning's gravedigging.

Lumine's eyes lidded closed as she deadpanned him. "We've been building hundreds of zombies, digging up graves, and now you let us know that you could have made them be quiet and follow orders? Do you know what it's like to sleep in a kid's bedroom over a container with five hundred groaning zombies all night!?"

"Uh, yeah," Lucian looked confused, "I thought me being a master necromancer would," he twirled the caliper, "kinda have that ability."

"So, you're just lazy."

"Bingo." Lucian snapped his fingers and another zombie rose. To hammer his point home, Lucian willed the last corpse in the wheel-barrow to move of its own accord and lay on the Christmas tree crates for the soul-binding. "See that? That took extra effort, my pupils. That little spell could have been the difference of life and death if the Society of Deus ever figured out our little plan here. What if guards showed up and I'm just so tired?" He held a hand to his forehead and pretended to faint.

"I'd use you as a riot shield." Mike came inside and dusted his hands off while leaning against the Halloween gravestones for a different time of year. A small spider shook and made pointless spooky noises. "Seriously, it's been a few weeks since we crossed the threshold. Nobody has noticed us digging up every cemetery in Hopkins and anything else nearby. We done with this yet? Every damn garage is filled to the brim. Every shipping container we could find is packed up, and let's not forget the amount of closets on that one block with houses that look exactly the same loaded to the brim."

Lucian finished the last corpse and shambled outside to gaze up. Minneapolis-St. Paul was only a sixteen-minute drive away, and the western chain had more than enough holes in the links for his plan to

work. *Well, it had enough holes after the first three days, but if you are going to piss in a lich's kitchen sink, you want to make sure you've at least finished the bottle of rum first.* "This is going to be beautiful." Lucian smiled as he basked in the rays of the black sun that peaked through the gaps in thick thunderstorm clouds. "Yeah, I think we are done. Go on and let them out." He waved his hand, activating the second half of his spell.

The suburb of Hopkins came to life with a roar as hundreds of bodies threw themselves out of every exit they could find. Corpses flung themselves from second-story windows, burst through wooden doors, and railed against the inside of rusted shipping containers and backyard sheds. With each container made of a different material, the zombies (each in varying states of decay) freed themselves in waves. Each wave set themselves on a shambling march toward the heart of Deus.

Lucian licked his thumb and held it aloft. "I wager," he flipped a coin passively, "they will be upon the city center in about four hours."

Mike's cigarette hit the floor, and he flung his arms in the direction of the fleeing zombies. "I just spent two weeks packing all these dead fuckers up! Why?!"

"Well, you needed something to make you feel useful. Come, come. Time to go shopping downtown before the zombies arrive. You know the drill. Zombies crave brains, and when they kill someone, you've got a new zombie. So on and so forth. Classic trick." *I have ALWAYS wanted to do this.* Lucian laughed to himself and twirled his bone-cane as he scurried to the front of a wave. *Who knew that I'd find such an opportunity in Midwest America? Of all places, I thought Arizona would have been first.*

Lucian turned and saw Lumine and Mike still standing in the garage. Lumine's hose was only a small sprinkle as they watched more undead than even they recalled pouring out of houses. "Come on, you two. Did you really think the only dead in Deus were buried in graves? I've been busy while you slept." Lucian flashed them a wink

and kept marching. He knew they wouldn't stay behind and miss the show.

Lucian thought downtown Minneapolis had a cute rustic vibe as he strolled over the stone bridge of a river that cut the city in two. The soft yellow streetlights didn't do Lucian's natural pallor any favors, but his appearance was the furthest thing from his mind since he had been wearing the same pelican Hawaiian shirt for over a month. He gave the city a flourishing bow before stepping into downtown proper, a final farewell to the city of hubris.

Unlike his impromptu soul-fused Misfortune charge in New Orleans, the Society of Deus required a more delicate touch. As Lucian passed the Seventh Heaven Tea shop tucked in the corner of a squat ten-story concrete building, he only needed to bump into a university student—spilling the hot lavender tea all over this evening's arcane homework. "Sorry, sorry!" he professed against the panicking student.

"Shit! Shit! Fuck! These... these are from the Society Library, you idiot!"

"I'm really sorry, garçon," Lucian lied. "Here, here, let me pay for this." He chattered on as he fished through khaki pockets looking for an old bullion coin. Three pockets later, Lucian produced an old, rusted copper coin and pressed it into the student's hand. "That should set you right. They can't be that expensive; it's just paper."

"They are original writings from Jack Parsons! Irreplaceable!" The student pounded his temple in self-inflicted frustration. "I'm so dead. I'm so fucking dead..."

"Look on the bright side. Everyone ends up there eventually." Lucian laughed with a pat and kept strolling down the street. In short order, that student would race inside and scream for help and cause a

scene. When the cops arrived, he'd flee into the street only to be hit by a car, which would veer and crash into another building, setting off further chain reactions. *The plight of orderly civilizations—tug on one thread and the sweater unravels.*

Merely one coin would not topple a city. The Alice in Wonderland-themed Korean restaurant would soon have an outbreak of their pills suddenly having catastrophic side-effects. The Beez Kneez biker who delivered raw honey for both arcane and delicious reasons would find their antennae-themed helmets catching on unfortunate wires in gruesome ways. A shoemaker from Rome would unlock his husband's phone to discover infidelity at the wrong time. A bone-themed bookstore peddling forward-thinking literature staffed by volunteers would find that a young wizarding session would *actually* produce fireballs on this day. Even the bubbly and happy Pet Paws filled with adorable and fluffy familiars would see one cage of a teleporting bobcat left slightly unlatched.

One street after another, Lucian merely tipped a single domino, always producing a small coin from holed pockets as if it were a beggar's magic trick. No violence. No grand displays of arcane might. Just a little bump, nod, or phrase uttered at the right time in order for Lucian to tug on a strand of misfortune he saw all too clearly. What happened after was entirely the choice of those affected with a glance of misfortune. *The student didn't need to panic, the Italian couple could have talked it out, and maybe the bookstore shouldn't run classes with pre-teens and live faerie blood. I mean really. Think of the children.* Lucian scoffed.

Just when the city would be mobilizing their emergency services (which would soon face calamities of their own), the zombie hordes an hour behind him would be arriving. *And we've all read that story before.*

Lucian came to a stop in the middle of the street leading up to Walsh Tower, the iconic building where Charles Walsh of the Unification helped direct the construction of this ritual site. "So

that's where Mike beat the head off that little lich, eh?" Lucian wasn't impressed. There were so many layers of control by the Unification, and somehow the Society of Deus still pulled off the greatest arcane betrayal in, well, Lucian supposed since Lucifer fucked Eve. *At least back then, both people got their desserts.* "I wonder what good ol' Walsh is up to with his time magic. Did he wither and die from using it too much?"

"Nah." A new voice spoke behind Lucian. "He's still the same moral goody two shoes and a pain in my ass when I need to kill a bitch."

Lucian looked up at the six-foot six-inch scrawny blond gentlemen who had strolled up behind him. Dressed in white gym shoes, classic Levi jeans, and a university hoodie, the fellow didn't initially stand out as odd. Unless, of course Lucian paid attention to the two glowing arcane swords strapped to his back, the newcomer might as well be named Frank Smith. *He does have pretty blue eyes though.*

"Name's Gabriel," he leaned in and added, "you aren't my type though. Sorry, bones." He circled Lucian, studying him with a cocky smirk on his face. "Lazarus's Death Lord... here in the ... Hawaiian, I suppose. I just come back to town, and here you are, trying to fuck up my house and my favorite bookstore to boot."

Just as he was studying, Lucian peered back. Gabriel wasn't a vampire but had clearly eaten a heart, and instead of seeing strands of fate for Lucian to tug around him—all Lucian saw was a pure white field. *Warding magic. Oooooh, it's Gabriel D'Angelo! Vryce's little apprentice! The Italian sorcerer.* Lucian tapped his teeth. *Doesn't he come from a family of Italian fate witches? Bah, I can't remember. I think I was elbow deep in cocaine at the time.* "Salut, friend." Lucian smiled. "Might I interest you in a sudden case of groveling?"

Gabriel unsheathed the Calvary Saber. "Well, a little case of misfortune for you, I suppose, but yes, my sisters are indeed vengeful witches."

Lucian thrust his hands stick straight up over his head. "Wait! I surrender!" *Baiser! I was never good at keeping my thoughts hidden. Maybe if I think in French?*

"Nope, won't work. I've been following you for about three blocks, buddy. Zombies? Really?"

"Can't blame a skeleton for the classics, can you?" Lucian pulled back slightly. "You are going to stab me with that thing, aren't you? Looks pretty nasty. Lotta souls sittin' in that blade. They say soul blades are forbidden magic, you know. In MY humble experience, they tend to be pretty pissed off souls when released."

"Oh this?" Gabriel pointed at the blade. "No, this isn't for stabbing you." He snapped his fingers.

Lucian felt the agonizing gout of white fire erupt beneath him. Under his illusion, what little rotting skin he had boiled and blackened nearly instantly as he screamed in horror. "MY PELICAN SHIRT!!!" he exclaimed before madly cackling and dropping any pretense of appearing to be something normal. Lucian relished the pain. His deadened nerve endings rarely felt something so tantalizing, and if Gabriel's flames were strong enough to melt the Mask of Misfortune—then perhaps a silent freedom awaited Lucian as a pile of ash under a red light. *But that pelican shirt did nothing wrong, you abomination.*

Gabriel gestured, picking Lucian up telekinetically, and slammed him face first into the curb. Lucian felt Gabriel's boot on the back of his head as he kicked down, shattering his fangs and cracking his jaw wide open. It happened again, nearly decapitating Lucian who rolled off to the side, gurgling on his own black ichor that spewed out from his putrid cheek before simmering into vapor.

"Waltz into my home," Gabriel said as Lucian felt lightning crash down, blasting off his left arm. "Fuck with my people." Lucian felt a needle slam through his psyche, shattering rational thought. "And think we wouldn't notice?" Gabriel ripped out the black vitae within

Lucian like a stream of flowing liquid and poured it into a clay jar. "Much less alone? I'm honestly hurt."

Lucian struggled to heal as fast as the wounds were inflicted, and his left arm was probably gone for good. *That fucking soul blade* was all Lucian could focus on. The weapon that allowed this upstart sorcerer to summon knowledge from centuries of magi. With a feeble hand, he reached out to tug at a soul, any one of them would do, just to start a chain... any chain of misfortune.

"No coins." Gabriel snapped his fingers to burn him again. "No misfortune, but would you just fucking die already!"

"Please!" Lucian cackled as his vision darkened, not from the embrace of death, but simply from his one good eye exploding from the fire. "Un ... fortunately ... you ... are ... in ... a VERY ... long ... line." Each pronunciation was truncated by Lucian being slammed into something, the Mask forcing his soul to repair what it could within his bones.

Then, faster than a suburban mom wanting to complain to a manager—the pain ceased. Blind and broken on a street, Lucian silently begged for Gabriel to continue, but no further spells came. Physical pain was common to Lucian, and his body had been broken hundreds of times before, but the pain that caused his tear ducts to simmer was that of regret. Gabriel had almost done it, almost killed him, but some earlier strand of misfortune finally caught up with the soul-thieving sorcerer.

And Lucian couldn't tell what calamity befell Deus's defender.

CHAPTER 26

Old Uploaded Video: An old man with a cabby hat and cigar stood over Mike Auburn with a wooden stake in his heart inside a dingy warehouse. "Tough love, kid. You're a Nosferatu now, a vampire. It's slightly different for each of us, but there are a few ground rules you gotta learn. Eating a demon heart kills the body and keeps your soul inside. You replaced your old heart with the demon's. Impale it and your body can't move. Tacos are a thing of the past now. Blood is how you stay young, whole, and moving," the old man said to Mike in a shaky cell-phone recording.

Two hours ago.

Mike and Lumine stared in disbelief at Lucian marching ahead of the zombies like a parade marshal. *He's totally fucking oblivious.* Mike pondered the absurdity of Lucian's plan while passively packing a fresh pack of American Spirit Yellows. In his eager zest for whatever diabolical chaos the Lord of Misfortune had planned, he was completely oblivious to the pace at which he walked... and the pace that the very slow shambling dead folks walked.

"How long until he notices?" Lumine asked before deciding to water the garden and pack away the hose.

"Pretty sure, never." Mike lit up.

"We, uh, just gonna let him go at it alone?"

Mike gave it the briefest of thoughts. "We'd miss the show."

"We would miss the show."

"Take the minivan?"

"Sixteen-minute drive? It will take him an hour."

"He's the idiot who decided to march."

"What would we do?"

"Get a drink and good balcony seats."

"I'll get the keys."

Twenty minutes later, Mike Auburn and a non-shifted Lucky Lumine stood outside of the strangest bar either one had ever laid eyes on: an Alice-In-Wonderland-themed Korean restaurant. Apparently, for the low cost of one thimble of blood, someone could take a pill, shrink, and get piss fucking plastered on the largest bottle of home-made Shōchū. *At least, relatively speaking. The overhead on this joint has got to be so cheap.* Mike inspected a train carrying bite-size desserts around the Jabberwocky as tiny people picked up massive plates, if they weren't wobbling. "I gotta say, Doc would have killed for this place during college. Chicken-on-a-stick is his kinda dish, and those portion sizes? In this economy? You gotta be shitting me."

"I'll take fifty of them," Lumine asked the Hatter. She tapped her thumb on a small silver needle and offered a prick of blood. "No pill needed. I like being big."

"Then you should come to late night tea party." The entirely androgynous person with fantastic eyeliner smiled. "They say it's a party worth dying for."

"Oookay, that's enough of that." Mike grabbed Lumine's shoulder with his fingerless glove. "She's like fourteen, dudes."

"Sixteen."

"I'm not a dude."

"Stuff it. I'm from Chicago—everything's a dude. You're a dude. That little chap down there, dude. Her? Dude. The invisible cat? Freaky dude." Mike effortlessly dragged Lumine out as she stuffed her mouth with twenty chicken skewers, setting her back down right as some guy in a bee-helmet whizzed by on the sidewalk. "WATCH IT, ASSHOLE! USE THE STREET!" Mike raised his fist.

"BEES!" Lumine raced off in pursuit.

She's like... like... I imagine Jane would have been. He sighed as he watched her wild hair filled with bones and trinkets bob after the beekeeper. Mike watched Lumine stand on her tiptoes, each shoe of a different make, in her patchwork clothes as she struggled to barter for a jar of honey with nothing more than a rat skull she wore on a bracelet. Mike honestly felt that she belonged here more than running around with two dead things. *Ghost? Vampire? Ironworker? All three are going to get her killed. Unfortunately, can't exactly drop her off at sorcerer foster home here. An hour of fun won't kill anyone though.*

"Oh, my god," a fifty-year-old stranger with silver hair and a dark-gray speckled beard and the most impressive set of wing tipped shoes stopped right in front of Mike, "you are the spitting image of Mike Auburn. That coat? You even replicated the buttons. Can, can I see?"

Mike blinked. "This thing? Oh, I've built these over the years. Every job I've done or bar I've closed out I'd get a new patch or pin." Mike started showcasing the buttons. "These ones are my union pins, this guy right here was my grandfather's Korean war pin, this Chicago Firefighters patch was from good ol' Captain T before he died. Lucifer Saves Lives is from this crazy burlesque show at the Vic." Mike rambled on reflexively with the guy, easily sliding into stories about the wear and tear his coat had seen.

"That is so authentic!" The guy patted Mike's bicep in a flirting manner. "Mind if we take a photo?"

Mike smiled. "Fuck it, I'm dead, you've got style—how do you want this selfie? Hugging, demon horns, or me dipping you down?"

"Go with the moment." He stepped into Mike's arm. With a quick innocent dip, a single flash, and intense eye-contact—the nearby crowd applauded. Mike easily flicked the gentlemen back up on his feet. *MAN, I love being real here. It feels good to have this strength back and no lust for blood. Maybe being a ghost isn't so bad.*

Lumine snickered and hooked elbows with Mike. "Didn't know you had a type, big guy."

"I've got many types, little L. I think I'm attracted to fashion. I'm also not talking about this with you after you just ambushed a bee guy with a rat skull."

"For a guy who thinks fashion is hot, you sure dress like something out of the road warrior. Patch green coat? Torn jeans? Untied combat boots? Fingerless gloves? Pirate bandanna?"

"Listen here, you little shit," Mike said as they walked down the street toward a bookstore, "fashion is all about personal style. My personal style is curb stompin' rat-bastards and brotherhood. Besides, I still get plenty of ladies." Mike winked as he opened the bone-shaped handle of Skull & Tomes.

"He thought you were cosplaying—squirrel!" she shouted as she ran inside.

The warm smell of incense washed over Mike, and a small woman in a green apron with red glasses bowed slightly. "You dropping her off for class today?"

Lumine had already run over to several other young adults and teenagers in front of an obvious vampire with classic jet-black hair and dark European features. "Today, my children, we practice the basic principles of fire magic." He spoke with a heavy Ukrainian accent.

"Maybe, who's that?"

"General Dragosani." She blushed and turned to face him. "He's been donating his time on occasion. In a world like ours, I'm glad we have them to teach us."

"General, eh?" Mike scratched his stubble as he eyed up the vampire. Classically handsome, stocky build, black trench coat with a blue

ascot tucked into a decorative vest. Affixed was a symbol Mike knew all too well—Amo-a-Deus. Vryce's personal army. *I could take him.* "Anyone who wears an ascot is—"

"Well aware of you, Mr. Auburn." He smiled. "Did you not think I smelled you the moment the door opened? Come, friend. We are no enemies here. Your sister, she speaks highly of you." He extended his hand.

Are you the fucker she has a crush on?! Mike cracked his knuckles. "A proper gentlemen would have dived into Purgatory after her."

"Tsk, no no. Your sister is spitfire, yes? We have a date, but that is on her terms. Do not get all angry big brother here. What message would you send to your little sister here?"

Mike froze. A dozen or so people lingered inside the store, and none of them looked hostile, cruel, or even that stink of rich asshole. Even to Mike's deathsight, none of them were rotting in their soul. *Hell, even General Dragosani looks ... whole ... for a vampire.* Mike held his hands up. "Fine, but I don't think we are staying for class."

"Your loss. I can see it in her," he said, nodding to Lumine. "She's a natural at spellcraft. Rare too. I've not seen a shapeshifter with a heart like hers. But I do have a class to teach. Please, enjoy the streets of the Society. We do not get many ghosts, which is a shame considering the efforts that were made to make your life feel more accommodating." He turned to the class. "Necromantic charms are reserved for university only. Fire, however, it's like a driving test."

Once again, Mike snatched Lumine. "Let's go before we are screwed without dinner."

She protested a little as Mike tugged her briskly past a pet shop with freaky little demon creatures and cats with lightning for fur. They walked farther into the city several blocks, with Mike's boots falling harder with each block as he retraced old steps, subconsciously heading in the same direction he marched while still undead.

"I SAID OW!" Lumine suddenly shifted to twice Mike's size and yanked him up with a large claw and hissed at him. "I'D EAT YOU

BUT YOU ARE MADE OF GOO!" She chucked him backward as her bones snapped and shrank back to normal little L size. "Sorry." She winced as she rubbed her arm.

Goddammit. Mike dropped to a knee. "I'm sorry, I, didn't mean. I forget the strength."

"You publicly ate Golgoroth's heart on national television and forgot that you are probably one of the physically strongest vampires around?" She raised her eyebrow. "Try again." Her arms folded.

"I'm sorry I panicked because of Dragosani and Jane and dragged you out of there like a wet cat?" *Better?*

She tapped her eyes. "I'm a soothsayer. Try again."

Mike owed it to her to really think about what pissed him off so much. He took a good hard look at the setting they were in, and it had been itching in the back of his mind like a cockroach trapped inside ever since he stepped foot out of their green Dart. Everyone in this city seemed to live a cute, knowledgeable life where they integrated magic into what was otherwise normal urban life. A self-sustaining, contained, paradise. *Except...*

"Lumine, have you seen a normal ghost around here? Not just here but in the weeks since we came?"

She shook her head.

"What about a normal human?" Mike rose and rubbed her back as she shook her head again. "Yeah, me either. The suburbs were completely cleaned out. The cemeteries we dug up had plenty of fresh graves, and there hasn't been anyone normal. At all. The Second City is a melting pot of ghosts, demons, humans, homeless, rich, and just about everything in the middle. This place almost has a..."

"Supernatural purity?"

"Sort of like magical fascism. Learn magic, join the army." Mike pointed to graffiti on the side of a brick building that hosted "SEE THE GREAT QUENECO!" in bright yellow writing and a scrawny vampire mage in a classic mage top hat. "Or give bread to the masses. I know this place. I *know* the Society that was in THAT tower." Mike

pointed to the white skyscraper of Walsh Tower just a few blocks away. "They looked at regular humans like cattle. Food. When everything was going down and the sun was rising black, I watched the Society dispatch their army to give blood and guns to everyone who joined them in preparation for a Unification counterattack." He felt very uneasy standing so alone in the city. Here, as a ghost, he was practically flesh and blood. *It's not a charm to make my life easier; it's a ward to stop me from walking through walls or possessing people.* "Fuck me." He looked at his fingertips.

"Too old," she nommed a chicken stick.

"Sixteen?" he said with swift acknowledgement. "Yeah, you are way past experienced. You know your type." He ruffled her bone-infused hair. "Seriously though, I'm sorry. I suddenly realized we were both in serious danger and dragged you out like an overprotective asshole. One who forgot you can turn into Godzilla."

She patted his sleeve. "There there. You'll learn. Stick around me, kiddo. Come, let's walk for a bit more. Before you say anything, I don't want a lightning cat."

Not going to lie though, I kinda do. Mike and Lumine strolled through Deus with a fresh look at the city. Rather than be charmed by every oddity, they instead peered deeper into the industry of weaponized magic. Nobody in Deus was out of shape, people were constantly training physically or in class. Winged creatures occasionally perched on rooftops above like sentinels of a maze, and Mike and Lumine even noticed a Masonic police force implanting false memories to a witness of an escaped demon so they could take the heart for themselves. *Once you look beneath the glam, corruption is the same story everywhere.* Mike took a drag as they walked block after block on the unlit side of any street. At least, he felt at home again. It wasn't so different than any other city, and he just needed to find the right bar with the right whiskey to get the real story.

"Hey." Lumine stopped. "At least we aren't that guy." She pointed down the street at two silhouettes four city blocks away who stood in

the middle of busy city street. Walsh Tower's bright floodlights and the distance hid their identity, so Mike could only make out that they were talking to each other a few feet apart—before one ignited into a pillar of white flame, and Mike saw a hat go flying.

"That's not some guy. That's Lucian, and he's fighting fucking Gabriel. I know that fire anywhere. Tour's over!" *Even if Gabriel is on the wrong side most of the time, he at least means well. I'll be damned if someone else ruins my rematch. I fucking kicked his ass last time no matter what the cocky little...UGH! Why are you here, Gabriel!*

Mike raced over to a slow-moving sedan, yanked the door off with a metallic crunch, said, "Sorry, bub," and threw the driver into the road. "L, get in! You, wear a seatbelt to avoid car jackings." *Out of all the people I didn't want to see, why did it have to be him? Lucian's going to kill him.* Mike impatiently waited for Lumine to scurry around, get in, and put on her seatbelt before slamming on the gas.

Four blocks seemed like an eternity as Mike watched Gabriel launch an absolute onslaught of spells faster than Mike remembered was in his arsenal. *Leveled up, eh?* When he curb-stomped a Death Lord, though, Mike shouted at the car to go faster. *You stole my move, you cocky asshole!* They were almost there when Lumine shouted for them to look up.

Falling from the sky was a massive glowing green slice of metal. As far as Mike could tell, one of the chains leading up to the giant pyramid floating in the sky shattered. It was headed right for Gabriel.

"Mike, stop the car!" Lumine screamed.

"I've gotta save him!"

"—Crazy!" She ripped the seatbelt off and jumped out the passenger door seconds before Mike blindsided Gabriel and the cold-iron chain link cratered into the top of the car, flattening the rear seat and stopping all momentum instantly.

Mike, much to his instant dismay, was not wearing a seatbelt.

His face met the windshield as he crashed through and felt wind rush past his ears. Minutes crawled to seconds in the air as he

tumbled headfirst in Gabriel's direction. Reflexively, Mike latched onto Gabriel's hoodie, tucked his knees up and head down, and forced the pair of them into a long road rash inducing tumble down Hennepin Avenue.

When they finally stopped moving, Gabriel coughed blood and clutched his side where a shard of impaled metal stuck out of his ribs. *Not your lucky day, buddy.* Mike pried himself off the dual yellow lines, and for once, felt happy that he didn't have organs—even if he felt about as good as Gabriel looked.

"Did you," Gabriel coughed, "cover me in fucking ectoplasm?" He spat out clear liquid. "That's ... not good," he remarked after glancing down and plopped his head back down.

Mike raced to cover the wound and grabbed the metal. "This is going to sound odd coming from me, but I never thought you should die. Sorry, man." He ripped the metal out and applied pressure to the stomach. "Uh... Gabriel. Fire boy. Weld this shit shut or something. Clearly, you are still mortal."

Gabriel's gaze darted around in a haze. Mike tried snapping, "Gabriel! Burn yourself!"

"Mike? I'm dead after all?" he wheezed. "I almost had him."

"You sure did, man, but you aren't going to hell yet. Can't you cast a heal spell or do some witch bullshit?"

The cars around them had all come to a stop. One by one, then two by two, and soon entire waves started running out of their cars in panic as screams and explosions started down the street. *Come on, Gabriel, pull your shit together. Lucian's curse has started.*

"You working with him?!" Gabriel found focus as Mike's thoughts centered him. "What did you do, you idiot?"

"It's not what you think. Just hurry up and close this wound." *I swear on my last taco, you better fucking seal this shit, or I'm going to knock your teeth out. I lured Lucian here to get wrecked. Who else could do it but a bunch of magical warmongers?*

Gabriel tried to summon fire with bloodied fingers, but his shaky hands couldn't pull off the spell. "Just... if you ever see my sisters, tell them to return my videos."

Mike straight up slapped him and fished out a lighter. "Look at this. Fire, not complicated. Caveman do it. Click click flame! MAAAAGGGIIC..."

The little flame was all Gabriel needed to turn a small lick into a swirling ball of fire like a miniature sun and slam it into his side as he bit down on his wrist.

Mike reflexively ducked when a loud impact shattered a car nearby. When he saw the zombies suddenly race and tackle a running person though, it was time to go. "We, uh, need to move. I don't even want to test what happens to me if that pyramid falls on me."

Gabriel weakly stood, only managing to rest on a nearby concrete barrier. He finally looked at Mike through the shaggy blond hair just over his eyes. "I'll live, but man, what the fuck are you doing here? You are *literally* the last thing on earth welcome here after what you pulled. And you drag... you drag that thing with you?"

"Apparently," Mike tied Gabriel's shoe, "I'm saving you from yourself. Who the hell takes on a Death Lord alone? Besides, you should not cast stones. I'm not the one who tore a portal so deep the sun turned black." *Also, zombies will eat your brain if you don't move. Just saying. Did we make zombies? Yes. Did we bring magic back into the world so we COULD make zombies? No. No, that's all you.*

"Mike, I can handle some zombies. Seriously. They move slow and a giant storm of pure fire does wonders."

"No, then you just have *flaming* zombies," Mike remarked as he put Gabriel's other shoe back on a swollen and broken ankle. "Should have been a vampire."

"It doesn't fit my namesake. Besides, what are *you* doing working with Lucian?"

<*I'm not. He bound me. Kinda. Fine.*>

"Win-win?" both said at the same time.

"Yeah, fine, either Lucian dies, and I get freed, or you know…" Mike waved his hand at the unfolding destruction. "The guys who broke the world finally get … commupance?" Mike mispronounced the word he was thinking of and knew it was slightly off.

"Come-up-pance." Gabriel hopped on one leg, allowing Mike to be his crutch as he guided them across the street. "I'm just going to say this shit once to you. Then we are parting ways. I've got a city to evacuate. You soap-box having motherfucker, listen here. You are stubborn as shit and have an immaculate iron will. Even Primus Vryce couldn't dominate you into submission. Are you really chained by that madman?"

Mike rested him on a flowerpot filled with blood-red roses and venomous alien herbs. *This fucking city.* "Not … anymore. It broke. But I'm dead man. Lucian could just put it back up whenever."

"For all your talk of revolution and the common man, maybe you should fucking attend a class on the basics of your craft, eh? He can't. Sure, a different necromancer could try, but for a full year and one day, you are free."

"Well, then help me. There's a prison under New Orleans loaded with gods. Tie me to one and bring me back. It's like Lazarus but angry."

Gabriel tried to laugh at the absurd thought but clenched his rib instead. "Hell no. First, only Vryce, the centuries-old prick you punched, knows that ritual. Second, that's a stupid idea. You don't need it. You want that, or you want Lucian dead. At this point, your only option is to drag that skeleton down below Walsh tower to the Library you know all too well."

"Either Vryce kills us both or decides to switch sides?"

"We both know only one of those is going to happen. Besides, leave my topside alone," he grimly remarked as clouds of fire started raining down coating every single body in sight. "We aren't some evil fascist, magic-supremacist group. We do, however, live in reality. Shit sucks. If you want revenge that badly, crawl down to Vryce's sanctum

and see how you fare. If I could get that close to killing that madman, Vryce won't have a problem in his own house."

Mike hunted in his field of vision to their crash and where Lucian might be. It was pretty easy to see on account of a giant lizard fiercely guarding a broken body on the ground that was unnaturally pulling itself up at all the wrong angles. <*Well, least this time I kicked your ass.* >

"It's only half-a-point if you use a car. I'm still up a point. Go now before I change my mind."

"Fuck off. I took you out with a boot last time." Mike ran to the middle of the street to quickly fetch the pair of scattered swords and handed them over to Gabriel. "Don't make me regret this. At least save as many as you can."

"Yeah yeah, enough cheesy shit. At least your sister does it with a Texan accent and dimples." Gabriel shooed Mike away with a blast of telekinetic energy before any further questions could be asked.

Did Jane flirt with everyone up here? The hell has that girl been up to? Mike pushed the thought out of his mind and ran to peel Lucian off the cement and get them under city. "Elevator. White building. Magic shit" was all Mike said to Big L as he shouldered Lucian and started jogging to Walsh Tower through the unfolding chaos.

"Yannoe, my boy," the sack of bones spoke. "You've got impeccably good timing. Just give me five, and I'll be right as rain, and you can make all the righty jokes about me you want."

"Nuh uh," Lumine spoke. "I've got your left arm right here." She held a black, charred, burnt stick up.

"Real useful. Good job." Lucian's sarcasm was on point.

CHAPTER 27

"You died. Now what? Have you recently discovered that your god has forsaken you? Has the escape from Purgatory left you confused and isolated? Helldiver Incorporated is your pathway to a profitable existence as a newly escaped spirit. Offering contracts to fresh ghosts and poltergeists across the globe, Helldiver Inc. will finance your return to the real world—by employing your talents down below! Survive for only two years as a first-entry scout and a cozy home in the Appalachian Mountains awaits!"

—Flyer stapled to bathroom wall

Jane sneezed for the third time this training session. They were the annoying kind of sneezes that lingered for a second before exploding, and each time one fired off, Jane bounced. "Turtles!" she exclaimed after the third, waving her hand in surrender. "Hold up. Someone is absolutely talking about me, one sec, one sec..."

Vryce thwacked her thigh with a dead stick. "Gesundheit," he continued, pacing over the still river that flowed beneath their feet. "The three underlying principles of magic are?"

This is some Jedi bullshit. She winced, rubbing her thigh while hopping on a leg—and never once did her new LexCo anti-gravity

boot dip into the stream. Jane lost count of how many days and nights the duo had been in the Texan backwoods training. Everyone else nipped out after the first night, and the moment they did, the insanely cruel teaching methods of the great, all powerful, magnificent Damien Vryce began. In short, it consisted of beating each lesson into Jane's memory. Rest wasn't even *on* the menu because it turned out, much to Jane's complete surprise—neither of them *needed* sleep. Or food. Or water. *Which, just like an inside-out-cow, is a heck of a sight considering he's in the body of a very living teenage girl!*

"Trick question, twinkle toes. There are *seven* principles of hermetic magic." Jane held up as many fingers. "Mentalism, since the universe is all mental. Like Avalon's faerie dream pillows. Correspondence, since as above, so below; as below, so above is apparently a thing. Basically, how helldivers think they go down into Purgatory, when really it's the same as above. Vibration," she grinned wildly and kicked up her sultry voice, "because everything vibrates. Nothing rests. Not the dead, not energy, not the divine, and certainly not the Dark Path line of unending monster—"

Jane could see Vryce's posture recoil as if he had blushed behind the mask. At least, Jane inwardly chuckled—she had learned that this old cat could not handle anything with spice.

She continued, "—fruit baskets. I was going to say fruit baskets. What are you so worked up about, hon?"

He narrowed his eyes. "Enough, continue. Fruit baskets aren't magical."

Did he really just say that? "'Scuse me, when was the last time you ever came home to a pile of deliciously chocolate-coated strawberries, blackberries, and a banana arrangement? My fans used to send all kinds of things my way and let me tell you—when you are on a 30,000-a-day calorie diet, that shit is honkin' magical. OW!" Her other thigh suddenly felt a sharp pain. "Fine, polarity. Because everything has a pair of opposites. Which is frankly good branding. Make some red fuzzy slippers and... well, I'm not exactly sure how you'd sell

nothing. RHYTHM." She quickly blurted it out before her arm got hit and lowered another finger. "I mean, that's self-explanatory, even with Metallic Jack's rhythm 9000 dance package."

"That's five..." he said flatly.

"I gotchu. Cause and Effect. This one is real important. You do a thing, like make a doll that represents someone and stick a shit ton of needles in it and then that person gets dead. You know they don't sell those anymore? Turns out it was bad for the bottom line." *Okay, shit, what's number seven?* She tried to recall what was explained, in her imagination, eight-friggin-months ago.

Vryce thwacked her on the left ass cheek as he paced around her with the stick. "If you can't focus on the principles in combat, you are toast. Each one allows you to modify any spell you cast, and you never know what twist is needed."

"Yeah, so this last one doesn't make any sense." *I think it's this one?* Unsure, she took her shot with a shaky voice. "Gen ... der?"

Vryce paused for a second and gave her a *flicker* of approval. "Gender is in everything. Everything has its masculine and feminine principles and manifests on all planes. Left-handed paths, right-handed paths, push, pull, hard, soft... Yin and Yang."

"So, like," she protested, "what does that make you, then?" She flailed futilely in his direction.

With a quick glance down at his chosen body, there was a soft "ah." "Both. Just as you are. You swear endlessly but know when to smile and put on a mask. Everyone, and everything, has both energies flowing through them. One can be protective and also nurturing. Imbalance yourself, and your magic becomes specialized. It's a common trap for many upcoming magi. Males often gravitate to offensive magic or strong defensive spells, and females are often viewed as the healers and soothsayers. Yet this doesn't need to be the case. A fire sorcerer can just as easily channel their fire to breathe new life and rejuvenation as equally as turning a room into ash." As if to make a point, Vryce patted his stomach.

"What? You uh, hungry? On your period? Need to rip ass and make thunder?" Jane teased.

"Your mind goes in the strangest of places, Jane." He looked exasperated. "I've been sustaining myself with feminine energy this whole time. It's why I haven't needed to rest or eat. Fortunate for you because we only have six more months to go since you drank my potion. What takes some students years to master, you'll learn in weeks." He raised the stick. "One way or another."

"Well, buddy, if you find a way to bottle the whole *not eating* for weeks on end trick, you've got yourself a billion-bitcoin franchise overnight. The ladies would slay... wait, what? Six more months! All I've learned is a bunch of fucking theory shit!" She kicked the river, sending a splash forward. "Jane, ghosts can't go under water. Jane, all magic spells are real. They were just missing the components from correspondence and the realms above and below to create the proper polarity and set the vibration into motion. Which, mister, shove it in your food hole because the reason you recite incantations is to keep solid rhythm and focus your mind to create the desired cause and effect. Which apparently has something to do with a uterus."

Vryce gave the most demeaning golf clap. "See, you are learning. Good girl. Now put it into practice," he said, throwing a small vial of blood from the Cherubim heart her way.

She snatched it effortlessly.

"Go underwater." He pointed down.

With one look, Jane knew that was impossible and shuddered at the thought. An earlier lesson centered around her being dared to cannonball in, and she still recalled that embarrassment. *Then when you dragged me in, I practically discorporated entirely.* She looked at the vial and frowned. "I'm not getting out of this, am I?"

"Nope. You, savior of Dystopia, slayer of Death Lords, are a ghost. Submersion in bodies of water is impossible, and only sends you screaming back into Purgatory." His head tilted. "Or Oblivion, jury is still out that. Magic makes the impossible, possible. As both

a ghost and a descendant of Lazarus, bending Purgatory and space comes more naturally to you. Do you think me possessing this body full time is ... possible? Or because I've spent centuries mastering the art of possession. To the point where any form I wish to take is simply a matter of utterly shredding the soul and mind of its prior inhabitant."

"Wait, so you killed that girl? Who the hell was she? Why don't you just possess, I don't know, Lazarus?"

Vryce thwacked her again. "I'd start casting if I was you. How will your will manifest?"

Jane hated when Vryce ignored a human question. Every time she got the tiniest peak into his real past, a veritable iron wall seemed to manifest between them. *There is so much more to you than the rumors of being an unholy lich.*

"There is, now cast."

<And don't read my mind! I do not consent!>

"Apologies."

Jane expected another hit and reflexively recoiled and shut her eyes. When nothing came, she peeked open with one and simply saw her teacher standing there still picking dirt out from under his nails. *Oh, thank fuck.*

"For the record, Gabriel is vastly more specialized in mind reading and prediction than I. You are just terrible at hiding your thoughts. Your mind is an open book. Mostly filled with commercial jingles, crushes, a wish for super speed again, and an unending fascination with putting yourself in situations that spike a feeling of danger. Anyone who has consumed the heart of an angel or has psychic affinity can read surface thoughts. They are rarer than the more vampiric demon style creatures or the cryptid shapeshifters these days... but if I were you, I'd play up the commercial jingles. It's hard to read thoughts of someone either focused or listening to music."

"Oh. Here goes attempt number eighty thousand." Instantly, a boppin' Halloween song popped into her head. Vryce raised his stick. *Right casting!* Jane popped the cork and looked at the river below.

Okay, let's walk through this. Below this river is Purgatory, but I also know Purgatory is all around us. There isn't a river there, just the lands of endless dead. I'm in motion, so I just need to... Jane replayed each step in her mind and started singing to find her rhythm as she decided that she would use a more masculine energy and push her way through. The Halloween-themed song made her envision ripping open the paper-thin barrier between worlds, not unlike when she would bring herself near death.

She could feel the touch of death easily and had always been able to, but with the vial of blood in her hand, it was like holding ropes. Jane lunged forward with both hands and grabbed the river, ripping it open like it was a fruit—tearing away the current world and opening a portal directly into Purgatory beneath her.

"Holy shit!" Jane marveled at the sudden view of decay and entropy that filled her vision. Vryce appeared entirely different. He was slightly taller than her, with dagger-cut short brown hair messily sticking every which way. He was skinny with angular features and not an ounce of facial hair this side of a baby's ass. Yet, several shadows all loomed around him despite the presence of any direct light source, and she almost lost herself in those heterochromatic black and golden-green eyes that glistened and retained their color in an otherwise muted world. He was contrasted only by the Ouroboros amulet that writhed with the same-colored eyes dangling over a black v-neck shirt. Vryce, Jane realized, was very much a young man. *He's actually gorgeous. Despite the stitch marks binding those shadows.*

Jane didn't have long to gaze on Vryce's true soul on account of the giant hole she tore open beneath her, and she found herself tumbling down with a yell into Purgatory. Endless bridges with blind marching souls shambled to no particular destination everywhere. But falling was her jam. Jane kicked her new boots into action, fired a quick rocket boost, and pivoted her direction upright. With another kick, she vaulted herself back up, firing the jets like an expert skater, hopping off imaginary walls of air until she vaulted out of the very

same tear she just made. She was happy as a clam when she performed a double somersault before skidding to the side of the riverbed with a perfect landing. "Ten points for JK-47! The crowd goes wild!"

With her concentration lost in her own applause, the world faded back to normal, returning everything in her field of vision back to a boring dead forest with a running stream.

Vryce tossed the stick behind him and folded his hands behind his back as he paced over on the waves. "Congratulations. You've passed the entry exam." Jane could *feel* the looming threat mixed with an ounce of praise in his voice. Despite his best efforts to hide it, Vryce loved being a teacher. *A murderous teacher but a teacher none-the-less.*

"Notice how the vial is slightly drained. Blood is your fuel, no matter the form of magic. Even in those technological abominations you call shoes. When we bring the mystical into the material, there is always a cost. Those who consume hearts are specialists and can produce their own, at the cost of their humanity. There is, Jane, always a cost. A divine being died so that you may cast your spell. Be it dragon, demon, or faerie... each gives something for us gods to bend reality. There is a reason they put up barriers to keep us out of their worlds."

Jane felt saddened by the thought as Vryce walked past her to his belongings and pulled out his viola case.

"Much like cattle, some can be farmed harmlessly, so think of the little ones as chickens. It's why demon blood is so common. They are born from human desires and concepts. Fairies rely on dreams... but you," he thrust the viola case in her arms, "need to go to New Orleans and practice. Our sessions are over."

"Wait... what? We just got started! And you! You with the pretty face and amulet! What was that!?"

"Jane, I do not believe you understand that you are currently holding a fragment of my soul," he stated flatly as he slid on the Praenomen's mask and donned the trench coat. "It will empower you tenfold. Music will come naturally to you and focus your will like no other. As you practice, those portals to Purgatory and shaping the

very lands of the dead will be yours to command in time. Lose it, and I will not be able to teleport to you directly. Don't be afraid of going alone either. I can always sense when a portion of me is in immediate danger. But even if you do, remember that the entry into the lands of the dead will be your greatest spellcraft. Just don't run out of blood."

She hurried herself in front of him and grabbed his arm. "Is that why you are bailing? Something's wrong, isn't it?"

A flash of lightning sparked behind the eyes of the mask. "Very much so. It appears that New Orleans is empty." His voice changed to reflect both masculine and feminine energy. "Some foolish cunt has decided to wreck my house."

"I'm going with you. I'd like to submit my resume of me kicking a shit ton of ass on camera and in war as proof I should come." She thrust the viola back.

The second it was in his arms, Vryce shoved it back into hers. "I haven't pulled off the impossible without planning ahead. I'm not sending you to New Orleans to keep you safe. I'm taking advantage of distance."

Vryce fell backward into the river without a splash. Jane watched as the reflection broke like shattered glass and consumed the Praenomen before the crunching sounds of reality repairing itself restored the stream. He was gone.

And she was alone.

CHAPTER 28

We stand on a bed of razors. Our vaulted libraries and gardens are in peril. Bastions of the past lay siege to cities along the Eastern seaboard with a single aim: slaughter. Your training within the Society of Deus has not been for naught, and the time will soon come when Generals Alexander Lex DuPris and Michael Dragosani call upon your talents in the heat of battle. If you are ready to fight, not just for your survival, but for the right of all magic to survive without restrictions—join Amo-A-Deus today.

The great libraries of Deus represented more than centuries of occult artifacts and libraries to Damien. They represented his dream. A dream he foolishly imagined would grow like a planted seed into a voracious garden without his guiding hand. As he flowed through the single mirror within his inner sanctum, those wishful dreams withered and died. *You do not steal from the heavens without consequence, but divine rule is about to learn a valuable lesson.* "Do not tread on the souls of spiteful immortals."

Over the past year, Damien's inner sanctum maintained itself exactly as he left it. A small, severed hand with a single eyeball still swept rows of original texts while homunculi made of blood and paperclips ensured any spellcraft reagents never spoiled. Tiny

household gargoyle-esque cats worked diligently, ensuring every ward and component within his pyramid remained active. It took Vryce centuries to build a sanctum in Purgatory and the mirrored polarity of a massive pyramid floating so high over Deus and one in the gardens below. Without even searching the room, he opened a small cherry-maple box and pulled out a spool of silver thread and two cold-iron forged needles, deftly pocketing them in the Praenomen's trench coat. *If one must stitch souls to bodies, the classic tools work best,* he mused while recalling the excruciating pain he felt tying fragments of his own soul into his bones of a now broken body. *Time for a new one.* He did, however, notice, that Delilah had helped herself to several of his possession nails. Not that he needed them any longer since becoming a lich, but still, he made a mental note to punish her for the polite theft at a later date.

The inner library of Deus served as more than just one of the world's great arcane wonders. It housed over a thousand years of forbidden and outlawed magic deemed heretical by the Unification. As Vryce quickly strolled out of the entry chamber down the long oaken staircase, he passed hundreds of shelves littered with books that detailed how to devour souls, steal power, forge gargoyles, and other left-handed paths. There was no such thing as a forbidden spell in his mind, and it offered comfort to think that he'd become so infamous for enacting the very ritual which led to his current predicament but achieved the goal of bringing access to magic back.

Farther down beneath the great library, the lich continued down into the widest section of the underground pyramid. A massive prison chamber unfolded before his eyes. Within each cell lay bodies. Vampires, fae, shapeshifters, and other former members of the Unification that Delilah and Vryce had betrayed on the final night before Lazarus's glorious return. *Although, I am proud of you, Delilah, for it was your idea to use weapons-grade nerve gas to eliminate an entire room at once. Effective.* His pace slowed as he shopped for a new suit. Vryce's current body had advantages, but they weren't suited for war.

Jane was wrong about one thing—Damien never killed the girl he possessed now. Rather, the current body was a ritually grown child with the exact vibration frequencies as his original form before he became a vampire, and then a warlock, before ascending to lich. *I'd be a fool if I thought the Unification was going to sit back and do nothing, so... back up.* Since his female form was, well, him, it was easier to hide and vastly more unassuming. It did, however, come with several other social challenges he hadn't expected. His aim had always been to avoid consuming a heart in the form, lest he risk undoing the seams of his soul-stitching, and even with Lucian assaulting his own city—he was not ready to make that sacrifice. "I need something ... more expendable."

A werewolf perhaps? They regenerate naturally, and Lucian seems ill equipped to carry silver. But he is older than I and might know curses against lycanthropes. He strolled past the catatonic row of shape changers Delilah had organized by both species, status within the Unification, and age. *Don a vampire again? The sun is no longer a weakness, refillable blood supply. Then again, Lucian works with misfortune and necromancy beyond any other creature. My mind might be safe, but the body itself is still very much dead.* Vryce tapped the glass with his knuckles and dragged them across the chambers as he strolled past sharp angles and dizzying turns within the maze. The prison wasn't based off a new concept; in fact, it was a rather simple Unification prison design. Housing catatonic bodies within Purgatory itself and a few wards slowed drastically any sense of decay. One could house a prisoner for thousands of years and still maintain some semblance of functionality. *I wonder how Lazarus felt being chained so long in the original cells.*

His mind wandered to ancient times before his own birth in the 15th century. Even as a young boy, he always dreamed of dragons flying in the sky and the great wizards of legend to be real. "To think how far I've come." He stopped outside a single cell. "Hello..." Inside rested one of the ambassadors from the Fae Court. An elven creature of

nightmares rather than dreams slumbered. The male form was tall, over six feet, with short, bright white hair and short pointed ears. Vryce opened the chamber door and came in to inspect further. *You once represented the Emerald Isles for the Unification. Unlike most of the Society's allies, you remained staunch in your loyalty to the Unification, believing we stood no chance, didn't you Prince Alil Merovingian?* Vryce lifted the catatonic body up and saw the seared wounds where wings once attached. *Faerie. Naturally immortal, magic resistant, weak against cold iron, and creatures of chaos. Perfect for Lucian's particular brand of magic.*

Vryce pulled out his needle and thread and removed his garments. "I know your mind still lingers within your dream, so this is a temporary arrangement. If your body survives when I'm done with it, you'll be free to contemplate the consequences of your betrayal to the Society, Alil. Until then, I make no promises about what state you'll be in."

The teenage body collapsed on the stone slab next to the faerie as Vryce's mind untethered itself, floating free in the astral sea several feet above both forms before diving in the fae. Slipping in and taking the first breath felt like sliding on fresh socks for the first time, as Damien shot up and quickly stretched his new frame. He could feel the instant pangs of hunger and thirst as the form's motor functions and nerve clusters breathed to life, but he had little time to satiate the basic needs. Possession was merely that—possession. A simple puppet suit with little risk and no inherent magic. *I'm going to need a little more.* With deft fingers, the lich started breaking stitches on the fragments of his soul and sewing them, not into the body of the elf, far too risky for that, but into the chain links on the Ouroboros necklace itself. *When people aim to kill another, they destroy the body and loot the corpse. Just in case.*

Vryce was getting better at this ritual, that of transference, and what once took him hours took only several minutes with the right tools. In under fifteen, the Praenomen was fully dressed, equipped,

and ready to step out into the geofront just in time to welcome his new visitors. After of course, sealing the entry to his suits and ensuring that even his teenager form was safely secured. He'd hate to lose bodies with so much latent potential after all.

The large geofront was a hollowed-out cavern deep beneath the Twin Cities where the true beating heart of the Society of Deus rested. Within the hollowed-out cavern, the veil between realms was non-existent, represented by the soft light that danced along the jagged ceiling from the astral and heavenly realms all the way down to the soil fertilized from the depths of several hells. It was within this chamber that hovered between worlds that Vryce worked with other Unification warlocks, each within their own chamber, to resurrect Lazarus. Of course, he had other schemes that day, and the majority of warlocks also had little intention of letting Lazarus return.

Apparently, we were only half successful. Vryce marched out of the stone pyramid with his gaze fixed entirely on the clear glass elevator shaft that descended from the basement of Walsh Tower. He didn't have to wait long before three people were visible descending down the hundred-foot-long shaft. *Mr. Auburn, Lumine the talented prophet, and Mr. Montague himself. Should I bother with etiquette and simply challenge Montague to a proper arcane duel? He showed me no such courtesy when he held me captive. Then again, I did just break Mr. Culmen's hospitality to illustrate a point. In for a penny...*

"Let's cut right to the chase." Vryce levitated a few inches off the ground and twisted the cavern skies into thunderous storm clouds with his first spell. Stepping forward, he summoned two massive golems out of the nearby plant life. With his second step, arcs of lightning streaked across the sky down to his position in the palm of his hand and arched across his body. The third step ripped all vitae

from the Cherubim heart that remained in a circle around him for easy access. The fourth sent a telepathic message to every member of the Society to evacuate the city and head south for war. The fifth step, he activated arcane sight to better see weaves of hostile magic. With the sixth step, he fortified his skin into that of cement. *Just in case Mike gets too close.* And with the seventh step, he waited at the base of the elevator.

When the glass doors opened, the three entities inside were met with the visage of the Praenomen, albeit with pointier ears, wielding several lethal arcane spells ready to be unleashed with a single snap of his fingers.

Lucian, who had apparently lost an arm, stepped out first and waved for the other two to stay back. "This one's on me," he said flatly before turning his attention back to the Praenomen. "A soul is a soul no matter what mask you wear, Vryce." He flicked a coin in the air and sprinted, far faster than any normal skeleton should move.

It didn't matter. Seven lightning bolts fried Lucian into a pile of ash with a single snap. Daggers of blood fired forth and impaled Lumine against the glass elevator and began digging themselves into her veins as she raged and screamed. As for the last, Vryce reserved the only spell that wasn't hung for the great Mike Auburn. He simply looked into his eyes and uttered a single word.

"Kneel."

"No," Mike snapped back before ripping Lumine free and throwing her with unnatural strength in Vryce's direction. The two golems were quick to uncoil themselves and intercept the were-crocodile's vertical assault, tackling her into the blood-rose bushes that flanked each pathway.

Vryce both hated and respected Mike at that exact moment. *I applaud the strong will, but I will not apologize for this.* "You could have joined—"

A raspy voice cut Vryce off as Lucian's cackle turned into words, coming from multiple directions as his spirit reformed. "Your power

is not in question, Lich. You could smite and destroy me a thousand times over, but now you stand before divine judgement. You who violated the principalities of heaven will be shown the hubris of your ways. We are *all* chained, heathen. You do not get to roam free."

Vryce felt Lucian's will press into his Sanctum like a worm, attempting to inflict a curse of misfortune throughout the cavern. Unseen to everyone else, their minds clashed for control over reality within the geofront. Lightning above became erratic, smashing down near them or simply spiraling in the sky as if two sorcerers were wrestling for control over a garden hose. Lucian's ghost slowly manifested and reincorporated itself, stepping calmly over the pile of ash.

The Death Lord continued, "You set your inner sanctuary within Purgatory to hide from the eyes of angel and demon alike. Yet you know not how ancient some of us bastions of death truly are. I have stood knee deep in mud and bone. I have filled my lungs with the ashes of volcano and mustard gas alike in war. I have seen brothers fall. I have lain with holy wars and copulated with the forgotten. I have dug trenches for the slaves; I have murdered dissidents where the ground never thaws and starved the masses of fortune so they may know truth."

Vryce quickly ran left and ignited Lucian with a pillar of thirty-foot white flame. Silence followed for but a moment.

Lucian continued. "This is your coming millennia? This is the thousand years of darkness you wish to be wrought upon the world? Let me tell you what awaits..." The skeleton marched forward relentlessly as its skin reformed around his bones from the ectoplasm within Purgatory. "They will eat them, Vryce. They will eat every creature of magic for power and dine on their blood until they are human no longer. They will become pigs. And in the end, they will stick their snouts into your ribs and eat *your* heart."

Vryce didn't panic. *Just how many souls will you burn, Misfortune?* He stayed just out of arms reach of the Death Lord easily on his march, and thanks to his new body, any curse effects of rolling misfortune

were buffered by the fae's blood—for a time. Lucian died again, and again, and again. A dozen spells each more powerful than anything Gabriel could bring to bear instantly incinerating, boiling, shocking, crushing, and more shattered Lucian.

Yet each time the Death Lord manifested again.

"We can do this dance for a hundred years, Damien." Lucian laughed. "Isn't it great! You and I, locked in battle within your sanctum, where you are god! How does it feel to have a devil in your kingdom? A worm you can't get rid of. A pathetic, helpless creature who can do *nothing* to you with all your wards, levitation, magic, and control of reality. This is YOUR kingdom. I'm just visiting. Yet you cannot deny fate; you cannot deny misfortune."

"Everyone has limits," Vryce intoned and smashed a torrent of rainwater to both crush and obliterate the Lord. "Even gods rid themselves of their demons." *You, however, enjoy this. I have a world to conquer. There will be no centuries-long battle between us while Lazarus's armies wreck my future and undo everything.*

"Hey, buddy." Mike had closed the gap during the duel and swung directly at Vryce's head once again. His fist nearly struck true with all the strength of Golgoroth behind it once again.

This time, Vryce deftly caught his hand without a flinch. "Absolutely not. I was waiting for you."

"Goodbye, Lucian." Vryce smiled. "Oh, by the way, your pupil has potential. You should consider enrolling her." Vryce expanded his mind to the fragments of his soul. Gabriel wielded both blades and had just left the city, Delilah was distant and possessed several nails, and then he felt Jane. In his mind's eye, he could see exactly where she had gone in this short time. *Did you bend space and travel through Purgatory to New Orleans?* Unfortunately, that didn't seem to be the case. She merely walked down a long highway alone with her belongings and her thumb out like a hitchhiker. *Close enough, I suppose.* Disappointed, Vryce quickly loosed a sewing needle into Lumine's

thigh as she tussled with the golem and tugged on the thread bound between his fingers and the needle to activate his final spell.

Mike, Lumine, and Vryce were all pulled from the heart of Deus to an empty highway where Jane lugged his viola case on the side of the road.

"We have work," Vryce said, walking briskly to New Orleans. *Not every battle is won through annihilation, Lucian.*

CHAPTER 29

"And I beheld another beast coming up out of the earth, and he had two horns like a lamb, and he spoke as a dragon. Beware, ye sinners, for the beast walks among us, cloaked in human guise, whispering false promises of power and salvation through the arcane. Those who heed its call will find their souls and bodies bound in chains, dragged into Purgatory to suffer the torment of endless waiting. The Church of Lazarus offers sanctuary to the faithful, a shield against the dragon's fire. Let the sorcerers tremble, for their end is nigh, and the righteous shall rise."

–Broadcast in Arcadia, Texas

John let the smoke trail from his lips as he toured the antiquities within St. Peter's walls while awaiting his speech. He had come to enjoy the moments of private clandestine meetings between the fire and brimstone propaganda he spewed forth from his high walls to feed the ravenous masses. *Don't kid yourself. You enjoy both.* He took another drag of the joint before looking up at a glorious naked statue of Aphrodite. Bacchus, Heracles, and Osiris awaited his presence farther down the hall, or at least their statues, but he was always a personal fan of Aphrodite. A goddess of beauty and fertility on the outside, but with a litany of tragedies and secrets hidden in history behind her ascent to power. If only he'd been around to consort with the real one back in ancient times.

Alexandria of Ur trailed her fingers along the railing as she sauntered in his direction. "You know, most tourists are confused about why so many pagan and demonic gods are revered within the Vatican walls." She rubbed his back and lowered herself to take a hit from the joint.

"People are idiots," John remarked with a sneer. "The secret to power has always been on display within this city, but hey, if they don't see it, makes it easier for us."

"Weed, Lazarus, does wonders for you. You are looking better since I saw you last. No coughing?"

"I hope that is not your one question for the session." John exhaled and walked fully upright. He wore now more than just grave clothes but openly sported the heavy armored cloak for the Lord of Heaven's Wrath. Made from threads of spider silk and woven Kevlar, the cloak also had ceramic-plate reinforcement in several places—each one specially enchanted to reflect a spell back upon its caster. A mere week ago, the thought of taking a stroll with the robe seemed a titanic feat, but he barely felt the weight. "Come, let us walk and talk this day. I'm feeling," he pondered the correct word, "satiated."

"We have only just begun, and you are already getting results. Fascinating."

John's cracked and bleeding lips smiled as scabs fell pathetically to the floor. "One does not shape the world with talks of peace and unity. Fanaticism drives the crazies to take action, and the rest of the masses cower in their insignificant burrows. I love the Catholics. Not because of their..." his finger twirled as he waved to the statues of conquered gods, "historic achievements. But because they knew how to conquer the world from the start. Appear meek. Unite the masses. Then one brick at a time, build a global empire."

Alexandria rolled her eyes. "Oh yes, let's glorify those who burned us on stakes, and for the record, there are *several* faiths that very much disagree with Catholic dominance. Holy wars exist for a reason."

"And every one of those religions followed the same blueprint. Co-opt, build your base, and demonize. You are right; they are wrong. You are godly; they are scum. You know that you are big enough to conquer a kingdom when your own religion has their own regional sub-branches."

She couldn't help herself as they passed Bacchus, pausing to place her hand on his chest and floating up to plant a kiss on his marble lips. "You, old friend, made immortality worth it."

"I never said he couldn't return. Dionysus, Bacchus, Agrios, and his thirty or so other names might be one worth returning into the mix when we win."

She looked forlorn and let the sounds of a thousand chanters waiting in the courtyards flow down the halls before acknowledging it. "If we win Lazarus. *If.* The war is not going well. No major territorial gains have been achieved. Japan and Korea have proven nearly impossible for the Lord of Pollution to crack. Eastern Asia: the whole bloody region has been nothing more than a standstill. Hell, even Australia has their own damned ancient sea gods. Few if any, are buying your propaganda."

"We disagree." John gestured to the masses.

"Please." She crossed her arms. "I figured you smarter than a fascist who surrounded himself with sock puppets who praise the shit you take at noon every day."

"You misunderstand. History has done this dance before. You of all people should remember that gods and magic once walked openly on barren and fertile soil alike. The Gardens of the old. Eden. Avalon. Atlantis. Elysia. Valhalla. Of course, they will return and have *power.*" His fist clenched. "Many new ones will appear. Yet let us not forget our garden is that of Purgatory. Each soul that perishes strengthens our legions. They are weak now, but on their lips, they pray to me for

escape. For I am their god. We only need to stoke the fires of conflict, and the blood will fertilize our gardens. If the whispers are true, then we have even proven that arcane heathens can fall. Our wayward Lord of Misfortune seems to have been a boon for us."

As they neared the podium where guards from the Church of Lazarus stood ready for the big speech by Lazarus, Alexandria stopped and pulled a small silver flask from her purse and slipped back the Lady of Suicide's feathered mask. "I need a drink." She eagerly devoured every drop contained within. Every drop except the rogue trace of blood that ran down her pale neck. She smacked her lips and offered a sip to Lazarus, knowing he would refuse. "Between Lucian laying siege to a single city, or the Lord of Murder's forces conquering nearly the entire East Coast except New York and D.C., I think one is faring better than the other."

John took her flask and sealed it up. *Yes, yes, Lord of Murder. Good at killing. What would I ever do without his ambition? Yet a few hundred thousand souls are a droplet compared to a single cut on an unchained lich.* "I have a question. What do you think Damien Vryce would do with an army of gods and demigods? Honestly." He glanced over to Osiris.

Alexandria fixed her hair and contemplated a true answer while her mask fastened into place. John was mildly amused as he watched her lips purse several times as she weighed options. "Tricky. His quest for power has always been about a ... righteous sense of tyrannical freedom. So, he would either steal their power to become *the* God of Magic. Or he'd set them free and enjoy a thousand-year-long cage match to prove his own worth."

John nodded. *That's the problem. It's a good story. The masses love a good story.* "I figured as such. We need to wound him deeper."

"Why are you afraid of him? Honestly." Her fanged smile grew wider by the word.

John pulled up his hood. "Because every Death Lord, except you and me, is a lich. Their souls shredded and then shoved back in their

withered stolen hearts like a stuffed turkey and then bound to eternal servitude over the souls in Purgatory, and those Lords and Ladies, my dear, are godlike children. They will not tolerate a brother who escaped a spanking by an absentee pantheon. If Damien's freedom goes unchecked, their jealousy will claw at their minds like centipedes in their skulls until they snap. They'll make a rash mistake, and the bastard will earn a victory. Which," he fidgeted with a strip of cloth as he studied the microphone waiting thirty paces away, "will have a domino effect. Not in his victory, no no, but in causing even more temper tantrums from those who command the faith and obedience of legions. Legions that will then utter his name, while carrying banners of mine. We cannot afford an equal."

"I see. That explains why it is only Misfortune there. If he dies, the others will not mourn." She helped dust off his clothes. "A bit of unwanted advice then. Our little pet project in the Sanctum is a useful tool here, so we should delay me undergoing the rituals of lichdom. I've got plenty of power, and the Mask of Suicide suffices. So instead... I could send a little whisper to Katrina and offer her select gods from our prisons for revival. With Dystopia's assistance, a few old gods with new corporate messages might create enough white noise to buy you more time. If they carry our banners into battle..." she mused.

Lazarus knew this was her opportunity to rescue a few old friends. Releasing old deities from prison would be akin to suicide for him. Their wrath upon the Unification would be swift after centuries of bleeding. *Unless...*

"You still have that informant Morris close to the Second City forces?"

She nodded.

"Tell Katrina and him that New Orleans is theirs for the harvesting. Let us sacrifice the Seat of Golden Tears."

Alexandria looked genuinely shocked. "That makes no sense. They are tentative allies of Deus. Wouldn't it be better for us to hold their chains?"

Lazarus smirked. "Do we have confirmation that Vryce is dead?" he asked rhetorically. "Do you think he will kneel before the Second City Boss? No. He is too prideful for such actions. Katrina will see it as an opportunity for her own ascension, and every capitalistic pig in that silicon freakshow will want in on the action. It will be, as you said, chaos and white noise. Noise we can ignore while we turn our attention to the rest of the world."

"Very well." She bowed. "And what of Delilah Dumont? She agreed to meet."

"Make her wait. I have a speech," he said, turning and hunching his back as he shambled up to the podium.

Lazarus gave his speech to thousands of followers in Rome. Followers who had held pure and rebuked the easy path to power of imbibing divine blood or devouring hearts. They were the masses of the meek, and they were his secret weapon against the inevitable arrival of unwanted gods. As the words of fire and brimstone echoed off concrete walls, the masses were oblivious to the vampires, ghosts, and demons that sulked in the shadows, avoiding the sun's rays. A tide had begun to turn within the Vatican Palace, and each of the lurking monsters could feel the shift infinitely more than the cheering crowds. The sun's rays, even if still emanating from a black sun, caused the skin of monsters to itch.

And while Lazarus's gaze fell upon many, there was one face in the crowd who Dr. John C. Daneka focused on. A single, bold demon, who sat in a lawn chair with a can of beer, sunglasses, and a Lucky Strike smoke proudly enjoying the coming of a sun which would cause magic to cower back to the shadows.

"Leaders have always said that their war is for peace. A means to an end. A war to end all wars. This has always been a lie. Shame is a prison. And so, we shall live in shame and deception no longer. There

is no grave that will hold my soul down. There is no trumpet that will bring us to kneel. Fear may be a liar with a smooth and velvet tongue. But we shall not turn our backs! Our war between death and life shall crucify the lamb of god, and we shall all rise as lions upon our garden! And so, I promise all of you. Our war is only the beginning!"

Lazarus basked in the raucous cheers that chipped away at the lie he sold one death at a time.

CHAPTER 30

"::click:: Experiment 6,023. Recording Date. May 2nd, 1957. Subject: Dr. John C. Daneka. The demon heart of Mammon, formerly known as Greed, has continued to survive with electrical stimulation from a vintage polyphase induction motor since 1889. All prior attempts to extend human life span without ingestion have failed. I will now attempt to implant the heart within the corpse of a freshly deceased U.S. Senator and make an offering to Greed. Extend my life without use of blood or consumption in exchange for freedom to walk. May god have mercy on my soul. ::click::"

—Old Tape Found by Doc Daneka in his father's desk.

Lucian bit his tongue inside the vaulted stone entry of the great Deus library. The massive metal doors loomed in front of him. Each door was elaborately decorated with the Tree of Life and annoyingly warded to an absurd degree. *Is there a key under the mat? Do people do that?* Lucian had peeked and snooped at nearly every corner of the pyramid for hidden doors or escape hatches, anything that would allow him to avoid using the front door, but to no avail. The

locked doors were his only option, and other than a smooth crimson orb set on a pedestal to his right, Lucian was coming up empty-handed.

He kicked the door and quickly regretted it. "Son of—!" He hopped while holding a freshly stubbed toe that stuck out of his boots. "Come on! Let me in! I've got uh…" He fished for something random in his pockets and only produced two six-sided dice and a business card for ten percent off honey delivery. "Coupons! Everyone loves coupons!"

Nothing happened.

Over the next hour, Lucian tried breaking the orb, pried at the door with a large stick, and even tried carving out the grommet that held a brick in place. The latter he really thought he had a shot at. *I've got centuries! I can dig at it like water wearing down a mountain.* He lasted about five minutes of scratching at brick before he got bored and went and sat on a step to sulk.

"This is bullshit." He buried his head in his knees and sobbed. Every single time he tried to do something good for the world, it always went south, and this time was no different. "Ironic isn't it, Lou? You trip down the stairs, and a war is averted. I topple an empire and can't even loot the king's vault." He brushed wet soil off the steps to clean the stone with resigned sigh. The little act of cleaning and tidying did make him feel at least a little productive. *Can't believe I'm going to do this, but hey, maybe this is my garden now.*

Lucian found himself a set of brooms in a garden shed that survived his duel with Vryce and got to work. The pyramid was covered with debris, plant matter, golem guts and several lightning scorch marks that the Death Lord found himself cleaning as he contemplated his predicament. Never before in history had someone just … abandoned post. *Every other king shields themselves with their armies or clings onto their paradise until their dying breath. Even the ones who flee leave behind sacrifices to "hold the fort."* Lucian was so frustrated at Vryce's impromptu teleportation that he pretended to strangle the

sorcerer's scrawny neck on the broom handle—before apologizing to the broom itself.

The problem, Lucian realized after a few hours of sweeping and helping broken plants back into their soil, was that nobody was left in Deus. *No souls. No ghosts. No vampires. No shoe vendors. No Mike and no Lumine. How would I know that Vryce would just ... quit!* His brand of misfortune magic, unfortunately for him, required people. Lucian wasn't a Death Lord of Famine, so causing plants and insects to malfunction wasn't his specialty, and if he was honest with himself—he wasn't good at high spellcraft. All of his magic was street level and relied upon either dead things or living things. "Hell, even if he left Lumine around, I could start a chain reaction with her misfortune. All I've got is a city of zombies ranging from Jeff to Jeremy, to Jebidiah..." He kept rattling off their individual names, each beginning with a J (except Frankie, who was the only zombie who named himself), as he replanted a blood-rose bush. "There you go, little guy. Sorry about that fight. It wasn't your fault. Your master is just a jerkface."

Maybe if I have the zombie family form a big-ass battering ram? He shook his head and dismissed the thought. Misfortune, curse, and necromancy magic functioned when there *was* a society. There needed to be order for Lucian to find the entropic cracks and threads to tug upon. Here, he might as well be standing in an empty forest and wishing bad luck upon a spider. *And a spider getting eaten by a bird isn't bad luck... That's just fucking life. God dammit.*

Hours later, after Lucian was satisfied that the landscaping and flowers were replanted and watered, he felt much better about himself. The truth had always been that his heart was never in the game. Mike had several good points about the nature of Death Lords and Lazarus. Chief among them was that Lazarus was just another dictator in the making, and for someone like himself, Lucian would just simply find a cheap apartment and wait out the reign until he died. For people like Mike and Lumine, though—they had to suffer through it. When

you add immortality into the mix, even Lucian would be waiting a long time.

"I only ever said I'd *come* to North America, Lazzy baby, never said I'd end up winning. But here you go! Your prize awaits! The locked library of Deus!" Lucian shouted into the cavern. "Look at me go! Lucian Montague! Death Lord of Misfortune topples another kingdom! Kinda?" He pressed the elevator up button and waited. *At least Vryce didn't fry the elevator. Granted, that was probably because he didn't want to pay the repair bill. The elevator's union is scary.*

Stepping out into topside of Deus was eerie. Cars were abandoned in the middle of the road, their doors ajar from a quick evacuation. The lights of the city shone brightly. Automated sprinkler systems still showered hanging gardens, and an occasional dog or small familiar feasted on restaurant food left on the table. Lucian felt like he was strolling through the ruins of a city devoid of human life, and it was perhaps the most peaceful thing he'd encountered this decade.

"Evenin', Jacob." Lucian tipped his hat as he passed by a zombie standing idly by a streetlamp with nothing to do. Jacob groaned.

Looking up to the sky, Lucian saw the massive pyramid only had one of the three chains snap and crumble down. "So Vryce's absurd creation stills stands? A crown without a head. He he he. Well, can't say I'm bothered by that. My whole domino plan kinda revolved around enough chaos that would spiral out and... kablammo! It would have been a show worth watchin', that's for sure."

If nothing else, Lucian figured he learned a lesson about his powers. In such isolation, the chain of misfortune gets snapped. Now, the only hope for the city to be turned to ashes was if he got several gas cans and became the world's loneliest arsonist—and that wasn't exactly entertaining. *It's no fun when YOU burn the buildings themselves.* "But looting..." Lucian's attention was drawn to the dying embers of a fire near a row of downtown businesses. "Don't mind if I do."

For hours until the black sun rose, Lucian helped himself to curiosities and oddities that caught his attention. A new set of boots was first on the list, along with a fancy new seagull shirt, but he did borrow a new left arm from one of the fresher zombies and spent the time healing himself. He filled a small backpack up with self-crawling slimes, rare coins from a currency exchange, and a new set of poker cards before getting completely lost in what he considered his finest artistic creation.

With a spark of inspiration, Lucian set about creating an economy of zombies. Grown in number since their invasion, but with no human brains to eat, his minions would just stand there until they crumpled. *That would just be a travesty!* One-by-one, Lucian saw to it that every one of his thousand plus creations were freshly clothed and given new roles. Jimmy would be a bartender, and Jenny was the flirty but sassy streetwalker. Jessica would work in the department of motor vehicles and issue tickets to jay walkers. Every single one got a new purpose in the city and set about on the most mundane tasks in an elaborate scheme that would breathe new life into Deus with Lucian as their mayor. Except Frankie, he didn't need a job; he was a cab driver. So, he got a cabbie hat and was shooed off. *It's pretty strange to just dig up an already animated zombie, but I mean, magical place, magical corpses, I suppose.*

When Lucian was finished with his scheme a day later, an entire downtown sector of St. Paul was a self-sustaining autonomous city of zombies complete with soap-opera level drama. They had romance stories, would break up, hold weddings, and even break into dance at programmed intervals. Setting it all up was a much-needed distraction for the Death Lord, mostly because he had no damn clue what to do next other than start a really long walk back to his Seat of Golden Tears. *Whoever finds this city, or if the residents of Deus come back, they are going to LOVE this! Imagine getting a ticket from Jessica for crossing the street wrong! I LOVE IT!*

By the third day, nobody had come back within the city's walls to Lucian's chagrin, and he got bored of waiting. In truth, he was more saddened that he couldn't stick around to see their faces when they were treated to a lovely dinner in the newly renovated Bones Bar by the waitstaff. *Bastards are probably scryin' in with some magic shit just waitin' for me to leave. They really didn't just like ... move, did they? Can they afford to do that in today's world? Ooof... to be rich.*

Lucian strolled into the Sonder the Fitz hotel, a huge gothic hotel in downtown St. Paul, and had Jared the bellhop bring him an old phone. With bony fingers, he slowly dialed a number he never really wanted to call. *Can't believe I'm doing this shit.*

The black earpiece nestled between his ear and shoulder. As it rang, Lucian took a hit from a vape until Jared held up a no smoking sign. "Rude," he responded.

"Rude? Who is this?" A female voice spoke on the other line.

"Sorry! Lou! Hey girl! Sooooo, how's it going?" Lucian twirled the cord around his finger.

"What in the hells do you want, Lucian? And why are you calling me collect internationally? Don't you have a cell phone?"

"Really? You think I could afford that? Anywho, how's my favorite Lady of Fate doing?"

"What did you do, Lucian?"

"Well... I'm standing in an empty city, sorry, a newly inhabited city with extremely hospitable guests and was wondering if you wanted to come visit."

"You claimed Deus?" She silenced someone else in the background. "Isn't that a bit grand for your stylings?"

"Eh, I kinda went with the flow on this one. I saw a thread on one of yours, a Mikey Auburn. Seemed like the right one to tug and just sorta ended up here."

"I mean, I'm certainly not going to complain to hear how my favorite bartender and his crew are doing. If you see O'N—" Lucian

held the phone off his ear as loud feedback suddenly came through. "-e better come visit. It's been too long."

"Yeah, yeah, I'll pass it along if I can get back down there. Hey, so, I was wondering. You wouldn't happen to have a spell for me, would you? Maybe like … a magical fated steed shows up, so I don't have to walk across this country? I can't drive."

"Lucian, where is your army?"

"You mean Murder's? I have no fucking clue. I cut those losers loose weeks ago. I think they are blowing up Florida or something, which really is a win for every sentient creature on Earth."

"No, Lucian, where are *your* soldiers? Our treasured children."

"Well… so… you won't believe this. Some dumb ass dropped bombs on Samhain and cracked open the Seat of Golden Tears. And since Lazarus has all these grand plans to turn everything right, I decided to set them free and left the vault open. They'll find their coins and move on. It's about time one of us Death Lords actually did our divine job, right? I mean, since heaven is all empty and there is no *reason* for them to stick in Purgatory… I uh…" He tapped the desk nervously. "Let 'em go? Except Lumine. She decided to stick around by my side."

"So where is Lumine?"

"Oh, Vryce stole her. Along with your Mike."

"The sound of my voice is the sound of my general disappointment in you right now. We've always looked out for each other, and things are getting strange here in the Vatican. Lazarus is…"

"Off the deep end? Honey, I knew that guy was a nutjob from his first speech. I don't exactly toe the party line as it were. How's that killing all the humans thing working out for you?"

"I think it's starting to work. The sun over Rome makes the monsters uncomfortable. The problem is the killing all the humans part."

"Well, you are the Lady of Fate. Go empower a champion and give them Excalibur or something. Isn't that what you do? Make heroes?"

"Excuse me! Pot calling the kettle black there! Where is your empire-crumbling magic at, eh mister? Do I need to hit you with a spoon?! Both our hands are tied, and you know that. We set things up, but we need others to rise up."

Lucian grinned. He loved teasing Fate just a tad, and she was easy to rile up. "So... am I hearing that you aren't drinking the Church of Lazarus kool-aid either? I learned a pretty funny thing about our limitations here in Deus. Without anyone around, we are..."

"Empty."

"I mean, Famine and Pollution will probably have a field day. All puns intended. But seriously, can you get me a ride?"

"That depends. Where you looking to go?"

"I dunno, *mon cheri*. I was thinking of going to visit Haiti. I've got to update some family trees with a branch of J's."

"Mmmm... I don't see that for you."

"You never see anything for me. That's why you like me."

"Shut it," she whispered. "So, I can't really talk much. But, and this is *not* because I see anything. This is me, Lou, just helping out an old friend. If you left your Seat open and unchecked... did you ever pause to consider what else is being held there?"

"Oh! The food? What about it?"

"Did you ever think that someone else might *want* that food?"

"The hell would anyone want with a bunch of drained, dying demigods? I mean, munch away; it isn't going to change anything. Lazarus is going to kill everything, and then we might finally get to die. A few nibbles won't change the war."

"Ahem. Who *else* did we have O'N—" the phone screeched again, "nailed to a tree?"

"Okay, whatever name you are trying to say is totally bugging this thing out. Please stop. Nobody is going to find Balor, unless you are Lazarus's..." Lucian stopped speaking as his eyes went wide. "Descendants."

"I hear Katrina and the rest of Murder's over there are starting up operations. Do you think Murder has forgiven you for the last time you plucked his souls?"

"Oh, Lou, what would I ever do without you?"

"Probably spend all your time trolling casinos, but I've got to roll. One of my newer souls, a girl named Phoebe, is still freaking out in the background."

"You're too kind to your prophets, Lou. Sometimes, they just need to learn the harsh lessons."

"That's the problem. She's not mine. She's Murder's, and that's why she's freaking out."

"Oof, rough. Some chap killed one of yours, eh? OOOH... wait... I'm not responsible, am I?"

"Enjoy the walk, buddy. This is a tangled ball of fate, but I'll figure it out eventually."

The line went silent, and Lucian was still no closer to getting home. "Where's a damn taxicab when you need one?" he whined to Jared, who simply pointed outside. "Shit, Jared! You are a genius! Why didn't I remember that Frankie can drive! Here's a tip. Four out of five stars. This should be a smoking establishment; it's not like anyone is going to get cancer here." Lucian slid over a small plastic container with a purple slime pet inside. "On me, buddy."

Lucian shouldered his bag and went off into the city to hail a taxi.

CHAPTER 31

"You know we've seen this movie before, right?" Mike said from the back of a police car. The camera picks up fires burning in the background of the West Loop. "Some douchebag flips the switch and releases all the ghosts into the world. So it's important to remember that as we go through this, if someone asks you, 'Are you a god?' you say yes."

—Chicago PD Footage Released

Mike was speechless. One minute earlier, he was watching two ancient bastards duke it out with zips, booms, and sparkly fireworks, and now he was standing on the side of a road in bumblefuck nowhere. Lumine lurched forward and puked all over his boots with a combination of sweet treats and bite-sized meat skewers. She looked up after the third heave and mumbled something of an apology. Mike just patted her head and shouted over to Vryce, who had only mentioned something about work and bolted off in a power walk.

"Sparkle-Fingers! Slow the hell down! If you are going slam people across space and time, you could at least…"

324

The faerie wearing the Praenomen mask froze in his tracks and looked over his shoulders with murderous intent. His head shook as he warned Mike with a wagging finger.

"Alright," Mike conceded. It took him a moment to study Vryce's new form. Taller and more lithe than the teenage girl he wore earlier, there were still several shadows instead of merely one at his feet, and the Praenomen's porcelain mask wasn't there to hide his appearance but as part of some artifact to empower his magic. The form paled in presence compared to the first time Mike saw Vryce's true body with all his souls unified into a single form. *At least I was able to save the world from something with that much power walking around.* "You've got me, Primus Vryce. I concede. To be real, I know you are out of my league. Still, I have seen Jane," he yanked his sister in front of him to serve as a far cuter body shield, "and Lumine here clearly does not teleport well."

"I think I'm still sick," Lumine groaned.

Vryce slowly turned and started back. "You, of all the creatures on this planet, have no right to disrespect me. I've tolerated your existence up until now. Worked with your band of merry little anarchs and their ignorant schemes. I've sat quietly and observed your pathetic attempts at revolution." Vryce marched back closer and closer with each sentence. Jane, Mike, and Lumine all raised their hands, expecting some arcane assault to be launched their way. "You even destroyed the lives of an entire city with almost every civilian more curious and more adept at navigating this world than you. So no, Mr. Auburn, I shall not wait for you to get your bearings. We have work to do before either Peter Culmen and Katrina rip open a prison of gods and seal them under contracts, or a Death Lord finds his way back to us. Now move."

Sorry about the Twin Cities. Not exactly a lot of options on my plate there. Mike rubbed Lumine's back as they started walking, letting Vryce take the lead a few good paces ahead. The pointed elf-ears sticking out from behind the mask would probably allow him to hear

anything said regardless, but Mike at least felt a little better talking behind his back that way. When he was a good twenty or so ahead, Mike finally looked down at Jane in her new clothes. Jane had managed to enchant some fingerless gloves, fresh skintight jeans with several rips, a set of Dystopian rocket boots, and a fitted T-shirt from a band called Zombie Girl to replace her old ghost clothing, and judging from a backpack brimming with fabric, she'd been collecting. The one object that didn't seem to fit was the viola case slung over her left shoulder. "You've been busy. I'm assuming that's his?"

"Mmmhrm." Jane's energy was anything but friendly.

"Good to see you? What uh... What have you been doing these days?" Mike adjusted his bandanna.

"Stuff."

"She's pissed," Lumine chimed in. "Here! I have..." She searched her pockets and found a small vial of honey. "Have some honey! It will help you feel better."

Jane rolled her eyes and walked faster, shouldering Mike in the process and leaving Lumine confused.

"One sec." Mike trotted up to Jane's other side. "Jane, what's wrong?"

She puffed a lock of blonde hair out of her eyes and threw her hands up in frustration. "Really? REALLY? Did you EVER stop to think that maybe you shouldn't fling casual insults and disrespect the very people helping us?"

"Who—him?! Helping? Trust me, Jane, if there is anything he's doing, it's for his own benefit. Vryce has no problems murdering anyone who gets in his way."

"Correct," Vryce said without the slightest turn.

Mike continued, "Point. Also, it was either the Second City or the Twin Cities. Lucian was on a tear, and he was going to trash one of the two cities. I figured, if anything, that in the Twin Cities he could at least be stopped."

"I don't care about that," Jane retorted. "When was the last time you showed anyone genuine respect? Boss? You give him sass endlessly."

"You do know Boss rammed a piece of wood through my heart and left me in a barrel under the sun as my hazing, right?" Mike realized he was reflexively arguing and held up his hands. "Okay, before I offer some hollow apology, tell me why this..." he struggled not to say *jackass,* "person gets respect."

"He actually takes the time to teach you. Mike, don't you get it? He could have killed you multiple times."

He DID kill me multiple times. Mike felt like he wanted to scream but kept his tongue bit.

"Plus, you should have seen him in Dystopia. Things didn't go as planned, and I'm prrreeetty sure that my favorite city is about to have Lazarus branding at the current pace." She punched him in the shoulder. "AND HE SAVED YOUR ASS! He could have had you fried just like Lucian. So, you owe him."

Mike sneered. "That one has me confused. Either Lumine really is lucky, or he's up to something. Why pull the pair of us back to you?"

Vryce made a *hrmph* sound under the mask but offered no clarification.

Jane whispered, "Because he secretly likes ghosts, it turns out. He spent like two weeks teaching me spellcraft."

"Which you did not put into practice," Vryce chided. "I had expected you to bend Purgatory to your will and already be in New Orleans."

"Excuse me, buttercup," Jane fired back. "You only left me with a few angel blood vials. What if I got there and had to use them for an emergency? I. Was. Rationing."

Great. My sister is now not only dating Dragosani, but she's also taking lessons from Glower McGlowery.

Vryce paused and tilted his head back slightly. "You are dating Dragosani, Jane?"

Suddenly Jane's cheeks turned an eerie white as her eyes went wide. "Uh, not... officially... sir. We have an arrangement for when I return, but... I have yet to see him."

"I will need words with my general then. We will rendezvous at our destination."

I hate mind readers. Mike had just barely gotten used to the idea that Gabriel could lift his thoughts, and now he had to guard them against everyone. "Speaking of meeting up with people. Jane... why are you alone? Where, uh, is everyone?"

"They took the car to New Orleans a fortnight ago. So, I've just been trying to hitchhike a lift. I was kind of ABANDONED in the middle of the woods abruptly."

Mike checked on Lumine, who still trailed along, pretending not to eavesdrop on the only conversation taking place for a few miles. "So, why are we walking all the way there then? Can't you just teleport us there?"

"I'm rationing," Vryce responded, but everyone could tell he was smiling under that mask.

"Torture. Got it." Mike shrugged. "So, we good now, Jane?"

"If you think so."

Lumine piped in from behind, "That's girl speak for absolutely not. Just in case you need a translation."

"Peanut gallery comments are not welcome." Mike decided to drop any further prying and change the subject. Jane was her own brand of badass, and he wasn't going to allow himself to battle a deep difference of opinions just yet. If she thought the Society of Deus was so great, maybe watching their ruthlessness in action would change her tune. "So, are we onto plan B? Or C now? Break out all the gods for some extra support?"

Vryce nodded. "Something to that effect. Jane is here because she has potential and can alter Purgatory. I've kept you around in case I need a door opened."

Lumine hugged herself as if she was cold and strolled behind with a frown on her lips, her posture appearing very closed off. Vryce slowed his gait. "Lumine back there has true talent, and I respect her craft and determination—despite her choice of company. And so, when we get to the prison site, we will rendezvous with the Sons and Daughters, dive on in, clean out any resistance—and judge the entities held within. If the Church of Unification arrives, we will have reinforcements."

Mike grumbled, "So, what happens if Lucian returns home? It is kind of his personal domain."

Nobody felt like answering the possibility, and they walked in silence for several more miles under the night sky.

Mike thanked the stars when they found an abandoned car the next day. A six-day walk in current company would have driven him insane, so he was more than glad to play the part of driver. After scrubbing the dried blood off the driver's side window, Mike was behind the wheel of a yellow Jeep complete with a fully charged mp3 player— loaded to the brim with some playlist called Swifties. *Absolutely not.* In the absence of tunes, their only option was the endless prattling of political talk radio. The one unifying trait all four of them agreed upon was how gross they felt listening to some senator talk about how Pride was going to save the nation. The world may have ended, but it was payday for any of the god-fearing types. Radio channel after radio channel featured everything from sermons to bigoted rants to insane claims that isolated the listener further and further from reality. *Some things never change. God, I hate the south.*

Silence became the universal peace of mind for everyone in the Jeep within short order as they pulled into the blasted landscape of New Orleans.

Calling it New Orleans was a bit of a stretch. The city had always been a squat city as far as urban development went, but now, it looked nothing like its former self. Mike pulled over before they hit the remains of a concrete highway and got out. The violet Lilith Moon clashed with a neon orange light that boiled up from the hole in the ground. *Fuckin' el.* Jane plucked a smoke from Mike's box and fished out her own flame as she pointed.

"We were standing over there on the edge near the industrial district as the bombs fell. When it happened, the city was already cleared of most people from the prior angel attack. All that remained were Church of Lazarus forces, monsters, and Lucian. Dystopia had some sort of special bomb that targeted spirits or energy and, according to the commercials, was supposed to nuke the spirit side while leaving the city alone." She lit up and pointed to the lakes. "The fleet of ghost ships that had docked there got taken out, and we knew the plan was working. The initial blasts melted demon and cryptid alike but left everything this side of Purgatory only a little bit rattled."

"Like an EMP for spirits?" Mike pursed his lips. *That's actually a damn good idea.* He gestured to the far southern side of the downtown by the Mississippi River. "So, just across from the Algiers there, Lucian, Lumine, and I were in his Seat of Golden Tears. Far enough down in Purgatory that the only buildings were a mix of old tunnels and crypts. Pretty close to where you and I found the prison. We felt the ceiling start to shake and had no idea what was happening. Suddenly water and sewage started crashing in, and Lucian almost embraced death. To be honest, I was ready to hold him down and drag him for the ride. Then he started doing the erratic laugh and cry simultaneous thing and reached his hand up."

Jane wrapped her fingers around his free hand. "That was probably when this happened. Everything went haywire and just started malfunctioning and... well... Phoebe froze when we tried to escape."

Wait... Phoebes? Mike laughed. "You're joking? She joined us on the ghost brigade? That girl never freezes though, so what spooked her so?"

"I don't think she's joining the ghost brigade. She stayed right when a spirit bomb exploded."

Mike freed his hand and plopped up on the hood of the Jeep as he felt hollow inside. Not because of sadness, just... numbness. He didn't feel an ounce of sympathy or regret that Phoebe died in such a way, not because he didn't like her—far from it. He loved Phoebe. *That girl could drive anything, and her insight into the machinations of the power players was incredible. She also cooked a damn good Barghest burger.* The problem Mike struggled with was something that plagued him his entire life. Everyone wept at funerals or mourned the loss of their loved ones, and he never had. Except for maybe when his grandmother died at a young age, he was entirely hollow around death. So many people around him had died before he even turned eighteen that when one of his friends died of cancer, he just went back to work like normal. It was a dark trait in himself that always made him feel outcast from everyone around him. *Death happens. ALL the time. You are there, and then not.* "Fuck" was all he said.

Vryce stretched and popped his back after freeing himself from the nightmare of Mike's driving. "That's not abnormal, Mr. Auburn. You were born around death, are connected to it, and surrounded by it. There is a reason the Chicago Outfit recruited you as one of their helldivers and why you found Lazarus's prison beneath Deus. Despite your lack of complex planning, you and your sister were always children of the grave. Imagine what happens when your human friends have the life span of gerbils in your eyes? Connection ... proves difficult."

"You must win awards for your inspiring speeches. Generally," Mike shook his head, "you kinda let the unspoken truth remain unspoken, eh?"

"Ignorance is a vile enemy." Vryce wagged a finger. "Besides, Phoebe's death was not in vain. Far from it. A prophet lives far beyond their life. Besides, I'm not entirely ruthless. Your existence proves that I do not wish to slaughter every enemy I come across. That would make the next thousand years ... boring."

A thousand years of this? Excuse me, I need to go return some video tapes. Mike tried to wrap his head around what he would do in six hundred years and what kind of person he would be. Ultimately, he figured there would always be assholes who exploited the masses and figured it would be a long time before he was out of a job. "After that, I suppose I'll just get really good at underwater basket weaving or something." He hopped off. "So, the prison is there, near the French Quarter. I'm assuming that is where everyone headed?" he asked Jane.

"That or the Waffle House," she said with a shrug. Mike noticed Jane kept quiet during Vryce's speech on death. Part of him wondered if she felt the same awkwardness as him about it. Jane knew how to put on a fake smile though, which helped her mask in social situations, and given the little tiff they had yesterday, Mike felt it best to stay quiet.

"Well, one way to find out." Mike jumped off the broken highway and started trudging his way over shattered concrete. "Let's head to the prison. If I was Akira, I'd go where the loot is."

CHAPTER 32

"Wanted: Medical subjects for alchemical trials. Must possess functional set of organs. Compensation pro-vided. Elcoll Pharmaceuticals is launching a new clinical trial to test our latest product: JK-69! Enjoy enhanced speed. Punch that vampire in the teeth or pull his tie closer into you! JK-69 provides you with all the benefits of 47 without the risk of rot or being mindwashed by the liberal elite."

–Pervasive Internet Ad

Jane hated feeling like a bitch. It wasn't her MO to be sassy. Instead, she pretended to be happy despite the wreckage around her. Modern day buildings had either been toppled or were broken facsimiles covered in holes from flying debris. Yet despite the city being blown to hell, somehow, beggars and panhandlers still found an excuse to rattle a cup for donations. One of the two reasons for her current emotional state was that she only carried Bitcoin, which was utterly useless to everyone they passed. *Here! Take this electronic widget! If I really think about it, this country really had its pants pulled around its ankles.* She kept uttering apology after apology to total strangers, most of whom were in some state of decay or already dead,

for not having a single coin on her person—which was apparently the main desired trinket.

The other reason she was salty was the big trench coat-wearing idealist who marched past, or weaved through, the growing crowds of looters like it was nothing. Jane never *knew* her brother growing up, but as an adult, he clearly had a chip on his shoulder. Anyone in a position of power seemed to be in his crosshairs, and he didn't seem to care in the slightest about kicking in heads with his combat boots. *And of course, one of those heads happens to be my new mentor! Smile on, Jane. It will be fine! Mike isn't entirely wrong about Vryce, but fuck that lucky asshole and his stupid superpower of failing upward.* The mere fact Mike worked with a Death Lord, toppled a city, and got out with no scratches burned in Jane's gut as simply unfair. She may have gotten her speed from drugs, but it was she who killed every CEO more concerned with whatever EBITDA profits meant. She killed the Lord of Suicide. She had the connections to fire the first volley of bombs. *And I'm the one who actually is studying!* It was a complicated set of emotions that she didn't have an easy answer to. *It was much easier to love the blockhead when we were isolated in Purgatory.*

At least, Jane reasoned, they were both heroes to the average citizen. She had her sex appeal marketed to the masses which helped convince regular people to actually *try* new products. Or if it wasn't about her blonde-haired blue-eyed demeanor—she was the vile corporate demon worshipper which really got under the Church of Lazarus's skin. She enjoyed that last bit and found herself smiling as she jumped over a puddle of water.

Ultimately, what really bothered her wasn't that Mike was kidnapped, marched to Deus, and came back. It was that Vryce *chose* for him to come back. She didn't want her brother dead by any measure. The opposite in fact. She wished for him to lead a nation in every regard. She just hated the idea, that she, herself, was second fiddle by age alone. *All the time in the woods studying... for what?*

Navigating Samhain streets, Jane spotted a tiny curiosity that made her feel a little better. Mike, Lumine, and she would spot the souls that Vryce was oblivious to. Jane apologized to the sixth zombie on this street alone when she realized that Vryce's neck never even pivoted when one would ask the group for a coin. Where Mike would occasionally hand one out or offer a smoke to someone instead, Lumine would give out a trinket or bauble taken from her dress, and Jane offered smiles and apologies—Vryce didn't even grant the slightest acknowledgement of their existence. The survivors, in turn, never even asked. As if they knew not to even try.

Cutting through an alleyway that opened out into Bourbon Street, Jane was surprised to see just how packed the main artery was... and how little had changed. The modern façade had been burned to cinders, but many of the old buildings still remained and stood defiantly next to broken balconies and simmering ashes of their modern counterparts. *Starbucks didn't stand a fucking chance, I guess.* Any structure that was burned down in a prior event and resided in Purgatory was now gloriously returned beyond the barrier. When she saw empty slave gallows had returned to street corners, her eye twitched. *Can we just ... let some history burn, please? Why did you have to bring that back?*

Bourbon Street was the most challenging. Not just a few hundred people remained as survivors in the city but several thousand. *Did nobody evacuate? The fuck is wrong with these peeps?* And these—recognized Mike and Jane.

"Oh shit! It's the flyin' chick. Hey girl, wanna come party?" the first called out, quickly followed by several other versions of the same. Something about Jane on TV. Something about her being a chick. Something about an invite.

Mike got fist bumps, devil horns, and high fives.

Jane felt obligated to give autographs and pose for polaroids.

She hated it.

By the time they reached the very same exit Mike and Jane left Purgatory from, the brand of JK-47 sank in her stomach like a bad period. She felt like someone who let everyone down, even if she knew that was wrong.

"You know, if you fuck with me, I might just change your life," she sang entirely out of the blue. "Let's not be modest. If it wasn't for me, none of you would be standing here..." There was no rhyme or reason to her sudden melody. She uttered them over the gaping, glowing neon-orange pits emanating from the Sea of Golden Tears as the occasional looter crawled with as many coins as they could hold. *What am I so salty about? I'm a fucking badass, and I know it. Snap out of it, girl. It's okay if you feel bad. I don't need to be hollow like Mike.*

A thought intruded her mind. <*You are indeed. Gods, Jane, you are famous. It's what makes them and what destroys them. Never regret your achievements, for it is how you shape the world.*>

The Praenomen merely touched his mask before flicking a dagger with razor wire into the wall of a falafel restaurant before falling backward into Purgatory.

Jane didn't even need theatrics to fall deeper into Purgatory. She simply allowed her dead form of failure to fall deeper into the prison that held the great Johnny Appleseed. *Because apples will save us from the Catholics.* She muttered to herself as she materialized out into the colorful prison before Mike, Vryce, or Lumine descended.

Amongst the random ghost or looter, Jane planted her face firmly in her palms when she saw the Sons and Daughters. *UGGHH! I'm going to kill 'em!*

Akira was perched over a corpse with its chest cavity already ripped open. Doc Daneka was sitting in an open cell, attempting to calm the emotions of a giant blue ox. Lucy flipped a heart casually in her hand as she strolled through the prison. *I keep a record of the wreckage of my life, but this is a bit much.* Jane kept quiet as she saw her colleagues already feasting upon the spoils.

It was her older brother who spoke first.

"Hey!" Mike picked up the body belonging to the Beast of Bray Road, a large werewolfish creature before it was killed, and flung it over his shoulder before charging in front of Akira. "Akira? What the fuck? Are you *really* eating Apple's heart?"

The small purple-haired gutter punk looked back with confusion evident in her wide eyes as if she was a Golden Retriever who was just caught wiping her ass on a carpet. "Yes?"

Mike sighed. "Akira. What exactly are you going to do with John's heart here? You already ate like ... fifteen different hearts by now."

Jane slammed Mike in the chest and took over. "These prisoners are literal soldiers in our army. Eat any more, Akira, and I'll—"

"I disagree," Daneka cut in. "The blood of gods is what they imprisoned here." The balding blond strolled out with dilated pupils and a massive swordfish dangling over his shoulder. "Let's not sugar-coat it, Jane. We are at war, and we need strength. Where is Morris? Where is Boss? If Resurrection Mary can allow me to teleport, why should I not claim her gifts?"

Jane clenched her fists. *Because you don't need to.* "Because you don't need to!" she shouted. "You were supposed to be at the Waffle House! Waiting for Mike and me! Not feasting off the spoils of war! We found this, not you! You were meant to free them!"

Akira blinked twice with her bug-like eyes. "But we did free them, Jane. They are ours now."

Mike put his hand on Jane's shoulder to stop her from throwing a right hook. "It's war. Get over it."

Vryce chuckled. "And you thought we were so different," he remarked, pulling out a spool of blood-soaked threads. "These peons think they can master the magic of Gods, but Jane... if it's not us, it's Dystopia."

Jane needed a rewind. An hour ago, she was almost making amends with her brother and the guy who brought magic back to the world. She'd been through hell-in-a-handbasket and had her own expectations about what she thought she would see. Akira kept her

cats alive, and Jane did NOT expect her to be eating and killing low-hanging gods in a Death Lord's prison. Jane truly thought that the Sons and Daughters would be freeing them or waiting outside with the other survivors conducting rescue operations.

"Welcome to the cost of war," Vryce said casually as he strolled past Monsier Assonquer's locked chamber, the deity of good fortune and, with a twist of an arcane lock, opened the door for Akira.

Jane stewed as she watched her crew of the Sons and Daughters devour the hearts of demigods for power. *I've worked for pennies. I've already sold my soul. They say all I do is cry. They dress me up, and they plaster my name. I've got the life I wanted. It's time I put your teachings into practice. It's time I take tradition... and put it into practice.* Her mind rambled and jumped between incoherent thoughts and schemes.

"No," Jane said. Her will manifested, shunting every door in Purgatory closed and bending time and space simultaneously with a loud crash. Every vampire raiding the Seat of Golden Tears was thrust out of their rooms. "I won't let you desecrate them. Mike and I found them, and they can help us."

All eyes fell upon her as the broken chambers within the Seat of Golden tears began to heal itself and reconstruct themselves at Jane's behest, sealing off the comatose prisoners from the hungry wolves.

"Jane..." Akira hissed after being forcibly cut off from the prize, "how do you think we win?"

"I dunno." Jane sighed. "By being better than cannibals?" She held up her arms. "I know, I know we were expecting everyone else to be here. I don't know where Morris is or where the rest of the Sons and Daughters are. Still, the plan was to bind..."

"Bind," Vryce chimed in behind the Praenomen mask, "them to corporations? To sell them? Most of these prisoners in Lucian's tomb don't even know what radio is... much less a bomb. As much as I think the Boss's mindset is barbaric, your plan to open the prison had merit, Jane." He plucked a blackened heart that Doc was holding out of his

hands. "I've no use for this. I think it belonged to Paul Bunyan." He lobbed the heart over to Jane. "But if you don't eat it, it's only a matter of time before Lucian's army does. Don't worry. Nobody imprisoned here is of any consequence. When the Unification hunted in the old days, we rarely went after the big ones. Odin and Amma still walk this Earth. These are..."

Vryce looked up and down the hall before bringing everyone's attention to a cell door painted in shades of white and soft blues. The symbol reminded Jane of two V's overlapping each other served as a silver arcane lock. "Let me give you an example. This is the Loa of Ayizan Velekete. She was already old, wise, and a primordial spirit to be treated with great respect. There was a time when she could be counted as one of the greats, and she certainly stood above the petty machinations of the old Unification." Vryce slowly twisted the symbol against Jane's will. "But she stood against the pilfering of fae and exploitation of magic—magic we needed in a dwindling world. So, the Unification sent their hitman. Now, in this world, what use does a god of business and roads have but as food for the warriors of the future?"

<You can't believe that. > Jane glared.

<Not in the slightest. But in case you didn't notice, the forces of Lazarus are closing in. Free them, we suffer their wrath. Let them be. They will be eaten. What solution do you see?> Jane saw the sorrow behind Vryce's mask.

Mike cracked his knuckles and stood by her.

<Jane, > Vryce said telepathically, <I will not tell you to stand down. Neither will he. Yet these gods were put here by the very Boss of the Chicago outfit. He helped harvest them. These gods failed, and their popularity waned. It was easy for the world to forget them. Everyone knows Odin. Loki. Zeus. Legba. Jesus. Do you know Ayzian? Be honest? Obscure. Minor. Only kept alive by the beggar lord out of pity. But fortune is a gift we need to kill the Lord of Misfortune.>

Jane raced forward and grabbed Vryce's hand off the door. "Not like this. Just let me think... Can everyone give me a minute?" she pleaded. "All of you... just listen. You are all friends, and I know pilfering the blood and hearts of these prisoners for extra power is kind of your modus operandi. Hell, I listened to Mike's whole rant on TV a thousand times over about eating hearts for power—but in Dystopia, we did it differently. Our power wasn't up close and personal; it was refined and injected," she chuckled, "usually with a cheeky advertisement."

Jane recalled the flashback of when she threw the CEO of Avalon Entertainment off a twenty-story-tall building into a billboard. *Guess I'm no better.*

<*You are.*> Vryce's voice invaded. <*You and Mike both are. I have not destroyed his soul because you have potential. This prison of gods is what the Church of Lazarus uses to bind the souls of any ghost with necromancy. Is Akira wrong for eating a heart? Lucy? Nay. But is it tactically smart?*>

Akira wiped off her fingers on Doc's houndstooth coat. "I'm just sayin', toots, that if we didn't come when we did, all these creepo zombie chaps would have taken their fill. Remember that one village in Alabama with the Huggin' Mollys?"

Jane snapped her fingers. "You're right! I've got it, okay? Hear me out. Vryce said that these people fell because they weren't popular."

"He did?" Doc raised an eyebrow.

"Shush, mind thingies," Jane flustered. "Anyway, eating their hearts only makes us stronger as individuals. Which is what you all *think* you want. And Vryce here is probably afraid of the retribution coming his way by letting them out unchecked, am I right?"

"Afraid is a strong word," he replied with a hint of acquiescence in his voice.

"What we really need is more soldiers. People to join our cause. So, why don't we use the law offices of Amon, Abraxas, & Asmodeus?

A simple sponsorship contract from us, bound in blood, and we help integrate the gods back into North America in exchange for their help."

Mike chuckled at the name. "They really do think of everything, don't they? Devil law firms. Okay, I'll bite. Let's do it."

A soft applause echoed down the hallway from behind Jane. Swiveling, she saw Edward Morris holding a door open for several bikers who entered first, followed by a tall old man with a cabby hat that gave slow claps as all attention in the room found itself focused on the Boss. "I know, I know, perfect timing." Despite the height of Vryce's faerie body, Boss's presence seemed to dwarf the lich. "You should know better. I'm disappointed."

Edward slammed the door, stormed past the old man, and stuck his ugly mug right in Doc's face while jamming a finger into his shoulder. "This is why you aren't the captain. The ox? Really? Akira and Lucy I expect—they are hatchets. But you? Not so cowardly anymore, are ya? Now sit the fuck down and listen. The lot of you. We've got things to say."

Akira, Lucy, and Doc instantly planted their butts on the prison floor at the command, as if suddenly controlled. Jane and Mike both seemed unsure if that was meant for them as well, and Vryce just leaned against the wall. Morris cracked his neck. "Might be losin' my touch, but then again, I haven't been popping cryptid hearts like candy. In case I weren't clear, that means you two as well. I know I ain't telling the Praenomen to sit, but let's not forget who's in charge 'ere, eh? Sure, as fuck isn't you two. Y'all lucky we got wind of this little operation before you went and did something stupid."

Hell of a time to show up. Jane sat. "How long have you been here?" she asked while tugging Mike down next to her.

"Boss," Morris gestured, "floor is yours."

The old man fished a weathered bronze key out of his suit pocket. "Since just before you arrived. We have a habit of going unnoticed, but you always learn the most interesting things." The key was handed to Vryce. "There are fifty-eight prisoners within these walls that are

worth the salt in their souls. You used to be a warlock, so here's what you are going to do: stitch them. Not to any of you." He waved his finger. "You lot have eaten your fill. No, rather, you'll be stitching them to some old friends of mine, and some of yours as well. They are dead, ghosts, mind you, and we've spent considerable efforts to free them from chains." The old man put his finger under Vryce's Praenomen mask and slowly pulled it off. "You do not get to hide from me, Damien. I suspect you know a few things about me these cats don't, so I know you'll obey."

Ooooh... shit... He did not just do that. Jane felt Mike close her jaw as they both felt small and eagerly studied Vryce's reaction to such an overt command.

Vryce's eyes flared as the mask was removed, but he refused to look away from the Second City Boss.

"The body of a Merovingian," Morris whistled. "Prince Alil, no? I always wondered what happened to our friends that you and Delilah gassed."

Vryce bared fangs and shot Morris a deadly look. "I may listen to him, but you, pirate, are still just vampiric ocean sludge. I'd be wearing your skin if you had the courage to visit Deus instead of sending your cannon fodder." He gestured at the sitting crew.

Boss snapped, "Enough. We've neither the time nor patience nor privilege for the classic tit-for-tat. Save it for court. Right now, you need to get your hands dirty. We've heard rumor from the Vatican that the sun, the *old* sun, is starting to come back around Lazarus. While we are stuck standing around with impotent dicks in our hands dealing with Misfortune, the rest of the world is losing their battles. It's only a matter of time before his plan works at this rate, and we all know you would seethe at watching the world tumble back into monotheism."

"Let me be clear with you, Mister." Vryce reached up and brushed off the bartender's shoulders. "I'll stitch your ghosts to gods. The gods have bodies, and your ghosts need power. Clever. You put them all

here, and now you get to bring them back, just... loyal and in debt. I'm envious that my army didn't get here sooner. I had..." he winked, "similar musings. But I don't work for free. What do I get by doing this for you rather than myself?"

The old man rocked back and forth on in his fine Italian shoes with a knowing grin. His gaze fell to Jane. "Tell me, little lady, you learning a thing or two from this old fogie?" He pointed to Vryce.

"Oh," Jane blushed, "I get to be a part of the conversation?" She stood up and mockingly made jazz hands. *Wooo.* "Right. Yeah, I am. Actually, I'm learning more from this diabolical possessing jerkface than I ever did workin' for your outfit. He's a good teacher. Yanno, he actually explained how Aunt Jemmy's demonic toaster works."

Vryce looked *very* confused.

She continued, "So. Gramps. Yeah, you should give him something. Like, fix his city or something." Jane crossed her arms. *I mean, I think that would be nice.*

The old man put his arm around Vryce and ruffled his silver hair.

Vryce looked *very* annoyed. Jane quickly added a checkmark to a hidden list she pulled from a back pocket with a look of amusement.

"Look at you, buddy. A little humanity has done you wonders. It does you good to leave your sanctum and libraries and walk among the world we built. Reminds me of the twenties. Don't worry. I'm not about to mete out divine justice on you for..." He tapped Vryce's necklace. "Your payment for my ask is your continued independence and a favor from me. Even you need information from time-to-time. So, for each god you revive and bind, anyone in my organization will answer your call."

Vryce freed himself. "So, you get an army of gods with their souls swapped out and in debt to you, and I get intel? I've got my own network, thank you." Vryce coiled a bloody thread around his finger. "And unless you've got a better offer, I'm the only one here who can perform the ritual needed. Remember? It's why your Unification *made* the likes of us warlocks in the first place."

"A network that hasn't even informed you of the sun returning over the Vatican is a poor network, child. Besides, I'm not hearing a price between all that spite, Damien. Surely surrounding yourself with dominated yes men and brainwashed soldiers hasn't dulled your negotiating skills. Is he always this angry?" Boss asked Jane.

She nodded a bunch as she wrote with a stubby #2 pencil. "Oh yes. SO angry. ALL the time."

"*Et tu*?" Vryce clutched his heart. "I'll accept this offer of a favor and open information for the next thousand years. However, you are also going to do one other thing for me. I want this hit on my back removed from the angels. I've earned the right to become a god of magic in this world. Let it unfold."

The old man whistled. "Big claim, that one."

Jane chimed in. "Don't you know everyone? I'm sure a connected boss like you can get it done. After all, you have the better network, no?"

He regarded Jane kindly and rubbed her back. "You are really swingin' for him. He's got a hell of a past."

"Don't we all? People change. Hell, didn't *you* change? CLEARLY Morris changed if he was a pirate or something. Look at him now! He's like a Boston mobster ready to break kneecaps. Those three," she leaned into the rubs. No matter how scary the old man was, he always seemed to give off a feeling of being a best friend. Someone trustworthy. *Kinda like Fredrick was outside of his Suicide mask,* "have clearly changed. I've totally changed. Mike is probably the only person standing here that's still the same Mike."

"Therapy does wonders." Mike gave a two-finger salute. "You should all try it."

Doc and Mike made a silent nod of mutual agreement.

Boss held out his hand to Vryce. "You'll have to give me time, and I'll need these agents to get it done. No promises on clearing that hit before Lazarus's forces get here. Morris's contact on the inside says

they are about a day behind us. But when the dust is settled, I'll make some calls."

"Accepted. A day isn't enough time, so we better get started. Who are we stitching?"

"Some of the ol' boys and lasses that fell along the years. Some really old, some newer. Few of them Delilah knew. I owe her a favor. This scratches off her debt." He gestured to Morris and the others. "Let's head back north. This fight is one for a god of magic. Akira, Lucy, Doc... you are coming as well. We need to have some lessons about what happens when you eat too many hearts."

Everyone stood up, including Mike, and shared uneasy glances.

"Not you two." Boss pointed at Mike and Jane. "You two haven't lost your minds yet, and let's face it, you'd probably go insane if I tried to keep you out."

Akira raised her hand. "I will also go insane. I go where Mikey goes."

"Negative." Morris grabbed Akira by the scruff of her jean vest. "You've got a backlog of assassinations. Time to get back to work." Akira frowned and blitzed to give Mike a big hug before getting tugged off again.

"I'll never forget you, Jane," she pawed. "I'll keep Sparkles fed! You better come visit!"

Akira! Ah, you cutie. Jane waved. "We'll be fine. It's just one Death Lord, right? We are already dead so... easy. But you better keep the pizza away from Sparkles. He's no longer chonky. He's now CHONKY."

Doc and Lucy were less theatrical in their goodbyes.

"I'm assuming I'm coming because I'm also leverage against my father?" Doc asked while exchanging a farewell fist bump with Mike.

Boss winked. "Can't exactly have Daneka's kid running around against the likes of Lucian, can we? That's just asking for trouble."

"I suppose that makes sense." He feigned a punch on Jane's cheek and kissed her forehead. "See ya soon."

Lucy just gave them a silent motion of *I'm watching you* and picked up her axes.

Jane, Mike, and Vryce watched the Second City crew head up the stairs. Despite their farewells, each of them looked a few shades paler over the looming fear they were in trouble for killing a few gods. Akira, most of all, seemed to walk the slowest and occasionally backtrack a step before Morris pushed her forward. *Nobody likes getting fired from a job. Hope Boss isn't too hard on them.* Jane watched them fade from view as a line of ghosts started to fill the hallway in their place.

"Wow, that was intense. So, how do we get started?!" Lumine suddenly spoke from behind the trio, causing Jane, who forgot she was there, to yelp in surprise.

CHAPTER 33

"This is a public service announcement. All classes held at Trismegistus University are canceled until further notice. All travel to and from the Society of Deus or the greater Minnesota region is forbidden. All prospects are to wait until further notice. We apologize in advance for any acts of misfortune, curses, or unforeseen calamities that may befall you or your loved ones during this time. Thank you for your understanding."

–Radio broadcast

Vryce dropped his bag on the ground the second Boss and the remaining anarchs left the Seat of Golden Tears. "We start now. Time is not our friend." *If only Charles Walsh were here at this very moment. What is the use of keeping a director of time magic on your payroll if they are perpetually late?* Kneeling, Vryce began pulling out several chalk sticks, sewing threads, a needle kit, and a stew of random paper clips and everyday office supplies. "Lumine, your first lesson begins now. I need you to find me seven small demons, cryptids, or regular animals roughly the size of a chicken. Jane, I need more components. Get me as many bowls as you can find, anything that is made of gold that isn't nailed down, and an object from a religious

institution. Mike, you are on crowd and god control. Get these souls in a line."

An average of one hour per ritual. Ten minutes between rituals for new components. Add in another ten to implant mental triggers or silence any errors. Fifty-eight stitches. Seventy-seven hours. Just over three days of no sleep. Assuming Lucian is smart enough to figure out the scheme, it will take him eighteen hours to drive. Which means I'll be at his mercy mid-ritual. Vryce pondered several different options to accelerate his casting time and kept coming up empty. Soul-stitching was not an easy spell and required precision. Even Gabriel was not skilled enough to perform the spellcraft required, and no other warlock was close enough in proximity to assist... much less get a message to them. *Although, this city is not empty...* Vryce pondered possessing several civilians simultaneously. Fifty-eight at once was an extreme stretch, and his true limitation was limited by the special needles required. He only had six. *I could do six. I ... could do six.*

He nodded to himself as he stared at the components in his bag, oblivious to anyone trying to flag his attention.

This body and five others. That cuts my time down to seventeen hours. I'll risk Prince Alil wresting control of this body, but it's within the framework of time. Of course, this assumes that Lucian won't arrive sooner. I'll have to add two hours to find possessable candidates above... and... Vryce finally looked to Jane, Mike, and Lumine. "You'll have to defend me. Wait... Why are you all standing there with your hands up? I gave you orders."

All three pointed back to the stairwell. The old man had returned, not alone, but rather leading twelve members of the Sons and Daughters into the prison. The Boss was standing patiently, waiting for Vryce to finally acknowledge their existence.

"Judging from what I know of you," he patted one biker on the back, "you are going to need some extra hands. Let's avoid randomly snatching people off the streets, eh? Do try and return them?"

"I'm infinitely curious," Vryce studied each of the twelve. None of them had a spark in their eye that marked them as particularly determined, but they could hold a shotgun—probably all the old man needed them for, "how you manage to spy into my secrets with such precision. But thank you. That saves me two hours."

"Spy," he chuckled. "My boy, you are fueled by spite and wonder. Stick around on this wonderful planet for a few rotations and people stop surprising you. There are a few exceptions though." He winked.

Be coy all you want; I'll figure out what you really are eventually. "So that's the real reason you pulled out the rest of the misfits? You knew I'd come to this conclusion and borrow something with a bit more ... *value.*" His words dripped as he studied the soldiers deeper. Nothing identified them as anyone of significance or power.

"Like I said, there are exceptions. I'd wish you good luck in your ascent to becoming a god of magic, but..." he waved his cigar around the prison, "I think we both know there won't be any in a bit. Oh," he snapped. "Don't get too carried away with your mind-control tricks. Vegetable gods won't do you, or us, any favors. I know you'll implant a few things, but... try and keep it above the belt, will ya?" He shooed the volunteer force forward before heading up the stairs.

Akira took one last opportunity to peek around the corner and wave.

That short one is practically pure devil at this point. He shook his head. It wasn't time to ponder the implications of people devouring hearts like those alchemical coffee drinks Delilah inhaled. Vryce paced over to the first of the volunteers and didn't even deem them worthy of a greeting before glaring into the eyes of the first. Possessing him was as easy as dipping one's hand in a bowl of cool water.

The first in line turned around to face the second, and then the second to the third, and so forth like a running stream. By the sixth, Vryce felt the noise of mind chatter eke into his conscious thoughts. Number 4 was hungry and thought about pulling a Snickers from her pocket but worried it was melted. Number 6 was terrified that he'd

be late for a Sushi dinner date, and Number 2 believed they were in some movie and kept humming a song about an impossible mission.

Vryce closed all their eyes and asserted his will. Stark silence filled his mind, with the singular exception of Prince Alil's nightmares—a recurring memory of a Ukrainian vampire sawing off his beautiful metal wings to mount on a wall like some trophy. Stretched so thin, the various Vryces were stuck dealing with the strongest subconscious among the lot. *The problem with inherent magical resistance is... well... magic resistance. If I knew I'd be doing this, I would have picked a different body.*

Opening his eyes was a dizzying affair. He focused on Jane but saw her simultaneously from several different heights and minds at once—tethered only by his own consciousness. If Number 3 felt queasy to the stomach, all of them felt the same sense of vertigo. *Okay. That's a single point. Let's try...*

All of him promptly turned outward, and three of himself fell to the ground as the five senses each felt six different sensations. Three of himself falling caused a chain reaction that brought down the others, given the sudden movement.

Jane slapped Number 1. The echo of Alil's skin getting cracked echoed down the hall from how hard she hit him, and the pain was instantly felt across the rest. Instant anger arose within Vryce. It wasn't just a single slap. It was multiplied over again and again, along with the feeling of shame and lack of control. Lightning danced through their fingertips as the pain provided focus. All of himself pried up off the ground, intent on bringing pain back to Jane. *Dangerous girl.* He steeled himself from lashing out as he seethed through his teeth and clenched his fist—six times over.

"Thank you," they all said. "Pain is useful to focus."

"You're welcome, buttercup. I'm going to get some bowls before you, uh, decide to find long sticks again. Don't fall again. Mike punches harder."

"Pain is a focus, you say..." Mike smiled and cracked his knuckles.

"If I fail here, then punch away. You might as well be useful for something," said Vryce, and each of him strolled to separate prisons and set about unlocking the wards that contained them. It took several tries before his dexterity was up to the task, but in short order—controlling six bodies at once felt like operating several spells at once. Rather than focus purely on a single form, he let his mind passively ride the bodies... and whenever he needed to focus on pain, Prince Alil's nightmare provided the perfect fuel.

Damien Vryce, an architect of impossible ambition, stood at the epicenter in Purgatory prison, orchestrating a macabre symphony with the deftness of a deranged conductor. Six bodies, each a puppet to his will, moved in disjointed harmony. Their actions bound by the bloody threads of spectral sinew wove the very fabric of the Boss's dark designs... and a little of his own machinations.

The gods of American folklore lay before him in several cells, comatose and inert, their once-mighty forms reduced to drained and starved husks. Some bore the grandeur of majesty—Paul Bunyan, a colossal figure of muscle and myth, his skin marred by the patina of neglect. Others were less impressive but no less pitiable, like John Henry—a relic of a bygone era, only identified by his rusted hammer still within the cage.

Vryce worked with a surgeon's precision and a madman's glee, stitching the ethereal essence of the Second City's ghosts into these vessels. Each stitch was a struggle, the threads slick with spectral ichor that clung like tar. When the marionettes twitched and convulsed under the invasive process, Vryce eagerly took mental notes as their dormant power reluctantly awakened. *Perhaps I only gave the world a nudge. I wanted gods to rise when I started my betrayal. I wanted modern humans to discover the wonder of magic and lay claim to their own.* "Maybe I needed to be a better father and push harder."

John Henry gasped for air underneath Suit #3 in the central chamber. Quickly, Vryce dropped his needle and pried his eyes open. "You inside. You who wear the face of Mr. Henry. You wield

impossible stamina that puts vampires and zombies to shame. You will race against time, wield your hammer, and inspire those around you to greatness. Do you understand?" Vryce waited for recognition to dawn in the soul's eyes. If the old man wanted his dead soldiers to wield the power of gods, it would also rely upon them believing that they *had* those abilities. Without the luxury of months to merge the souls, Vryce could only rely on his own skill of mental command. He figured it was, as Mike would put it, like taking a sledgehammer to a Tic Tac.

Damien watched the crimson light of Henry's original soul begin bleeding into the new spirits by staring into his eyes. It was like watching a battle of dominance unfold between territorial predators locked in a cage. Imprisoned for so long, Henry's original soul stood little chance, and within minutes—they were as one. *Now, Mr. Henry, if you are strong enough... in time, maybe you'll be the one in charge of your body.* Vryce lifted the legend up as color flooded into his skin, and the shirtless black man looked every bit as powerful as the legends. "One more thing," the legend's eyes met Vryce's, "if you yourself ever think, or you hear of anyone, that will move to harm, betray, or destroy anything belonging to the God of Magic Damien Vryce, you will stop what you are doing—walk to the nearest phone or communication device and contact the Society of Deus to tell them every ounce of information pertaining to such plots."

Vryce snapped his fingers, implanting the mental command deep within the subconscious of both entities. Even though referring to himself as a God of Magic was a lie, he had to start somewhere. *If the legends believe it to be true, then in time, perhaps it could be. Then I could walk openly.*

"Next one, Mike!" he shouted from Suit #3 as the rest of him worked, repeating the same steps as Jane and Lumine raced to keep the ritual supplies in stock. One body, a hollow-eyed specter of a Native American legend, twitched violently under Suit #2 as Vryce tugged on a particularly stubborn thread. "Ah, Wovoka," he muttered

through gritted teeth, his frustration manifesting in the grinding of all six sets of molars. "Could you be any more difficult? Even in your sleep, you're a pain."

Controlling six bodies simultaneously proved no small feat, particularly when gods like Wovoka still had plenty of fight left in them. Even if their end result was the same—sewn, merged, and mentally hammered—each one that resisted only hastened Vryce's exhaustion. By hour seven, one body—Prince Alil's, or what was left of it—began to wobble precariously, its balanced threatened by a phantom breeze. "Focus, Damien," he chastised himself, the sarcasm dripping as thick as the ectoplasm pooling at his feet. "Can't have you faceplanting into the abyss now, can we?"

<Oh, I'm sure we can, Vryce.> Prince Alil's consciousness bubbled up in the back of Vryce's mind. *<Nice party you tossed. I particularly enjoyed the weapon-grade nerve gas. Remind me to never come to your house again unless I'm there to shit in your toilet and not flush.>*

"Jane," Vryce spoke as he wove threads into the hurricane tamer Pecos Bill, "would you kindly find a way to cause me an excruciating amount of pain in very short order? Someone is being a rather rude host."

Jane poked her head into the stone prison cell from the edge of the door frame and used it as a chance to grab an empty bucket. "Uh, lemme see..." She surveyed the room. "You're a pathetic excuse for a sorcerer. You let your city fall to a sack of bones with a bit of bad luck and terrible fashion, and to make it worse, you let the Boss usurp our entire plan of freeing the gods. You aren't bringing magic back into the world. You're *actively* destroying it with each stitch." She smiled and tugged at her cheek while sticking her tongue out.

All six suits of Vryce stopped as he was taken aback by her words. He had imagined a slap or a dagger through the thigh.

"Truth always hurts, love," she said while Lumine handed her a fresh bucket of drained blood that Jane set at his feet. "Nothing cuts

deeper." She made a *boop* sound as she touched the point of his elven ear and skipped out of the room.

At the very least, he reasoned, Jane did get Prince Alil to silence, but Vryce couldn't help but feel he was laughing somewhere deep within his body.

One of the bodies, the Beast of Bray Road, jolted up and howled in Suit #6's chamber, nearly toppling over Mike who raced to hold the werewolf back down on the table. "Dammit, Bray," Vryce growled, a flicker of his old self resurfacing despite the exhaustion. "I need you upright and stitched, not performing rebellious interpretive dance."

Deity after deity, they worked in tandem to bind the Boss's soldiers into the captured legends. The violet Lilith Moon rose in the sky, only to set hours later and bring Antihelios's black rays cresting into prison's ceiling. When one of Vryce's bodies would collapse from exhaustion (or get ripped to shreds by the likes of the Slenderman), he quickly possessed one of the other remaining twelve and continued his work. When a stitch was completed, Lumine would bring them up to the city proper, Mike would fetch another from a prison, and Jane would ensure that Vryce remained standing and stocked.

He was rather sure that, at one point, that Jane had procured cocaine for him from above ground just to keep #3 standing for an extra two stitching sessions.

As the final hour approached, Vryce's vision blurred, and only three marionettes remained on the verge of collapse. The bloody threads that had once moved with fluid grace now trembled with each motion, the weight of his task pressing down like a millstone. Yet, through sheer force of will (and several arguments with Alil), he persisted, the final stitches falling into place on the last god—Ayizan Velekete. *Number fifty ... eight.* Vryce bit the thread off with Alil's teeth.

<You did that on purpose.> Alil's voice bubbled up.

<Did what?>

<Stitched wrong. Did Jane's words cut deep?>

Vryce took a second look down and realized that he left out several key ritual components and Hermetic principals during the casting, and it wasn't the eyes of a soul that looked up at him—but an invigorated Loa who devoured the energy of the dead man he'd stitched inside. "You, madame, are free to go" were the only words that Vryce spoke to her as he bowed in deference, allowing her bare feet to walk out of the Church of Lazarus's prison a free goddess once again.

Even if Vryce wanted to rebuke Alil's musings, he already knew his words to be true, and thus, so did the mind of the possessed faerie. *<Fifty-seven completes the deal.>*

<The deal was for fifty-eight. Do you truly think that entity isn't going to remember? Just think, he was the hitman who locked up most of these. You know what happens to liches like you. So kindly, before he chains me in this banal hell for eternity like Lazarus, release me.>

"I've got time to find one more. We finished early." Vryce felt the other two bodies collapse in other cells as his full attention focused on pushing Alil back down. Still, Vryce could only leave the room by using the wall as a crutch, and as he stepped into the hallway, he allowed the cool brick and arcane wards to tingle against his skin as he slid down a wall.

The world was now a stage for his unholy orchestra. Gods were never meant to return, but Vryce still surveyed the empty prisons of Lucian's grim domain with a mixture of pride and exhaustion. He'd certainly pay to see the look on the Death Lord's face when he realized that celestials didn't play by the same rules of Fate and Misfortune. *Oh, let's see if the world can handle the havoc to come, or if I just thrust the world back into the age of Prometheus.* "Well," he panted, a weary smile playing at his lips, "that was ... invigorating."

CHAPTER 34

::Sealed CIA Evidence from the Unification investigation::

"Where are you taking me?" A female voice, nervous, speaks to an unseen stranger.

"You asked to be on top of the world? Come on! It's 1999!" The male voice got closer to the hidden phone. "Look, TPK is going to happen, and everything begins anew. So, let's have fun tonight. I'll tell you a secret if you stick by me all night though."

"Okay..." she responded.

"There's this group on Wall Street into some fucked up shit, like drinking blood and talking with Satan, but let me tell you—they are behind every major trade and global policy. Turns out, they are recruiting before the end, and your date tonight got three invites."

"So where is the third?"

"On her way. She said to pick up dinner first." ::end::

Lucian applauded the greatest monument he'd seen in North America: The World's Largest Ball of Twine. Apparently it was constructed by a Frances A. Johnson between 1950-1979 and weighed over 17,400 pounds. The Death Lord couldn't help but see the ironic beauty in its simplicity. It was a perfect day for the viewing, as even the black sun shone a little brighter today than in the past weeks. Still a gloomy apocalyptic ball of darkness, but there was a slight hint of a brighter gray to mark the special occasion. Maybe it was good luck.

"Did you know," he chattered to Frankie, who was an equally chatty zombie at least for one so marred by giant tiger claws, "that right here in Darwin, Minnesota, an absolute spit from the Society of Deus, that there was this glorious beauty? I didn't either. I mean, can you imagine what an insane soul-stitching warlock would do with miles of twine? I bet you, that's *exactly* why they chose the Twin Cities as their ritual site."

Frankie shrugged and continued to stitch up gaping wounds. "It'ssssh, not the largeshet." He struggled to finish words and threw his hands up in frustration.

"Oh, come off it. Who cares if Kansas has a bigger ball? Nobody likes Kansas." Lucian slammed a brochure in the zombie's chest. "Stop picking at the wounds. You're a zombie. You need rotten faerie blood and a taxidermist. Come on, no more detours. We've got a city to get back to. I can't believe you talked me into visiting this fat beauty. What kind of taxi driver are you?"

Frankie was a master of the deadpan look that said, "Are you serious?" without saying a word.

"We better be there on time. Nothing, and I mean, we stop for *nothing.* Not even Missouri's World's Largest Rocking Chair." Lucian crawled into the back seat of the yellow cab. He tried to put the feeling that the black sun seemed a tad brighter than usual out of his mind. If Lazarus's insane plan of killing everyone would actually work, then Lucian would have to suffer eternity under the self-righteous prick.

Which meant he either had to actually do his work and part in the slaughter or go back and face an ever-growing god. *I wonder what everyone else is up to. Certainly not enjoying the best vacation ever. Fuck me, man, do I really want to let Lazarus win? He isn't the type to care about the odd or absurd.* "Maybe the hair museum..."

Chapter 35

"And the seven angels which had the seven trumpets prepared themselves to sound. The first angel sounded, and there followed hail and fire mingled with blood, and they were cast upon the earth. In this age of darkness, the angels' trumpets herald not just divine wrath, but the fall of the false idols of magic. Hail of brimstone will rain down upon the sorcerers, their blood turning the rivers into torrents of decay. The earth shall quake, swallowing the heretical enclaves, and only those who kneel before the altar of Lazarus will be spared. The Church of Lazarus beckons the pure, and the wicked will face the angels' wrath."

–Priest's speech in Germany

"Your guest has arrived." Alexandria closed the large cathedral doors behind her. Her hands stayed planted high, as if she was under arrest, and she peeked back at Daneka with a coy wink. "Along with some unwanted guests. We could keep the doors barred and hide within, whatever stupid name this chamber has."

Lazarus sat on the high-backed chair within the San Giovanni and fought back human desires to ravage the vampire presenting herself across the room. To say she was wearing a black dress was an

359

understatement. *She keeps trying her charms. But like a succubi, only death awaits the weak.*

"I can see why you were gifted immortality back then," he complimented to feed her ego. "But if we have unwanted guests, a show wouldn't be what they are here to see."

She flipped over, rested on the middle of the door, and toyed with a red tie that helped frame her form by cutting down the middle of her chest. With the feathered Mask of Suicide, she was the spitting image of a consort attending a Masquerade sex party. "I'm sure we can make sounds that say otherwise." She winked and then flipped off the seduction like a light switch. "Delilah Dumont awaits outside, along with the Lords of Murder, Pestilence, and Lady Pollution with an honor guard and several council members of the Unification. They are calling for a Praxis."

"Mutiny?" Lazarus chuckled. "They intend to vote me out from under my mask. Pathetic." He gestured. "On what grounds?"

Alexandria pointed through the stained glass windows. "I'm pretty sure the fact that the sun is burning them again is top of the list. The upside is umbrellas are back in fashion." She lifted a purple and green parasol.

"And you still choose to stay, now seeing what happens when my plan begins working?"

"Lazzy," she popped the umbrella open indoors and walked slowly to the window, "I always preferred that creatures like us stay in the shadows. It's more ... elite. Unlike them, I do not fear Heaven's Wrath; instead... I rather prefer being the devil in the shadow. I suppose today will see what happens. Considering I doubt you are strong enough to face three Death Lords all at once, you sure you don't wish to go out on terms pleasurable to you? I can make your ... transition one of ecstasy rather than sorrow."

"Well, if anyone is going to rebrand the role of Suicide, it would be you. I'm pretty sure many in the world will be thankful you aren't selling some myth about comets with kool-aid cups." Lazarus

grabbed a cane that sat near the gold-encrusted chair and rose. "Send in Delilah first."

"As you wish. Summon me if you survive. Otherwise, nice knowing you, John." She muttered something about foolish men as she left the room.

The second the door closed, John invited a different guest into the room. "Mr. Morgan, I think it's time we came to an appropriate arrangement."

The smell of Hal's cigarettes was evident before his form manifested next to John on the dais. Wearing a classic Italian suit with a red shirt and long skinny black tie, Hal lowered his sunglasses to stare at the door with his golden-hued eyes. He pressed a button on his Walkman, killing the glaring sounds of Metallica that echoed from his headphones. "I love quick deals. Great terms. High Interest."

"I've certainly considered letting you possess me or drinking your blood for a quick dose of power."

"Not seriously though."

"You already know what I want to ask."

The demon put out his smoke on the back of his hand. "To go to war on your behalf. Let me guess: Murder, Pestilence, and Pollution need to lose around the world. Tall order, a lot of guns. Murder *kinda* knows what he's doing."

"It was inevitable. I never thought I could hide my plan forever."

"It is easier to hide in the chaos of war. Alright, I'll get started. Just don't expect results overnight. My ask is simple. The Church of Lazarus will do *everything* in their power to hunt the abyss when it starts leaking in through the cracks of this fractured world. Even if it means you putting aside that pride of yours about being some god. You, uh, might have to work with a few undesirables there, buddy." Hal patted John on the back. "When I *do* win later though, I might have some recommendations for vacant seats. Purgatory needs its keepers after all."

There wasn't any point in John hiding the chess game from his own personal demon. Both he and Hal knew that there were two outcomes. If John won, then he would be the de facto God and could easily set the world back to a state of balance, which would give Hal exactly what the demon of War wanted on multiple fronts. If John's gamble in sabotaging his strongest armies led to his own downfall— then whoever came out on top would achieve the same result. Either way, the demon of War won. *Either way, new friend, my thesis is proven. The world is shaped by mortals, not monsters.*

When the two doors reopened, Lazarus hunched his back to appear weaker as Delilah Dumont strode with purpose across the velvet carpet. She sported an olive-green suit and carried a briefcase with a small red ribbon coiled around a locked handle. *No doubt some gift or peace offering.* He didn't care. Lazarus only wanted to speak with Mrs. Dumont to lay eyes upon Vryce's disciple just once. If she was going to be a fly in his web, he felt it was only proper to visit the prey before eating it.

Delilah didn't appear to be the least bit nervous, gladly looking him right in the eyes with determination. Her eyes, framed by golden spectacles, clearly bore the markers of a supernatural creature—given that one of them was entirely demonic gold. She kept walking, past the point where most visitors would stop and kneel before their god. He raised his hand to signal that was enough, but she still strolled closer. *Is she insane enough to kill me here?* John refused to flinch as the vampire stepped onto the dais next to him, her eyes never leaving his.

"Greetings." She extended her hand. "Let's cut to it. I'm not here to kill you, and you are in the middle of a Praxis, so I know your time is short."

Looking down at her hand, Lazarus sniffed. "And what makes you think you can stand here with me like an equal? I've gifted you with an audience. Kneel."

Her lip curled a fraction. "Respectfully, no." She set the briefcase down next to him. "You'll need this. Do not be fooled into believing it

to be a peace offering. Rather, it's a list of every single nuclear weapon the Archive has managed to usurp control of since the fall and the coordinates of every Unification blood factory that's been built over the past five hundred years. You'll find ample evidence that, if pushed, the former United States military possessed enough power to blast this world into oblivion. Kill or delay me, and your supply lines will be cut off within a fortnight."

Excuse me? Lazarus straightened and stepped closer, looming down over the petulant diplomat. "If you've such power, child, then why even accept my summons?" *Is today filled with disrespect?* John resisted the temptation to just pull out his gun and shoot her.

"Where there is chaos, there is opportunity." She curtly pulled a small journal from her pocket filled with checklists of impossible tasks. John clearly saw "Test god" as she crossed it off. "You aren't a god yet. You have dissension in your ranks, and you possess no supernatural presence about you. Anyone with two brain cells and knowledge can see your plan. Kill everyone who doesn't worship you?" She tapped the pen to her lips. "No... it's more than that. The sun here in the Vatican... hummmmaaannnittyy..." she said with widened eyes and jotted down another note right where he could see.

- Hide pure humans from The Church

"Now," she continued, "feel free to carry on with the mass extermination. When you are done, I'll have a few humans worthy of also being God." She tucked her journal away and dusted her hands. "Now that's just for *me*. Let's not forget that Vryce *also* has his human soul back and, unlike your Death Lords, isn't shackled with divine purpose. Didn't ... we in the Unification *teach* warlocks how to do that? To bring you back?" she *tsked*. "All of them are still alive, aren't they? Can you imagine THAT secret getting out. Man... I would not want to be you."

John had imagined many different ways this conversation could have gone, but this was not on the list. Delilah had once been nothing more than the logistical liaison for the construction of a ritual site, and clearly, John realized, she had been let off her leash. "Impressive." He turned to face the doors and stopped looming over her like a threatened animal. "Of course, you do realize that you may have one god in your corner near the end. I'll have every other Death Lord and the consensus of the masses. I think that wins."

"Maybe," she folded her hands in front of her, "except for the obvious weakness."

"I don't even have to ask because I know you are going to gloat, child."

"Our side doesn't need a leader. We aren't trying to rule the world. We just need to kill you."

"And if you do, the world will slowly crumble and fade into oblivion or fracture into a thousand realms ruled by different gods."

"Eden for the masses." She quickly plucked out her journal. "Makes a good campaign slogan. Thank you."

John gave an exasperated sigh. "Well, let's have it. Why are you still standing here? Might as well hear the rest of this before I have you executed."

She nodded. "I've served the Unification prior and am familiar with thousands of its members and cults, along with the candidates for future Death Lords during elections. We both know they are self-serving morons who cheated their way to power. How many of them went to college? Have led a nation? Dealt with logistics of a military?" She held her hand up. "Don't answer. We both know everything was completed by those at my rank. Directors, grunts, diplomats and bureaucrats on the payroll. Out of your Death Lords, I'd say only four are truly terrifying. You are one of them, so take that as a compliment."

Oh, lovely. I'm charmed. Smitten. "One, I don't need them to lead nations. I need them to kill. It's in the name. Two, you are rambling. Get to the point." John was already tired of the conversation. Blowing

up the prison sites with nuclear weapons wouldn't even cut off their supply of blood thanks to the proliferation of magical creatures. But he already knew that was a known fact; it was diplomatic power play, nothing more. *The warlocks, however, could be a threat if unified again.*

"You were in Purgatory when the Soviets were in a cold war with the United States. The only reason the world didn't end was cooler heads prevailed. Peace isn't on the table for us; ideologically, the stars are closer in proximity than our end games. But do you want more warlocks or liches in the world?" she asked. "Lady Alexandria has ascended to the Lord of Suicide but is still just a vampire."

"You wish me to burn the other ritual sites," he mused. It was a decent proposition. Vryce may have taken advantage of the first great ritual, but with enough sacrifice—any of the remaining warlocks could, in theory, reach into the heavens and hell to stitch their remaining souls back together.

"That or kill the other warlocks. Peter has removed himself from the equation already by going in a new direction. I'm just saying, wouldn't the battle be much easier if you *only* had to worry about the known commodities?"

John pondered for a long minute in silence. It was a trap and served no purpose to his greater schemes. Furthermore, the Death Lords' jealousy over someone like Vryce usurping their divine right kept them focused on the *potential* of more. Which meant they paid less attention to him.

"How about," he held up his finger, "you go fuck yourself? I am done dealing with heathens for today."

Lazarus slammed his cane down onto the dais. The large double doors ripped themselves off the hinges and flew into the foyer, revealing the three Death Lords and their high-ranking captains. Any flecks and stone debris rotted away into ash before touching even a single one. Lazarus let the power of the heavens flow through him at last, burning through his eyes and ripping out his back as six wings of

pure white light erupted in the throne room—igniting any tapestry they touched as they unfurled.

Delilah quickly rushed to the side to avoid Heaven's Wrath as the three Death Lords walked into the chamber. Murder, nothing more than a blackened and charred skeleton with vampiric fangs and a shroud of black entropic energy, forced his way to the front.

"Lazarus. You have betrayed us," he boomed out of thin air. Behind him in the hall, guards suddenly began stabbing and killing each other as the Death Lord incited murderous hatred in any of weaker minds. "We have no wish to be shackled into the shadows once again, and your sun reveals the truth of your aims."

Pestilence, a man of perfect health with a mask made from the skin of lepers, flanked Murder's left and calmly folded his hand. "You can either die a thousand ways or cede the Seat of Heaven's Wrath."

A woman with short hair and a slick black mask made from oil clicked a ballpoint pen in perfect timing with the sound of her heels echoing off the chamber floor. "I think we can remodel this church. I'm thinking ... more purple."

None of the Death Lords showed any fear over John's display of divine strength. Nor were the sun's rays strong enough to send them screeching into oblivion. *None of them will ever fear a god, for they've seen too many pass. How sad that they are wrong.* "To think," when Lazarus spoke, his words traveled across all of Rome, "you've forgotten your birthright as disciples of the divine. Heaven's Wrath has but one mandate: to ensure you shepherd the souls of the dead. Your coup is a month too late."

"No," the Lady of Pollution remarked. "We brought you back from the dead to usher in a new age, not return us to some biblical hell. The world needs a god, but we've got other candidates."

"You do not have a say in what I become, wrathful or benevolent," Lazarus intoned. "Faith is your only recourse."

The Lord of Murder brandished a ferryman's scythe. "This could have been avoided. But our loyalty comes at a price. One you refuse to

pay. Murder the world, you said. Sounds great." The shadows boiling around his feet chuckled. "Restoring the sun like a poison that slowly banishes us back into the darkness ... is not the Unification's agenda."

"I think you forget," Lazarus looked over to Delilah who cowered in the farthest corner she could crawl into. The bold diplomat was trapped in the one place she never wished. She wasn't wrong in her demands, just misguided. "That we are no longer the Unification."

His wings lashed out at the speed of light, each light hitting the eyes of the Death Lords right through their masks. John felt their souls, coiled his will around them, and ripped them out of their abominable husks before they could react. Each Death Lord fell to their knees.

Three small sparrows were pulled back to Lazarus's healed hands and chirped happily in his palm. He petted the stolen mortal souls that made them proper liches. "These belong to you." Lazarus floated to the ground, and his wings retreated. "These are what allow you to govern your Thrones of Purgatory. You falsely believed that Heaven's Wrath was physical judgement. To wreck your bodies. Smite your kingdoms." He kissed a sparrow. "Nay, it is judgement over your souls."

The Death Lords were speechless as they struggled to comprehend what had just happened.

"Isn't Pollution and Pestilence a little bit ... redundant?" John smiled as his hand squeezed around a sparrow. "Now, you incomplete three will have to earn back your divine right. You have until the next ascension ceremony to prove your competence. A few years should be enough time for pathetic warlocks such as yourself to slaughter a few countries and earn back your true souls. Do not concern yourself with the wrath of my sun any longer. For in the end, the loyal shall be rewarded."

Lazarus held forth his ring in front of Murder, who promptly kissed the ring in defeat before leaving without protest. The other two mimicked the acceptance of their fate. Once they left, he turned

his attention back to the pompous diplomat who suddenly found the willpower to have terror in her gaze.

"It takes courage to be afraid, Delilah Dumont, as you should be. My quarrel is not with the supernatural, despite the rhetoric. It is with those who have forgotten what true divinity looks like. I do not need to fear a rogue lich, a Death Lord, or even a warlock who ascends to one. I have my own fears, but they are not of your get. Do you understand?"

She rose with her hands pressed firmly on the marble wall. "More than you realize. I see your limitation," she said, finding her courage again. "Thank you for the lesson, Lazarus."

"Purple would look so gaudy in here, don't you agree?" He crushed a sparrow in his hand. "Now what have you learned?" John could feel hope wither and die in the Lady of Pollution. She knew that she would never again be a true Death Lord, merely a sorcerer who wore a mask imbued with power. *Let this be a lesson to you, Murder. My seat alone holds power over the supernatural.*

Delilah was unfazed at this particular display as she responded, "That even I can cut god." She turned and bolted out of the altar room as a small clank echoed on the floor. John saw the pineapple grenade bounce, and his eyes widened when he saw a single iron nail sticking out of his shadow, preventing him from fleeing the room.

Dr. John C. Daneka always knew there would be challenges in pretending to be a god. Yet in the few seconds before the grenade went off, he found it ironic that it was such a uniquely normal mortal instrument that would set back months of healing. Something so insignificant that any vampire or sorcerer could easily handle, and thus, something that his guards would never check for.

He curled into a ball beneath his armored robes, clutching the sparrows to his chest, and for the first time in his existence—prayed. A prayer that only caused more panic because he knew deep down inside, at best, he could only pray to himself.

CHAPTER 36

Unearthed Scroll. B.C. 878. Translated Version. "Eat thy Demon's heart if thou wishes to roam the Earth ravenous. Eat thy Angel's heart if thou wishes to be trapped in a prison of thy mind. Eat the hearts of the Wild Ones if one wishes to roam among the beasts. Any will make a mortal feel as if they were a god. This is fallacy. Worse yet, those who devour more than once wield untold power—yet condemn themselves to invisible prisons of divinity. Forever barred from eternal rest. Forever cursed to wander as soulless revenants between realms. Woe will be mankind should one reclaim their soul. May the wrath of all realms strike down such ambitious monstrosities."

"You know, maybe we should go visit that rocking chair," Lucian said as they crossed into southern Louisiana while he looked out the window. The taxicab slowed down to avoid running over legions of chained ghosts shackled to vehicles containing Church of Lazarus necromancers. *Can't Murder's dumb army travel in Purgatory like a proper spirit horde?* He sighed. It was unavoidable that he'd have to work, he supposed. If he didn't, then every thread of misfortune he tugged upon since his arrival would never see its final crescendo—and that would just be a waste in his mind.

"You can stop here, Frankie." Lucian ripped a coin off his mask and chucked it on the dashboard. "That tip's worth more than you know. You look like you've had a spot of bad luck, so… I dunno, go hit Vegas or something."

Frankie snapped his jaw back into place as he pulled over to the side. "Thanksssss, muffin." He snatched the coin and traced its edge with an unblinking gaze, mostly because he lacked eyelids.

Lucian wished the zombie well. *Poor guy was buried unalive for a few years now. That kinda torment really fucks with your mind.* He shuddered as he recalled a time he was stuffed in a crate and chucked into the ocean for a decade. With a shiver, he slammed the door shut, looked to his home, slipped on his mask, and gave a big grin. "Daddy's home, bitches."

Lucian admitted to himself there were times he enjoyed slacking off, perhaps more than any other lich that sat on the council. So much so, he often let others take his voting seat just so he could travel the world. Yet every few centuries, he got to have a burst of real excitement, and judging from the strands of misfortune he saw—this was one of those centuries.

His city, his Seat of Golden Tears, his Samhain, was at war, and everyone fighting was oblivious about its true battle. Months ago, Lucian had shattered the barrier between realms in a twisted parody of Vryce's ritual and left that door wide open. Purgatory, the heavens, several hells, and even Lucian wasn't fully sure of what exactly he dialed into. *And sure enough, someone dropped a bunch of bombs on it. Because that is surely going to help.* To him, it looked as if his city was a beautiful wart upon the cosmos. Bubbling with energy like a pea soup that someone vomited in and served for afternoon tea.

High above the city, the black sun shone its pathetic rays down, as if Lucifer the Morning Star was ashamed to look upon the zit Lucian had made. In the heavens, angels of wind, sound, and light scrambled like sailors on a leaking ship, trying to fix the hole before their boat sank. Closer to reality, where mortals walked, the city was at war with

two armies. The Church of Lazarus and Murder's North American branch were the invaders. Lucian strolled through their ranks first as they handed out shiny new weapons from Dystopia to any ghost with strong enough will to hold one. The rest would be ectoplasmic meat shields.

For an hour, Lucian strolled through the endless ranks of lesser ghosts, both curious as to whom they were fighting and also just how many people they'd slaughtered on the coast. *Seriously, I think all of Florida is here...* He performed a Christian cross sign upon seeing bound ghosts race forward wearing crocs and Miami muscle T-shirts with nothing more than a dagger. They made it just across the river before a raging firestorm incinerated the entire lot.

"So that's where the Society of Deus went!" Lucian laughed, slapping his knee and begging a necromancer nearby to do it again. The result was exactly the same. *So, it's Deus, eh? I mean, I expected Texas, to be honest. They sent the bombs. Or hell even a branch of the U.S. Military. They love being the world's police, but Deus?* He dusted his hands off. "Time for round two."

His very presence emboldened the actual soldiers of Lazarus's army, the vampires and necromancers who made up the real troops, to charge with him across the bridge. Lucian raised his cane high and shuffled faster with a battle cry that bubbled up from within, and in the middle of spells and fire raining down from rooftops—nobody noticed Lucian just kept shouting the word "Penguins" over and over again.

Much to their surprise, it wasn't a small squadron of Deus forces that were holding off a single bridge. It was one. A lone vampire with dark features and slicked black hair stood on the remains of a three-story apartment complex. The decorations on his blue military trench glistened off the black sun's rays as he summoned forth torrents of blood from the river and daggers of wind to slice through the racing horde. Unfortunately for everyone *around* Lucian, they seemed

to always get impaled first, and with every step they took, Lucian expected that the building would collapse.

Any moment now. The Death Lord ducked as a Honda Civic was thrown clear over his head at the general's command. Faster Lazarean vampires raced with unnatural speed and climbed like spiders up the buildings' side, only to discover that this general wasn't purely long range. Lucian scurried underfoot between the buildings as he heard the sickening sounds of wet thuds from the Deus general punching vampires to death with his bare knuckles. A fang from one unlucky member in Murder's ranks flicked Lucian in the ear as he ran past.

"Good luck, guys! I believe in you! Don't worry, eventually that tower will topple!" Lucian wasn't going to stick around long enough to find out. *I'm a Death Lord. I've got better places to be. Like... over there!* He ran into a small gas station and locked the door behind him, chucked bottles of Windex on the ground, and quickly wiped off the dusty window so he could peer outward. Normally, his misfortune magic worked a little faster, and something felt a bit off.

The city was in full-scale war. The forces of Deus fought entirely differently than the rank-and-file of Murder. Murder utilized hordes of dead, albeit slightly better equipped than past centuries, to overwhelm basic defenses while actual serial killers would stalk in the shadows to assassinate any true threats. Yet Deus relied on extremely skilled sorcerers with gargoyle bodyguards to shape the battlefield to their whim, and if a sorcerer appeared in true danger—a whole pack of gargoyles would slam down to defend their comrade and evacuate.

But when Lucian saw the largest Black man casually smash a Dystopian semi-truck on its side with a hammer he hissed through his teeth. *John Henry? Who let you out, buddy? Maybe...I really shouldn't have visited the world's greatest ball of twine.* Suddenly, Lucian found himself genuinely pissed. Not that someone had broken open the gates to the prison and freed the gods; no, no, he knew that was bound to happen. But rather it was the forces of Deus. After all, he didn't get to break into Deus's vault and steal *their* secrets, so why

should they have his! "I swear, the audacity of that cretin." He took a swig from a bottle of Windex. "No matter. Misfortune brought their downfall before; I just need a little more juice."

For the next fifteen minutes, Lucian shuffled, ducked, and sprinted through his city. More than once, he pretended to be a mindless zombie just to be left alone. Particularly when a well-groomed blonde gentleman he knew as Charles Walsh froze time on a city block and had his gargoyles systematically snap the neck of every necromancer foolish enough to step foot in his web. And he certainly didn't walk down the street that Ayizan Velekete operated her prayers of fortune on to save a rustic historic building from her past. That was just asking for trouble. No, Lucian sought the right strand of fate to tug upon, and that meant he needed to see everything in play.

But he wasn't alone. Each street the Death Lord walked down he found a panhandler, and to each he gave a coin from his mask. Even though the world crumbled and burned around them, they never seemed bothered or shaken by the chaos—or impacted. To them, it was business as usual, and they just needed a coin to watch the show, of which Lucian gladly abided. *If my wish comes true,* chéri, *then when I am free of my curse, all of you will be richer than you can ever imagine. Forever spared misfortune's touch.* He helped a ghostly panhandler off the ground, a battlefield medic caught in an unfortunate grenade misfire, and pointed to Ochsner Medical Center. "Might want to set up in there, bub. A little work will help you feel better. Thanks for comin'." Lucian patted the ghost on the back and got him on his way right when a gargoyle landed behind him.

"Heh, heard you coming. You are as stealthy as a bag of cement." Lucian turned around and held his hands up.

He wasn't expecting the gargoyle to be feminine and carved of intricate jade. She moved with the grace of a panther as she closed the distance to grab him by his neck, easily lifting his torn boots off the ground. Lucian smiled as he gazed into her extremely human eyes.

"You aren't a construct like the others," he choked. "You were stitched. You belong ... to Vryce."

Her lips curled into a smirk. "We've been hunting for you. Did you think you could hide forever?" She began to bend his neck at an angle bone wasn't meant to bend.

No amount of strength in Lucian's possession would free him from her grasp as his legs dangled uselessly. He tapped on her arms. "Wait... words" was all he could say before she snapped his neck and ripped his head off like a dandelion.

Lucian's spirit fell to the ground, with his mask falling right into his lap as he watched his material husk get ripped asunder yet again. Jade felt a sense of momentary accomplishment and pride in killing a Death Lord until she looked down and saw Lucian simply sitting there at her feet.

"I was going to say, it's pretty pointless for you to kill me here. It really doesn't do anything." Lucian stood up, grabbed his mask off the pile of ash that was once his head, and slipped his mask back on. "But it is like shattering a mirror. Things aren't going to go so well for you, Janine Matsen." Lucian smiled as the whites of her eyes appeared. "Thanks for that."

Even the brief connection with his immortal curse was enough for Lucian to see the final set of threads he needed: Purgatory. While angels raced above, and war waged in the middle; below, his stragglers of misfortunate souls recovered their artifacts, all before tethers of the abyss feasted upon the souls sent teeming down into his Seat of Golden Tears like a garbage disposal. It was everything Lucian had ever hoped for—both Lazarus, Deus, everyone, killing each other above a pit of no return that would only grow stronger the longer the fighting went. The roaming gods were a bit of a pickle, Lucian figured, but he had seen enough to figure out how they were returned. All were connected to Vryce, and an old friend Lucian couldn't quite remember. *But Vryce is arrogant enough to attempt a binding, I bet.*

He fingered a wooden six-sided dice. "Tell you what." He held it out in the palm of his hand. "I'm going to have a gamble of my own. Why shouldn't you? I'll cut you a deal, Janine."

"It's Jade... Janine is..." She struggled to say "dead."

"Yes, yes." Lucian waved his hand. "Vryce mindwashed you to the point of no return. I get it. Still, you wouldn't recognize your name if his magic was absolute, no? Here's the bet. You call evens or odds. If you win, you can fly away and resume your fight. If you lose, you have to listen to me say a single phrase."

She folded her arms and looked around for any signs of danger as her claw tapped the curb and her wings twitched like a cat's tail. "Screw it." She grabbed the dice and shook it. "Odds."

She tumbled the dice off the broken sidewalk, and they both watched. It rolled a three.

Lucian chuckled. "Well, hot damn. Intentionally, my bets are never rigged. You, lass, are free to go. I was looking forward to ramblin'." He was genuinely surprised that the stitched gargoyle took the bet because nobody ever trusted the Lord of Misfortune. *Unfortunately for me, that means I'll have to test my anti-god defense plan on the real deal.*

A bolt of plasma sliced the air between them, followed swiftly by a curse, as Jade quickly took to the skies and went back to her battle.

Lucian checked to make sure his nose was still missing.

"Stop playing games and kill them!" Katrina hissed as she chucked the rifle into the gutter and pulled out her rapier, raising Lucian's chin with the deadly end. "Just where, oh where, have you been? I've been burned, flung, teleported against my will, and I had to kill Florida, Lucian. FLORIDA."

Katrina's normally stark white hair was matted with brown dried blood on the right side, but her fierce eyes and exposed fangs told Lucian instantly that she wasn't being coy. *Lady, if you were here like, a minute ago, you would realize how little I care about this stick.* He reached out, grabbed the blade, and held it steady as he

stepped forward—impaling himself through the throat to get closer. The rune-marked rapier caused agonizing pain to his undead flesh, cooking his throat like bacon in a frying pan as small flecks of blood and skin-grease popped off. When Lucian reached the hilt, he tilted his head to look up at the taller vampire and pressed a single finger to his rotting lips. "Shush."

She didn't expect such a craven display and wiggled her blade in a vain attempt to free it. Behind her, her personal guard consisting of a tall Italian man wearing a jet-black suit with a skinny white tie cocked a shotgun. "Ma'am?"

"Stand down," she relented. Her shoulders slumped, and she pinched her nose in frustration. "Why. Why do I have to work with idiots?! I flipped a kingdom of corporations to our side. Did what was asked of me. I hate America. Hell, I hate *this* city. It stinks. Does the Lord of Murder care? Nope. Do you care? No. Everything is a joke to you. So, what's your master plan then? I'm winning this war with or without you. Lazarus at least recognized my name." She planted her boot in his stomach and tugged in failure. She growled as she mounted Lucian with both feet and yanked her sword free as if she was freeing Excalibur.

Ooof, someone had a bad month. Lucian chuckled and fell backward after being freed and allowed himself to lie in the gutter for a minute. A bolt of lightning arched horizontally across the rooftops. *Winning, eh? I suppose that is a thing.* "Alright, fine." He felt the pain of thirst as he channeled his blood to close the wounds in his neck. "What, dear Katrina, does victory look like to you?" Long spindly fangs slowly sprouted as Lucian looked to her bodyguard, judging if he would make a solid snack. "Sorry, mate, but I've recently had to reform my whole body. I'm feeling a bit ... peckish."

The bodyguard curled an eyebrow and flicked the safety of his gun off.

"Xavier is off limits." Katrina sighed and pulled a bottle of demon blood from her backpack and chucked it over. "Victory, you

incorrigible tampon, is finishing our contract with Dystopia and binding the prisoners here to their companies. Orders from on high."

Lucian caught the bottle with a single hand, and as he guzzled the peach-tasting liquid, he flailed at the city streets with his free hand. "Ahhh! That hit the spot." He burped and threw it behind him. "I think someone already beat you to it."

"Really?! I didn't notice that Slenderman was giving loving embraces again. You don't say?"

"You uh, got anymore?" He licked his lips. She glared. "Awww, fine then. Seriously though, you don't notice anything different, do you? Are your hands all tingly? Feeling a bit hollow on the inside? Maybe your necromancy has shown signs of age and gone a little ... limp?" Lucian's wrist flopped backward as he toyed with the lieutenant. Katrina was an extremely competent killer, but noticing threads of fate wasn't exactly her forte, and Lucian had spotted the absence of Murder's tie on every priest the moment he stepped foot on the battlefield. She was no different.

"N-no?" She lied. "Besides, everything is still going to plan. We captured these prisoners before, and even if we don't—the chamber houses plenty of cryptids and other lesser gods. This isn't our first war, you realize? Block by block, we eventually close in. The Society is competent, I'll admit," she widened her eyes, "but they lack numbers... and now you are here. Do the thingy..."

He laughed. "Oh dear, I did *the thingy* months ago. You are standing *in* the thingy," Lucian paced around the leather-clad vampire and trailed a finger along her shoulders. "The fact you *are* standing here in my city means maybe you were never meant to work for Murder after all. I mean, can that *le con* really be a great boss? I mean sure he's got the biggest armies. Humans are experts at killing each other... and nobody really wants to work for Pestilence. But you don't find it odd that you have to manually bind and mark the people you kill now? Wasn't that ... automatic for you priests before?" Lucian picked up the energy rifle out of the gutter and held it away like a pair

of used socks. "And really? Since when did the armies of death itself need trinkets? You should be ashamed."

Xavier spoke. "Can't fault a man for adapting to the times, Grandpa. Our job is to kill, so we do it with the best tools available."

Lucian rolled his eyes. "Ah yes, let me guess, you're going to say that you like to see the lights of their eyes go out."

"Ew. No." He shouldered the shotgun. "Quick and filled with lead. I hate it when they make noise."

"ENOUGH!" Katrina tugged at her hair. "Okay. Something happened. I don't know what, but it's different, and I don't care because I'm still here. I've been offered a role in the Sanctum, and I finally get to have intelligent conversations with people outside of Italy. I'm not just stuck in Purgatory, poking at Murder's prisoners for years on end or corralling demons. So, Lucian, Lord of Misfortune, I'm asking you. I need this. I don't want to be so far down the ladder anymore. It feels like I'm in my own grave. So just this once, can you please help us win? Or at least make it easier?"

I wonder what happened to Murder. Why didn't Fate clue me in? Lucian mused and found himself slowly nodding. He would help Katrina. After all, she was placed in his web of misfortune for a reason, and he never knew exactly how things would unfold. *Besides, I can't let Vryce win either.*

"Alright. I'm just going to pretend I didn't hear something about a Sanctum, or whatever the hell bullshit ol' Lazzy is up to now. He's probably making his move. One way or another, the world is screwed so might as well have a good time along the way, no?" Lucian gestured for the duo to follow him closer to the heart of the French Quarter.

"I can handle the gods. Not in the way you might like, however. So, here's the deal." He held out his hand. "You let the ones who walk out of here... walk out of here. Understand? Spread the news to your forces on the outside that anyone who walks out is free to go— including the Society of Deus. Fighting ones are fair game for your

troops to swarm like ants and capture. Whoever is still in my prison of Golden Tears is yours for the taking."

She contemplated silently as they walked on the sidewalk, with Xavier switching between three different guns to take precision shots at gargoyles or sorcerers who left themselves open. Lucian stepped on the chest of one fallen gargoyle and remarked that Xavier had a talent for hitting the eyeball. *Humans never cease to amaze me.*

Rounding the corner to the Saint Hotel, Katrina, Lucian, and Xavier stopped. The black marquee sign with yellow bulbs and white marble construction stood mostly unfazed by the war. A single palm tree still survived right in the middle of the double entry glass doors. It was an odd sight given that on each side of the hotel cavernous pits directly into Purgatory sprawled in either direction. The rest of the street was now dominated by old, centuries old, buildings that had long been demolished. The Saint was the last bastion of modern New Orleans that remained as Purgatory had fully crossed the line from a hidden realm and into reality within this region.

And standing right in front of the hotel were the main forces of the Society of Deus. Blue military clad vampires with masks and a menagerie of weaponry were issuing commands to others in the city. Of course, several of the newly unshackled gods stood guard with them. Lucian didn't recognize any high-ranking generals other than the black-haired sorcerer from the earlier bridge, and he felt a twinge of sadness that Gabriel wasn't among their ranks. He wanted a rematch. Still, the elevator he wanted to use happened to be within that hotel.

"We are a bit far forward, no?" Katrina whispered.

"Nah, they already know we are here." Lucian shrugged. "Besides, what's the point of having endless hordes if you don't let them crash against the walls for hours while the heroes do the real work?" He extended his hand to Xavier. "By the way, I'm Lucian, nice to meet you, pal."

Xavier was counting bullets and bit a round to return the shake. "Xavier Hood. Hitman for hire."

"So, what's the other part?" Katrina asked. "You said a deal. So, what do you want from us?"

"Oh! Right. Uh..." Lucian scratched his chin. *The hell do I actually want? That she can achieve.* He snapped his fingers. "I'm tired of being the only grandpa, and you have some new secret force you are a part of. So, wake up the old guys in Venice. There are a ton of ol' vampires there, and in France, England, Poland. When this is over, I want you to go pull out the wooden stakes from the ancient ones. If the world is going to chaos, I at least want some crotchety people to piss off in seven hundred years."

"Surrreee..." She narrowed her eyes. "So, gods?" She pointed forward.

Lucian batted her hand and danced across the street with a whirl. "Gentlemen and ladies! Hello!" He smiled while flicking a coin up into the air.

Three miles back, an impossible chain of events had been unfolding for the past hour. A three-story apartment building began to collapse while Michael Dragosani beat skull after skull in with his bare hands until a gargoyle ripped him off to the safety of the Saint Hotel. A racing caravan of Lazarean forces sped through the collapsing checkpoint, hoping to exploit the gap. A single fang from a vampire's skull wedged in the cobblestone road stuck up, popping a tire and sending the truck careening out of control into a nearby gas station.

The explosion shattered nearby windows and sent a billow of smoke up in the air, but also triggered a cascading burst of power lines snapping like brittle twigs and dancing into the streets. Sparks danced across wrought-iron fences, igniting ancient oaks that lined the

avenues. The flames licked hungrily at the dried branches, spreading like wildfire to nearby rooftops, where centuries-old homes burst into a cacophony of cinders and ash.

The heat rose to a ferocious intensity, warping the air itself, causing a blinding mirage that sent (of all creatures to survive in the apocalypse) a flock of pigeons veering wildly off course. Their flight ended abruptly as they collided with precariously perched scaffolding on the side of an old cathedral. The structure groaned under the sudden weight before collapsing inward, sending a spire crashing through the roof and into the sanctuary below.

There, a forgotten cache of ancient relics—bottles of holy water, vials of sanctified oil—reacted violently to the intrusion. They shattered in a flash of searing light, sending shards of consecrated glass flying in every direction. One fragment, sharp as a dagger, sliced through the air and struck a jade gargoyle perched on the nearby church tower. As her mouth snapped, she grasped a nearby lightning rod while uttering a swear, accidentally letting loose a spell of lightning down the road. The surge channeled into a long-abandoned underground gas line, creating a thunderous detonation that spread like a shockwave in each direction.

As Ayizan Velekete's beloved house was blown to smithereens, she unleashed a primal scream that reverberated through the astral plane, further ripping the tear between worlds and unleashing every soul bound to a grave in cemeteries for miles on end. The ghosts, wraiths, and phantoms spilled into the streets as they unleashed centuries of torment.

In their wake, the very fabric of reality began to warp. Time itself fractured, moments from the past and future bleeding together. Fates that could have been crossed with unlucky events. As the madness of Lucian's chaos spread, the streets of New Orleans/Samhain became a twisted labyrinth, where echoes of jazz from the 1920s played alongside the hum of future tech, and horse-drawn carriages shared space with Dystopian armored carriers, all moving in discordant rhythm.

Amid this maelstrom, a lone street musician, oblivious to the chaos and satisfied with the coins in his guitar case, strummed an upbeat chord on his guitar. The sound resonated impossibly, rippling through the broken city to the tune of *In the Hall of the Mountain King*, and somehow, beyond all known means of sorcery, caused the Mississippi River to swell and churn. A massive wave rose up, crashing over the levees, sweeping away debris, vehicles, and the remains of battle-worn soldiers alike.

Katrina and Xavier quickly took cover as a massive wave washed through the very street Lucian stood upon. Dragosani and the forces of Deus standing outside of the Saint Hotel abandoned the nearby gods and raced inside to avoid the maelstrom of chaos and water.

And yet, as the flood waters receded, they revealed Lucian Montague, Death Lord of Misfortune, standing atop the rubble of what was once a market square performing a simple bow to the two gods who remained. Lucian's arrival was marked by the final, fatal act of a thousand intertwining fates. The air was thick with the scent of burning wood, ozone, and despair.

Lucian inhaled deeply and surveyed the wreckage, a smirk playing on his lips as he felt the strings of destiny tighten in his grasp. He eyed the only two deities with enough courage to stand their ground. One was a werewolf-shaped beast strong enough to hold on. The other, a native American in a wide-brim, black hat, seemed unfazed by the waters of the Mississippi.

Lucian lifted his hand, and with a casual flick of his wrist, the dying embers of fires behind him flared back to life, igniting anew. "Oh, Beast of the Bray and Wovoka, aren't you two a little far from home?" His voice dripped with sarcasm and malice. "I bring intent to harm the one known as Damien Vryce." *Oh, please, PLEASE let that work. I get one really good spell. That was good entrance, right?* Lucian hoped that Damien was dumb enough to implant mental commands regarding his self-preservation because if not, the Beast of Bray Wood was about to turn him into a bloody soup, and Wovoka would bind

his ghost into a dream catcher for the next decade, and he would rather avoid that.

The Beast of Bray and Wovoka looked at each other, looked back to Lucian, and turned around to walk inside without so much as a word.

"Ahahaha! Yes! Take that!" Lucian hollered. "Okay, Katrina, my job's done." He dusted his hands and hopped off the washed-up rubble. "I've been setting that up for ages. No idea what happens next, so when they come out of that building to kill us... go get 'em, tiger."

Katrina and Xavier looked several shades paler, which was an impressive feat for a vampire, and they looked around at the total chaotic destruction that washed over from behind them. Any rampart or fortified position from the Society was in total shambles, even if their sorcerers were lifted out of harm's way by their guardians. Thus, the fifth wave of Lazarus's legions could wash into the city unchecked and reinforce Katrina or take territory. If they still wanted to, that is.

Katrina held out her hands at the futility of the situation. "Well, I guess we weren't trying to live in the city afterward."

A dead pigeon fell into her right hand.

CHAPTER 37

"Look, Frank, hunting for good Mexican food is a fine art. It takes skill and patience. Unlike Chinese food, which throws itself at you like a lemur, fine Mexican cuisine is like a seven-horned, white-tailed buck. The Chicago Tamale Guy is the prize stallion. His mom spends all day making tacos and tamales, and he wanders north-side bars with a red cooler in hand by night. Like a god delivering soma to the masses drunk on Dionysus wine."

–Footage of Mike Auburn outside of a Division Street bar next to a cab driver wearing an aviator coat on an Instagram reel

Mike shook off organs from the pot-bellied, three-eyed demon that slowly dragged down the stone wall with its dying breath. He licked his fingers first before wiping his hands off and took a moment to light up and survey his handiwork. *Little sister had the right idea—getting back clothes makes a ghost's job much easier. Fuck, I love this coat. I wonder what patch or pin I should add for this battle, though?* The most recent demon was something from another culture that Mike wasn't familiar with, so other than its chicken legs, tiny bird wings, and three eyes—he didn't know what to call it. *Or*

the rest of them. Down the corridor lay thirty-two demons that Mike had crushed, smashed, or ripped in half. "I think I'm getting pretty good at this, wouldn't you say?" He grabbed the demon by the back of its head and smooshed its face against the strange arcane glyphs that warded the prison chamber he currently stood at. *One of these arcane glyphs would make a really cool patch.*

When it didn't work, he just discarded the dead corpse and grabbed another. *Shiiit, don't make me do all thirty.* It was tiresome work, freeing captives when nobody noticed. The psychopath Vryce was moving from one god to the next, and sure, Mike knew he was responsible for helping facilitate that. Yet the rituals took time, and when Jane and Lumine were focused on other tasks, Mike was alone. In the heart of the Unification's prison. There was no insane Death Lord or armies of vampires to battle. All that remained were just the natural guardians he'd seen time and again in Purgatory. He held a female demon with seven eyes and sixteen horns up. *Mostly seen.* Her face was still smashed into the door without a second thought.

The Boss's intel was off. There weren't merely fifty-eight demi-gods within this prison. It went far deeper than any of them realized. Granted, he wasn't sure if half the prisoners he'd freed between rituals were genuine gods or just prisoners of war, but the way he figured it, if they were locked up by his enemy—then freedom it was. The pulsing purple wall of energy faded, revealing the musty stone cavern inside with a lone figure sitting on a bench barely visible in the darkness.

"Alright, buddy." Mike stepped in and gestured. "First, I come in peace, and second, if you need some demon guts to heal a wound or something, I made a buffet outside."

The scrawny old man rose and dusted off a black hat. "Can I trouble you for a smoke?" His voice sounded musical and like trouble at the same time.

"Oof," Mike joked and counted his six remaining. "Ever since I died, I think I chain gun these more than I ever did alive... but screw it. I'm not the one who's been locked in here for how long?"

"June 1st, 1868," he said, plucking one from the pack. "The day the Navajo officially signed the treaty. So... a while."

When Mike lit the smoke, he saw the man was certainly humanoid but had distinctly coyote features with sharp eyes, furry animalistic ears, and rows of pointed teeth that glistened off the Zippo lighter. "Well, unlike most here, you can still walk and haven't been drained of blood like some of the others. Hell, they decapitated Balor and impaled him to a tree several leagues down deeper."

"Kid, they certainly tried," he held the smoke between his teeth as he donned a duster coat that was hanging inside his cell, "but some people still worship me, so I've got a few tricks up my sleeve. Alright, what's the catch. Favor? Boon? Make you a king?"

Mike waved. "Nah, not my style. Just don't get caught on your way out. Take the back way through Purgatory." He gestured down the hall away from Vryce. "It's a deeper walk through the deadlands, but you'll pop out somewhere in the west if you don't get eaten by a demon. Texas is the first stop on the that train if I recall right."

Coyote stared at Mike in silence for an awkward minute. "Take caution when playing with fire. Gods, particularly European ones, can mete out far worse punishment than mere death if they catch you doing this. So, do us both a favor and don't get caught, eh?" He patted Mike on the shoulder and stepped over a demon on the way out.

No shit. Mike chuckled. Ever since he crawled out of Purgatory, Mike had one string of bad luck after another. Now, for hours on end, he had been freeing prisoners in the shadows and not asking a thing for it. If Boss, Vryce, Lucian, or hell, anyone really, except the freed, caught him, he was confident he'd end up like Balor. Forced to endure an eternity of torment. The prospect certainly wasn't something he looked forward to, but he also didn't have the cowardice to do *nothing*. And this realm of the dead was the one place Mike felt capable within.

Unlike most ghosts, he could see and hear normally, and that always allowed him to get the drop on demonic guards. *And the strength of Golgoroth certainly doesn't hurt either.* He surveyed the

rest of the hall to ensure that everyone in this corner of the maze had been freed and took one final look. It was a bloody mess of chaos and smashed open doors. Certainly not something that was considered subtle by any measure. *Even if I get out of here today, it's not like they won't figure it out later. Eh, fuck it. That's tomorrow's problem.*

He grabbed a smaller demon for Lumine and took rugged stone steps up two at a time back to the main floor where the cabal of Vryce's stitched souls happened. Everyone had been at it for a while now, and when Mike saw that Vryce was down to just a single body, drinking a tall glass of vitae that Jane provided, he steeled his thoughts away from his ulterior activities. *Tacos. God, I miss tacos.*

"So, we done?" Mike lightly tossed the chicken-foot demon on a pile of other smaller ones used to fuel the ritual.

Lumine, Jane, and Vryce all looked like their best friend just died of cancer.

"This motherfucker," a familiar voice from behind Vryce echoed. "Caught in a battle with the Lord of Misfortune and he's thinking about tacos," Gabriel said, stepping out.

Mike felt the smile grow despite wishing it hadn't. "Oh, the cat does drag in roadkill. You are looking better than last time."

"Can't say the same. You're still dead."

"Don't be a speci-ist. Ghosts have rights." Mike flicked him off as he entered the main chamber where everyone stood.

Several more figures had appeared since Mike had gone down the last time. Besides Gabriel stood Onyx, Dragosani, and the Beast of Bray. All of them except Gabriel had water-soaked feet.

"Mike," Jane smiled, "meet Michael Dragosani, Onyx the Gargoyle, and the new Beast of Bray." She skipped over and grabbed Dragosani's hand. Mike thought they looked like a couple coming out to their parents for the first time.

"Jane." *Oh, for heaven's sake, really? Alright. This is happening. It's happening. It's fine.* "I'd like you to meet Dragosani, a general in Amo-A-Deus, Onyx, formerly known as Officer Winters of the Chicago

Police Department, and... and..." Mike flailed his hand at the Beast of Bray. It wasn't *really* the Beast of Bray, just a soldier from the Second City soul-stitched in. Mike could see clearly the threads of Vryce's handiwork. "Well, I don't actually know your name."

"It was Jebidiah, but I'm going by Bray now," the werewolf responded.

Gabriel clapped his hands. "Fantastic, we all know each other in different ways. Those two are fucking, Onyx's a former Second City cop before Bollard betrayed him, and Bray here is just lonely. Ya missed Wovoka, a real ball of charisma. Came in, said that Lucian is here, and promptly fucked off."

Bones is here at last? "Good thing we are done then, right?" Mike looked at Vryce.

"Yes."

"So why does everyone look like you dropped a slice of pizza? Let's go kick his ass!" Mike clapped his hands.

Lumine elbowed Mike in the ribs. "You don't mean that."

"Fuckin' hell I don't. Look, you can have pity for him all you want, but that prick totally needs to be locked in a barrel and have the shit slapped out of him. Besides, wasn't the whole point of this to knock another one of Lazarus's Death Lords off a pedestal? You know, before they friggin' kill everyone?"

Dragosani rubbed the back of Jane's neck like an owner petting a cat and spoke casually. "The problem with that is they *did* kill everyone. There are more forces outside than we can hold. Legions of dead from who knows where, along with other necromancers and vampyr. We bought time. But cannot win. Not with him here."

Mike's eye twitched at the public display of affection. "Okay, true, they have an army, but we have," Mike flailed at Vryce, "the guy everyone hates. Go out there and blast him."

"It's not that simple." Vryce sighed. "Winning here would only be a pyrrhic victory with little reward."

"So, you are telling me you can't beat him then?" Mike folded his arms.

Lightning arched in Vryce's hair, bouncing off the tips of his elven ears as his fists clenched. "I DON'T KNOW HOW!" he screamed, causing every torch in the prison to ignite in a six-foot long flame. "We are trapped! They have our exit surrounded. He is older than I. Killing him does nothing. He fails upward. Raw power is useless against misfortune. So no, Mike, I can't BEAT HIM! I cannot summon storms to eradicate him. I cannot possess him. I cannot curse him." As Vryce walked forward, blood boiled and popped out of every carcass on the ground, and Mike watched his soul separate from the body he possessed at times.

"The sun sets, big guy." Mike held his hands up. "Easy... you are losing control."

Everyone winced.

"Control?!" Vryce's eyes widened to reveal their whites. "We have no luxury. If I was whole, I could have beat him in Deus. But where are we, Auburn? We are in *his* sanctum. His domain, and thanks to you, I'm but a pale shade of myself."

Mike braced for an arcane onslaught and winced his eyes shut. When none came, he peeked open to see Gabriel's hand on Vryce's shoulder.

"Don't pop your suit," Gabriel said in a low tone. "He's not your enemy today."

Mike's mind raced to think of ideas. *If I remember right, Lucian's misfortune doesn't work well inside Purgatory. Or we could maybe send Lumine out to chat with him. Raise a white flag? Or...* He clapped his hands. "Can't you just teleport us out?"

Gabriel shook his head. "Delilah was the one to invent the spell to move armies anywhere. Vryce is bound to his fragments." He tapped the swords on his back. "We've got most of them here, and he hasn't mastered his own apprentice's spells."

Well, that's unlucky. "Okay, sooo... let's just take the back door?" Mike pointed to the shadowy depths.

Onyx and Dragosani shook their heads. "We can't navigate the depths without helldivers. We'd get lost."

"Plus," Vryce sighed, "I am not a creature who can step foot in heaven or hell without luring far greater threats than what we face. That way lies suicide." He clutched his temples to silence a headache as the flares died down. "I believe I'm also at my limit."

Jane leaned up, kissed Dragosani on the cheek, and tugged him into the middle. "Hey, don't worry about getting lost, guys. Mike and I can navigate, no problem. Easy peasy. I mean, isn't that why you brought along two of the *best* underworld guides this side of the Mason-Dixon line?"

Mike nodded. "I agree. Come on, big guy. You just teleport back to a different fragment, and Jane and I will get everyone else out. You don't strike me as the kind dumb enough to put ALL your fragments in the same spot. So, the rest of us run recoup and study a means to win the war."

Everyone seemed to weigh the option.

"While that seems logical," Vryce said at last, "you would still be fleeing through a Death Lord's realm. I've put too much investment into the lot of you only to watch each of you be captured and imprisoned."

Mike caught Vryce's gaze shift to Jane's hand with a slight hint of jealousy.

"Fine." Mike folded his arms. "Here's my real plan then. You let me go kick Lucian's skinny ass down the streets of New Orleans. I just need your help to do it."

Everyone laughed.

"You think I'm kidding, but need I remind you, I've uh... kicked both your asses before?" Mike put his arms over Vryce and Gabriel. "I just need you to stitch one more soul so I can actually *do* it outside of Purgatory. Remember, down here I can touch things. Up there... I'm

a ghosty boi. Plus, he's kind of a necromancer, and sending me up as a ghost is just asking for disaster."

Mike was flung off the duo as each sorcerer telekinetically flicked him back.

"If I was to even *consider* bringing you back to the mortal world, Mr. Auburn," Vryce hissed, "I doubt any of the prisoners left would give you the strength required."

Mike dusted himself off and stretched. "Oh, I wouldn't worry about that. Ya see, deep down inside this place. Waaaaaaayyy down there lies Balor One-Eye. Decapitated, impaled with spears, and chained to a tree. Fucker is massive. Like Golgoroth sized. If Golgoroth helped me kick your two lily asses six ways to Sunday, imagine what Balor's heart could do."

"Balor, king of the Fomorians, vile of the fae." Vryce's features darkened. "Under no circumstances will I bring back such power into this world. That's like asking me to return Jesus or Loki."

"So, what I'm hearing is you know it would work." Mike smiled.

"Let me ask you, Mr. Auburn, if your goal is to prevent Lazarus from obtaining deification, then what makes you think it is a wise idea to aim for the same? Do you not despise concentrated power?" he mused.

"First off, that ain't Lazarus." Mike shook his head. "The real one died in Purgatory. Asked for freedom. I've no idea what, or who, this new one is. The way I see it, it's probably someone just like us—a mortal grasping at straws to survive. Second, it's not power I despise; it's how it's wielded. For centuries, you hid all these secrets from everyone. Dude, you could have cured cancer with this demon-blood shit. But no, you let people suffer. You *chose* that."

Gabriel stepped in between the two. "Technically, we chose to give that magic to everyone. It's the legion of people trying to kill us outside that kept it hidden. Don't confuse the two. We wield magic, but we are miles apart."

Vryce turned his back. "The answer is no. Now, Onyx, tell everyone to flee and return to Deus. There is no longer a reason to fight on these shores."

"As you command." The massive gargoyle bowed and instantly left up the stairs without another word.

Vryce continued, "The rest of you, our choice is war. Jane, Dragosani, and I will engage. Gabriel, you flee the moment we step outside and get as far away as you possibly can. If you can get beyond the reach of New Orleans, I will grab them and teleport to your location."

"Hold the banana phone," Jane protested. "That still leaves Mike and Lumine here, and you can barely fucking stand, cupcake. Nah." She picked up the viola case. "I've got an idea. I didn't spend weeks getting thwacked with a stick to sit by idly. Everyone's big concern here is Purgatory and this place being Lucian's. Wellll... I'm about to go make it not his."

Rather than wait for anyone's response, Jane grabbed Dragosani by the tie and led him up the stairs, muttering something about not letting him out of her sight again and something about a "good boy" echoed down that made Gabriel snort. "Oh, he's not living that down later."

Great! Great! Mike chucked his hands up. "See what we did? The youngest of us is now going out there to fight a Death Lord alone."

"Well, she did kill one before." Vryce grinned. "You should have more faith."

The sound of clapping hands echoed from the shadows behind Mike, followed by the slow tap of dress shoes echoing off the stone floor.

Everyone readied themselves to annihilate whoever revealed themselves.

"Faith is something you each are sorely lacking," the man said, stepping into view. Red aviator sunglasses rested atop the demon's head. He was dressed in a black suit coat with a red button-down

shirt that was more opened than closed, and Mike could spot several wicked occult tattoos etched into his skin. The handsome man with 5 o'clock shadow casually smoked and glared at each of them with serpentine eyes of pure bright gold that glistened against the darkness around them. "Apologies for interrupting. You can call me Hal Morgan, and I'm your local Demon of War." He pointed to the sky. "I couldn't help but notice you find yourselves in... oh, a fancy little spat on this continent."

Wait, didn't I kill the Demon of War? Mike scratched his head and worked his jaw. "Wait... you? Bit ... small? Aren't you?" Mike judged his height somewhere around a few inches shorter than six feet.

"Mike!" Hal held his arms wide. "Bring it in! Oh, man." Hal lunged forward embracing Mike like an old friend. He smelled like sulfur and napalm. "Man, do I owe you some thanks. Without you, I'd never have been promoted. Golgoroth was a right Nazi asshole. Seriously, down in the pits, we were all cheering for you. But really," he held Mike's shoulders and nodded back, "did you really have to kill so many minions? You know good help is hard to find in hell."

Vryce and Gabriel quickly compared demonology notes to see if either of them recognized any fragment of a true name from a Hal Morgan and came up empty-handed.

"True names there, y'all just don't know me yet. You will. See, Pride got to come on out and play, along with Azmodeus. Mammon is always looking for his break, and we really don't want to mention that you mortals let Karen out. You'll regret that later. Trust us." He rolled his eyes. "We don't have long, so I'll cut to the chase. The actual forces of hell." He pointed down and mouthed the word *Lucifer* without saying it. "Not the help and wait staff we stick up to tend to Purgatory, the real ones all have a vested interest in the Lord of Murder getting knocked down a peg."

Mike freed himself from the grasp. *Guy's got style, but seriously does EVERYONE just show up here?*

"Right, Mike?" Gabriel chuckled. "It's like, I dunno, you are standing at ground zero where everyone is looking. So... I bet everyone shows up."

"Please no." Vryce slumped against the wall. "I was so close to being free..."

Hal snapped his fingers and pretended to shoot Vryce in the chest with finger pistols. "That's right, buddy. A lich? Dipping your toes into Purgatory, buddy, pal, buskha, you GOTTA know Purgatory is part of hell? You think we didn't notice? And in the middle of a WAR? Baby, call me on the cell phone next time you want a booty call. I've got blondes and gingers for days, just pick your flavor."

Mike asked, "You here for him then? Not us?"

Hal nodded. "Oh yessss, he broke the rules. Big bad warlock trying to become a teeny wittle god." Hal booped the nose of Vryce. "See that?" Hal pointed to a defeated Vryce who allowed it to happen. "Even the great and mighty know their place. Lesser demons and angels he'd slaughter for days. Real ones with influence show up WHEN YOU ARE STANDING IN OUR KIDDIE POOL, and he buckles like the good little soul-stitched he is."

Gabriel drew his two swords and cracked his neck. "I think you misunderstand, Hal. He isn't hiding from you. Angels kill demons, demons kill mortals, and mortals with angel hearts kill both." Both swords ignited into flames as Gabriel twirled them.

"Whoa!" Hal dropped to a knee and raised a literal white flag on a tiny stick. "Easy! We can all get what we want here."

Gabriel held the flaming sword to his throat. "One sentence."

"You need my blessing to allow Vryce down to Balor's prison."

Oh? I like where this is going. Mike took up position behind Hal and leaned down. "This prick right here is called Gabriel D'Angelo, pretty on the nose for smiting demons. He even comes equipped with flaming swords. So just level with us: what's that blessing going to cost?"

"War, of course. You wage war. Without it, the world doesn't have a concept of peace. I know, we demons go about things backward, but if everyone loses here... then what follows is really a slow slaughter of the whole world. You need bigger guns to beat the likes of Lazarus. A few bad asses can't stop millions of faithful. You *need* to bring back real gods."

Vryce's head bounced off the stone wall as he stared at the ceiling. "What is one more binding?" He sighed in reluctant acceptance. "Fine."

CHAPTER 38

"Critics around the world have labeled our city Dystopia, all because we place the future of sentient species first. Through hard work, cohesive mind-melding, and an upbeat attitude, the corporations of our Utopia have revolutionized a world where the sun rises black each morning. Where others see endless working hours and a concrete paradise—we see a city where everyone is equal. And so, we proudly announce that we will treat the world as equals. Now, no matter what nation, faith, or creed you hail from—all our approved products will be available. Any time. Anywhere. We invite you to join our team. Help us make the world a more equal place."

–Triumvirate Enterprises

Jane dragged Dragosani by the wrist into the small wooden elevator and kicked the gate closed before pinning him up against the wall. *I've waited way too long for this.* She let the world fade from her mind as she kissed the vampire. In that moment, she didn't care about the Death Lord, or anything really, only that he desired her in turn. Her lips danced along his as she bunched up his black hair and pulled him even closer. *Dating in the apocalypse doesn't leave a girl with*

396

many options. I got lucky. She let out a gasp as she pushed herself off and let the tingle settle into her lips with a coy smile.

"I, assume," Dragosani took her hand and kissed the back of it, "that means you miss me, no?"

"No, not at all. We only met briefly on a battlefield, had some sparks, arranged a date, and then I spent the next year dead. Minor long-distance problems." She chuckled and activated the rope-bound pulley system. *You'd think that with all their resources, they'd install something a little more advanced than rocks tied to ropes.* She made sure they were moving vertical by looking over the edge with a nod.

"We not waiting for them?"

"Oh, hell no. They are big boys. Besides, I couldn't date you in front of my brother and your boss." She intertwined her fingers with his. "One nice thing about being in Purgatory is we can touch each other."

"I'm not complaining, but this is a little rustic for a date. I'm more of a ... toasting glasses over a fine meal with music kind of vampire."

She poked his nose before folding herself into his arms with her back to his chest. "If you don't mind, I'm going to pass on your dinner dates. That can be a you-thing, honey. Hey, question."

"Answer?" He looked down easily into her eyes.

"Do ghosts age?"

"You never age, beautiful." He kissed her forehead.

Ack! Cheesy! Jane elbowed him. "Okay, Casanova," she joked. "Cheesy romance aside..." Jane's thought trailed off. Truth is, she actually knew very little about him. Not that that was a problem given that he was cut from the mold of dark-sexy-European-vampires, but they should go on a proper date at least once. She gave one last squeeze of his arms before pulling free. "Okay, let's do this."

Dragosani looked very confused by the sudden pull away, and he glanced down at his belt before going back to her face.

"Not that." She nodded. "Maybe that. Not yet. Date. You. Me. We are on it. Yes? You asked for one?"

"I did lay it on pretty thick in Michigan, so I'd say yes."

She clapped her hands. "Fantastic. You!" Jane suddenly jumped closer. "Our first date is an elevator ride out of Purgatory. You rescued me from an eternity of endless boredom. What did I do?"

Michael Dragosani raised an eyebrow at the game but slowly nodded. "You ... made an undead lich blush, who happens to be my boss. We met at a work event, and it was all sparks from there."

She leaned up and gave him a peck on the lips before suddenly slapping him. "How dare you not wait for me!"

His fangs appeared. "It wasn't my fault; she was texting me!"

Jane huffed and turned around. "I waited for a year in Purgatory for you. Did you come?"

"I tried, but you fell in Dystopia. They won't let our kind in. They are rather discriminatory against vampires."

"Excuses," she lowered her head, "but I can forgive you." She turned around and unzipped her jumpsuit slightly. "Promise you only flirt with girls and guys who are at my standard?"

He swooped in and bent her down. "Oh, I promise. Only creatures as magnificent as you..."

"Introduce me to your parents?"

"Parents are dead."

"Do you have any children?"

"Do we count vampires I've embraced?"

"Yes." She nodded. "Absolutely. Wait, you have children?! I don't know if I'm ready for children!"

"I... uh..." Dragosani let her go and turned his back. "If you can't accept my progeny, then we won't work."

Jane held her back to his. "Then I suppose this is the end. I need a life of being free, finding hot vampires and fae to ride. I can't be tied down being a ghost mom."

The elevator reached the foundation of the Saint Hotel with a dust-laden clatter. Jane opened the gate into a small five-foot tall crawlspace with unfinished gravel floor and a single bulb light with

a silver chain. Even as short as she was, it was easier for her to crawl on all fours until they reached the staircase at the end. *You better be soaking in the view, buddy.* "I can't believe you couldn't keep your fangs in your mouth. So, what hussies have you made immortal? Who are your children?" She looked back and saw his glowing red eyes cut through the darkness, absolutely fixated on her position.

"Child. Nathanial. He's a proper badass in his own right. Still in Europe though. I haven't seen him since the 1960s."

"Lost the custody battle?"

"That's not how ... vampires ... work?"

"Yeah, you lost the custody battle." She nodded to herself with a smile as she crawled out by the stairs and extended a hand to help him up and dusted him off. "Okay. I think we should break up officially." She extended her hand.

His smile slowly faded as he realized she was being serious. "Wait... you aren't playing anymore?"

"Well, this is our first sequence of dating in five minutes." She reached up to straighten his tie. "Cut through all the Tinder bullshit in an instant. We met, we kissed, almost got busy, but I need to spend the next two weeks ghosting you to figure out if I'm ready to be with a guy that has a kid, and then I'll suddenly text you to come over one night when I'm drunk."

"Oh..." He shook her hand, *slowly.* "I am very confused."

"Don't worry. If you are good in the sack, I'll just end up never leaving and stealing your T-shirts. But uh..." she thumbed up the stairs, "we are... kinda... just a little... about to go fight a Death Lord. Usually, one of us ends up dead in these scenarios." She gestured his way. "So—"

He put a finger on her lips to silence her. "Do you know the best part about being immortal?"

You have really good compound interest on your 401k? She shook her head.

"A year is nothing. Thus, when you die out there, I'll still be there for our second date when you dig yourself out of the next sewer cesspool." He flicked her forehead and took the lead up the stairs. "What's the plan, lass?"

What makes you think I'm going to die? She huffed and straightened the viola case. "You are so lucky you've got one of those lumberjack butts. The plan, dark-and-stormy, is to put your boss's lessons to work. Apparently, by combining music with what I've learned, and this bad boy here," she tapped the case, "I should be able to raise the barrier of the Innocence once again and push Purgatory back down to separate it from the real world."

"...and given that Lazarus's army is mostly filled with ghosts..."

"Bingo. Untrained ghosts can't do anything but walk through walls then." Jane rounded the third staircase up and stood by his side at the door leading into the lobby.

"What about you then?"

"Eh," she poked her forefingers together, "I'll find my way back out later. There are like tunnels everywhere. Just keep them off me while I play, okay?"

"You have a deal." He began to open the door, and she quickly slammed it shut.

"But then you run." She held her pinkie up. "Promise." *None of that self-sacrifice bullshit.*

He took one look at her and grew six-inch talon claws from his fingers. "Absolutely not," he said, shouldering the door in the opposite direction and barreling into the lobby with unnatural speed.

Jane kicked her rocket boots into action, burning the lacquered wood-slat floor of the lobby as she took to the air and skated through the thirty-five-foot-tall white drapes to keep pace. If there was anything she missed about being alive, it was the sense of vertigo from the adrenaline rush of aerial maneuvers. She dashed past the lush red bar with checkered floors and the pristine-white reception desk toward

the front doors, inwardly marveling at the magic that must have kept this hotel identical on both sides of the shroud.

Tucked away in a corner was a velvet red door with massive magenta drapes decoratively folded open and a massive Victorian-era throne sitting right in front. *Perfect.* She kicked above her, instantly changing directions and somersaulted backward into a perfect landing right as Dragosani crashed through the glass lobby doors. She wasted no time in unlatching Vryce's viola case.

The wooden instrument was a hand-crafted masterpiece, older than she could place but perfectly maintained. *All the time in the world to master bartending, being a badass, but never learned to shred. Do you even shred on this?* The cherry-stained wood that comprised the base had decorative but functional etchings of Gnostic hermeticism laced throughout, and the translucent blue strings glimmered in the little light that emanated from the nearby candlelight. As soon as she wrapped her fingers around the fingerboard, she felt the surge of power course through her soul. Vryce's knowledge of sorcery became an instant memory in her mind, as intimate as knowing how to breathe.

Threads of magic were visible to her everywhere her eyes darted. She could see Dragosani's heart out in the street, pulsing with demonic grace as it fueled his vitae in a battle with another vampire, a vampire who wielded an enchanted rapier laced with necromantic magic. Their bodies weren't visible, but it didn't matter to Jane—she could see every attack and spell channel through the vitae in their bodies before it manifested. Jane could see the threads of Purgatory, the middle world, and even torn gaps in the heavens as clearly as stars in the night sky. There was no creature, ghost, gargoyle, or thread of magic within a city block that Jane couldn't sense. She even noticed that only one person had boarded the lift she and Dragosani took and could feel the blades fixated to Gabriel's back as if they were her own fingers. *Jesus, Damien, is this how you see the world? If so, no wonder you became so depressed in a world without magic.*

There was, of course, one figure that stood out differently in her arcane sight. Lucian Montague leaned against a lamppost, occasionally puffing from his obscene e-cigarette amid the chaos outside. His aura radiated a palpable black malice of misfortune and hatred. A hatred, Jane realized, not for any person or object in particular—but existence itself. Even though he was behind a wall, she saw his entire form clearly in all his homeless floppy broken boots and khaki outfit and as a full emaciated and starved rotting zombie. Off his regal mask made of coins, she could see waves of unheard sound, sound she understood to be the tears of a thousand souls who lost their fortunes—all wondering what went wrong.

Just like the Lord of Suicide, your life has been filled with misery and torment. Sorry, Lucian. Consider this a mercy killing.

Lucian looked directly at her through the wall.

Determined, Jane placed her chin on the rest and focused on the spell. In her mind's eye, it grew like a small flower in an empty and desecrated garden. With the stick, the first note of strings began to play, and with the talent of a virtuoso, Jane began weaving music with magic on the greatest stage in New Orleans—over a pit into hell outside of a bar.

Buildings and physical objects faded from her view as she focused on Lucian, Purgatory, and the other realms. First, around her feet, a small microcosm, she rewove the barrier between worlds and slowly pushed her will outward. As her spell spilled into the immediate street, the distance between realms grew into an impassible cavern. Stores and structures healed themselves to their pre-Purgatory status, and Lazarean ghosts found themselves trapped once again in the endless prison of Purgatory. They could no longer see, hear, smell, or taste. In a single piece of her song, they were condemned to being lost once again.

It was then she truly understood the potential Vryce saw in her and understood that this wasn't a spell he was capable of. Perhaps only she, Mike, and Lazarus were connected to the realms of the dead so,

and with that polarity, Jane was uniquely positioned to fix that which was broken. Even Vryce would be struck blind and deaf within the microcosm, for all mortal souls were inherently designed to wander endlessly. Since she wasn't, the crescendo continued, spilling out through the rest of New Orleans. Jane may have been barred from physically seeing her results, but she could sense them. She just *knew* in her gut that block after block was put back into place from her will alone. Jane could feel the confusion of ghosts and the panic of necromancers as they quickly activated spells to cross back over into the material world as easily as she could hear the strings sing at her command.

The heavens weren't spared either. The realms retreated peacefully once her spell touched their tethers and healed the wounds caused in the fabric of the Innocence by every errant sorcerer who dared to dabble with divinity.

At the farthest reach of her spell, nearly a mile away in every direction, Jane reached her wall—but discovered something new. The lands of the dead, the very realm she once longed to escape to, moved at her command. She could create bridges and mazes. Close doors and create monuments. So lost in focus she was, she didn't even have time to marvel without losing the feeling of absolute power at her fingertips. Instead, she focused on isolating the legions of dead now trapped in Purgatory far away from necromancers who attempted to drag them back into the living world with spellcraft and chain alike.

"They are not yours," she uttered through her teeth as she battled Lazarus's forces across the city from her sitting position on the Victorian throne. They were tenacious in their attempts to violate the sanctity of Purgatory—constantly tearing new holes in the fabric of the Innocence and yanking out the souls they slaughtered to refill their ranks. She violently played, her fingers dancing along strings that cut as she opened new tears to suck the necromancers down—and then removed bridges or streets from underneath them, hurling them into the abyss. She created gardens on a whim when the music was

uplifting and spectral hurricanes in the labyrinth when the music was violent. For the minutes that she played, raw, unhinged emotion was her muse, and her soul felt at one with the torment of disappointment and wonder that Vryce felt on a daily basis.

Finally, the outro of the song came to an end, and Jane stood firmly within the realm of Purgatory, no longer straddling multiple worlds. Initially, when she realized that the chair and Saint Hotel around her seemed present but distant, she felt a twinge of regret and loneliness after her hand phased through the chair. She couldn't interact with the physical world easily anymore. *Well, girl, back behind the wall again.*

Physically, her location hadn't changed, so she could still see Dragosani cracking his knuckles before squaring off with Katrina. The vampiric or undead troops with more skill still existed as they emerged from positions of cover or other hidden places to avoid the spell, but their ranks had been heavily weakened without their reinforcements. *You're up, big guy.* She began packing away the viola and already found herself musing about the possibilities of becoming a traveling musician, fixing the world one city at a time when she heard the applause from behind her.

Lucian Montague looked like he was standing on the other side of a slow waterfall to Jane, but he clapped his hands regardless. "Gorgeous." His raspy voice emanated from the shadows around Jane, rather than from the mouth of the Death Lord himself.

Oh yeah, forgot about you. Jane bowed. "Thank you, I accept tips." She rotated the case and was surprised when Lucian flicked two bronze coins in from across the shroud. *Here's where he kills me, isn't it?* She pushed down the feelings of imminent demise, put on her smile, and stood back up. "Thank you, sir. I'm also available for weddings and funerals, but those require advance booking. But for real, why didn't you stop me? How come a chandelier didn't fall on my head out of the blue or somethin'?"

"Why would I?" He placed his hands in his pockets. "You were playing a magnificent piece, and it was heartwarming to see you heal my city. It was also rather cute to see your nose wiggle when you felt hopeful."

"Well, it worked." She reflexively touched her nose.

"Yes, it did. You've successfully put all of Murder's ghosts out of my hair." The waterfall shroud between them began to boil and pop as one of his eyes lit into an eldritch green flame out of the skeleton socket. "But your hope was in vain. Now every soldier here has nothing else to focus on but killing your precious gods and friends."

With a bony hand, Lucian parted the shroud like he moved aside a set of the Saint's white drapes. Jane heard the tear of stitches and weaves she just repaired and felt the moment of panic—yet felt the rush of adrenaline and embraced the fear. *Yes. Let's dance...*

"Don't you see!" He cackled as Katrina stabbed every one of Dragosani's organs in alphabetical order behind Lucian. "Life just fucking sucks, girlie."

"It's got its perks," Jane and, to her surprise, Gabriel said at the exact same moment. She heard the sound of fingers snap and kicked her boots into gear to dash over the Death Lord before the massive gout of fire erupted at Lucian's feet. With two kicks in the air, Jane fastened the strap on the viola case to her back before tumbling into a side-twisting kick—this time connecting directly with Katrina's perfectly cut jawline and sending the vampire crashing over the reception desk.

Before Lucian, Gabriel, or Katrina realized just how fast she could move, Jane quickly channeled a spell to suck Dragosani into a portal and sent her vampire crashing down into a garden in Purgatory. *Time out for you, buddy.* "And time for a rematch, you pale-ass bitch." Jane landed on the reception desk—ignoring the flames spiraling out of control in the lobby as one set of drapes ignited another and another to the sound of Lucian's laughter.

CHAPTER 39

*"Reality is a simple construct, defined by the perceptions
of the masses. Reality, unfortunately, is not governed
by truth. It is as ethereal as the very strands of magic
we use to shape our kingdoms. For centuries, alchemists
have merged the worlds of science and magic to discover the truth and their findings … are disheartening.
Magic, and faith, will fade from this world. To combat
this, our fractured societies will need to band together
and, forgive my words, steal the power of gods if we
wish to exist. With the rise of the renaissance, our hunt
has already begun. The very wine you drink tonight is
a gift from the Unification and the Lady of Fate to you,
stolen from the heart of an unworthy deity. We must
burn the old in order to usher in the new."*

*–Archives of the Unification. Speaker:
Apprentice Vryce of the 3rd circle*

"**N**o," Vryce pointed to the elevator and freed his leg from
Lumine who attempted to latch on, "you, of all creatures,
are absolutely not allowed."

"I'm a soothsayer! I can be useful!" She lay prone on the ground and pretended she had no bones. "Besides, everyone else is gone. You really are going to abandon me here? Alone? In a pit of hell?"

Hal patted her head. "Oh, this is a far cry from a pit, girlie. They've got far more style and a lot more screams. Pick your religion, any, and there is a pit for it. Besides," he sat down on her back, "the deal isn't for you anyway. You're stuck."

I can't believe I'm saying this. Vryce's shoulders slumped. Today really had not unfolded the way he'd imagined. "You have potential, but you are still a child. So lie there. Stay put. When this is all over, head to a Deus university and drop my name."

"I hate school." She spoke to the floor. "Can't believe you are betraying me, Mike."

Mike mouthed *absolutely not* to Vryce before speaking down. "Look, I'm sure this demon is a super nice fellow. Maybe he'll take you to buy snacks or something. Besides, you aren't missing anything. It's really just lots of walkways and an eternal abyss."

"Betrayer!" she shouted before relenting. "Fine… whatever. Go get lost and forgotten below."

"Nah, I'm a natural. I'll be back in no time." Mike chuckled.

"I wasn't talking to you," she sneered.

"We don't have time for this." Vryce glared at Morgan. "We have a deal. Now grant me your blessing."

"Sure thing, bucko." The demon leaned back and folded his legs. "You've just gotta kneel."

The request made Vryce's ears twitch, and he felt a spark of rage fly up from his gut. *Absolutely not.*

"That's not a request. You grasped at straws. Stole your soul back from the heavens and hells. I shouldn't even be letting you stand. I should be shackling you in pits of mud and slowly torturing you beyond the existence of this very planet. Hell, letting you walk gets me in trouble. So, kneel."

"That wasn't part of our deal, demon. I do not worship you, and you are not my better." Vryce mentally catalogued the opening components for several offensive spells at his disposal. "Why?"

The Demon of War flipped his shades down over his eyes and took a long drag from a smoke while simultaneously giving Lumine head scritches. "Why doesn't matter. I know you are packing enough heat to make my life a literal heaven, and I'm enjoying not being in a pit at the moment. So, I'll play nice. Nothing, and I mean nothing you do will convince any other demon to grant you passage deeper into our realm. You mortals can mine Purgatory for all the hearts you want and explore your forgotten trinkets. You've got me, right here, right now. Willing to grant your request... but even I'm a tiny bit narcissistic. In a thousand years, I want to be sipping martinis as nuclear bombs rip the cosmos to shreds and know... I had the magician who cheated God itself kneel."

Vryce recalled Phoebe's last words and wavered at the feeling of déjà vu that washed over him. *"The only way we win is if you take a knee before Daneka's champion. And trust me, I'm just as confused about how Daneka has a champion!"* she had said. Vryce had contemplated her words a hundred times since, and the problem with prophecy was not knowing who Daneka's champion was, or even if that this was the right one. Was it Father? Or the awkward psychologist that trotted around with Mr. Auburn? Either way, it put the concept of kneeling, an act he loathed, as a needed tool within his menagerie until he cracked the puzzle. *I murdered her for a reason, but damn do I hate the threads of fate.* Slowly, Vryce lowered himself to the floor before the Demon of War and let his knee touch the cement in the Seat of Golden Tears. He knew that there would never be a world without demons or angels as long as he existed, and if the Old Man could silence the wrath of Angels... "This is my repentance for stealing that-which-is-mine back into our world. Grant me passage once more into your realm; otherwise, I'll have to rip it open to claim what is needed."

Hal showed no emotion. Neither a cocky sense of victory nor a forlorn sense of regret was betrayed to Vryce in his posture. A single head nod to rise was all the demon did, a request Vryce quickly heeded.

"You have my blessing to dive deeper. Mike, it was a pleasure meeting you. I sincerely hope you both discover what you are looking for down there. A war of gods can usher in a thousand years of darkness, and that, my friends, is a razor's edge." Hal rose and picked up Lumine, flinging her over his shoulder. "Let's go watch the show. Do you know where we can get some lawn chairs?" he asked as they began walking away.

When Vryce turned back to Mike, he noticed the anarchist had turned around to give Vryce a modicum of privacy during the display. He appreciated the sentiment. "Hopefully, you remember where you are going."

"I hope you aren't afraid of heights." Mike's patched-green trench coat flowed behind him as he began a jog forward.

It had been centuries since Vryce stepped foot deeper into Purgatory. Nothing had changed. Landscapes of prior civilizations long since destroyed or forgotten marked the passage of depth as the duo descended, and unlike Mike who marveled at architecture from the late 1800s, Damien wasn't enamored until ghostlike fragments of fur trappers from the 1600s started appearing. The rest of the inhabitants were, to Vryce at least, the typical fare. The occasional wandering or lost ghost or demon that Mike had slain on an earlier visit marked their passage through the silent canals and pathways of America's history.

What was new, *very* new, to both of them—was the ever-changing landscape that moved and shifted in real time as they walked. Every textbook or helldiver manual Vryce had ever read detailed the lands of

the dead as equally endless, bottomless, and mirroring the time period of their passing. The nearest lair rested alongside their current reality and became more ancient the deeper one descended. When ancient columns began shifting under their very feet and rotating bridges into perpendicular angles, Vryce was concerned.

Vryce had been following Mike's parkour for a while now, watching the ghost jump off one bridge and plummet down effortlessly to the next lair, and he would follow with a quick levitation spell when suddenly their destination bridge unshackled itself from its supports and became a set of stairs. Other columns folded themselves together to form modern-day skyscrapers, and canals of water pooled themselves together to sprout floating gardens complete with bird feeders.

Vryce made the judgement call to keep levitating as he chuckled at Mike's endless string of swearing. *I wonder if his sister will tell him that ghosts can fly in the dead lands.*

"I can see that smirk." Mike flicked him off before vaulting himself from a hanging garden down to a horizontal skyscraper that manifested. "Do you mind NOT changing reality down here? Unless you want to get lost?"

"Do you label me as the villain for all your frustrations?"

Mike walked to the edge, gazed down to get his bearings, and quickly jumped off to fall farther. Vryce followed until he was just behind Mike once again.

"Are you saying that you aren't responsible? You are floating around like some masked Dr. Doom with that creepy mask, buildings are moving around, and this shadow gunk is creeping in everywhere. I don't think the deadlands like you."

"I think your sister is more responsible for the current changing landscape than you realize. So no, I am not responsible for..." He sighed. "I'm only *slightly* responsible for the current changing environment. I did arm Jane with the tools and knowledge to bend

Purgatory to her will, I suppose. But should I hold your father responsible for your penchant for punching and killing? He did hit you as a child, no?"

Mike pointed at a mass of writhing black tentacles that coiled their way up several columns on nearby bridges. As they writhed upward, the columns they rested on crumbled into a green ash that flowed down into the endless void below. "First, fuck you. Second, you taught Jane how to unravel Purgatory? Real smart. When she dies, she's going to end up here."

Vryce tilted his head and studied the location Mike pointed at further. He didn't see anything, or rather, all he saw was the devoid presence of magical traces, life, sentience, or any sort of arcane trace that would otherwise bely an entity that was devouring the columns. *That's interesting.*

"Explain that further," he said as he touched down on a bridge.

"Right there, on that third bridge. There are these... I dunno, giant squid-like tentacles made of solid black ink wrapping their way around the infrastructure and snapping parts off as they crawl up. They are also up there... over there on that wall... on the bridge above us... two are trying to latch onto that hanging garden up there... you blind, man?"

"No..." Vryce followed his finger each time and hunted for traces of auras. Each time, he realized that he'd missed the obvious *lack* of something. The entire time he was here, Vryce was on the lookout for demons looking to attack him, and it had been an eerily quiet journey as far as creatures were concerned. He wasn't looking for something that wasn't even supposed to exist within the celestial sphere. Something that perhaps only Mike or Jane could see in this realm.

"Mike," his voice leveled, "whatever you do, do not come into contact with that. As much as I would enjoy your soul being unmade, we have something of a current agreement. What you see that I cannot is the abyss. Someone has summoned it and allowed it to feast on things falling down through the cracks of reality. Worse, they are

not mindless. They are fingers of those who were never born. Entities scarred and burned on the edge of creation itself. Truly, the origin of universal secrets. With the right spell and sacrifice—they'll teach you anything you wish to know. Each bit of knowledge they leak into this world is one step closer to its undoing."

"Oh," Mike folded his arms, "great. They sound peachy. So how do you beat them?"

Christians. Vryce spat. "Unfortunately for us, divinity and faith. Something the world has been lacking for a very long time."

Mike gave Vryce the side-eye. "You've used them before, haven't you?"

"Mayhap. One does not uncover the secrets to stealing back souls from the gates of heaven and hell by simply reading a textbook. Find me a sorcerer over two-hundred years-old who hasn't plucked a secret or two."

"And you wonder why I punched your head off? This is exactly what I'm talking about! Yo—"

"—are equally as ignorant," Vryce cut him off. "Before you rant and rave yet again about your superior moral virtues, let's take a moment to consider the fate of humanity. Human masses are trivial slobbering idiots. They wage wars. They ignore the world around them. They pollute oceans and destroy the wondrous. Even when I was first brought into the fold, young Auburn, they oozed hypocrisy from prince to peasant alike. The downfall of mortals began the very same day they forgot their own divinity and were lured into the promise of worshipping empty thrones. Spare me your prattle about the downtrodden and consequences of actions until you look into the mirror yourself. For the path you are on will see chaos unfold in your wake."

Mike sneered and jumped off the bridge without a response, then down six more before coming to a stop. Vryce found himself amused at Mike's thoughts as they descended. *<Well, at least I'm taking action to fix it,>* to *<Maybe he's right. Fuck, I hate that he's right,>* followed

at last by < *This should be it. I remember that door.* > When Vryce set foot on the last bridge, he was already braced for the rant that was soon to follow.

"Okay, smart ass," Mike cracked his knuckles, "yes, people are ignorant masses, but there are good eggs among them. Hell, otherwise, you wouldn't be recruiting people, right? We were dumb enough to wield nuclear power, and apparently you asshats were wielding shadow Cthulhu secrets that did the same thing. We both want to fix the world and make it a better place, though no? So, for now... as we walk through that door, I'm going to suggest we bury the hatchet and call a truce. We can duke it out over the future of humanity at a later date, deal?" He stuck out his fingerless gloved hand for a shake.

"Correction." Vryce walked past Mike to the thirty-foot-tall double-wide concrete doors with embroidered stags and hunters carved into the walls. "I seek to usher in a new era where all humans can ascend to godhood. You," he flicked his wrist and flung the doors open effortlessly with a spell, "seek to return to the old. You are a dead vampire. One that shouldn't even be walking as a ghost. I chalk that up to your stubborn nature and ancestral lineage. You have a second chance," Vryce turned to face the stocky construction worker, "so I will accept your truce on one condition. Refuse to accept, and I'll simply walk away here and let the world unravel and Misfortune win."

"Anybody tell you how much of a prick you can be?" Mike peeked over his shoulder at Balor's grave behind him and marched forward to look down at him. "What is it?"

"When you are granted this power within, you swear that you will never make someone kneel before you."

Vryce smiled behind his mask as Mike was taken aback by the request. *Oh, no doubt you expected it to be something selfish, young one.*

"I..." he stammered. "I'm ... actually okay with that." He held his fist up to seal the deal. Vryce rolled his eyes as he gave what Gabriel called a fistbump.

Balor One-Eye was a giant. A literal, red-skinned giant that had been decapitated and impaled in the center of a garden to a fifty-foot-tall glowing violet willow tree. Unlike the prisons above, Balor was not here to be farmed for blood by thirsty members of the Unification. Rather, he was one of the gods that the founders buried and locked away—before throwing away any records of his location. For centuries, some groups within the Unification had constantly been helldiving in the British Isles to harvest his heart, but even Vryce had never been privy to his location. *Sure enough, Misfortune kept it hidden and on a different continent entirely. Although, I suspect the old man knew exactly what was here, and that this is the real reason why he left Mike behind.*

Mike stepped over the bodies of countless fallen demons, Barghests, and other guardians as he made his way into the patches of flowers that bloomed from Balor's spilled blood. Vryce contemplated the variety of ways at his disposal to avoid stitching Mike into a new form and was coming up empty-handed. If he had the time, he could have forged a new soul blade and simply stolen Balor's power into that of a weapon, perhaps gifting it to one of his generals. A possession suit was useless here, as the moment the deed was done—possession would be impossible, and his new form in the teenage girl was better left as strictly human. With a few decades, he could mentor a pupil to be the perfect receptacle... *but I'm rather short on decades for now.*

"Well, Mr. Auburn," he mused as he pulled forth needles from his satchel along with the remaining spools of bloody threads, "I suppose if any frustrating mortal is going to wield chaos and destruction, you certainly fit the bill. Fair warning, what you are going to feel is," Vryce stepped into the garden, "the most excruciating pain you've ever experienced. You will black out. This is not unlike me creating a gargoyle, so rest assured I'll succeed. When you wake up, your body will feel as if it's on fire, and you'll hear voices in your head. That, my stubborn boy, is Balor. For a little while, you'll be yourself. Then for

a little while longer, you'll be both. But eventually, in the end—you will just be Balor."

Mike raised his hand.

"Lower your hand, you idiot. You are the wrong Auburn to be my student."

"Right." Mike fidgeted with his lighter. "So, all the other gods we released that Boss wanted. Eventually they'll..."

"Yes, just be what they are. By then, I imagine the old man will have everything he needs from his soldiers. The process could take days, weeks, decades, or even centuries. It's a battle of wills, and given your penchant for having an iron will, I figure you'll have some time. It is inevitable."

"Can it be reversed?"

"You should have asked that before you had the bright idea to suggest this."

"That's ... a no. Okay, last one, I swear. Will I be a giant, or will the giant be me?"

Vryce chuckled. "Last one? If I were you, I would ask questions for the next day. Time is different here at our depth. Only seconds have passed in the real world, remember? But unfortunately for you, you'll just be..." Vryce held his hand up to Mike's head, "you. No giant-sized, red-skinned Mike."

"Do you know what kind of power I'll wield?"

"I thought you said that was your last one. Keep the coat on and lie down. That coat, given its history with you, is a part of your soul. And no. I do not. I do know the more of Balor's power you draw upon, the faster you will cease to exist."

Vryce watched Mike hunt around like a dog trying to make a bed in the flowers before lying down in a pool of blood. Once he was in place, Vryce allowed himself to feel the still beating heart within the giant's chest and uttered the incantation to telekinetically pull out one of the massive spears before plunging it directly into Balor's chest cavity. Once. Twice. Twenty times. Each thrust sent showers of

blood raining down upon them as Vryce dug his way into the god's core by shattering bone. Once exposed, Vryce mounted the potbelly and pried the heart free, more with magic than the paltry physical strength of Prince Alil's form, and set to work.

Vryce figured Mike's unnatural strength would pose a problem, and before he set about causing unholy pain to someone who could shred through him like wet tissue, he impaled Mike to the ground with the very same spears used to imprison Balor. Despite Mike's scream and struggles, he was still a ghost, and the spears had imprisoned a creature far stronger. For a second, Vryce honestly considered just walking away with the heart on his own, but at this point—he had to admit he was curious. *Will these gods be the same in the long run? This ritual was only performed by religious fanatics looking to take their gods' place and... well... is this not a mortal becoming a god?*

Mike only lasted minutes into the ritual before he screamed himself unconscious. For the remainder, Damien was allowed to have the world fade away and focus on his craft. Nothing was more calming than being entirely alone and conducting blasphemy. As he stitched each fiber of the heart into Mike's soul, he found himself musing about the future. These new gods would have the memories of current mortals, and perhaps, just perhaps, they would be grounded in reality once again. *Plus, even if other cultures free their gods, humanity also wields divine power. Both Pandora and Prometheus should be proud.*

Fiber by fiber, Vryce meticulously threaded Balor's heart into the location of each vein and artery as he continued to craft a god out of blood, not superiority. With each sinew, he slowly killed the last remnants of the King of Deceit, villain of the Tuatha, and herald of destruction all to give new life to a dead anarchist. With each thread, Mike's naked ghostly form became more tangible inside his patchwork protest coat.

"You will be a gospel of rage and bring terror to the world, Iron Heart Auburn, or should I call you... Balor Béimnech? Which of you will awaken?" He allowed himself to smile. "Nearly my finest work.

We all can't have seven stolen souls, can we?" He bit off the last thread and stepped back as Mike's eyes opened first, and he let out a deep gasp for air that didn't exist. As he struggled against the restraints and suffocated in Purgatory, Vryce idly cleaned his needles. "You aren't undead anymore, nor a ghost, nor blessed with passage. Stop trying to breathe. You don't need it."

A third neon-bright red eye suddenly opened in the center of Mike's forehead, filling the room with a dark orange color as the fae soul awakened.

"Gorgeous." Vryce found himself taken with wonder by the presence of ancient magic filling the room. It was rare, and wonderful to behold, and in that moment, he bathed in the presence of a giant—even if in the form of a man.

He didn't notice when his own elven hand passively grabbed the Ouroboros amulet off his chest, snapping the thread. A command he never issued to his body continued, as Prince Alil hung the amulet on an iron spear sticking from the willow tree. He was merely a passenger when the Praenomen's mask was taken off and hung atop the same spear, and only when Alil's delicate fingers let go did Vryce realize he was no longer in the body.

"That's enough of that, thank you very much," Alil said with a flick of his wrist.

I... Vryce's thought paused as he panicked. Neither Alil nor Mike could hear him. There were no demons or mortals to possess within range. He panicked as he stretched his shadows out around the tree and nearby gardens, hunting for any single body he could possess but found none.

Alil summoned roots from the tree to bend and free Balor's restraints.

Focus. Without limbs or blood, he couldn't cast. He was at the mercy, the off-shot hope, that Mike would somehow notice that he dangled uselessly from a willow tree. He watched as Alil broke an iron spear in two, melding metal into two curved iron daggers and tucked

them behind his back. "Let's go. The battle will not last forever," Alil said with a tone of voice that mimicked Vryce's cadence. He had the gall to impersonate him.

Willpower. He mentally stretched himself, hoping to feel the other fragments of his soul. Even a sliver, the tiniest sliver, would allow him to possess the wielder, but the moment his mind attempted to leave Balor's prison, it was as if he was trapped under ice, only able to scream to the very same walls that held Balor's mind warded from reaching his faithful for centuries. A prison built to contain a god now contained a different ward.

Notice me.

Please.

Vryce watched as Mike and Alil left the tree behind and saw Alil wink back as the doors to Balor's prison were shut. He knew right then that he was sentenced to divine punishment. Trapped in Purgatory by the same demon who granted him passage in... but never mentioned leaving.

It was his punishment for daring to be divine.

Vryce frenzied without being able to make a sound.

CHAPTER 40

"My bartenders, they tell me things, Lucian. Secret things. Like how the Unification is planning to resurrect Lazarus. I wonder, which Jesus do you think will give protest, if any? The Catholic one? Protestant? What about Ahriman? Osiris? It never bodes well to trample upon another man's garden. Every century I check in with you, and every century you forget me. So this time, I'm writing it down. I'll play hitman. I'm just an old forgotten grandfather. But trust me when I write this—once mortals get a taste for the blood of Olympus, the Seventh Age will truly begin."

*–Crumpled parchment discarded in
the Seat of Golden Tears*

Lucian cackled with mad glee during the orchestra of violence that unfolded around him. Gabriel's fire spread along drapes, filling the room with blackened soot and ash that made mortal eyes water, but the relentless sorcerer kept summoning fire as Lucian slid and jumped around the foyer to narrowly dodge attacks. *I am going to rot the very skin off your bones, betrayer.* Lucian grabbed the table leg of a piano and skidded in a half circle to change directions before launching himself at his foe.

A massive onyx hand oozed out a marble column and grabbed Lucian's Hawaiian shirt in midair, causing a *gurk* sound as his momentum suddenly stopped—inches away from his bony hands touching Gabriel's nose. "Gargoyles? Really? That's not fair." Lucian watched as the massive creature, uncreatively named Onyx, flowed itself free from inside the marble as if it were stepping out of a pool of water and grabbed his right leg. With a swift yank, Lucian felt his leg dislocate. "You are going to beat me with that, aren't you?"

"Yup." The gargoyle dropped him to the floor, and both Gabriel and Onyx proceeded to bludgeon, shred, and incinerate Lucian with his own limbs.

It was charming for a stretch of time, but after his left arm had gotten involved, Lucian was getting bored. *Show me something new. You idiots already lost. If fists and fire could end me, I'd have loaded myself into a canon ages ago.* Lucian allowed his body to fade into a cloud of ash and set his soul free from the broken prison.

"We got him?" Onyx seemed cautiously optimistic.

"No." Gabriel twirled a blade and cast a quick spell to peer beyond the veil... with his gaze settling right on Lucian's ghost. "We need to try something new."

Lucian clapped as he burned another soul from his Seat and stepped back across the barrier between worlds without a scratch on him. "At least rocket boots over there put up this fancy wall..." He nodded to Jane, who ducked and weaved between Purgatory and the real world to frustrate the ever-living hell out of Katrina. "You there... mortal!" Lucian shouted at Katrina's bodyguard. "Break this one." He nodded to Onyx.

Xavier Hood cracked his neck. "Right..." He looked unsure of himself as the barrel of the shotgun slowly raised ever higher up to Onyx's monstrous face. "Time for the children, I suppose." Throwing the shotgun up, Xavier pulled a pistol from his sixth holster and ejected a clip of full bullets to the ground while backpedaling and reloading with a strange type of ammunition. He fired two shots,

one each into Onyx's clear blue eyes. Onyx charged blindly forward, crashing through the column.

Gabriel muttered something about fucking his life. "You know he can sense anything on concrete, right Lucian?"

"Oh, I'm aware."

Xavier continued weaving backward and pulled pistols from holsters three and two before charging into a slide between Onyx's legs. Each of the bullets fired reacted with the chemicals from the prior shots and created deafening explosions and concentrated blasts of fire right into the eyes. Without hesitation, he grabbed a sawed-off shotgun, loaded in a wooden stake, and thrust the pig nose barrel right into Onyx's armpit. The backblast sent Xavier backflipping onto the piano, where he swapped ammunition yet again with a glowing bright blue bullet into a small machine gun—and riddled Jane with some type of ammunition that disrupted her form right when she Purgatory jumped behind Katrina.

"Ooohhh… that's gotta hurt." Lucian cringed as Jane yelped. "Oh yeah, forgot about this." He flicked a coin in Gabriel's direction, who sliced it cleanly with the green-flamed soul blade as if it were paper right when Onyx's massive frame crashed to the ground—paralyzed from the wooden stake.

"Try again," Gabriel sneered as he telekinetically levitated Lucian up, spinning him so his boots were pointed at the burning ceiling.

"Shouldn't I be saying that to you? Going to smash my skull? Rip off my head? Break my mask? Go on! Try to get rid of me like you do a cancer, but it never works."

"No." He threw Lucian across the lobby, forcing Katrina to swear and jump over the Death Lord… then suddenly duck when Gabriel yanked him back like a yo-yo. Jane, now hiding on the other side of Purgatory, unfurled the long set of soul-forged chains and lashed them across the barrier to bind Lucian's feet and began racing to the door—dragging him like a sack of trash behind her. "Let's just bury you."

Oh no... soul chains. He rolled his eyes. Out of all the things he mourned, it was that his latest hat bounced off and was catching fire by the reception desk.

Jane managed to kick open the front doors before suddenly stopping. Lucian peered between her thighs and saw a battalion of necromancers and vampires armed to the teeth level their weapons and reliquaries at Jane. The majority of them were the forgotten homeless beggars that had been scraping coins or scraps of food out of the gutters of New Orleans—who now wielded the weapons that Murder's forces found themselves, suspiciously, freed of.

"Fuck me," she said.

"Did you forget we *also* have undead?"

Gabriel began swearing in Italian as he found himself fighting a vampire swordsmith and her gun-toting bodyguard.

"You uh, wanna untie me there, *mon cher?*"

"Where the fuck is our army?! Did they just piss off?" Jane dropped the chains in frustration and flopped her arms next to her side. She winced when a bullet hole oozed green from her ribs.

Lucian wormed his way out of the chains and dusted himself off before standing behind her and putting his bony hand on her shoulder. "They did exactly that. Here's the thing about bad luck: it doesn't turn a good day bad... really, it makes a rotten day terrible. Right now, you and your lot are standing directly in the path of my army. An eccentric lot sure, but everyone ignores 'em."

The glass from the front doors exploded into a thousand shards as Xavier went barreling across the street into a trash can. Everyone who saw it cringed when they heard his thigh snap at a ninety-degree angle.

Jane pointed. "He yours? Because if so, we might be winning."

Lucian shook his head. "Not yet. But you might be. When has your life ever gone well?"

She held up her hand. "Nope, not doing it. The Lord of Suicide tried to recruit me, and frankly an eject button sounds more damn appealing than having to endure your stupid laugh anymore."

Fredrick found kin. I'll miss that child. "You know, Fredrick only wanted to save people from suffering in a world of monsters. Go quietly or watch as your neighbors rip your heart out for blood—and potentially leave you a trapped zombie."

"So, what do you want then?"

Gabriel shouted from inside, "A little help!"

Lucian twisted his head one-hundred and eighty degrees. Katrina had managed to close the distance, and despite most of her blood floating in the air above her like a rain cloud, continued to parry, lunge, and pressure Gabriel. "Man up and hit the bitch!" Lucian shouted. "Win the duel like your daddy wanted."

Katrina chucked a dagger into Lucian's back for the insult without breaking flow.

Yeah, I earned that. Lucian returned his focus to Jane. "Sorry, Gabriel needed a little motivational help."

Jane brushed his hand off, but when several soldiers raised green manacles, she went back to surrendering with her hands held high.

"I'm a simple skeleton, Jane. I just want to teach everyone that their ambitions, empires, godly goals, and money mean nothing. We are all six bad days away from shitting in buckets. So, since nothing really matters, just go with the flow and enjoy life."

"Oh, fuck right off," she spat. "That is the most privileged immortal undead bullshit I've ever heard. 'Oh, look at me, I'm the kooky Death Lord,'" she danced. "You can't kill me, and I can't die, so I'm salty that I've work to do. Boo hoo. Let me kill everyone on the planet or make them worship my boss so I feel better...'"

Everyone who is short lived always says that. Lucian sighed. "Say that after a thousand years. Because from where we sit," he stepped in front of Jane, "when everyone is dead, then the only place we have to go is up..." Lucian flicked her forehead, catapulting Jane back through the building and into the vortex of white flames Gabriel summoned around himself as a ward and watched as her magical clothes and

boots melted into slag and her soul was sent screaming across the barrier she erected.

"Right," he clapped, "you unlucky sons of whores. Welcome home at last. Our Seat of Golden Tears is yours to pilfer. For far too long you've suffered in poverty and misfortune, and so I open my vault to each of you. This world is going to shit, and our job is done here. Go forth. Be rich. Cause chaos. Make a few friends and don't come crying to me when it all ends."

Lucian's smile grew as he jutted his claws into the shroud and focused his will while chanting, slowly ripping the floor of the Saint Hotel in two, causing the building to start collapsing in on itself, and revealing the prison and Jane's unconscious soul curled in a naked fetal position clutching the only object that survived Gabriel's inferno—Vryce's viola.

You sent them to die in your stead. Pathetic.

Katrina, half her face burnt beyond recognition, limped herself out of the collapsing building with her fangs bared past Lucian without a word and lunged into the neck of the nearest mortal with blood—her own bodyguard.

Lucian saw the threads of his life fade away as the vampire drank deeply to heal her wounds, which mirrored the dying embers of Gabriel's inferno and vortex as the weight of a full hotel slowly collapsed on top of him. In truth, Lucian felt remorse for his actions. When he walked to this continent, he mused that the people here would stand a greater challenge. *If they couldn't defeat me, then they never stood a chance against Pestilence or Murder.* "Oh well." He let the spell collapse, unfinished in his hands, letting entropy and chaos take care of the rest.

"This, gents," he turned his back, "is usually where Fate kicks my ass and one of her stupid tricks saves everyone, but really, no Director Walsh stopping time?" The building fully imploded and sent debris flying everywhere as it tumbled down into the pits of Purgatory. "No Second City Boss breaking my knees? No great liches channeling

lightning? Or techno-fucking warlocks and their ghost bullets?" With his shoulders slumped, he went and sat down next to the dying Xavier and Katrina—who was looking a little better.

She looked at him with a hint of pleasure, from the feast or combat, Lucian wasn't entirely sure. "I had my reservations, but... that was *fun*."

Lucian nodded to Xavier. "Just when I thought you had a chance to be free of Murder..."

"He was skilled," she closed his eyes, "but I'm not authorized to carry the blessing of Raphael De' La Corizone."

Lucian bumped her shoulder while his helldivers and army began their descent into the depths. "What if, and hear me out here, you broke a rule?" He winked. "I won't say a word. The Lord of Murder is on the way out, but the throne..." He whistled. "That goes back to the days of Caine, and while Raphael wears Murder's skull, you do carry one of his seven swords. A sword that can cut even the dead themselves. Don't tell me you haven't noticed the inky-black abyssal heart stored in the hilt?"

She glanced at the rapier sheathed along her belt and covered it with a worried look in her eyes. "How do you know about that?" she whispered.

"Please," he felt his own chest hurt from memories of his past, "when you young ones worship us Death Lords, do I strike you as the wise one? Or the one who is so desperate to escape I'll walk to the edge of reality to look for a way out?" He choked back a tear-laden laugh, barely allowing it to eek through his words. "Only to discover that the outside is just as miserable as we are in here. So, I brought some back." He rose. "If I were you, I'd take your freedom and build your army. Feed him the heart, then run far away. Get to Italy and wake up the old vampires sleeping in Venice. You'll need leverage if you want to be voted in as a Death Lord in a few years. If this mortal survives, then maybe you have a different sword."

She clicked open the sword's hilt and held a small pearl-sized perfectly black orb that refused to reflect light. "Why help me?"

Because I need you stronger to kill me. "You're cute and look great in leather."

Lucian elected not to watch whatever choice Katrina made behind him as he walked to the hole he created, intent on at least stealing Vryce's prized viola before he forgot about it. *I do have to hand it to Jane, though. She really patched this city up. Look at this. I only broke ONE hole this time! Ugh, I'm getting rusty.*

As he approached, he saw a color that wasn't typically associated with the lands of the dead.

"Since when is my realm red?"

CHAPTER 41

"Well, I'm going to go on official record and state that the entire Unification plan is stupid. Next time they want to open a gate to hell, don't pick a fucking populated city."

–Mike Auburn. On the record.

Mike felt the concrete pillar shatter over his forearms. The impact caused his knee to buckle slightly but also brought a rush of heated air and concrete dust that set his lungs on fire. It was the first time he'd felt a living pain in years. It was the first time he woke up since he was with Vryce. *I'm alive! I'm already fighting! Why does every joint hurt?!* Mike's eyes watered as more concrete and debris fell into the prison from above, and he kept his hands as a shield. He needed to get his bearings, and most importantly, he needed to figure out why someone was trying to bring a building down upon him.

I've still got the strength of Golgoroth. That's good. A discordant noise of a piano crumpling down nearby diverted his attention. Mike watched as Jane tumbled down between broken sections of walls and glass. Covered in concrete dust, Jane looked sickly dead. She was naked, pale, and curled in a fetal position clutching a pristine viola with glowing strings. The viola didn't have a single scratch on it. *Okay, maybe not on me. Bringing down a building on Jane.* Mike heaved

forward, pushed a mountain of rubble off, and cut his leg on something sharp. Gabriel's calvary sword gashed through his right calf, and the pain in his lungs was suddenly a second thought.

"Fffffffuuuuuuuucccccccccckkkk...." Mike seethed and kicked the sword out of Gabriel's limp hand. Gabriel was what Mike had been shielding, it seemed, and he didn't even realize it. The sorcerer also looked on the brink of death and had several bits of rebar sticking through his thighs and abdomen. *Next time you fall, don't land on the pointy parts, dumbass.* Mike clenched his fist and channeled his pain into the debris to his right. A flash of red light washed over the prison as the ground shook.

Suddenly, there was a hallway where debris once stood.

"That's new." Mike checked his knuckles, and despite the fact he needed new gloves, they were unscratched. No mysterious claws or flaming energy emanated from them. He didn't have time to inspect further as more tears from above kept appearing. Direct rifts from the surface world poured in everything that rested above them. Someone was trying to bury them alive.

Mike felt his shoulder blades pop and shatter reflexively as his body was wracked with pain, this time tumbling him down on all fours as he sweated profusely and silently seethed. The red light washed over the tiny pocket he guarded. Even though Jane was several paces away, he felt every impact on his back. With a glance, he saw why. A gigantic bloody angel wing of torn flesh and metal spikes shielded his sister on one side and guarded Gabriel and whomever else fell on the other side.

The wings flexed, sending the metal rebar-shaped spikes jutting out into a web of pylons that crisscrossed in their pocket to provide support. The searing and flesh tearing feeling that washed over him caused Mike's grip to shatter the concrete under his fingertips as he screamed. He felt his teeth extend into fangs that tasted metallic followed by an absolute hunger for any source of blood to fuel the

transformation as his heart beat so loudly it sounded like it would punch out of his chest any second.

He loved the pain. "I'm fucking alive!" He forced himself to rise and let the subconscious destruction wash through him. It was reflexive to shatter anything that caused him pain into a thousand pieces. Either his newfound metal wings would twitch and send iron rebar spikes into a hostile object, or he'd headbutt, kick, or on one occasion shatter an annoying piano simply by gazing at it with an eye that seethed hatred. Mike thrashed underneath the Saint Hotel like a dragon defending its horde until the ground finally stopped shaking.

At last, there was silence.

Only after Mike pulled Gabriel, Onyx, and Jane to a spot of safety did he allow himself the chance to figure out what happened. *You three need to file OSHA complaints... and need blood badly. Or major surgery. Now where the fuck is Vryce?* Mike stood up and surveyed the prison, or rather, what remained of it. There wasn't much to see given the extent of debris, and so Mike could only make out a few broken rooms where soul-stitching had taken place. Even the hallway he and Vryce had left down was completely buried. Going up to the surface was certainly possible by simply climbing. *Hell, going back down the hallway is possible. I love having my strength back.* Mike choked on the dust-settling air and regretted the thought. "Take that back a little bit... There were perks to being dead. Fuck, can't believe it worked."

The first rule of any rescue operation was always to keep track of your own injuries, and Mike began his survey. For the most part, he was very much ... *himself.* He felt the stubble along his face and still had hair apparently. His shoulders were still wide-brimmed and thick, and his hands felt stronger than ever with an incredible grip strength. The wings were certainly new. Mike could move them like any arm, and honestly thought they looked metal as fuck. A cross between old bone and flesh with modern construction steel laced through them— steel he could bend and shape with a thought.

He checked between his thighs with a sigh of relief to find out that he was still, well, intact, and continued to pat down. *Wallet, watch, testicles, and keys. Check.* The gash in his calf was very much still bleeding and hadn't miraculously healed with some sort of god blood magic. *Okay, so I don't heal like a vampire, and I should avoid pointed objects. Probably means I'm not bulletproof. Makes sense. Most demons think they are, and well... then they wake up in a city and find out the hard way.*

Mike sensed a presence in the back of his mind. A soul that he felt a kinship with crawled out of a nearby shadow before manifesting into Vryce. Mike knew he was *looking* at Vryce, but it didn't feel to him like he was. Something was off as the elven creature let the shadows melt off his form and the color return to his cheeks. Once Mike could see his purple eyes, he knew without a doubt that Vryce wasn't there any longer but rather the soul of some faerie who felt ...*familiar.*

"Where's Vryce?" Mike rose.

"Ah." Prince Alil tapped his lips. "Probably back home. He exhausted his time in my body. That's irrelevant for now. You don't need him at the moment. You need me. Your body is undergoing some changes." He stepped forward, crouching slightly and keeping his palms up. "You and I are something of distant relatives. You, well, I suppose are Balor now. A legend in the flesh. Flesh that can be cut."

Mike glanced at his calf. "I figured gods would be more durable."

"Strength, destruction, smiting." Alil lowered himself and inspected the wound. "Those are your domains. You aren't Atlas or a Titan. It will also take time for the blood to settle."

Mike felt an icy chill as Alil summoned shadows to stitch Mike's calf closed and reduce the swelling. "So, I can't heal?"

"Not without magic, and I'm guessing that isn't your forte. So, I would suggest finding a friend who can. Like me." He smiled. "In war, Balor typically destroys any object before it hurts him, so lean on that. Because, my old friend, we are very much still at war. I wish we had time but..."

"Yeah, I know. They are coming..." Mike could sense souls starting to descend even though he couldn't physically see them. *That is going to be handy.* "What's with the metal in the wings?" Mike rotated his thigh to test the stitching and painfully discovered just how far he could push it.

"That's new, and I'm jealous. You are both Balor and this Mike Auburn person. Iron in the wings and metal-clad teeth must be a Mike trait. Welcome to being one of the fae where self-actualization is paramount. You're a creature of dreams and nightmares. As for me, my wings were cut off. Maybe if I help you, we could get them back."

Mike wasn't sure. The sharp-featured shadow wielder had the air of a trickster spirit around him, but Gabriel needed medical attention. Jane just needed a shot of ghost-coffee or something. "I really should have paid more attention to the ghostly medical practices." He sighed. "Right. You make sure these three are operational and at least limping by the time I'm done with Lucian, and we will talk. No promises but consider it an audition."

"I'll ... do what I can." Alil checked Gabriel for a pulse. "Why is the first test always a nigh impossible task?"

"Less whining and more stitching." Mike ignored the scoff and began barreling out of the prison at full speed, effortlessly shattering debris that sealed them in.

His fists smashed through the last of the debris, and with a surge of primal strength, he propelled himself out of the suffocating grip of Purgatory. Mike vaulted up the debris like a feral animal, eager for the upcoming fight. Helldivers had already begun to descend, and Mike grinned as he used their faces for leverage with his boots, catapulting himself up further at an ever-increasing velocity. Yet he didn't abandon them to the prison below. Mike's wings shot rebar and impaled and hooked those he passed, dragging them up as they screamed and fought to free themselves. By the time Mike reached what was once a basement, he carried dozens of bodies behind him like a bloody chocolate flower arrangement comprised of vampiric assholes.

The first true breath of outside air tasted of ash and blood, the stench of war hanging heavy as if the world itself was bleeding. He rose, his winged form casting a shadow over the shattered basement that remained, eyes burning with a fire that mirrored the furnace of his newfound power. The bulk of Lucian's forces looked at Mike like an abomination. It reminded him of the United Center in Chicago years ago when he devoured the heart of Golgoroth and spoke to the crowd.

He loved it.

A wave of silence swept through the ranks of Lazarus's minions who stood around the pit. Necromancers froze mid-incantation, their hands trembling as they felt the shift in the air and the red light that washed over them, and they watched as Mike's rebars impaled their brethren onto any disjointed structure that remained. The vampires, once ravenous and eager to helldive, recoiled as if struck by an invisible force and fled from the steps they took to loot the prison. Mike didn't care that they weren't wearing the cloaks of Murder, and he could tell that every homeless or rugged-looking creature was truly one of Lucian's get.

"Evening, gents." Mike waded into the ranks of the undead. The first vampire that dared to approach him was met with a backhanded blow that sent it careening into a broken wall, its body crumbling to dust on impact. Another lunged, only to be caught midair, crushed by Mike's iron grip before being flung aside like a broken rag doll.

Even the necromancers soon discovered that their desperate chants to summon and call forth reinforcements were futile—even the dead hesitated to rise under the shadow of Balor.

As the last of the cowardly undead slowly withdrew and gave space, Mike stood tall and fixed his gaze on the one entity standing calmly in the quiet battlefield. Lucian Montague waited for him like the final boss in a rigged game, or he had at least decided that Purgatory suddenly glowing red was a future problem.

The Death Lord's expression was a twisted blend of annoyance and amusement. His bright Hawaiian shirt fluttered in the wind, and his ever-present smirk widened into a full toothy vampiric grin as he lazily clapped his hands. The sound echoed in the stillness but carried the sarcastic mockery with perfection through his ranks.

"Well, well, if it isn't the walking embodiment of ironclad stubbornness," Lucian drawled, his voice as raspy as ever. "I must say, Mike, you do know how to make an entrance. Though, I can't decide if it's bad luck or sheer audacity that brought you here. Either way, it's impressive … in a reckless, suicidal sort of way."

"Probably." Mike pointed up to the night sky with the purple Lilith Moon now hanging clear overhead. "A satellite going to fall on my head?" He stepped forward. "Or is some battleship off the coast going to drop a nuke right around now? Or will I simply trip on a rock and bust my new skull? What kind of misfortune do you have up your sleeve?" The beggar lord's army parted for Mike to stroll right up to Lucian. "Do you really want to win?" Mike asked seriously.

Lucian tilted his head, his smile never fading. "Oh, I wouldn't have it any other way, Balor. The problem is I'm not in a fucking pickle! Lazarus on one side... you on the other. I'm like a bone sandwich. Can you really outrun your fate? And how long will you," Lucian reached up and fixed a union button on Mike's green coat that had come undone, "still be you?"

Up until now, Mike hadn't encountered any invasive thoughts in his mind, and he still felt very much like himself, but both Vryce's warning and Lucian's statement did cause the thought to cross his mind. *How long?* He chuckled. "Well, I'm on borrowed time already. So probably long enough to kill Lazarus. I definitely could make it long enough to eradicate that mask of coins... but I'm not going to."

Mike reached forward and plucked a set of dice from Lucian's chest pocket. "Let's play a game. Everyone else has tried to kill you, but I've been with you long enough to know that is as practical as wiping your ass with a pinecone. If I win, you just quit. That's it. Just walk

away from Lazarus's ranks. If you win… then I'll play along and keep fighting you until one of us dies. Eventually you'll run out of coins to burn, or I'll become some ancient god with no memory of who I am."

Lucian eyed the dice and placed his bony hands around Mike's fist. "I'm the Lord of Misfortune, and you want to toss bones against me?"

"Evens or odds?"

"No." Lucian wagged a finger. "Stakes are too high. If you are going to challenge fate, my boy, you need to roll the unluckiest number on these bones. You roll a seven… you win. Any other number, you join me in proving that nothing matters. Even if you are a god."

Mike rolled the six-sided dice around in his hand. *Can I really take him? Fuck around and find out, I guess.* Mike gave the bones a proper shake and rolled them between their feet, watching them bounce. The first settled instantly on a six, and the second spun around like a top.

"Oooooh… come on, just start punching. You know you wanna…" Lucian taunted.

"Shush." Mike stared. "Trust me, the thought crossed my mind. I'm trying something different here. Punching things is if this fails."

The dice settled on a side. A single, filthy pip was face-up.

"BOOM!" Mike cheered.

Lucian looked speechless at the dice as if it had betrayed him. Without saying a word, every onlooker from his armies began to take a knee and bow their head in Mike's direction.

"Fuck my life and call me Suzy." Lucian laughed. "I knew someone was going to have a bad day when I saw you… I knew that this was a remote possibility. Everyone gambles knowing they can lose every-thing, but the wins… that rush… make it worth it. The best part of being me? I'm okay with losing." Lucian knelt. "So, I'm going to up your gamble, buddy. I want to see where this long game of yours goes, and you lot are way more fun than Lazarus. Ergo, I, and the ranks of Misfortune, abandon the Church of Lazarus and am happy to pledge our faith to you."

"Whoa whoa," Mike backpedaled. "You, uh, nobody has to kneel! Stand up!" Mike watched as more ghosts and people from the streets that comprised the army of Misfortune took a knee in unison with their Lord. "Seriously, I'm not that kind of god..."

Nobody rose, and even the footfalls of Jane walking up went unnoticed by Mike.

"Unlike Lazarus," Lucian said without raising his skull, "you are unbound by fate and misfortune. A ball of chaos in a scripted world with the shadows of the abyss stitched into your soul. You should not exist in this world, and thus, this world does not bend you to its will. You ... are the perfect god for us to kneel to."

Oh, this is not how I thought things would go. This cannot be good.

"That can't be good," Jane muttered from behind as Prince Alil laid down Gabriel and took a knee.

"All hail Balor," Prince Alil intoned. "High King of Chaos and Destruction."

Mike looked back to Jane and saw the panic in her eyes.

"This really isn't good..." Mike muttered. *Vryce is going to fucking kill me.*

CHAPTER 42

"America is a divided country, and that's why Noblesse Oblige Incorporated is taking action. Ever since the black sun has risen, our leaders have run and hid within their bunkers. Yet with a newfound Pride in our government—fair and balanced elections are required. Coming this November to a city near you, the Nobel voting machines will magically store your vote, no matter where you are at. Safe. Secure. Easy. Trust in nobility."

–Late Night Cable Ad

"'Scuse me." Jane dropped the viola onto Gabriel's unconscious body and proceeded to march through the kneeling crowd to grab Mike by the back of his coat. "I need to talk to my BROTHER." She glared while properly donning the Praenomen's coat that Alil had draped her in. "His name is Mike Auburn, by the way." *Get over here, you idiot. I get knocked out for ten minutes, and you are off playing God.* Mike gave zero resistance to the rough dragging, but Jane still couldn't believe it.

One minute, she was kind of kicking ass, and the next she was waking up buck naked to someone who very clearly was not Vryce speaking some flowery dead language. Gabriel was nearly in a coma,

436

and the big black gargoyle was a fucking statue. But rather than reinforce them and join them in the actual plan of evacuating everyone to regroup, these idiots went down to pinch Balor. She was half tempted to quaff another vial of blood just to slap Mike straight. *No, no, be calm, Jane. Might need it when the McDonalds of bad luck goes back on his word.* Jane made sure they were a block away and tucked Mike behind a red-brick wall that used to be an entire building.

"Speak." She glared up at him. Mike certainly wasn't a ghost any longer and his puppy-dog brown eyes were still there, but he had these annoyingly large wings that clanked when they twitched nervously.

"So," he fidgeted, "you were up there, and we were going to follow, but this demon showed up—"

"Don't even finish that sentence. Listen to the demon? Really? Dog ate your homework? You went back for Balor because you wanted that heart ever since we found it. Remember, *we* found it."

"Hey! I found it well before I ran into you down there. Still, I'm not playing finders keepers. Jane, we didn't have much of a choice. Vryce agreed with the demon's deal, and I don't know why myself, but this is his work. You think I know how to perform magic like this?" His wings flexed out.

"Put those things away..."

"I don't think I can."

"Put. Your. Toys. Away. Or..."

The wings suddenly snapped back into Mike's body, and Jane inspected his back. *We didn't go through all this to give up. You better be okay.* There were no signs of tears through his coat or visible scars when she pulled it down to check. She lifted his shirt, forced his jaw open to inspect his teeth, and patted the rest of him down. Outside of the occasional stitch, Mike appeared to be a perfectly normal soldier who ran hot to the touch. *Except for the giant strange shadow he produces that follows him around, he seems him.*

Jane squished his cheeks and rose to her tiptoes. "You are normal. Except for that big ass shadow stitched to you. You still you in there? Any feelings of bloodlust?"

Mike's eyes darted to the shadow, and they widened slightly. *Blockhead didn't even know it was following him.* Jane patted his stubble thrice before stepping back and uncorking a vial of blood. She held it out like she was giving an alligator a piece of meat.

"None?" He shrugged. "Look, Jane, I'm still me. Other than the period in Purgatory where I blacked out because I couldn't breathe, I've been me the whole time."

"Blacked out? Did you just appear up here?"

"No, me and that other guy, Alta or whatever, found you and Gabriel as the building was collapsing. That's when I woke up."

"Ah, so the shadow possesses you when it needs you to keep alive. Kinda like taking a shot of the Kraken—one shot is liquid courage, but three shots and you wake up surrounded by naked people the next morning."

"Exactly!" He leveled a closed fist expecting a bump.

She left him hanging. "Now explain the bowing. I watched you gamble with Lucian. Those odds? Really? If you lost, you would have been stuck fighting him for who knows how long. Centuries probably. But the worship? If you have any semblance of being a member of the Sons and Daughters, you knock that shit off right now."

"Okay, I can't explain that." He waved his hands frantically. "I absolutely, under no circumstances, wanted them to bow. That's... no. In fact, Vryce *actually* made me promise to not ... do that."

"Oh, so you're fucked then. Which body is he in?" Jane peered around the corner and saw Lucian and the rest of his survivors huddling with hushed whispers while they occasionally glanced in their direction. *Yeah, keep gossiping.*

"I don't know. I think he is probably back in Deus or something. When I came to, he was already out of the body."

Knowing him, I highly doubt that. Something doesn't sit right. She paced back and forth. They had just spent all this time bringing back gods, gods which cut and run, probably into the arms of Lazarus's forces. Vryce wouldn't have just skipped and ran, but it was possible that if Gabriel was unconscious, he went to Delilah instead? She wasn't sure, but she knew it was suspect.

"Okay," she said at last.

"We good?"

"Not yet. You are going to do something for me. Without protest. Without complaining. You are just going to *do* it. I'm sure Boss probably saw this coming, and if you really don't want to be worshipped, you are walking away right now. No saying goodbye, no final speeches. You are going to walk right down that cobblestone street until you find the nearest working vehicle. Get in and drive straight back to the Second City. I don't care if you gotta walk so far out of town that you hail a damn taxicab in the next city. I'll clean this up."

"You're extremely bossy, you know that? This isn't over here, and I'm not exactly seeing any allies on our side. Akira and crew got pulled."

"And it was Boss who provided the rank-and-file to get soul stitched. We know we aren't lucky, so they probably ran or got out to make the same journey. You," she jammed her finger into his chest, "aren't the sibling that's used to people turning you into propaganda. That faerie is going to use you, and you just got a Death Lord to fucking kneel. Useful, sure. Extremely dangerous. I put an entire army *into* Purgatory, but they are skilled sorcerers and will eventually crawl out. So, before that happens, get out and regroup. Before bad luck *does* find you."

Mike looked down at her and gave a warm smile. "Fuck it." He gave Jane a massive bear hug. "Who knows? Maybe staying will cause my morals to decay. I'll go. But you better float your sassy ass up there when done. Besides, you've still got me beat. Between the two of us, you've at least killed a Death Lord."

Ugh, sappy, but take care, you idiot. She took a deep breath to remember his smell, iron, cigarettes, and dust all mixed into one, before prying herself free. "Well, between the two of us, only one of us managed to come back to life. Now I can't copy you, so I've gotta one up you another way." She pushed him off down the street.

As Mike walked away, the shadow boiled and loomed behind him on every surface that was devoid of light. The way it moved was entirely unnatural, like a skittering caterpillar being tugged along on a leash. She knew that Mike was on a ticking clock. Hell, she knew that all the returned legends were on a ticking clock before their sense of self would decay, and she hoped that everyone would carve out something before that happened. *Or at least be strong enough to knock them off their pedestals.*

Once Mike was off the main street, Jane turned her attention back to Lucian and his stupid army and double knotted the coat shut. *Bad enough I'm buck naked under this. Am I going to make him or Gabriel pay for new enchanted clothes?*

As she approached, Lucian shooed everyone away. Only the Faerie-formerly-known-as-Vryce had the gall to stay close.

Lucian sat cross-legged down on the ground and stretched his back like a cat. "Well, looks like you're in charge. Bold move sending him away. What makes you think I'd keep my word?"

"Because doing nothing is vastly easier than doing something. So, out with it. Why did you let him win?"

For once, Lucian didn't laugh or cackle. He just leaned forward and rested his head while looking up. "I always thought Lazarus's plan was stupid, and before you get all huffy about it, I didn't let him win. Unlike Vryce, I'm not allowed the same freedoms. I know you are all murder, death, kill against the Death Lords, but did you ever think that not all of us sign up for genocide?"

"It's kinda hard to get that impression when you blast cult-like messages, send armies to do exactly that, twice over, and prop up a god."

"Everyone has a web that binds them, even if they don't see it. We imprisoned those gods for many reasons. The Lord of Heaven's Wrath?" He lowered his voice. "Lazarus has a real shot at undoing all of this. Still does." He tapped the ground and pointed below. "If he's right and wins, I don't care because I'll be free. But if cracking vaults and bringing back the old guard works... maybe it's worth sticking around."

"You could have just done that from the start," Jane flicked him off, "instead of getting that many people killed."

"Ah!" He held up a bony finger. "I didn't really do that much killing. Technically, the army you fought belonged to the Lord of Murder. All I did was come along for the ride and set a few dominoes in motion. From where I'm sitting—Murder's forces also had terrible luck. What did they accomplish? Kill a few states, grow a big army, and then get trapped in Purgatory? Lose a bunch of gods to the enemy? My guys mostly just chilled. HELL! Even when I went to Deus, all I did was send a message!"

So, you're the useless Death Lord. No wonder you gave up.

"Careful..." he hissed. "I may have agreed to quit fighting, but that doesn't mean I can't make you stub your toe every day for eternity."

Jane let her shoulders slump. She didn't know about the inner machinations of the Church, and maybe Lucian had a few solid points. "Well, if you genuinely mean to quit working for Lazarus, then I'm sorry. I'm just not used to people..."

"Actually letting things go?" He finally gave a soft laugh. "Yeah, well, if every soul that I laid claim to just let things go—they wouldn't have suffered. Many times I have heard someone beg for one more spin of the roulette wheel. If they walked away, maybe they would have lived on. Now that they are all dead though... they've learned that lesson. Unlike some other Death Lords, I teach mine."

"What are you going to do now then?"

"No clue. Probably ask you to grab that viola and help me fix up the place. Maybe give my mask to Lumine for a while. I love this

city. I'm not stupid, JK-47… I know I've got info your organizations are itchin' for. That, however, is barter for a different day. Mike got me to quit. Maybe you'll convince me to do more than drink blood out of coconuts and take a vacation. I could teach you way more about Purgatory than Vryce could… Ever think about building a city? You've got it in you. By our powers."

"Hold that idea." She quickly shifted over to the faerie who stood there in Vryce's clothes. *Well, I suppose they are his? No, the Praenomen's. Ugh, I'm going to get real annoyed at all this body hopping. BRANDING, PEOPLE. Be yourself!* "Where is Vryce?"

The faerie narrowed his eyes. "You know I'm the victim here, right?"

"I ain't punchin' you for answers, am I?"

"Touché." He reached out and adjusted the collar of her coat. "But I also healed you, and you happen to be Balor's half-sister now. That almost makes you royalty and certainly in the High King's court."

"His name is Mike."

"For now. But since you are so intent on knowing, Vryce and a demon made a deal. A demon of war, to be specific. So, if you want to find your teacher, who has a *lot* of complicated emotions about you—I'd start looking below. And before you do decide to start punching, like Lucian here… I'm a Prince with plenty of ambition and information. The lands of the dead aren't exactly my scene…" He gave Jane a flamboyant pat on the head and began sauntering away. "I like my cities to be a little closer to the seat of power. Toodles."

Lucian clicked his tongue. "That bastard was magnificent at the Unification Christmas parties back in the day."

Great. Great! This is Jane speaking; we have a clean in up in aisle three. She tossed her hands up in frustration, walked over to Gabriel, and picked up the viola, then downed a vial of blood and cast a spell effortlessly to open a portal right to where she stored Dragosani. The vampire casually lay on a bed of violet flowers like he was basking on a sunny day atop one of Jane's hanging gardens.

"Hey, sleepy, get up here... your boy needs medical, and we've got helldiving to do. Someone misplaced a centuries-old asshole. Oh. We won, but I need muscles and real skin now." *Vampire-in-a-pocket. I should market this.*

CHAPTER 43

"You and I are not so different, Mr. Auburn," Vryce said. "We both want humanity to succeed in the face of adversity. The room behind us contains power. That is true. These are creatures who have mastered their changed states. But they are the weapons that will be used to save those below. Those people below are being given a choice, to become something more than what they were or face oblivion. We are not hoarding our power as you championed. Today is a holiday, and the world is changing. If it could be stopped, would you really want it to be so?"

–Eve of the Black Sun. Society of Deus party.

Was it weeks or months? Vryce lost count. His world was a static and never-changing prison. In the early days, he held out a modicum of hope that Gabriel or Delilah would use their gifts to locate him. He even held out hope that Mike would return to Balor's grave. Those hopes faded like wilting flowers as the silent march of time ticked forward. Hour by hour. Day by day.

Look at you, wallowing in pathetic lamentation again. There is no logical reason for you to be discovered. Even if they helldived for you, Hal Morgan could have simply moved the location, destroyed a bridge,

or shifted space to hide this location. You are but a needle in the floating sea of oblivion and despair.

Vryce had replayed the conversation with the demon over a thousand times in his mind and hated himself for not catching an obvious loophole. He was promised entry into Purgatory yet nothing about exit. A honey trap. Desperation and ambition created the perfect scenario. He'd fallen exactly into the trap that every heaven and hell wished for—eternal damnation. *How dare I claim what is rightfully mine. God abandoned his post when humanity was crafted in their image, leaving the celestials to tend to a broken machine. Humanity can rot.*

Every calculated plan he'd ever conceived centered around the wonders of magic. Ever since he was a young boy, tales of fantastic and hidden secrets lured him like a moth to the flames. Over the centuries, he had walked both left-handed and right-handed paths, mastered spells in witch's houses, collected the forgotten, and idolized the philosophers who came before him. When his first master, Sydney DuWinter, a fellow warlock in London, saw promise and leapt at the opportunity to rip Vryce's soul apart and make him his equal, not out of spite or hatred, but in Sydney's mind—Vryce was the perfect determined bastard to betray the Unification and pluck their souls back. The perfect one to unearth the secrets of lichdom.

A lot of good that did us, Sydney. Back then was different. You served under the Lady of Misfortune, and Lucian masqueraded as a simple warlock hiding under the Lady of Age's skirt. I can't believe his ruse worked during the great ritual. Have I been played from the start?

Vryce's mind went back to the start. Thirteen Lords of Death that changed hands every three years under the Treaty of Unification. An ambitious conspiracy of over three hundred disparate occult groups from around the world—all jockeying for position to wear the coveted masks of Death Lords. All coveted the power that came with being a lich.

The Lord of Murder held the leash on Warlock Mortiemer Ploutuns in Jerusalem. The Lady of Age shielded the "warlock"

Lucian Montague in Haiti while the Lord of Starvation let Warlock Rasputin run amok to control Baba Yaga. So on and so forth between Drowning, Unborn, Fate, Pestilence and the others. Each Death Lord oversaw the creation of a warlock for the sole purpose of Lazarus's resurrection—or was it? *Many of these warlocks have been around for centuries longer than I, and the Death Lords, like Fate—even longer. What if this imprisonment is part of the process of ascension? The vaulted council got bored of their duties and made replacements, letting ones like Lucian take a vacation.* Vryce couldn't recall the name of his maker. The Lord of Heaven's Wrath that oversaw the Society of Deus had been absent for a century before Daneka was elected. Perhaps, Vryce hoped, this current imprisonment was merely training to take the role of Heaven's Wrath back under his mentor?

After all, I did return the heavens and hells back to this world. Have they not been wrathful?

He loathed his maker. Coy games, hiding behind the cracks of memory, and enigmatically abandoning post to pave the way for Lazarus. Vryce knew the trademark signature of being forgotten. He knew the Death Lords rotated but were always from the same pool of candidates. He felt the embarrassment of his idiocy. All of his machinations were calculated around the idea that they *wanted* Lazarus to return. Yet if that was merely a byproduct of their agenda, then Vryce was nothing more than a hammer to hit a convenient nail.

Here you go, Vryce, have all of the secrets to pluck a soul from oblivion. You are meant to grab only Lazarus's; don't you dare think of taking yours. Don't learn these secrets of soul stitching. Don't learn to become a lich. That is like asking a child to avoid a biscuit with tea.

Do I regret reaching into the heavens?

Vryce pondered the question for days, replaying every event in his memory. Every choice he believed he made was to find the hidden hands guiding him. Every morsel of information about the players within the Unification. Their pawns. Their sacrifices. Their victories.

Being hung from Balor's tree was a setback, a punishment for violating divine law... and yet, Vryce could only blame himself. Not blame his actions, or even Hal Morgan's deception, or Mike for being oblivious. He couldn't blame Alil for the act of revenge; rather, he respected the faerie more for it. *Even if I'm going to return the favor.*

No, Vryce resolved himself. He did not regret his actions and came to enjoy the unfettered freedom of thought. Free from responsibility and consequence. Free to analyze every word uttered from the lips of immortals for hidden context.

Free to lie to himself about his imprisonment.

Anything to bide the passing of stasis.

CHAPTER 44

"...and lo, the heavens wept."

THREE MONTHS LATER

Dr. John C. Daneka opened his eyes and felt the beauty of the sun's rays nearly blind him. A small beeping noise filled the room like a repetitive annoying alarm clock. *Where am I?* He tried to shield his eyes, but his arms failed to move, as if they weren't there. Slowly, his vision adjusted itself to the light, and the deafening roar of sounds crashed into his senses. The air smelled of fresh flowers, not a single kind, just an onslaught of bouquets. The beeping became headache inducing, and Daneka realized it wasn't an alarm clock, but rather the sound of his heartbeat hooked up to a machine. In between each beat, he could hear birds chirping happily nearby his bed.

His body failed to move. John was paralyzed. His gaze flicked to the left and right, taking in the elaborate flower-filled bedroom. He could spy a note on a bouquet of lilies.

Get well soon, my lord. —Lady of Age

Delilah Dumont. Memories flooded back into his mind. She had discerned he wasn't undead and taken advantage of the situation. *I*

448

will shred her soul. He closed his eyes and basked in the warmth of the sun's rays. It was stronger than he remembered. No hints of blackened rays or desecration. His power was growing. *My plan is working.* He felt the corner of his lip quiver through the numbness as he tried to smile. *In time, John. In time.*

He heard the door to his chambers open and the sound of footfalls as the windows were closed and shades drawn. Darkness washed over him once again. The echo of high heels on marble flooring betrayed Alexandria's presence.

<*Still afraid of the sun?*> John opened his eyes as Alexandra took a seat on the side of his bed and pressed a cold wet cloth to his burns.

"It gets worse every day, no thanks to you." She smiled behind her mask. Alexandria, for once, wasn't dressed as a sultry sex icon, but rather wore gray robes adorned with the Church of Lazarus symbology. "You've been out for a while, and you have no idea the number of vampires I've had to beat with a stick to stop from feeding you their blood. Seriously, John, we could have had you perfectly healthy in less than an hour."

<*I will heal. Flesh is but a prison.*>

"A prison that needs to lead an empire. Even the companies from Dystopia have sent medical equipment that can reattach your arm and leg. I killed them before they could operate. You're welcome."

<*Grazie.*>

"You know, John," Alexandria opened a nearby birdcage and forcibly snatched a sparrow from within, "your little stunt with Murder was an effective message. Fear is an amazing motivator." She kissed the top of the sparrow's head. "You should have seen the tizzy of destruction raised in the wake of your accident. You make a good little martyr. You've shown the Death Lords that godhood is obtainable, and you sit on the throne. They waged your war with more fervor than before, and the faithful have flocked to your banner. Letting an enemy thrive has also galvanized and emboldened your ranks." She gently bit the

sparrow and licked up a tiny drop of blood before returning the bird to its cage.

<What has transpired?>

"Glory, my dear." She lay in bed next to him and gently petted his cheek. "Damien Vryce was imprisoned, and a plethora of gods were freed from their prison. Some escaped, others... we let Dystopia hunt down. One of them, Balor, is walking again. Which sparked your little church into action to clamp down on Loki, Athena, and Set before they could be rescued. Across the world, we've been tactfully letting our enemies siege the vaults to free their legends at the cost of exceptional losses. Then, we outsource dealing with the gods to the corpos. Our ranks swell, their cities become kingdoms, and then the god of capitalism swoops in." Her fingers trailed in a circle on his chest. "One little drop of blood at a time, humanity itself slowly decays into something else. Monster? God? Dead? It's all rather fascinating."

<At great risk, no? Idols can grow.>

"Let them. I'm so bored, and that's why you are so fascinating. Let the world kill itself..." She nuzzled him like a cat before stretching her thigh over his waist. "As long as people keep eating and drinking the divine, you get your wish. The faithful, meanwhile, flock to your ranks. Some even willing to undergo vicious transformations to be your sword. The Sanctum is comprised of vampires and magi loyal to the cause of Lazarus above all else, knowing they've sacrificed their souls to shape a better world."

John wished he could smile. It didn't matter how far the world fell into rot and ruin. So long as he survived to the end, he could fix it all. *<And the Death Lords?>*

"Well," she sat back and patted his chest, "don't get mad, but I've had to make a few judgement calls in your absence. As your official voice and all. Misfortune has properly fucked off into the wind again, so he's out of our hair until the next election. Murder and Famine are determined to get back within your graces, but I think we need some fresh ideas. So, I've been letting people who have devoured the heart

of a god join up and start their campaigns. Everyone else is toeing the party line. Only Fate has remained truly neutral, which I suppose is typical. Between you and I, though, I don't think Murder is going to make it past the next election. He's got some stiff competition in that little upstart vampire Katrina, but that's just gossip. You don't care about that."

<*You are right. I don't. But we meet again. So let me ask you my question. What is the bad news I'm not being told?*>

Her face darkened as she crawled off. "I thought you'd never ask. Pandora's box is open. Shadows are starting to have voices. She-who-shudders-with-the-lidless-eye whispers on the wind again. Demons aren't just being summoned from hell any longer, they are fleeing, and all bear the whispers of those which were never born are seeping between the unseen cracks in the world." She gave John three pats on his forehead with her cold hands. "So. Get. Better. Because if you don't, we are going to need a new Heaven's Wrath. Elections are in three years."

Alexandria didn't ask John a question in turn, and he knew it was because he had nothing to offer. He closed his eyes as she left the room and set about the task of willing his body to twitch.

Even if just a little.

The End.
Welcome to the Seventh Age.
Magic has returned. For better or worse.

EPILOGUES

Akira dangled her bare feet off the Chicago Board of Trade as she hummed to herself while watching the city traffic below. A fat hairless squirrel-like demon imp lovingly named Sparkles by the crew devoured a plate of cilantro-free tacos behind her with everyone else, but the demon's thick rear kept bumping up against Akira's claws like a happy golden retriever. It was supposed to be a moment of happiness and reunion for the Sons and Daughters, but Akira was listless. Frankie, one of the Big Boss's primo zombies, had returned from the grave again and finally came home. Morris and he were old stomping ground friends, and thus, a party was in the works.

The Second City had been quiet since New Orleans. Boss refused to let them anywhere near the battleground, and so Akira didn't get to rip out anymore hearts. Hell, the whole time she didn't get to test her abilities. She wondered if that's what all-star athletes felt like when being benched, but she couldn't relate. Nobody ever picked the scrawny dirty kid for their team. That held true for Mike and Jane as well... since every night the Lilith Moon rose, Akira eagerly checked to see if they had returned.

Frankie turned out to be false hope. "Oh, yeah, I saw him," Akira mimicked. "Him and the elf got off back on the Appalachian trail." She grabbed one of the tacos from Sparkles and chucked it over the edge out of spite.

Sparkles looked betrayed and plucked the last taco before waddling farther away from her.

"What do you want?" Akira said, sensing Boss appear behind her. "Don't think I'm going to open up and be all squishy about how much I miss them? I'm bored! You won't let me hunt. I can't kill. Hell, do you know how many games I got to one-hundred-percent completion? Like fifty!" She huffed and leant forward. The streets below carried a soft green glow on account of the number of ghosts that inhabited their city. It had become a thriving economy where the dead and living equally worked together in some sort of anarchist commune. In their Second City, reputation was capital. Contribute and do well, and favors would be returned.

Akira was only good at hunting.

"Oh?" Boss lit up a cigar and planted one wing-tipped shoe on the edge.

"Okay, maybe seventy-six. Still, that's a whole library. They still aren't back yet. What if some demon ate them? Maybe they got lost in Purgatory. Maybe they decided to help rebuild Deus instead of here..."

"Really?" His bushy eyebrow raised under the iconic cabby hat.

"I think I should go check up on them. I mean, less than half the gods you had them bring back came up here. The rest are now fucking mascots for Wall Street."

"They could be anywhere..."

"Right!? So, I better start sooner? I'm glad you agree, Boss. Great talk as always." Before Akira could jump off the edge, Boss grabbed her shoulder.

"Hold it, hotshot. First, you need to take Doc with you. He's going nuts ever since he reopened his practice. Therapy for merged half-god half-ghost people is a scientific conundrum for him, and I'm sick and tired of hearing about it. Second, no more hearts for you. I like you as a capable assassin, not a ravenous berserk assassin I need to keep on a leash. Third, I do not want you to come back until you've made at least one new friend. Pet rocks don't count."

"Bullshit. You just didn't like that Stoney was a jerk."

"I didn't like you trying to teach Stoney to fly in my *bar.*" Boss held out his hand, the ironclad symbol of a deal.

Akira shook. "Fine, but I am taking the captain's car. Morris doesn't need it."

Boss smiled. "I saw nothing…"

Lumine waved enthusiastically at the crowd. "Come on up! Take a flyer. I don't bite!" Running for mayor of Samhain was exhilarating. For starters, her campaign manager, Lucian, was the official wrangler of public relations, vice president of infrastructure, and captain of rum, each title an official position Lumine promised to award upon her ascension. The city of New Orleans had a lot of rebuilding to do, and even though it had been months, they were still finding cryptids and reality-breaking loopholes in the darndest of places. The launch of her platform began when she started organizing the zombies to clean out pixie pests from the grocery stores and continued accelerating from there.

She organized the first city rebuilding efforts and managed to construct a single park in the past three months. Granted, it wasn't the *best* park, but it technically had at least one tire and one piece of rope. But her small efforts motivated others to renovate and fix their bars, start cooking food again, and even get the fishing industry operational again. She had plans for Samhain, and to enact them, she needed to be mayor. And so today, she offered free powdered lemonade mixed with vodka and free flyers for the upcoming Noblesse Oblige voting day.

"Remember folks, a vote for Lucky Lumine is a vote for easy street. We'll get the quarter rebuilt, a gambling house on every corner, and a local witch market that promises to keep out the big corporations.

Stay local, buy local!" She smiled and waved after passing out another flyer and red Solo cup that was mostly vodka.

"Uh, Lumine," Lucian sat nearby with his feet up on the table, "you know your crowd is filled with zombies, right?"

"So? Zombies have feelings."

"Zombies can't vote."

"Says who? They can press buttons on the machines just fine."

"No soul, no vote. Dem's the rules." Lucian lowered his wide straw hat over his face and leaned the chair back.

Angrily, Lumine snatched the vodka back and downed it. There was no lemonade.

"Ghosts can't vote, though. They have souls but don't have a body."

"Yup."

"Zombies can't vote. Body. No soul."

"A-yup."

"Vampires can't vote. Removed from time."

"That's just unfair."

"Shifters can't vote because animals can't vote."

"The living can't vote because nobody here is friggin' normal."

"Politics. Gets you every time."

Lumine grabbed the pitcher of vodka and flopped into the second chair beside him. "These elections are rigged. Nobody can vote!"

"I can vote..." He picked up his hat with a smile. "I've got a body, a soul, I'm not an animal, and I'm not a vampire. As a lich, I count as human to that machine."

Lumine slowly slid over a flyer.

"Yeah, yeah, I'll vote for you. I'd still keep campaigning though. Never overlook the support of labor when you run on a reconstructionist platform. Now I'm going back to my nap."

Lumine resumed her campaign in earnest. Even if they couldn't officially vote, she figured it was nice to have their support. When your home had perpetually bad luck, you already had rock bottom, so the only place to go was up.

"Look, honey, there isn't anything I can do," Lou, Death Lord of Fate, whispered next to Phoebe as they were escorted toward Porto Marghera. Lou's right hand never stopped rubbing between Phoebe's shoulder blades, offering what little comfort a Death Lord could to a ghost on a one-way ticket to a riverboat.

Nothing you can do? Nothing?! I shouldn't even BE across the pond for heaven's sake. Why couldn't I just be a normal ghost? Phoebe bit her tongue and focused on the pain in her wrists from the oversized spirit manacles that clamped her wrists and feet together. She was now nothing more than a prisoner in a line filled with hundreds of others, marching to the Lord of Murder's ferries.

She knew exactly what was going to happen, and knowing only made everything worse. Everyone in this line wasn't going to wander Purgatory. They weren't going to be conscripted either. Instead, all that awaited them were forges and furnaces on some remote island where their souls would be melted down into slag and forged into more chains, manacles, or other spectral weapons. Murder was not keen on keeping around souls he had to pry from the grasp of his competitors. Before she died, she saw herself screaming as she was fed foot first into a great machine with shadows for saws and slowly chopped up as her soul was unraveled into spaghetti.

She couldn't help but cry empty tears.

"Toughen up, girl." Lou elbowed her. "Just because I can't do anything doesn't mean you are shit out of luck. You are a soul with the power of fortune telling, which right now feels like a curse, I'm sure. You were also caught up in that adorable idiot's web of misfortune, so he has a claim. Clearly, someone murdered you, and let's not forget you've been with the Second City Boss for a long time now."

"If the Death Lord of Fate, literally, can't change my destiny. I'm…" She felt her lips quiver. "I'm… I'm…" Phoebe couldn't finish

the sentence as the visions of her screaming in a forge made of shadow filled her mind. She fell to her knees until the chains attached to those in front of her dragged her forward again.

Lou squeezed her elbow and yanked her forward. "No. Toughen up, shut up, and listen. You had a vision right before your death. In order for our world to survive, Vryce would have to kneel before Lazarus's champion. Let's cut the bullshit. What you see moments before your death are powerful. They will come to pass. Unless people defy them, which puts them in my camp. Who was Lazarus's champion? Who was Vryce meant to kneel before? What threat?"

"The shadow." Phoebe choked back the tears. "They corrupt and twist the gods. Cracks in the world. Unraveling. Souls being shredded. Purgatory being devoured. Mortals with the power of gods ripping apart continents. The black sun cracking. Existence fading."

Lou hissed and swatted away a rank-and-file soldier from Murder's camp who began wandering over to see what the delay was. With one glare, he quickly turned away, and it at least caused Phoebe a momentary smirk. *Lady has some rank.*

"Right, the abyss. Got that. So unfortunately, that means the Lord of Heaven's Wrath is correct..." Lou whispered.

Lord of Heaven's Wrath? A spark went off in Phoebe's mind, as she suddenly realized that everyone probably thought she meant the imposter was the savior. It's not like she had a long time to explain her vision after all. "No, no, uh, it wasn't like that. It was more, Vryce kneeling before an emissary, a champion, you know, someone who has power over you in that moment. Doing that would cause a chain of events where a descendent of Lazarus would master the skills needed to give the gods a chance to fight back against the abyss. I saw someone building cities in Purgatory and taking the war below— rather than up here."

The Death Lord smacked Phoebe on the back of her head. "Uh, of course. No wonder that bartender recruited them, and no wonder you saw that. You were surrounded by them. That's either Jane or

Mike, and if the rumors are true, now just Jane. Well, Phoebe, you might have just saved the world." She looked back at the walled city of Rome. "And I probably need to pull some strings to buy that girl some more time."

Just Jane? Wait… What happened to Mike? Fuck it, that means I'm saved, right? She felt hope well up inside her as the lines stood before the massive ferryboat. "Last chance? Please?"

Lou's attention snapped back, and Phoebe felt the large woman embrace her. It felt warm. "I'm sorry, dear. It's best if you don't think about your future. Your part in this web has played its course. I can't save you from Murder's grasp without bringing undue attention to myself right now. But I can ease your passing… You did well, my child."

Lou kissed her forehead.

Phoebe no longer had visions of her death. Rather, all that flowed in her mind was visions of what could have been. A happy life, partying late at night, and enjoying the world as an influencer who burned bright before being killed in a tragic motorcycle accident. There were no world wars, vampires, or black sun in Phoebe's mind as she was loaded onto the boat. She was just happy and completely oblivious to the forges that awaited her.

Hal Morgan sat in the New Orleans bar next to a pale gunsmith crying over whiskey he could no longer drink. While he listened to the black-suited gunman lament over the lack of drink choices for vampires, Hal idly drew on a tea-stained map of Purgatory. For months, he'd engaged in a game of cat and mouse with a rather experienced helldiver who kept getting close to Balor's prison. Whenever she got too close, Hal would scribble out a bridge and move the chamber to another lair. This helldiver, though, would occasionally rearrange the

entire map, and even Hal found himself hunting for Balor's prison like he was playing Where's Wally.

The Demon of War had no intentions of letting Vryce free any time soon, and at the rate Vryce's seeker was rearranging Purgatory, she would probably construct her own city before she found him. Hal wasn't opposed to the idea, so he never really erased her newer constructions that the ghosts took a liking to, but he also didn't have the power. He was a demon of war, not a God of Hades. All he could really do is pluck his prize from one location and redraw it into a different spot. Satisfied that it would take the girl another three weeks to get close, Hal folded up the map and turned to his new favorite person.

"I know, becoming a vampire has its drawbacks. I can help, you know?" Hal reached over and grabbed the glass of whiskey right from underneath the man.

The sound of a safety being released echoed from under the bar top.

"Semi-Auto." Hal winked and took the glass anyway. "You know how to flirt with a war demon."

"Don't touch another man's drink."

"Well, for starters, you aren't a man any longer. Second, you can't drink it, and third—I know why normal blood doesn't slate your thirst..."

Hal was not shot.

"The shadows. You can hear them, can't you?"

The man nodded, his short white hair falling down before his eyes. "How can you tell?"

"Where do I start? You keep talking to your feet, your eyes are jet black, and you don't cast a reflection. You look like a drunk Japanese Salary Man. Come here..." Hal reached over and fixed the crooked white tie. "You're shadow kissed, son. I could use your talents. Maybe even save your soul in the process..."

He grunted. "Not interested."

"I could show you how to stop being hungry all the time?"

He hesitated for a moment before finally sighing. "Fine, let's cut the deal..."

"Hal Morgan."

"Xavier Hood."

Hal shook his hand. He was *very* glad to meet a shadow-kissed in Samhain. Maybe the city wasn't so unlucky after all.

Delilah Dumont sat in a local café in Marseille, France, waiting for her contact to arrive. She idly stirred her oat milk, cinnamon mocha with a splash of pixie blood as she read the local news. In the past three months, Lazarus's Crusade swallowed Europe, India, and Greenland completely. None of that concerned Delilah any longer—what was more interesting were the places never mentioned. Japan, Ethiopia, or Venezuela, for example, never once made the paper, which meant they were victorious—or the Church was simply too afraid to invade. To her, that smelled like a fresh opportunity.

Life within the Church's borders was ... passable. Most civilians tried to keep their heads down and ignore the black sun or talked of migrating to Rome where it no longer shone. Commercial products were cheap knockoffs or smuggled goods since the Church frowned on magically convenient products. It made perfect sense to Delilah. Lazarus was trying to multiply his humanity, and she toyed with how she was going to break that. Part of her wondered if it was even worth building a cryogenic tank to store a human like a rare baseball card for a thousand years.

"I don't think baseball cards go in cryogenic tanks, milady." Her contact pulled out a chair. The vampire was faceless with empty sockets for eyes and smooth skin over his ears. Today, he wore the military uniform belonging to the Death Lord of Drowning.

"I don't think it's wise to pry into your boss's thoughts..."

"Apologies, madam." His face suddenly shifted to the recent target of his impersonation. A Pakistani man with a bald patch on his crown. "It's as easy as breathing without my mask."

"So, what is your report, Whisper? Did you locate Symon?"

"After three months? Yes. After the Lord of Suicide's death, Dystopia sat on his staked corpse for a year. A few months ago, they sold several unneeded vampires into the hands of Alexandria of Ur. Apparently, she's been buying her army one vampire at a time."

"No doubt using her old blood to intoxicate them into loving her." She took a sip. "Effective trick."

"Won't work on our Symon though."

"Nope. But given her proximity to Lazarus, Symon will be a perfect saboteur when the time comes. We just need to get to him."

"If I may," Whisper folded his hands, "perhaps you should return to the Archive. You are a wanted woman, and you no longer have the Praenomen's mask. Leave the infiltration to me. I'll locate Symon, ensure his loyalty, and embed with him. You go back and get your tools, train the army, maybe cut a deal with Pride."

Delilah sighed. She hadn't been able to locate the mask, or Vryce, for months, and it was something of a sore topic for her. She loved that mask. "That is the politest way to call someone a hindrance."

"Etiquette is forever," he started.

"Honor is a lie…" she finished. "This is the first vacation I've had in a decade, but I suppose you are right. In one year from now, at this very café, meet me with Symon and any other spies you lure over. I'll see about staking a few of our own to sell through Dystopia into Alexandria's clutches. Infiltration is a long-term effort, I suppose…"

"There is no better saboteur than Symon. That vampire can bring down a subway station with a single strand of piano wire and three toothpicks." Whisper chuckled. "Besides, don't look so forlorn. Balor has returned. You should be happy to return."

She raised her eyebrow. "The Auburns are stubborn. I highly doubt they'd be willing to break blood with me."

"Does it matter? You have vials of Balor's blood. You're probably one of the only ones."

She scoffed. "My dear Whisper, why do you think the Church hasn't panicked? The Unification mined every god in prison for decades. Now that we know Lazarus's plan, it's clear as day. When the gods come out, it will inspire more people to hunt for that same power, and less and less humans will exist. When all the forces of the world unite to lay siege to the Church of Lazarus, the strongest of them will find themselves suddenly surprised by the effectiveness of blood magic against them. The gods aren't a threat to the Church as long as they have the blood."

"So, what is?"

"Themselves," she sipped, "and thermonuclear warfare."

BOOK CLUB QUESTIONS

1. The Seventh Age *Decay* has several factions forming their ide-
    ology. Which faction do you root for?

2. If you could claim the power of a god by killing it, would you?
    Would you be afraid that you might lose your sense of identity?

3. Lucian has probably cast the world into an even worse battle by
    letting the abyss run unchecked, and few noticed until the very
    end. Do you think Lucian really wants to see the abyss defeated,
    or do you think he sees it as a means to end his immortality?

4. Gods and mythology have been with us for ages, but at the end of
    this book, now we start taking over their roles. What story would
    you tell in this setting if it was a tabletop roleplaying game? What
    about if it was a short story?

5. Do you think Vryce, if ever freed, will tilt so far down the path
    of arcane power he's unrecognizable, or do you think a sliver
    of his personality that admires competence and intelligence
    can be saved?

6. Demons fleeing hell to escape the abyss is bound to have con-
    sequences, particularly if arch-demons find themselves killed by

armies or bound by corporations. What is one human emotion or concept (love, happiness, loyalty, unity, etc.) that if removed from the world would cause its destruction?

7. Among the Sons and Daughters, Doc, Lucy, Akira, Phoebe... one of them has a power that allows the group to even dream of achieving their goals. Which one has the power that truly keeps the group focused and why?

8. In what ways did the characters and their challenges feel real to you? Were there moments when the story felt unbelievable?

9. Was there any part of the plot or aspects of the characters that frustrated or upset you? If so, why?

10. Which part of our world do you think has a strong enough connection to old gods and religions beyond the big three that they would thrive with the prisons of gods being opened up?

About the Author

Rick Heinz's inspiration for *The Seventh Age* traces back to his history as an electrician and especially to his love of crawling through the hidden underbelly of a city to uncover its secret wonders—not to mention countless caffeine-driven hours spent slaying his digital demons. *The Seventh Age: Decay* is the third book in the Seventh Age series that sets the stage for countless future stories within the world as we see the decay of society when magic finally returns. He's written many other projects both in tabletop gaming and literary form such as *The Crow: Prayers of the Past*, *The Red Opera: Last Days of the Warlock,* and *The Black Ballad.*

Go to http://www.StorytellersForge.com if you are curious about the gaming side of Rick's mind... which includes multiple novels, Seventh Age RPG tie-ins, and massive epic campaigns filled with metal music and badassery.

But no spiders. Spiders deserve to be ejected from this planet like the aliens they are.